NOW YOU SE

'Spectre,' he said aloud. 'Spectre.'

It was a Byker Chapter word . . . A Spectre was something that queered your pitch; it was something that screwed everything up . . . A Spectre could be the reason for the sound of police sirens somewhere out there in the night as a dirty wind rattled and clawed at the bedroom window . . . A Spectre could be the reason why your mother was crying alone in the kitchen, and she would not tell you why . . .

Richard shook himself back to the present. It was time to forget the Byker Chapter.

But something was soon to happen that would bring those memories back into sharp and horrifying focus.

Also by Stephen Laws in Sphere Books

GHOST TRAIN

SPECTRE

by

Stephen Laws

SPHERE BOOKS LIMITED

SPHERE BOOKS LTD

Published by the Penguin Group
27 Wrights Lane, London W5 8TZ, England
Viking Penguin Inc., 40 West 23rd Street, New York New York 10010, USA
Penguin Books Australia Ltd, Ringwood, Victoria, Australia
Penguin Books Canada Ltd, 2801 John Street, Markham, Ontario, Canada L3R 1B4
Penguin Books (NZ) Ltd, 182 190 Wairau Road, Auckland 10, New Zealand

Penguin Books Ltd, Registered Offices: Harmondsworth, Middlesex, England

First published in Great Britain by Souvenir Press Ltd 1986
and simultaneously in Canada
Published by Sphere Books Ltd 1988

Made and printed in Great Britain by
Richard Clay Ltd, Bungay, Suffolk

For
Robert Alexander Laws
(who started the ball rolling)

with special thanks to Terry White

and regards to Peter Cushing
whom I have never met but have greatly admired
for many years; an heroic adversary of
cinematic Spectres of all kinds

Contents

SPECTRE

PART ONE
THE STALKING

Like one, that on a lonesome road
Doth walk in fear and dread,
And having once turned round walks on
And turns no more his head;
Because he knows, a frightful fiend
Doth close behind him tread.

Samuel Taylor Coleridge,
The Rime of the Ancient Mariner

One

South of England, Thursday, 10.15 pm
Phil Stuart pulled the tab from his sixth can of beer and drank deeply. The previous five lay empty on the carpet of his plushly decorated sitting-room, beer staining the deep pile. In the kitchen, Stevie Wonder sang loud and strong from the portable cassette-radio. In the adjoining bedroom, his music centre blasted Bachman Turner Overdrive. In the hall, a small portable cassette player blared out Dave Brubeck.

Phil drank again and reached for the automatic television control. BBC2 were showing a wildlife film; the volume on the set had been turned up to maximum and the cries of animals from the tropical rain forests echoed and howled through the room, blending with the cacophony of music. Hastily he switched channels, searching in vain for some loud and gaudy variety show. Channel 4 were screening a concert by the Boston Philharmonic, playing a selection of music by John Williams from the *Star Wars* trilogy. It was good and loud; it would do.

The thumping on the walls from the neighbours had stopped some time ago. Phil prayed that at least one of them, outraged by the noise, would have reached for the telephone and dialled the police. Sitting unshaven in his armchair, dressed only in a bathrobe, he allowed himself a hopeful image of the police finally battering down the door and arresting him for disturbing the peace. If nothing else, he would then be among people; in company, there was protection.

He took another swig of beer, trying to quell the fresh pangs of rising fear. Then he remembered the portable television set in the bedroom cupboard. Dropping the beer can on the carpet, he ran into the bedroom and tore open the fitted wardrobe door. Boxes cascaded around his head as he clawed at the overhead shelving. Eventually, he found what he was looking for. Wrenching the portable set from the shelf, he scrabbled for the extension cord and jabbed it into the base of the machine, then hurried across to the socket in the skirting board. In an instant, the loud, brassy theme music from a detective series boomed out into the bedroom. Phil smiled—a nervous, palsied twitch of the lips, devoid of humour.

Turning, he went quickly through the sitting-room to the kitchen, heedlessly kicking his most recent beer can across the floor as he passed; it crashed, hissing, against the pastel-blue wall. There were a dozen more cans in the fridge; with any luck, he could drink himself to death before . . . before . . .

Before what?

When he returned to his seat, the Boston Philharmonic had finished their recital.

'And now,' boomed the television announcer, 'it's time for a classic tale of horror from those masters of the macabre, Hammer Films. Starring Peter Cushing and Christopher Lee, tonight we present . . . *The Gorgon.*'

No horror films, thought Phil. *No bloody horror films. Things are bad enough.* He reached for the automatic control and switched to another channel. An over-the-hill movie star from the 1950s was beating up a thug who should really have made mincemeat of him. The noise of the fight echoed harsh and loud. That was what he wanted: plenty of noise; plenty of noise to keep away the . . . keep away the . . .

Keep away the what?

The hammering on the walls began again and that, too, was comforting. At least someone knew he was here; Phil could pretend that he was not really alone.

He glanced nervously towards the picture window overlooking the city centre. He had drawn the curtains earlier that evening when the night and its crowding phantoms had gradually transformed his gnawing unease into outright fear. The window had been a frame for the night and he had felt too vulnerable as he stood, searching the glittering neon darkness for the source of his disquiet. It was as if he was exposed to the gaze of whatever watched from the shadows down below; the shadows inhabiting the rainwashed alleys; the cold, black, angular corners of office blocks and car parks.

For more than two months he had been trying to shake off the feeling of being hunted. In the early days, when the crowding fear had suddenly, and for no reason, entered his life, valium had kept it at bay; but as the fear had intensified, the valium had ceased to be effective. Every corner, every shadow, seemed to hold a hidden, lurking terror, and Phil had gradually withdrawn to his flat, shutting himself off from the outside world. In the last month he had felt totally unable to venture out at night . . .

It's been closing in. It's looking for me.

During the last week, he had realised that it was almost upon him—unseen, unheard, unknown, but not unreal. Oh no, it was real, of that he had no doubt, and he was hiding from it in the only way he knew. He had the booze delivered to his flat now. The last delivery had been made only the day before and had caused a lot of speculative talk down at Mason's Off-Licence.

'I'm telling you, mate. The door opened just a crack—on the chain, you know?—and this hand comes out with a ten-pound note in it. "Take it!" this voice says. So I says, "What?" And the voice says, "Just take the money and leave the crate there in the corridor. I'll get it later." So I says, "What?" again and he just throws the money at me. Creep! So I takes the money—no bloody change for him, mate!—shoves the crate against the door and comes back. Reckon that bloke's got some problems, all right.'

Phil had achieved his aim: the last three days had become blurred. The unknown fear had occasionally reared its sickeningly ugly head from the deep, dark waters of his subconscious, bringing events sharply back into focus; when that happened, it was time for another trip to the fridge and, soon, everything was all right again. But tonight the fear was eating through his alcoholic blur.

Time had lost its meaning; his mind was wandering, down long-forgotten, shadowed corridors. But suddenly he was brought back to reality by a sharp stab of anxiety in his stomach. There was a new, chilling sound in the room: organ music and a vaguely spooky female voice. He focused his blurred vision on the television screen. A dark castle loomed from a ragged shroud of trees—it was that horror film. Cursing, he groped for the control and switched channels.

No . . . bloody . . . horror films . . . Don't need that . . . Must have leant on the switch.

He became aware that a low, soft ballad was playing on the

cassette-radio in the kitchen. That was no use. It had to be good and loud; loud enough to keep away . . .

What?

. . . to keep away the darkness that he could feel crowding claustrophobically around him. It was like being on the bottom of the seabed, surrounded by cold, suffocating blackness.

But something's on its way.

Phil pulled himself out of the armchair and staggered into the kitchen. He fumbled with the dial on the cassette-radio and the myriad signals surging invisibly on the evening air whined and shrilled amid fiercely crackling static. Suddenly, Status Quo blasted into mid-song with 'Caroline'.

'Good,' mumbled Phil. 'A bit of head-banging.' He grinned an apish, drunken grin as an image came to mind: he was an entertainer on a variety show, with five plates spinning simultaneously at the top of long, thin poles. Every time a plate slowed down he had to hurry over and set it spinning again before it fell off.

That put him in mind of something else. He fumbled in the pocket of his bathrobe and, smiling, pulled out a colour print. The seven faces in the photograph—that terribly important photograph taken so long ago—smiled back at him, momentarily thawing his icy fear. One of them seemed to have become rather faint—almost transparent—but perhaps that was just his imagination, combined with the haze of alcohol.

'Time for another drink,' he mumbled, and reeled over to the fridge, fighting gravity all the way. He grabbed another can, nudging the fridge door shut with his hip. As he pulled the tab, he again became aware of the droning organ and the female voice.

'Look,' he snapped fiercely, 'I said no horror films!' He staggered back into the sitting-room, found the control on the sofa and stabbed at the buttons. Then, over the general cacophony, he realised that he could no longer hear the detective drama that had been blasting from the bedroom. Angrily, he blundered across the room and stood weaving from side to side in the doorway. The thin sounds of the solo organ and female voice were drifting from the portable television. Through the alcoholic blur, he felt another sudden stab of unease. He was afraid, but he did not understand why. First the television in the sitting-room; now the portable in the bedroom.

Growling, he lurched across and clawed at the controls. The channel refused to be switched. He could see on the screen that a man was picking his way through the dilapidated banqueting hall of a ruined castle. Something moved in the shadows at the top of a staircase. Phil scrabbled at the buttons, his anger briefly swamping the rising, unknown dread. Seizing the carrying handle on top of the set, he swung it viciously away from him in a swift underarm movement. The set jerked free of the extension cord, twisted in the air and shattered explosively against the wardrobe door; fine glass shards sprayed out, littering the carpet.

'That's shut you up . . . '

But somehow, he could still hear that eerie music. The fear clutched at him. Something was wrong, something terrible was happening, something that he could not understand.

He fumbled his way back to the sitting-room. The music was coming from the television set and, as he drew closer, he felt his eyes being dragged back to the screen. The man in the film was ascending the stone staircase . . . and something in a billowing shroud, with twisting, snake-like hair, was waiting for him. The noise of hissing snakes began to grow louder. Now it was issuing not only from the television, but from the radio and the music centre. Frozen in panic, Phil could only watch as the thing at the top of the staircase stepped out into view and the television set blurred into a hissing, static-filled snowstorm. Now the twisting, wriggling tentacles of snake-hair filled the screen, serpent eyes gleaming, tongues flickering. They were writhing outwards, crawling from the screen and reaching for him.

No . . . this isn't right . . . this can't be happening . . .

He scrabbled for the photograph in his pocket, clutching it tight to his chest like a protective charm. It had kept the fear away before, but this time it was powerless.

The coiling, spitting serpents were ravenously hungry as they spilled from the television screen and hunted for him. Terror engulfed Phil, surging in his veins, coiling like a snake in his throat, screaming in his mind: *Get away! Run!* But he could not move. He felt the clamminess of reptilian flesh on his face as the first of the snakes found him. He felt the sharp, savage bite of their fangs as they crawled into his mouth and down his throat.

Everything was misting over; the snakes were coiling around his throat, both inside and out, biting and tearing. There was the taste of salt in his mouth; his eyes clouded in hissing, red pain and the world tilted.

* * *

When the police sergeant and constable eventually arrived, summoned by enraged neighbours, the cacophony from Phil's flat still resounded through the building. After several forceful demands to open the door, one of the neighbours told the police that she had also heard . . . well, she could not be sure . . . but she *thought* she had heard . . . well, *screaming*.

The door was broken down immediately.

At first, the sergeant thought that someone had gone berserk with a red aerosol spray. His fifteen years in the police force had not prepared him for the sight that met his eyes, splattered over the sofa and surrounding carpet. Although it was impossible to tell, he presumed that the tattered mass had once been human. It appeared to have a stained photograph crumpled in what had once been one of its hands, a photograph of six people grouped around a sofa. He was glad that the young constable, green as grass, had lurched away into the kitchen to be sick. He would not have wanted the youngster to see him as he leaned against the sofa gasping for breath. The constable had just beaten him to the sink.

'Oh . . . sweet Jesus . . . '

Two

North of England, Thursday, 10.15 pm

Richard Eden sat in his usual place at the corner of the L-shaped bar in the Imperial nightclub. It was busier than usual tonight. On most occasions, he could see right across the plushly carpeted main area, strategically furnished with tables and chairs, to the lower level of the nightclub and the disco floor. Access to it was gained by two steps down—a hazardous arrangement for those who had over-imbibed—and through a fake proscenium arch. But tonight the view was obscured by the crowd. Red and green searchlights hunted the floor for talent while, above, a multi-faceted globe spun lazily, like Superman's home planet Krypton, reflecting apparently radioactive light into the crowd. Overhead, television screens displayed the latest rock and pop videos.

Richard sipped his whisky, watching the barman and barmaid mechanically and efficiently dispensing drinks. It was an odd fact that, the busier the club became, the more bored Josh and Angie seemed to be. The black waistcoats and bow-ties looked uncomfortable and inhibiting. Angie did not like the work, but it was the only job she could get and it helped her to support her two-year-old kid since her live-in lover had, as she said, 'done a runner'. She was an attractive girl and Richard watched admiringly as she used her looks to induce tips. She had had a hard time; she deserved to get everything she could out of life. Richard turned his attention to Josh: in his mid-twenties, retiring and gay—although his mates were not aware of the fact. Secretly in terror of being ostracised, he fought bravely—some might say manfully—to keep it hidden. And he suffered badly as a result.

Angie tossed her blonde, tightly curled, shoulder-length hair out of her eyes, loosened the bow-tie and sighed deeply, catching Richard's eye as he nodded understanding of her mood. It was a mixed crowd in the Imperial tonight, as usual; there were at least two hen parties, which had obviously started in the pub across the road—the Plough—and drifted into the nightclub before ten-thirty to take advantage of their 'Free-before-Ten-Thirty' tickets. He turned back to the disco floor and could just see the head and shoulders of Dave Johnson, the resident disc jockey—known as 'Deejay' ('The name's DJ and I'm your own Deejay!'). He was standing in the raised booth that housed his stereo equipment and record decks.

'And now it's Laura Brannigan singing "Self-Control". But don't take it too much to heart. The Imperial's the place where lack of self-control on the disco floor's no disgrace. Just don't let the bouncers see you!'

Richard winced. He was worse than usual tonight. The bottle of vodka stashed beneath the record deck must be fairly well depleted by now. The odd 'herbal' cigarette did not seem to be helping matters, and Richard shook his head at the unnecessary risk Deejay was taking. The local police station was just around the corner, and the boys in blue on night shift often popped into the Imperial for a quick drink after work. The infrequent punch-up outside was also sufficient threat to ensure that the cops kept an eye on the place. Troublemakers could be out of the club and into the nick quicker than they thought possible.

'Do you know what that bitch is planning to do?'

Richard turned back. Angie was standing directly opposite him behind the bar. 'Who?' he asked.

'The Woman. Do you know what she's going to do? She's going to stop paying for the bar staff's taxis home after the club closes. No reasons. Nothing. Well, she's on to a loser there straight away, Rickie. There's no bloody way I'm making my way home to West Denton on my own after this place shuts. There's been two rapes up that way, already.'

'Who told you about the taxis?'

'Deejay.'

Richard laughed. 'Take no notice of him. He's plastered tonight. It seems to me that he says that sort of thing just to get a rise out of people. He'll go too far one day and be out on his ear.'

'You reckon?'

'Of course! He's done that sort of thing before, hasn't he?'

'Yeah . . . I suppose he has . . . Like that business about Josh wanting to marry me, and all that.'

'That's just what I mean. Forget it. Even the Woman wouldn't do something like that.'

'You're right,' said Angie resolutely. She snatched Richard's drink from the bar, refilled it, winked and placed it in front of him, mouthing: *On the house*. Richard smiled and returned to his reverie.

The Woman. The mysterious Woman.

The Imperial was officially owned by Layla Management, with the Under-Manager, Douglas Pearson, handling the day-to-day running of the place. But the real owner was the Woman. She lived above the Imperial in splendid and mysterious isolation. No one knew her name; no one knew who she was or where she came from. Douglas Pearson was her barrier to the outside world; her dictates were issued through him. Speculation about her ranged from the imaginative to the wildly improbable, but on one point there was total agreement: she had money and, for some unknown reason, she had chosen to invest it in this former cinema/bingo hall, re-establishing it as the nightclub it had been in Richard's halcyon days. Whoever or whatever she was, her speculation had paid off handsomely: the Imperial was a popular and lucrative business, and the Woman presided over it, never showing her face. Local rumour and gossip-mongering, not to mention the active snooping of certain local inhabitants, had revealed absolutely nothing about her. The Woman was a mystery and seemed likely to remain so. Richard often wondered what it was like upstairs in her living quarters. Presumably she had also invested in sound-proofing, for he had heard that her private rooms were directly above the disco floor. He had long ago decided that the Woman—if she existed at all—was a pretty shrewd bird. The air of mystique that she generated looked like a deliberate ploy to achieve the very thing she was after: to draw crowds of curious patrons wishing to bask in her aura.

As Richard surveyed the crowds, he began to think about all the years he had been coming here. Back in the old days, when he was a kid, the Imperial had been a cinema; he remembered sneaking in there with his friends to watch the X certificate horror films. In the early 1960s it had closed down, re-opening again in the late '60s as a club for live bands. Newcastle's own home-grown band, The Animals, had played there. Even now, a picture of Eric Burdon hung in the reception, next to an autographed copy of the sheet music from 'House of the Rising Sun'. But then the management problems of the Imperial had begun and the licence had not been renewed. Once again the place had become a cinema and, in time, a bingo hall. Then, after a long period of dereliction when it had been used as a warehouse, followed by a short stint as the base for a community arts group, it had undergone its most recent transition and, after intensive restoration and redevelopment, had re-emerged in its former glory as a nightclub.

The new Imperial was not the same kind of nightclub that Richard and his friends had visited back in the 1950s. This was the modern, brightly decorated, plush, Star-Wars-style version of a nightclub with its flashing lights, spangled décor and completely impersonal promise of the 'good time', the drunken cavort and the quick fuck. For reasons he could not understand, Richard found himself continually drawn to the place, although sometimes it depressed the hell out of him. It was emotionally dangerous to hang on too closely to old dreams and memories. You had to go forward, not backward; sometimes it was better to forget the way things used to be. Richard knew all this, but could not change his habit of returning here, chasing ghosts from the past. In a way, it was the only thing he had, particularly since his marriage had broken down and his personal life had collapsed into ruins.

He finished his whisky and ordered another.

* * *

He left the nightclub at 12.30 am. The place was becoming too crowded and he was constantly being jostled in his seat by a group of drunken kids. When someone spilt beer on his jacket, he decided that it was time to go home.

The burly, dangerous-looking bouncer called Paul sullenly held the outer door open for him as he collected his overcoat from the girl preening herself in the full-length mirror in the cloakroom. Richard knew that, for some unfathomable reason, the bouncer had taken an intense dislike to him. They had never spoken, but he had a feeling that the squat, one hundred and eighty pounds of gristle was just looking for an opportunity to fill him in. He slipped out into the icy, rain-washed night. The nightclub door *whumped* shut behind him.

He stood for a while on the pavement. The Imperial was at the top of Byker Bank which curved away to the right, past the Plough and the massive council-house development known as Byker Wall, before vanishing steeply downhill. Sweeping round to his left was a huddle of derelict buildings and the main road leading down to Byker Bridge. The new Metro viaduct stretched massively overhead, racing away behind the nightclub to an overhead intersection with Byker Bridge, the Imperial squatting in the bottom tip of the 'V'. Directly ahead lay open, bulldozed land and the shadow of St Silas' Church.

'The old and the new,' murmured Richard. And then he

became aware of that indefinable sense of unease that had often crept over him in recent weeks. The empty streets, the shrouded car parks, the dimly lit alleys that surrounded him, seemed somehow threatening. The shadows and the dark places had an air of expectant watchfulness that made him shudder. Dismissing the feeling, he turned left into the main street, Shields Road. Within minutes, he was on Byker Bridge, spanning the valley below, and looking back to the brow of the hill where the Imperial crouched glowing in the phosphorescent blue of its neon sign. He walked to the apex of the bridge, looking down to Byker Bank running steeply and roughly parallel. He stopped to lean on the corroded rail and surveyed the shadowed Ouseburn valley stretching below him. Directly beneath, the Ouseburn itself wandered, glinting black through its labyrinthine, factory-shadowed, hewn-stone channel to the bright lights of its dark sister half a mile away, the River Tyne.

Away to the left, beyond the rim of the valley where the Imperial stood, lay the suburb of Newcastle-upon-Tyne known as Byker. Richard had been born there when it was a teeming, grid-iron pattern of tightly packed, two-storey houses on the steep slopes of the Tyne valley. Developed from 1860 onwards to accommodate workers in the nearby shipbuilding and heavy engineering industries, it lay only one mile from the city centre where he now lived. Designated a slum area, the old Byker had been cleared and demolished and a new housing development, the Byker Wall, had emerged, a concrete barrier against motorway noise for a by-pass that never arrived. A mile and a quarter long and between five and eight storeys high, people lived within the Wall and in the new village-housing development beyond. The back lanes and streets that Richard had played in as a child were gone.

He looked down again to the Ouseburn. Once, as a child, he had been told that in days long gone the valley had supported several thriving farms. But then industrialisation had come and, in Richard's own time, the banks of the Ouseburn had always been crowded with warehouses, paint manufacturers and ancient, crumbling factories, suffering from poor access and badly neglected roads. The steep valley sides had been rubbish tips on which kids had built helter-skelter slides using pieces of cardboard. As the new Byker had emerged, phoenix-like, from the ashes of its own destruction, the Ouseburn had remained as he had always known it: a largely dilapidated, mysterious place with its shadow-haunted, empty streets, tightly crowded buildings and black-flowing, effluent-polluted burn. To Richard, with his childhood memories, the Ouseburn valley was like a ghost town, a place that the grown-ups had left to be explored by children; a haunting reminder of old Byker.

In the late '70s, the Council had declared the Ouseburn valley an Improvement Area. The steep valley sides had been reclaimed and landscaped. Financial grants were regenerating industry and controls on pollution in the burn had been imposed. Byker City Farm, standing directly beneath the bridge on a three-quarter-acre site, had been established. But, in Richard's mind, the Ouseburn valley was still a haunted place.

The three viaducts that spanned the area—railway, road and Metro—only heightened the valley's dramatic appearance from above and below.

'The old and the new,' said Richard again. Below him, the Ship Inn and a huge, disused chimney, built for a former leadworks in 1871 and now standing like some monolithic tribute to the past, rose spectrally amidst the new development and industry.

The bad feeling had begun to creep up on him again. The shadows below seemed to be beckoning.

Something behind . . . something creeping up behind me . . . something rushing down on me, arms outstretched . . . ready to hurl me over the . . . NOW!

He looked frantically over his shoulder, crying out involuntarily, expecting to see someone hurtling towards him.

There was no one there. He breathed a sigh, shrugged off the feeling and walked on—back to the city centre, back to his flat.

And then he started to remember.

The Byker Chapter. That was what they had called themselves.

They had grown up together in Byker; together they had played in the streets and back lanes, had explored the Ouseburn valley. They had gone to school together, had shared the pains and ecstasies of teenage life. Some of them had even gone on to the same college, although taking different courses.

Bound by their heredity and background, their friendship had been a firm anchor. Later, Richard had read a social treatise on the area's strong sense of identity and pride—a tightly-knit community with highly distinctive characteristics and a visible neighbourliness. Many families had lived in the same area since the first houses had been built in 1860, with brothers and cousins still living close to one another. The area's sense of self-respect, individuality and friendship was a documented fact, and the Byker Chapter was living proof of that feeling. It had even survived when the old Byker had given way to the new.

Richard recited their names as he walked: Stan Shaftoe alias Stan the Man. Derek Robson. Phil Stuart. Joe McFarlen. Barry Clark. Richard himself.

Somewhere on the River Tyne a ship's siren mourned plaintively.

And Pandora.

Pandora Ellison had been the only female member of the Byker Chapter. She had been born in Cornwall but had come up north when she had been awarded a place on a course at Newcastle Polytechnic. She had moved into a flat in Byker while demolition of the area was under way. Six blokes, one girl—amazingly, there had never been any sexual jealousy or conflict arising from this situation. They were all free to sow their own oats elsewhere and Pandora had shared the same freedom of choice. They enjoyed and revelled in each other's company while still maintaining non-Chapter relationships. Even now, Richard was staggered by the strength of that bond; it had been a high point in his life, a thing to be treasured. The Chapter was a fortress, a refuge, where everyone was on even terms.

Until that last week of college when . . .

He discarded the memory. It did not belong. He just wanted to remember the way things were, not how they had eventually turned out. He kept walking. The ship's siren mourned again.

Three

Two hours later, snakes of rain were slithering down the window pane as Richard gazed out across the city centre from his tenth-storey flat. For an instant, the glittering neon mantling the city was swamped by a silent flash of electricity, followed in seconds by a landslide ratcheting of echoing thunder. His breath frosted the window, engulfing the scene in fog. Without looking, he groped for the vodka bottle that stood, two-thirds empty, on the window-sill beside him. His fingers brushed the neck of the bottle and it tipped backwards from the sill. He whirled drunkenly, caught the bottle in both arms like a father saving his child from a fall, and pressed it close to his chest as he staggered back across the room.

He flopped onto the sofa and drank from the bottle in what he knew to be a ridiculously over-dramatic gesture. He swallowed, grimaced at the burning sourness in his gut and then laughed at himself. His cynicism would not even allow him to get drunk properly. He glanced around the room.

'What a *dump*!' he said in a high, camp voice, imitating Elizabeth Taylor imitating Bette Davis. In the past week, he had really let himself go. Unwashed dishes lay in the sink and economics textbooks littered the furniture and stereo unit. The hoover stood like a sentinel beside the lavatory door. He had dragged it from the cupboard in a depressive rage, intent on cleaning the place up, but when the memories had set in again he had decided to clean up the vodka bottle instead. There were six framed cinema posters on the wall: Bogart, Cooper, Cagney, Lollobrigida, Bergman and Grahame. He toasted them all, with an extra swallow for his favourite dream girl, Gloria Grahame.

There would be no classes at the college tomorrow, so a king-size hangover would not matter too much. The Principal had called for a staff meeting but Richard had made up his mind that he would phone in sick. One missing Economics lecturer would not make much difference to the proceedings.

He wondered what his wife Denys was doing at this moment and felt the usual stab of hurt and jealousy. With an almost physical effort, he stopped his mind from wandering back over the three years of their marriage before the final break-up; he was depressed, yes, but it would only make matters worse to dwell on it. He lurched to his feet and made for the record cabinet, sweeping the textbooks from the lid of his stereo unit. A familiar album protruded from the ranks of its companions. Reverently he retrieved it and, seconds later, Derek and the Dominoes were playing 'Layla'. Richard slumped back and felt the music take over in his mind. It was a track from the good days. After a while, he turned up the volume, letting Eric Clapton's guitar concentrate his thoughts. He remembered the Byker Chapter's wild Christmas party back in '72, at Stan the Man's place. And then he remembered the photograph.

At the height of the party, Stan had mounted one of his many cameras on a tripod in the living-room. It was a time-lapse camera, enabling him to hurry back to the sofa, around which the other members of the Chapter had grouped themselves, before the flash went off. Richard had not seen that picture for years. God, that had been a great time, one of the best evenings he could remember. Suddenly, he had to look at that photograph.

He walked into the bedroom as purposefully as his drunkenness would allow. 'Messy bastard,' he growled at himself when he saw that the bed was still unmade. He knelt down, knees cracking, and reached under the bed, dragging out a battered brown suitcase. The locks were broken. Hell, they had always been broken. As he rummaged through old gas and electricity bill counterfoils, TV licences and Christmas cards, he remembered that the photograph had been mounted in a white cardboard folder. Finally, he found it at the bottom of the suitcase.

He restrained himself from looking at the photograph straight away; he wanted to savour this. Back in the living-room, he turned over the LP and sat down, took another swig from the bottle and then opened the folder. Instantly, he was transported back to that Christmas party so long ago, in another life.

* * *

'What do you mean?' protested Derek, turning from the ice bucket and confronting Phil. 'Course I don't drink too much. I spill most of it on the way to my mouth.'

'Well, pour me another, then,' said Phil, proffering his glass and turning back to the others. Joe was standing with his back to the window. Behind him, snow was gusting against the glass. 'Looks like we're going to be snowed in,' he said.

'Oh, my God,' said Pandora from the sofa. 'Just me and six drunken idiots. What a plight for a poor working girl.'

'Well, if we're snowed in, I suppose we'd better start drawing lots,' said Richard.

'What do you mean?' asked Stan.

'Well, you've heard all those tales about people being stranded on life rafts and on mountains for weeks on end . . .'

'I get it,' said Barry. 'Who's the fattest?'

'Leave me out of this,' said Derek. 'I solemnly promise to give galloping indigestion to anyone who tries anything. Anyway, it's time for a little entertainment, I think.' Reaching behind the sofa, he pulled out a suitcase, flicking open the catches.

'Oh no!' There was a general groan.

'That's your trouble, all of you,' said Derek. 'No culture, no appreciation for talent.' Sitting on the edge of the sofa, he pulled something out of the suitcase and sat it on his knee. It was a ventriloquist's dummy. The others began to throw sofa cushions at him but, expertly avoiding the missiles, he started to sing a ridiculously inept version of 'Sonny Boy'. The dummy, dressed in evening suit complete with tails, bow-tie and frozen grin, clacked its mouth in a complete absence of synchronism.

It was a standard joke whenever they partied together. The dummy, affectionately known as Charlie, had been bought years before and had become the eighth member of their clan, often to be found sitting in an armchair with a drink in its hand, or taking a bath, or on the telephone. A well directed cushion sent Derek sprawling. Feigning offence, he sat the dummy on the floor and went for another drink.

'Got any oldies, Stan?' asked Pandora, playfully grabbing at his ribs. 'Present company excepted.'

'Yeah, what do you fancy? Chuck Berry? Fats Domino?'

' "Blueberry Hill". Put that on.'

Stan began searching through the record cabinet, while Richard sat back and looked at the friends who meant most to him in the world. Something happened when they were all together; the chemistry seemed perfect. They brought out the best in each other and asked nothing in return. No backstabbing. No false expectations.

'What are you looking so down in the dumps for?' asked Barry, grinning. 'It's Christmas. Be of good cheer, you bastard.'

Richard grinned back. 'Pensive, old lad, that's all. Just thinking.'

'Who said that?' asked Pandora. 'Who's getting pensive?'

'This long-haired bugger down here,' said Barry, waving a glass at him.

'Okay, that does it. Up on your feet, Eden.'

'What?'

'We're dancing.'

'To "Blueberry Hill"? That's too slow.'

'And there'll be no "bump-and-grind" dancing in my flat,' said Stan, emerging with the single, 'unless it's my turn next.'

'Come on, up!' Pandora grabbed Richard's hand and dragged him to his feet.

'It's too slow, Pandy,' he protested.

'Stan!' shouted Pandora over her shoulder. 'Put it on 78 revs!'

'What?'

Derek burst out laughing. 'Go on, Stan. This I've got to see.' A falsetto Fats Domino began to give it all he'd got. Pandora and Richard bluffed out their own outrageous rock and roll manoeuvres while the others stood in a small circle, laughing and clapping in time to the ridiculous tempo. Soon, they were all dancing, roaring with laughter and blundering around the room. When the record finished, Richard collapsed onto the sofa and Pandora sank cross-legged in a giggling heap. The laughter was too intense for speech.

'A toast!' said Phil at last, holding up his glass. The laughter subsided into choked gasps.

'Lightly browned, lots of butter,' wheezed Barry.

'To the Byker Chapter,' said Phil. They drank.

'More music,' demanded Pandora.

'Music for the lady coming up . . . ' said Stan. 'But hang on for just one minute. I've got an idea.'

'This could mean trouble,' said Richard.

Stan clambered to his feet and vanished into a cupboard next to the kitchen. Seconds later, he emerged holding a tripod and camera.

'Oh, my God!' Pandora held her hands up to her face in mock alarm. 'Not artistic poses!'

'I want to get a picture of everyone to commemorate the best Christmas I've had for ages. Get yourselves sorted out over there on the sofa.'

Richard and Derek jumped up and grabbed Pandora by the arms and legs, flinging her squealing onto the sofa. They sat on her, proffering innocent, cheesy smiles to Stan. Pandora fought her way to the surface, insisting that she should sit in the middle and the others should place themselves around her.

Barry stood behind the sofa with Joe and Phil, a plastic daffodil from the vase on the window-sill clamped between his teeth. When Stan had lined up the tripod, he looked through the viewer and told him to get rid of it. Barry started to eat it, whereupon the others convulsed with laughter again.

'Come on, you bloody idiots,' called Stan. 'I want this to be a good picture. Pull yourselves together and look semi-sensible.'

He fixed the time-lapse, quickly hurried round the camera and jumped on the sofa beside Derek, leaning back and putting one arm around Pandora.

The cube flashed.

* * *

The thump and click of the needle on the record brought Richard back to the present. Memories of the Byker Chapter had temporarily vanquished the blues, but it was a very fine, precarious balance; the scales could easily tip over again and the depression might be worse. He needed more music—and more alcohol. Feverishly, he pulled out another record, also strongly associated with the Byker Chapter: Bachman Turner Overdrive playing 'You Ain't Seen Nothing Yet'.

'Play it hard!'

Richard picked up the photograph again. He had not taken a

close enough look at it the first time.

Something was wrong.

He rubbed his face sleepily. Something about the photograph wasn't right. What was it that seemed so out of place? His drunkenness might have befuddled his perception, but this was not the way he remembered it. Carefully he took in every detail: his own platform shoes and loon trousers, so hopelessly dated now; Derek's shirt, with massive spiked collar and kipper tie, his shoulder-length, feather-cut hair; the plain pastel walls of Stan's flat; the slight reflection of the flash on the outside window, snow bleaching down outside; Pandora's eyes, turned red by the flash, her beautiful smile and the hot pants; her brown hair; the golden bracelet around one wrist; Stan with his great bearded grin.

What the hell was it? Something was staring Richard in the face but he could not see what it was. Something so fundamentally wrong that in his present drunken state it was eluding him.

'This is stupid, Eden. You're drunk, that's all.'

Drunk, yes. But there *was* something wrong.

'All right, all right. Let's concentrate.'

Joe smiling secretly from behind the sofa, arm around Barry's shoulder; Richard's own face, beaming into the camera; the spot on his chin which had suddenly swollen up the day before the picture was taken. The glass of vodka held up cheerily to the camera as a toast; the single ear-ring, uncommon then. Richard continued to scan the photograph, his gaze resting on the back of the sofa.

You're looking at it! You're looking at it now!

Where was Phil?

He was not in the photograph.

'This is stupid . . . stupid . . .' Richard strained forward. Phil should be standing right next to Joe, his right arm over Joe's shoulder. He should be wearing a white, buttoned cardigan. Richard remembered how his gold ring had caught the flash in a small spark of light.

But he was not in the photograph.

Barry stood smiling on the left with Joe in the centre. But there was an empty expanse of pink wall on the right, where Phil should have been.

'No . . . no . . . this isn't right. He was there. *Of course he was there.*'

Something was creeping around the drunken edge of Richard's consciousness, something ugly, unpleasant and dangerous. He screwed his eyes shut and shook his head, which only made him feel worse. He banged the vodka bottle down on the glass table and turned back to the photograph. It made no difference. Phil was not there.

He slammed the photograph face down on the sofa and grabbed for the bottle again. It was halfway to his mouth when rage suddenly swelled within him. 'You stupid, drunken bastard,' he growled between clenched teeth, and hurled the bottle across the room. It bounced on the carpet and rolled clunking beneath the bureau, trailing a thin stream of vodka. He had so desperately wanted to dispel the blues and hide from the way things were. The booze should have helped him, but it had not —it had cheated him, just when he had needed it most, when he had needed that photograph of the Byker Chapter most. He was so pissed that he could not see straight.

Dragging himself to his feet, he leaned over and pulled the plug on the stereo. The music droned to a halt as he blundered into the bedroom, collapsing face down onto the bed and sinking almost immediately into a ten-fathom sleep.

There was only one dream, just before he slipped over the brink into oblivion. It was a dream of the photograph. Phil was standing in his proper place, beside Joe; but now Richard could see that everyone in the photograph, including himself, had no face. The features had been replaced by blank, pink masks of smooth flesh. Somewhere in the distance, a sibilant, hissing voice was repeating the same echoing word over and over again:

'Spectre . . . Spectre . . . Spectre . . .'

The photograph rippled away from sight and there were no more dreams.

Four

On the following morning, Richard felt just as bad as he expected. His head was full of broken glass and his epiglottis seemed to have swollen to three times its normal size, throbbing with dull pain on the roof of his mouth.

'Was it worth it?' he asked himself as he tottered gingerly into the bathroom. He really must do something about these masochistic binges.

He telephoned the college and told Admin that he had picked up a bug or something. A feeling of unease hung around him for the rest of the morning. He put it down to the hangover, not allowing himself to believe that it had anything to do with the person missing from the photograph. He had been pissed. He was not seeing straight; that was all. When he cleaned the flat that morning, he swept the photograph up in a pile of magazines without even looking at it and unceremoniously dumped the lot under his bed.

I was drunk.

Yeah, a little voice at the back of his mind seemed to say, *but Phil wasn't in the photo. He's gone.*

I couldn't see straight.

But what will happen if you look at that photograph now, in the clear light of day, and Phil still isn't there? What do you do then, Mr Rational College Lecturer?

Shut your mouth!

The remainder of the day was wasted. Richard tried to read but could not get immersed in anything; tried to watch television but was put off by the insipid daytime soap operas. Channel 4 usually showed a vintage movie in the early afternoon, but they must have known that he was going to be absent from work today, so they cancelled it.

The sky was leaden and overcast, with thin drizzle still drifting over the city in memory of the previous night's storm.

Richard began to wish that he had gone to work after all. He stood at the window looking out over the city, just as he had done on the previous evening, and caught himself wondering if his wife was down there somewhere in the crowd.

God, what a miserable day.

He looked at his watch. It was one-thirty and the pubs were open.

Better there than here.

He went to hunt for his jacket.

* * *

Meditating over his hair of the dog—a bottle of Pils lager—in the Portland pub, he found himself thinking about the Byker Chapter again. He had rationalised the business about the photograph and had been extremely firm with that small voice, although it still tried, as it was trying now, to let doubt and fear creep back in again. Despite his efforts, his mind returned to Phil Stuart.

Now you see me, now you don't!

Richard ignored that whisper and instead thought about Phil's brand of lunatic humour, how he had acquired some dry ice from the lab at college and slipped it into Stan the Man's pint of beer one night. Clouds of steam had begun bubbling over the brim, transforming it from a pint of bitter into a Jekyll and Hyde potion. Calmly as always, and to the general hilarity, Stan had quaffed his drink as though nothing had happened to it.

After the Byker Chapter had crumbled, they had all severed connections and gone their separate ways, but Richard seemed to remember that Phil had moved away down south and had finally made it in his chosen career—chemical engineering. That was all he knew.

The previous night's dream came back into his memory: the smooth, featureless faces and that hissing voice. It was a nightmare that had been born out of the booze, nothing else. But that flesh-crawling voice and its single, repeated word still haunted him.

'Spectre,' he said aloud. 'Spectre.'

It was a Byker Chapter word.

The term had been coined many years before, when they were kids, and it had stood the test of time, becoming part of their adult conversation. Richard remembered clearly how the word had acquired its special meaning. Joe had heard the word on the radio during a newscast—'The Spectre of Unemployment,' the man with the BBC accent had said. But what the hell was a Spectre? Chapter discussion while kicking a can in the back lane had cast no light on the matter. Derek seemed to think that it was the surname of a bloke who produced records like 'Be My Baby' by the Ronettes, but that could not be right. Someone had looked it up in the dictionary (after they had worked out the spelling). It meant 'ghost' or 'a haunting presentiment of evil'. But that did not seem right either. The whole thing had turned into one huge joke. Eventually, the Byker Chapter had given this mysterious word a new meaning. A Spectre was something that queered your pitch; it was something that screwed everything up. A Spectre could be the Bogeyman; it could be the mysterious force that made your geography homework go missing, ensuring a leather strap across the hand from the teacher. A Spectre was the strange guy who haunted the park, looking longingly at the little kids; the patch of ice that made you slip and break your arm; the group of big kids standing at the top of the street when you were delivering newspapers and you *had* to walk past them, drawing their dangerous attention. A Spectre could be the reason for the sound of police sirens somewhere out there in the night as a dirty wind rattled and clawed at the bedroom window and Dad was still not home from the pub. A Spectre could be the reason why your mother was crying alone in the kitchen, and she would not tell you why . . .

Richard shook himself back to the present. It was time to forget the Byker Chapter.

But something was soon to happen that would bring those memories back into sharp and horrifying focus.

Five

At 8.30 am on the following Thursday, Richard sat in the college staff-room hunched over a steaming cup of tea and listening to Peter Ives and Norman Potter chewing the fat over Newcastle United's chance in the forthcoming football game at

St James's Park. Somewhere along the way, he concluded, he had missed out on sport—that great national institution—both as participant and observer. His mates thought that there was something perverse about a thirty-two-year-old bloke who did not like football; perhaps he had spent too much time as a kid at home reading books, when he should have been out kicking a ball in the back streets (the Byker Chapter had upbraided him for the same thing). Whatever the reason, sport failed to hold his attention to the same extent that it did, say, Ives and Potter.

He lit a cigarette and glanced across the room at Crosse who was rummaging through his filing cabinet. At the flare of his match, Crosse looked over his shoulder at him, allowing his distaste of Richard's filthy habit to register before returning to the paper chase. Crosse was forty-two, Richard's elder by a full ten years, tall despite his stooped shoulders, bearded and bespectacled. Richard had often tried to work out why they should make such an open secret of hating each other. There was no single factor that could be attributed to their enmity, and he supposed that it was something chemical, something instinctive that could not be rationalised. Crosse slammed the filing cabinet shut with unnecessary force and headed for the door, making Ives and Potter look up quizzically from their conversation.

'Having a bad morning, George?' asked Potter, smiling his wide-toothed smile and looking more like the actor Tom Baker every day. Crosse grunted an apology and marched out of the office.

'You been riding him again, Richard?' asked Ives.

Richard raised his eyebrows in mock surprise. 'I *never* ride Crosse. You know that. I annoy him just by existing, I think.'

Ives laughed and shook his head. 'Anyway, Potter, he continued, 'it's all a question of defence, if you ask me. You know the problem we had last season . . . '

The outside door opened once more and Diane Drew entered. At once, the football conversation died as attention focused on the tall, blonde and extremely good-looking Social Policy lecturer who had just 'signed on' at the college at the commencement of the new term. Richard knew what was coming next and wanted no part of it. The conversation would probably take on a blatantly sexist tone, as if they were somehow testing her. It had happened before and he could tell by the expression on the two men's faces that it was going to happen again. But Diane had their number and Richard admired the way she was able to turn the tables on them to make it seem as if she was the one who was taking the piss out of them.

There was no doubt about it, she was extremely attractive. At least if he kept out of the ridiculous banter, she might not associate him with those other two berks—perhaps she might even begin to take an interest in him if she thought he was different? A direct approach from him was out of the question; he had given up such tactics a long time ago. After the split-up with his wife, it seemed as if something vital had been taken out of him, some kind of spark that would not ignite and allow him to make overtures to any woman, whether he desired her or not. It was not impotence: he had slept with two women after the separation, casual, one-off affairs that had been instigated by the women themselves with 'no-strings-attached', formal handshakes on the morning after and no heart-felt sadness at saying goodbye. For a while, he had wondered if his experience with Denys had turned him into some kind of misogynist. But, after analysing that, he realised that whatever had happened, he was not a hater of women. He just lacked that elusive, indefinable 'spark'. Sometimes he wished that he did not have to analyse everything he felt; it only led to confusion, and it was bloody stupid to try and rationalise and interpret every one of his emotions.

He allowed himself a 'good morning' as Diane dropped her attaché case onto a nearby bench and headed for the kettle, skirting around the over-jovial attempts of Ives and Potter to outdo each other in ad-libbing. She appeared not to notice as she made herself some tea and returned to her usual seat beside the door.

Her long, blue-jeaned legs conjured up a memory as she sat, stirring her cup: a memory of Pandora sitting on a sofa, surrounded by smiling faces. *And of one face in particular which should have been in the photograph, but was not.*

Richard shook off the bad feeling and looked up at Diane's face. It was pretty damn' near the most perfect face he ever remembered seeing. He might have used the word 'beautiful', but his inbuilt cynicism rebelled.

But she is *beautiful. The line of her face. Those diamond-chip eyes. The way her hair curls tight behind her ears and hangs perfectly on her shoulders. Look at those teeth: I wish I were a dentist. And she's so damned self-assured, I really envy her that. Not one concession to all the shit that's being thrown at her by Ives and Potter. They're rabbiting away, but as far as she's concerned, it might as well be water off a duck's back.*

Richard suddenly felt a strange pang inside. With an effort he pulled himself together.

'Christ!' snapped Potter, looking at his watch. 'I've arranged to have a chat with one of my students before the seminar this morning . . . ' Pushing back his chair, he hastily swigged his coffee and made for the door.

'That's the most pathetic way of ending a football argument I've ever seen.' Ives grinned and looked back at Diane, expecting an answering laugh which was not forthcoming.

'Good night, was it, Diane? Last night, I mean?' he asked, when he realised that he was not going to get the response he was after, and now looking far too innocent to conceal what was really going through his mind.

'Sorry?' queried Diane.

Richard had also seen the gleaming Mercedes that had been waiting outside the college for her on the previous evening. He groaned inwardly.

You're out of your depth, Ives. She'll chew you up and spit you out.

'You and your boyfriend out on the tiles last night? Having a good time?'

'Boyfriend?'

It's one against one now, and he'll never stand a chance.

'Yeah . . . you know . . . ' Uncertainty now. 'I saw you being picked up . . . . '

'Oh, you mean my pimp?'

'Your . . . your pimp?'

'Yes, that was him. It was a busy night, last night.'

She's really got him now.

Ives' face was a picture of disarray. Richard hunched himself further over his cup of tea, trying to suppress the rising urge to laugh.

'Interested in some business?'

'What?'

And now the coup de grace.

'Do you want to buy some of my time? I assume by the way that you and Potter have been ogling me since I arrived that you must be interested in spending a little cash.'

'Oh, really? . . . Well, I mean . . . we're all fairly liberal here . . . aren't we, Richard? God . . is that the time? Mustn't miss Maths Three. Must dash, then . . . ' And Ives was gone, the staff-room door slamming behind him. Richard gave in to his laughter at last.

'Superb! I've never seen him handled better! Congratulations!'

'Actually, I hate myself for making those remarks. Knowing those two, they'll believe it and have it spread all over the college by this afternoon.'

'Probably. But so will my account of what really happened, and how things really are.'

Diane seemed to melt a little at Richard's statement. She harrumphed philosophically and lifted her cup in a toast. For a second, he began to wonder if that 'spark' had been rekindled.

She finished her tea, stood up and retrieved her attaché case from the bench.

'Richard. You don't mind if I call you Richard?'

The spark rekindled after all! 'No, by all means. Please.'

'Richard it is then.' A pause while she moved to the door. She turned back and looked him straight in the eye. 'You're a fucking wreck. And unless you pull yourself together you're going to end up on the junk pile.'

Richard felt the spark vanish instantly. He spilled his tea into his lap and began to mop it up in confusion as Diane left the staff-room and headed for her first lecture.

Six

Richard read the entire newspaper article without it making any impression on him at all. His mind had been in neutral as he drifted from a column on inflation to the latest carefully and deliberately leaked exposé on a publicity-hungry film star. From there, he had wandered to the account of a murder in

Shepherd's Bush, a particularly brutal murder of a semi-reclusive type—no motive; no reason; no actual details of the death, other than that it had been the work of some deranged madman. Still drifting, he had moved on to the report of a tax fraud and was still halfway through it, when something began to niggle at him. He felt uneasy . . . no, worse than uneasy: he felt frightened, and he was damned if he could work out why. Had he forgotten to do something important? Was something going to happen?

No. Something *had* happened.

It was the article that he had just read. Something about it had registered subconsciously as he skimmed over the newsprint. He flicked back a page and read again.

'Police hunt savage killer. Ex-chemical engineer brutally slain.'

Ex-chemical engineer . . . ?

Richard read on:

> Circumstances surrounding the murder of Philip Stuart, a former chemical engineer with One-Ten Chemicals, are unclear. It is understood that the police were summoned following complaints from neighbours concerning excessive noise from Mr Stuart's television and radio which were still playing at maximum volume when entry was forced into his flat and his body was found. It is also understood that upon initial discovery of the corpse, police were unable to ascertain the identity or sex of the victim due to the condition of the body . . .

It was the final arrival of the Horror that Richard had sensed on that drunken night the previous week when he had looked at the photograph. Philip Stuart. Ex-chemical engineer. Ex-member of the Byker Chapter. Ex-face on a photograph.

Richard's hand began to tremble; his stomach lurched. He was cold but he was sweating. It was as if his grip on reality, his ability to distinguish between what was real and what was imagined, had been severed. He looked up. Students still buzzed along the canteen counter or sat laughing, smoking, joking or reading newspapers. Their world seemed unaffected. Norman Potter was standing in the doorway arguing with Ives about football fixtures. They, too, were carrying on as normal. The universe had tilted and only Richard was aware of it. He read the article again. Perhaps he had been mistaken? Perhaps it was coincidence? Another Phil Stuart who just happened to be a chemical engineer?

No! It's him. I know it's him.

It was a definite, irrevocable fact. Something deep inside, something that knew of nightmares and their insane logic had told him so. The Nightmare of all nightmares had caught up with him at last.

Phil was in the photograph. Now he's dead. And now he's no longer in the photograph.

Richard was not really aware of his journey back to the staff-room, head down, hands thrust into pockets, mind going over everything that had happened in the last few days. Occasionally, he would pull the newspaper out from under his arm and read the article again, searching for something—anything!—that would offer a rational explanation. But the facts obstinately refused to be rationalised. He continued on his way unseeing, students side-stepping to avoid him.

A shadow moved into his path.

Suddenly aware, he was too late to prevent a collision. There was a cry of pain, a clatter, and books were scattered on the floor.

'Sorry . . .' Richard stood back. It was Crosse, his face purple with rage. Stooping, he began to pick up the books he had dropped. 'Sorry,' said Richard again, bending to help him. Crosse slapped out at his hands.

'Leave them, Eden. Bloody typical. Charging around, eyes shut.'

'It was an accident, Crosse. I'm sorry.'

'Sorry? Sorry? I don't think so.'

'Look, Crosse. Just what the hell is eating you about me, anyway?'

Crosse stood up slowly, facing Richard squarely. 'What's eating me? Everything about you. You're living in the past. There's no difference between you and the kids you're teaching.'

'Should there be?' said Richard. 'I can relate to my students better than you and that's what's eating you, isn't it?'

'Take a look in the mirror, Eden. The world changes and you've got to change with it.'

'You're a nerd, Crosse. Give me one reason why I shouldn't knock you on your back.'

'Look in the mirror, just look in the mirror.' And then Crosse was gone, stalking away down the corridor.

Richard watched him go, unable to quiet that small, whispering voice in his head.

And what happens when you look in that mirror, just like the photograph, and you can't see your face?

* * *

Richard delivered his lecture that afternoon with all the conviction of a robot. He knew his subject-matter by heart and would normally have improvised, sensing the 'mood' of his students and attempting to develop his theme along compatible lines. But not today. The newspaper lay on his desk, folded open at the article which he had now read a dozen times at least. Something about the damned thing seemed to be mocking him, constantly demanding his attention as he stalked the classroom. His words spilled out mechanically, while his mind replayed the events of the last week, over and over again.

By the time the lecture had finished, he still had no answers. And by the looks on several faces, he had delivered one of the driest, most boring lectures ever heard.

'*. . . It is also understood that upon initial discovery of the corpse, police were unable to ascertain the identity or sex of the victim due to the condition of the body . . .*'

It was raining again as he made his way home on foot. He lived not far from the college in a privately owned, multi-storey block of flats. Traffic roared and hissed around him, commuters swarming and bustling against him as he walked. But he was aware of none of it. The rain soaked his hair, leaving spiders' webs streaked over his forehead. Purely by instinct, on automatic pilot, his feet propelled him homewards, alone with his nightmare thoughts.

* * *

A snap. Hissing, white snowstorm. Flashing lines. Somewhere beyond the glass, the sound of lost, faraway voices. A gabble of unfocused noise.

'It is time.'

'I'm frightened.'

'You have no cause for fear.'

'I don't like it. I don't like to lose control.'

'I will control you. I will guide you. I will direct what is within you. But it must be done.'

'What is it? What is this thing? What does it want? You mustn't let it out again. Please, don't let it out. Please don't make me . . . '

'Gorgus . . . Imago . . . Pacter . . . '

'Please don't . . . '

'Dark-Out. You must Dark-Out. It hungers to stalk.'

'Please . . . '

'Necrolan . . . Absavel . . . Gorgus . . . '

Seven

The lure of the vodka bottle was strong, but Richard resisted and drank coffee instead, scanning the city as the pastels of evening became the black shrouds of night, wound tightly against the concrete and mortar of the city. Vodka would only dull his senses and tonight, of all nights, he needed to think, clearly and concisely. He fought down what he knew to be superstitious fear (how he hated himself for being so weak-minded) and returned to the suitcase under the bed, groping in it tentatively, as if searching for a poisonous snake. Eventually, he found it again. Eyes shut, swallowing the bitter taste of his fear, he held the photograph in front of him.

It looked the same. It looked just as he had remembered it.

Except, of course, that Phil Stuart was no longer in it.

Sober and frightened, he tried to convince himself of a number of reasons that might explain the situation. His memory must be faulty. Firstly, Phil had never been at the party at all that night. He had not been able to make it. Secondly, Phil had been at the party but had left before the photograph had been taken. Thirdly, Phil had been at the party but had simply declined to be in the photograph. He had cried off. Despite the lunatic humour, there had always been a shy streak in Phil. He had gone off to mix himself another drink in the kitchen while the picture was being taken. Fourthly, Phil had been at the party and *he* had taken the picture, not Stan the Man.

Richard tried to make himself believe each of these hypotheses in turn, but after a brief period he was forced to develop another theory and eventually accept it as the only available alternative.

I am not mad. I am not insane. True, I drink too much, but it hasn't affected the balance of my mind. I'm sane. I'm rational. Phil Stuart was at that party. I can remember that party vividly; it was one of the high points of my life. Phil Stuart was there and he was in the photograph. Now, someone has killed him and he's vanished from that photograph. He was in it! The easy answer would be to say that I'm cracking up, but that's not true because, when Phil was in the picture, he had his back to the wall. Now that he's gone I can see a small framed print of Bamburgh Castle that Stan had on the wall and which Phil was obscuring. I'd forgotten about that bloody picture. But there it is now, as clear as day, now that Phil's no longer standing in front of it. A small framed print, which I'd completely forgotten about until today.

The walls of Richard's flat were crowding in on him. Suddenly, he felt terribly claustrophobic. He had to get out on the streets. He always thought better when he was travelling or walking. Perhaps a long walk would clear his head.

Half an hour later, jerkin zipped up against the snapping wind, he was wandering through the night. Unable to rationalise, his mind halted by a brick wall of potential insanity, his thoughts turned desperately in search of other preoccupations. But these could provide no temporary respite, no soothing diversion: he thought of Denys.

They had lived together for two years before getting married, but it would be too easy to say that marriage had been the main reason for the breakdown of their relationship; the seeds had been sown well before that. He had turned a blind eye, had kidded himself that it would all work out if only he persevered. He wanted to go one way and she wanted to go another: it had been as simple as that. And then, six months ago, she had packed her bags and left to live with the foreman of an engineering firm, some guy called Swan. Richard had never realised how much he relied on Denys just being there. Of course, her leaving him was not entirely a surprise—it had been on the cards for some time—but he had been more than hurt when it happened: he had been devastated; his personal life was in ruins. Denys was made of harder stuff; she had been quite philosophical about it. And all Richard could do at the moment was console himself with vodka and a string of over-the-top parties where companionship, even in a superficial form, could be found.

And now this bloody photograph!

The return to the photograph snapped him back into an awareness of his surroundings, and he cursed his subconscious mind for directing him to this of all places. He was standing in the centre of the new Byker housing development, overlooking a row of balconied, terraced houses. Directly ahead of him, in the centre of the terrace, shrouded by trees, lived his wife and that bastard Swan.

Undecided, Richard rubbed his freezing hands together, lifting first one foot and then the other in rapid succession. Just ahead, a pub beckoned. Behind him, the road home. Or a bus stop on his left which would take him back to the town centre. Depression hovered like a dark, threatening cloud. Perhaps he should go down there and try to talk to Denys? Maybe Swan was working on night-shift. On the other hand, why flog a dead horse? There was more than enough on his mind as it was.

She's my wife!

He started across the road towards the house. It was beginning to rain again. Street lamps cast harsh, orange slabs of light over him as he reached the pavement leading to Number 73. He hated this street. Still not knowing what he was going to do or say, he reached the large, panelled door and stabbed at the doorbell. Somewhere inside, a bell chirred. Impatiently, he stabbed again, standing back and looking up at the bedroom windows. There was no movement. He stabbed at the button again.

What am I really doing here? he asked himself. *What do I intend to say?* A secret part of him hoped that there would be no one at home. Then he would be able to go back to his flat in the city centre, feeling as if his mission had been accomplished. He cursed himself for not knowing his own mind. He was about to make a last jab at the button when he heard the sound of movement inside. A curious emotion seemed to swell from the pit of his stomach to his chest; a rush of pain that tasted of loneliness, the hopeless lack of direction in his life and the longing to see Denys again. Taken together, all these sensations coalesced into one: fear.

The door opened.

Denys was wearing a dressing-gown which, of course, made everything worse. Her reaction on seeing him only seemed to intensify the bad feelings inside. She groaned, turned her head away and began to shut the door again. Richard moved forward quickly, adopting the old salesman's trick, a foot in the door.

'What the hell do you want, Richard? I mean . . . what's the point?'

'I just need to talk to you, Denys. Just to talk.'

'You always were ripe with clichés. We've done all the talking we have to. It's always the same. Go home.'

'If I had a proper home to go to, I would. But you're not there.'

'Give it a rest, Richard. You know it's hopeless . . . '

A noise from somewhere in the house. A man's voice, slurred and gruff.

'You'd better go, Richard. I don't want a scene.'

'Look, if we could just talk . . . '

'Richard, go home!'

The door was suddenly pulled wide and Swan stood framed in the doorway: short dark hair, bull-browed, tee-shirt and jeans. One hand now draped protectively around Denys' shoulders.

'You again.'

'Yeah, me again.'

'Piss off, Eden. Do yourself a favour.'

'I want to talk to my wife.'

'She's not your wife any more.'

'She is until the courts say otherwise, Swan. I just want to talk. I'm entitled to talk if she'll let me. I'm half-paying for this flat, you know.'

'There's only one thing you're entitled to, mate!'

Richard never saw the blow coming; he had turned his attention to Denys again for a last, desperate plea. Swan should not have been here; it had spoiled everything. Swan's fist hit him between the eyes and the next thing Richard knew, he was lying on the pavement. The cartilage in his nose felt crushed. A gout of blood sprayed over his shirt. Denys had stifled a scream, but even from where he lay, Richard could see that it was born only from sudden shock. There was no pity, no love for him.

The door slammed.

Richard staggered to his feet, clutching his nose as blood poured over his wrist and down his forearm. There was no emotion in him, no rage at what had happened, no feelings of revenge or hate to make him charge at the door and batter at it until Swan came out again. No remorse. No love. Nothing . . . no, not even love.

Denys' reaction—or lack of reaction—had put a final seal on the affair. The confrontation, the fist, the degradation, all these things had brought about a kind of catharsis. Richard knew that, somehow, an old life had ended and a new life had begun. Feeling cold and hollow, yet knowing that from now on the only way to go was up, he turned and headed for the bus stop on Shields Road.

* * *

The flat was silent when he arrived home. Too silent. The silence and the darkness seemed to reflect the hollowness inside him as he entered, without flicking on the light, and pushed the door shut behind him. The picture window on the far wall framed the irregular city skyline in a jagged, peaked jumble of blue and black. The vodka bottle stood on the sill, occupying centre stage, cold blue light making its contents glitter invitingly like liquid platinum.

'Why not?'

Still not switching on the light, he made his way to the bottle, spinning the top from its neck, closing his eyes and drinking deeply. The figure of Denys standing in that doorway haunted the darkness behind his eyelids. It was a different Denys from the Denys he had known.

It's like being dead, he thought, drinking again. *Dead inside. Dead and buried.* He looked out across the city. He did not give a damn about anything or anybody. He was dead. His fingers found the table lamp at his side. He switched on. Before him lay the newspaper article and the photograph. And, of course, at the moment he did not give a damn about those, either.

Until he looked down.

Phil Stuart was not in the photograph and all the other members of the Byker Chapter were still grouped around the sofa—*all, that is, except Derek.* Richard felt horror thrill in his stomach, surging to his throat. Frantically, he snatched up the photograph.

Where Derek had been, sitting next to Pandora on the sofa, was an empty gap. It was as if he had never been there.

Richard cried out. A long, loud, wordless yell. The vodka bottle suddenly shattered against the far wall as he collapsed into his armchair, face buried in his hands. The floodgates of grief and sanity temporarily spilled over and tears of loss and ever-mounting fear flooded out.

God, no! No, no, no, no . . . NOT AGAIN!

* * *

In a fever-tossed dream, Richard found himself travelling north across the high-level railway bridge spanning the River Tyne. Standing distant yet conspicuous, he could see the Byker Wall beyond the crowded city centre buildings. Embellished with galleries and balconies, porches and pergolas, railings and weatherboardings, it looked like a barrier surrounding the village within a city.

Now, he was standing at the top of a street in old Byker, many years before the new development and the slum clearance. It was the deep of night and, from where he stood, he could see long, steeply-sloping streets, crowded with glistening terraced houses and their black slate roofs, all the way down to the River Tyne. A cruel November wind was blowing; ships' sirens moaned plaintively from the distant quayside. He knew that the houses were empty, all of them. He turned to look at the house beside him. Rain gurgled and splashed from a broken gutter. From a shattered upper window-pane a ragged curtain flapped and dripped in the wind. He knew that he must enter that house.

The door was opening and he was drifting inside, smothered by the blackness. He could smell the damp, pungent odour of decay and peeled wallpaper. Something scampered in the blackness. Another door was opening beside him and suddenly he began to feel dreadfully afraid. He did not want to go into that room, but he was entering anyway and could not tear his eyes from the terrible sight awaiting him.

Wallpaper flapped from the walls, huge flakes of scabrous dried and peeling paint hung from the ceiling like burst blisters. The room was derelict. Bare floorboards squeaked underfoot as he entered. A cold wind hissed through the broken window-pane. Only one piece of furniture stood in the room—a sofa. And grouped around that sofa in familiar poses were the Byker Chapter; all of them except Phil, Derek and himself. Again, as in his previous nightmare, their faces were horrific pink masks devoid of features: no eyes, no mouth, no nose. They were beckoning Richard to join them. Screaming silently, he tried to tear himself away from that awful spectacle. In slow-motion, body dragging and dull, he managed to turn and was confronted by an ornate mirror that had suddenly appeared on the peeling wall beside him. Now he could see the stark terror on his face, the wild horror in his eyes. His mouth was open in mid-scream. There was no end to the nightmare, because now he could see that his mouth was vanishing, to be replaced by smooth, pink flesh. His nose and ears were disappearing as he began to join the other members of the Byker Chapter and some invisible artist wiped his features away. He clutched in terror at the smooth blankness of his face. He was suffocating. And now his body was transparent, vanishing slowly from the mirror.

I'm fading . . . I'm disappearing . . . something's wiping me away.

His body had no more substance than a ghost, and his ghost image was slipping away.

No . . . no . . . no . . . NOOOOO!

*   *   *

Richard awoke, soaked in sweat, the unvoiced scream still lodged in his throat. Moonlight was streaming in through the window.

He was standing naked in front of his own living-room mirror.

Eight

'I was lucky to make contact with such a good friend of Derek's,' said Richard. 'When I rang Durham College, I really didn't know who I would get. I suppose I just needed to find out what happened . . . talk to somebody who worked with him . . .'

'Sure you won't have another drink?' said the portly man next to him. His hair was receding, making him seem older than he actually was; the thin woollen tie around his neck looked as if it was choking him. 'No? Okay, then. Yeah . . . I knew Derek pretty well. We lectured in the same subject. The sooner they catch the bastard that killed him, the better. For the first time in my life, I'm starting to regret that we don't have the death penalty. I was always against it before, but hanging's too good for that maniac.'

Derek's fellow lecturer, Robinson, ordered another drink at the bar. The pub, not far from Durham College, was filled with lunch-time customers. Richard had remembered that Derek had taken a teaching post at the College just before the Byker Chapter had split up and had prayed that, if he had moved on in the intervening years, the College would be able to give him a forwarding address. Luckily, Derek had still been working there when . . . *when he vanished from the photo*, thought Richard. He *had* to find out what had happened and when he had explained to Robinson that he was also a lecturer, the latter's frosty manner had melted and he had suggested the meeting.

'What happened exactly?' asked Richard, when the barman had brought Robinson's gin and tonic.' The reports I've read in the press seem a little muddled.'

'Yes, well . . . it was a little bizarre to say the least. I was there, you know. Well, by *there* . . . I mean that I walked in on his place when the police had just discovered his body. Perhaps I'd better start from the beginning . . .

'You see, Derek had been having a pretty bad time over the last few weeks. Depression; no real reason as far as I could work out. He'd had a minor tussle with his girl-friend, Linda, but he'd seemed to get over it. I don't know, maybe it *was* that. Anyway, he'd really withdrawn into his shell, wasn't socialising as much as he used to. For the last couple of weeks, he'd virtually disappeared from the scene. Valium. On the sick. Nervous exhaustion. So I gave him a ring. No answer. One afternoon after classes I went round to his flat . . . a private block up on Bymoor Road. The daft bugger wouldn't open the door! He just kept swearing at me to go away, saying really stupid stuff. Stuff like: "I know it's not really you. Go away." What a crazy thing to say—"*I know it's not really you.*"

'Anyway . . . I lost my temper a little and banged on the door, telling him to open it or I'd put my foot through it and belt him in the mouth for talking such idiocy. So he opened the door just a crack—it was on a chain—and I felt like telephoning for an ambulance straight away. He looked terrible! White face, sunken eyes, slurred speech. Just as if he'd had some kind of nervous breakdown or was suffering from the worst hangover in history—or both. He *stank* of whisky. I tried everything to get into that flat, but he just wouldn't budge. Tight, clipped, one-word answers—you know? He was looking at me as if he expected me to attack him or something. And he had his television set in the sitting-room blasting away like hell. I kept talking to him, and after a while he seemed to relax a little. But he still wouldn't let me inside. I told him straight: I didn't know what was wrong, but if he didn't pull himself together I was going to send for a doctor. In the end, I made him promise to meet me here on Wednesday for a chat, to see if I could help him. He seemed pleased at that suggestion.

'Wednesday came. Two hours after the arranged time, I realised that he wasn't going to turn up. So I went to his place, intent on smashing down the door and dragging him out by the scruff of his neck. Of course, I soon found out why he hadn't turned up. He was dead. Murdered. And the flat was swarming with cops. The minute I arrived, they dragged me down to the police station and gave me the old first-degree questioning. Made me glad that I had an alibi—chatting up the barmaid in here.'

'And just what exactly happened to Derek? Do you know?'

'Really bloody bizarre. You probably know all about that daft hobby of his . . . ?'

'Ventriloquism. He was hopeless at it.'

'Yeah,' chortled Robinson in a resigned manner. 'Hopeless. But it was a good laugh, because he knew he was hopeless and played it up for all it was worth. Always went down a bomb at parties.'

'Yes,' said Richard, remembering one party in particular, 'that wooden dummy of his. Charlie.'

'That's right. Charlie . . . ' Robinson's expression had darkened. 'Well, some bastard must have broken into his flat while he was there. Maybe he was in the bathroom or something, getting ready to meet me at the pub. He obviously came face to face with the intruder. And the bastard beat him to death. Beat him to death with the ventriloquist's dummy.'

'Bloody hell!'

'Yeah, that's right. Derek had been thrown all over the place. Furniture broken up, television smashed, books ripped apart, ornaments shattered to hell. They think the guy must have used the dummy as a sort of club. There was blood on the floor, the walls . . . God . . . The dummy was soaked in it. This fella must have been a maniac because he'd had a go at Derek even after he'd killed him. Torn him up, they reckon.' Robinson's face was white now. He finished his gin and tonic in one gulp.

'Drink?'

'Yes,' said Richard, horror seeping into him. 'Whisky.' Robinson ordered again, and they waited in silence until their drinks arrived.

'This may sound stupid,' said Richard, sipping at his whisky, 'but I'd really like to get a look at Derek's flat.'

Robinson looked at him steadily for a moment.

'Why?'

Richard toyed mentally with several fabrications and then, deciding that they were all too weak for credibility, opted for the truth.

'Something's going on. I don't know what, but I've a bad feeling that someone has got it in for a bunch of friends who used to call themselves the Byker Chapter. Derek and I were Chapter members.'

'Derek told me about the Byker Chapter. Go on.'

'Did Derek ever mention Phil Stuart?'

'Let's see . . . the comedian, right?'

'Right. Well, he was murdered last week. Somebody broke into his flat in Shepherd's Bush and tore him to pieces.'

'Christ!'

'He was killed in the same way as Derek. There must be a connection.' *The photograph. Tell him about the photograph!* And then: *No! that's too much. He'll think I'm insane.*

'Have you been to the police?'

'No, not yet.'

'Don't you think you should?'

'I can't. Not yet. There are other things going on that I'm afraid I can't tell you yet.'

'Maybe you're the killer.' Robinson lit a cigar, watching over cupped hands for Richard's reaction.

'I was getting pissed in Byker when Phil was killed. Arguing with my wife when Derek was . . . '

'I'm sorry. That was probably a stupid thing to say. You're obviously not a murderer . . . '

'No, you're right to think that. You don't know me from Adam. Look, before we go any further, I want you to make a few phone calls to substantiate what I've just said. I want you to be sure.'

'No, there's no need. I believe you. Why do you want to look at his flat?'

'To be honest, I don't really know. I've just got a feeling that if I can look round, I might find something that will make sense of this whole damned business.'

'The police forensic experts have been over that flat with a fine tooth comb. What do you expect to find?'

'That's just it. I don't know. But perhaps . . . *something* . . . How come you know so much about what's going on, anyway?'

Robinson reached into his pocket and pulled out a key-ring, jangling it at Richard. 'Because I own Derek's flat. I was renting it to him. Not only that, but my brother's the desk sergeant down at Durham City.' Robinson downed his gin and tonic and stood up. 'The police released the flat yesterday. If we leave now, we can be there in fifteen minutes. Come on, my Renault's outside in the car park.'

He rolled away towards the exit door, cigar smoke streaming from around his head. Richard gulped down his own drink and followed.

Nine

Brewster Dwellings was a six-storey block of privately rented flats overlooking Durham and giving a good view of the Cathedral. Its bland, stucco façade and balconied verandas seemed unprepossessing as they approached, but Richard guessed from Robinson's conversation in the car that the interior of the flats would be somewhat more impressive. On closer inspection, he saw that the windows of each flat were glazed with smoked glass, the sure sign of opulence and treasured privacy. *Not bad for a college lecturer. Wonder where he gets the money?* They parked in an underground bunker.

In a gruff, embarrassed way, Robinson told him that they were using Derek's identity pass to gain access.

'Controlled entry?' asked Richard unnecessarily as Robinson pushed a key into the communal flat door at the top of the underground car park stairway.

'Yep!' grunted Robinson, pushing the door open with his hip.

'And the police are satisfied that it wasn't another tenant who killed Derek?'

'Yep!'

'I should have thought that it was bloody near impossible to break into this place.'

'Security doors aren't infallible. All it takes is for someone to prop them open while they nip round to the shop for something.'

'Yeah, maybe in a council flat. But from what you tell me, the snob quotient in this place would make them all super-fastidious.'

'My view exactly.'

'Then how the hell did anyone get into Derek's . . . ?'

'My view exactly,' repeated Robinson as he guided Richard into the central foyer. The lift doors opened immediately when he pressed the switch inset into the wall.

Derek had lived on the top floor, the sixth. Within seconds, they emerged in the small, functional corridor that gave access to the top-floor flats. The carpet squeaked underfoot like compressed snow. 'Read any good "locked room mysteries" lately?' asked Robinson as they made their way down the corridor.

'No, why?'

' 'Cause Derek's door was locked when the police arrived. Locked from the inside. And the key was in his pocket. They had to break the door down.'

'Whoever did it came through the front door, locked it again with one of those skeleton keys or something and got away over the balcony.'

'Not possible. You'd need a hundred-foot rope and nerves of steel. Also, it was broad daylight and the street down there was busy. Someone would have seen him.'

'He jumped down to the next balcony . . .'

'Not possible. The overhang's too great.'

'So it was bloody Batman!'

'Don't get testy, Eden. I'm only telling you the facts.'

'Sorry.'

Richard's guess about the interior of the flat was well founded. A small entrance hall gave access to a spacious living-room area. A door on the left opened into a bathroom; on the right into a bedroom. Straight ahead, french windows led directly onto the balcony. Bright sunshine slanted from the windows over the living-room, throwing sharp shadows and highlighting the swirling dust motes in the air. Richard could see a profusion of potted plants and climbing vines on the balcony. They had not been watered for some time and most of them were dead or dying. Beyond the french windows, Durham Cathedral sat magnificently on the skyline.

Richard advanced into the centre of the room as Robinson locked the door behind them. A coffee table, one of its legs broken off and lying on the floor, sat crookedly in the centre of a rectangle formed by a sofa, two armchairs and a television set. On closer inspection, Richard saw that the glass top of the coffee table was transparently tattooed in a jagged cobweb. The tan-coloured carpet was marred by a large, irregular stain between the living-room and the bedroom. He tried not to look at it as he wandered round, examining the bric-a-brac. The room was like a jigsaw that had been scattered and hastily reassembled. In places, someone had hammered the wrong piece into the wrong gap.

Plastic flowers had been replaced in the vase on the mantelpiece, head first and with bare stems sticking upwards; a print of Durham was propped, upside down, on a table in the corner; the jagged filament of a light bulb dangled naked from the ceiling. There was a promise of bad luck on the wall beside the bedroom door: a broken mirror, the crack streaking across the glass like frozen lightning.

'I see the police at least had a go at tidying up,' said Richard bleakly, examining a shelf filled with popular paperbacks.

'Sort of. Look, Richard . . . what do you expect to find, anyway?'

'Like I told you. Something. Nothing. I don't know.'

The door to the bedroom was open. Richard went inside. The quilt on the bed was rumpled and pulled to one side. A window occupied half the wall on the same side as the french windows, height ensuring privacy. More bookshelves; a chest-of-drawers and two large cupboards. Richard opened one. Jackets and shirts hung from the rails inside. Below the clothes were two built-in shelves on which LP records and half a dozen singles were scattered. He picked up the topmost record: Derek and the Dominoes playing 'Layla'.

A Byker Chapter record.

For the first time, he felt a terrible sense of loss. Raw emotion began to swell in his throat. Until this moment, he had been living in a dream—a walking nightmare. Phil's death had been a horrible phantasm; the vanishing figure from the photograph was somehow a fantasy that he could not relate to the person, the flesh-and-blood mate he had known so well. The phantasm had gathered momentum when Derek had vanished from the picture; but now, in Derek's flat, holding that record which they had played so often and which had been one of the inconsequential yet emotionally tying bonds of the Byker Chapter, sorrow at last bubbled upwards.

'Find anything in there?' Robinson's voice drifted in from next door. Richard heard the french windows slide open as Robinson moved out onto the balcony.

He cleared his throat. 'No . . . nothing yet . . . '

'Take your time.'

Richard replaced the record. There was nothing else in the cupboard, other than a scattering of shoes on the floor. He moved to the next one. It opened with a soft, *snicking* sound.

A monstrously pale, grinning face leered up at him from the bottom of the cupboard.

Richard felt his heart lurch. He recoiled from the cupboard, bumping against the bed. Doll-like eyes glared upwards; crimson lips snarled in an unnatural oblong, framing square, shining enamel teeth.

The terror ebbed and he breathed a sigh of relief, moving forward again.

It was Charlie, Derek's ventriloquist's dummy. He stooped down to look more closely. The three-foot dummy lay huddled grotesquely on the floor of the cupboard. It was dressed in the same evening suit that Richard remembered from the Byker Chapter parties, except that now it was stained and crusted with something that did not bear close examination. Black coat and tails; white shirt; a blue-spotted bow-tie swathed around the neck like some vampiric butterfly—a bow-tie that would spin if Derek had remembered to renew the batteries in the dummy's top pocket. Painted black hair glistened on the grotesquely large head, one strand curling on the forehead.

Richard heard Robinson come back into the kitchen as he searched the cupboard. More clothes, shoes, an empty bottle of Jim Beam. He pushed the door shut and crossed the room to a picture hanging on the wall. Suddenly, he felt very uneasy. It was the same feeling he had experienced on that drunken night back at the flat when Phil had vanished from the photograph. Something he had seen was out of place. From somewhere in the living-room, he heard the clinking of glasses.

'Drink?' asked Robinson. A fridge door slammed. The clink of ice cubes.

'No . . . no thanks . . . '

Richard looked round the bedroom, trying to remember what he had examined. Perhaps whatever it was he had seen had been in the living-room, not in the bedroom. Behind him, there came the soft *snick* of a cupboard door opening again.

He turned.

The second cupboard door was swinging slowly open. It thumped lightly on its hinges, wide open to the wall. The dummy's hand had fallen forward out of the cupboard against the door.

Just as if the dummy had opened the door itself, thought Richard. And then, as he moved forward and watched, he could see that there was something else in the cupboard. Something apparently buried under the blankets and other household debris. Something that twisted and squirmed, making it look as if the dummy itself was wriggling and writhing, trying to clamber out of the cupboard. He moved cautiously round to the foot of the bed, trying to get a better look. A cat, perhaps? The dummy flopped out of the cupboard onto the carpet. And then Richard realised what had been troubling him: it was the dummy itself. Robinson had told him that it had been the murder weapon. There was no way that the police would have brought the major piece of evidence back to Derek's flat and simply stuffed it into a cupboard. So what the hell was it doing there?

The dummy's face turned to look up at him.

Gravity . . . that's all . . . it was just gravity . . .

But in that instant, he knew that there was nothing else in the cupboard that had given the dummy the appearance of movement. Its horrid wooden eyelids blinked with a dry, clacking noise. The marble eyes swivelled and fixed on him. The mouth began to open and close, a high-pitched yimmer-yammering sound issuing from the square orifice. Richard stood frozen as the dummy began to crawl slowly on all fours across the carpet towards him. Its mad, enamelled face remained fixed on him as it came, the head wagging from side to side, its horribly caricatured, child-like face full of horrific threat.

Behind Richard, the bedroom door opened and Robinson walked in, a tumbler full of whisky in one hand.

'Well, Sherlock, did you find anything? No tell-tale clues or . . . ' Robinson's words died in his throat at the sight of the ungainly midget scrabbling on taloned hands towards Richard. But the words broke the hypnotic spell. Richard stepped back and turned quickly to Robinson, an unspoken question hanging on his lips.

Robinson dropped his glass. The dummy's high-pitched gabbling was building to a manic crescendo.

'No . . . no . . . ' muttered Richard, as if refusing to accept what he saw with his own eyes. 'I definitely don't believe this.'

The dummy reared to its knees, arms flapping, talons gripping the air; eyes rolling, mouth working continually, *clack-clack-clack.*

It shrieked and flew at Richard like a wild animal.

Robinson blundered away as Richard flung his arms up to protect his face. A row of ornaments on the chest-of-drawers was swept to the floor. The dummy fastened on one arm, enamel teeth shearing through the cloth to his flesh, claws ripping and shredding his sleeve. Richard felt no pain; his terror overwhelmed all else. He swung his arm away from him as he staggered backwards, smashing his fist at the unyielding wooden head. The dummy clung on, savaging and worrying his arm like some large, rabid bat, coat-tails flapping madly. Richard uttered loud, hoarse cries of horror and fear as the doll tried to get better leverage on his arm. Instinctively, he knew that it wanted to get to his face.

. . . To my eyes . . . to my throat . . .

The doll continued to shriek.

The bedside lamp shattered.

Robinson's words:

They think the guy must have used the dummy as a sort of club. There was blood all over the flat. The dummy was soaked in it . . . must have been a maniac because he'd had a go at Derek even after he'd killed him. Torn him up, they reckon.

Richard crashed against the bedroom wall. The dummy lunged upwards. His fist caught it in the middle of its face. He felt the face crack, felt the enamel split. He swung his arm hard against the wall. The dummy slammed into the plaster, bounced back with an audible crunch and then, its grip lost, was flung clear across the room. It smashed into the wardrobe and fell to the carpet.

Breathing heavily, his arm tattered and bleeding as if he had just fought off a wildcat, Richard saw Robinson flinch in the bedroom doorway where he had been standing, frozen in shock.

The dummy squirmed and wriggled where it had fallen, as if in agony, but Richard could see that it was still very much alive and still yammering with rage. It was trying to rise again.

Alive! The thing's alive! And it wants to kill me!

'Quick, Robinson! Get out . . . get out before it . . . '

The dummy was rolling onto its front again, head turning to

look for them. Richard lunged forward and caught Robinson by the arm, dragging him into the living-room. Robinson had now recovered sufficiently from the shock to lean back and grab the doorknob as the dummy found them again, shrieked and flew at them.

'Jesus!'

The door slammed on the dummy's arm and the upper part of its head. Robinson kicked at the head, trying to dislodge it and shut the door completely. The head twisted, small taloned fingers tore shreds of wood from the door jamb.

'I can't hold it much longer!' Robinson had to shout over the doll's hungry shrieking and ranting. The door rattled and clattered under the onslaught from the other side, wood on wood. Desperately, Richard looked round for some kind of weapon.

The shattered coffee table leg.

Striding purposefully back to the bedroom door, holding the leg like a club, he moved round Robinson, knelt and lashed out savagely and repeatedly at the enamel head. Flakes of paint littered the carpet.

'Eden, I can't hold it!'

The door was wide open as Robinson fell back, and the dummy was scrabbling inside, head down, arms flapping. Richard stood astride it aiming blow after blow at the head.

It squirmed into the room on all fours, Richard walking grimly with it, each attempt of the dummy to rise or turn its face upwards being rewarded by a sharper, more savage battering. The ranting began to diminish; the insane, child-like yammering died away.

Richard stood on the dummy's back, swinging a two-handed blow at the enamel head. With a sharp crack, the head was severed from the stump of its wooden neck. He lashed at it again with his foot and it rolled away swiftly in a wobbling arc, like a grinning football. Richard kept his full weight on the body with his other foot as the arms and legs drummed a savage tattoo on the floor. He grabbed one of the arms, tore it from the body and flung it away across the carpet. The head came to rest by the sofa, eyes swivelling, jaw clack-clack-clacking. Richard began to stamp on the dummy. The arms and legs spasmed, the yammering head began to croak. The arms and legs flapped lifelessly. The eyes and mouth clacked shut.

The dummy was dead.

Richard dropped the table leg and leaned against a chair, fighting for breath.

'My heart!' exclaimed Robinson suddenly.

Richard moved to catch him as he slumped against the other armchair. His eyes were bulging, his chest heaving as Richard guided him into the chair. 'Oh God! I've had trouble before. I've got pills . . . '

'Where?'

'Got to take them with water . . . '

'Where are they?'

Robinson began to claw at his jacket pocket. Richard found the pills, loosened Robinson's tie and hurried to the bathroom, pausing only to look at the dummy. The head, the severed arm and the body lay still in the centre of the room.

Robinson tilted his head back, gasping in rags of air; the pain in his chest was crushing his lungs, his fingertips were tingling. He struggled to regain composure, trying to steady his breathing and the rhythm of his heart.

Richard blundered into the bathroom. The entire sequence of events during the last three minutes had been a nightmare that defied logic. What the hell *was* that thing? How could Derek's bloody dummy—an object of affection for the Byker Chapter for so many years—come alive like that . . . ? What was it doing here, anyway?

Back in the living-room, the fingers on the dummy's severed arm twitched and groped at the air. Unaware, Robinson groaned as another stab of pain pierced his chest.

In the bathroom Richard found a glass and filled it with water from the wash-basin. His hands were shaking badly as he examined the bottle of pills: 'Three to be taken when required.' There were only three in the bottle. The top flew off in his trembling fingers. The pills clattered to the floor.

'Oh shit!' Richard scrabbled on the floor, hunting for the pills. He could hear Robinson's laboured breathing from next door. *Alive*, he thought, *The bloody thing was alive. It killed Derek and it tried to kill me.*

In the living-room, the dummy's eyes opened slowly. The jaw clicked wide. Slowly and silently the head began to roll across the carpet towards the body.

'Just a second! Hang on! It's okay!' Richard had found two of the three tablets. If he did not find the third in the next few seconds, he would just dash and give him the two he'd retrieved. That would do until he had time to hunt for the third.

The arm dragged itself forward, fingers clutching at the deep pile of the carpet. Nearer and nearer. The head rolled past Robinson's feet noiselessly, face momentarily leering up at him.

Richards thoughts whirled crazily. *That dummy shouldn't have been here. No way, It should be under lock and key in the police station. It shouldn't have been in the bedroom* . . . And then, another more desperate and terrifying voice in his head: *It got away. It got out of the station and came back here. It came back to look for something. It was waiting for something . . . Oh, my God . . . It was waiting for ME!*

Something clunked at Robinson's feet. It made a sucking sound. But Robinson was too tired to look.

Richard snatched the third pill from its hiding place behind the drain-pipe, grabbed the glass of water and hurried back into the living-room.

The dummy was standing awkwardly in the centre of the room.

The severed arm was no longer severed. Both hands clutched at the now unsevered head in a parody of a human with a bad headache. The face was a black mass, the yimmer-yammering somehow distant. It was only when the dummy twitched and yanked sideways at its head, staggering slightly, that Richard realised that the black mass was the enamel hair on the back of the dummy's head. The head had been replaced back to front and now the dummy twisted it the right way round. The face turned to leer at him. The yimmer-yammering grew louder. It was weaving backwards and forwards drunkenly as Robinson finally saw it and began to scramble painfully sideways out of the chair away from it. The head did not turn but the eyes followed him relentlessly. They turned back to Richard; ugly, evil eyes, filled with malicious intent.

Shrieking, the dummy hop-skipped and jumped in a horrifying, loping motion towards him.

There was a plant pot on the television beside Richard. Reacting instinctively, he seized it and hurled it straight at his attacker. The pot exploded against the dummy in a spray of bone-dry earth, tangled roots and china shards. The dummy shrieked again and went down under the impact, whirling, squirming and wriggling on the floor. Its feet lashed the armchair as Robinson moved around it, his terrified gaze fixed on the outside door, looking right through Richard in his panic to get away from the flat. The armchair swung sideways on its castors into his thigh. He grunted, clutched at the air and sprawled awkwardly, off-balance. The chair tilted under his weight and he fell heavily, face down onto the squirming manikin.

Now it was Richard's turn to stand frozen in shock as the dummy's triumphant screams mingled with Robinson's cries of pain and terror. He staggered to his feet once more, and Richard could see that the dummy was fastened to his face, its claws gripping his head, enamel teeth working savagely. Robinson began to thrash backwards across the living-room, tearing at the wooden nightmare. A flap of his cheek had fallen lid-like across his chin in a flash of scarlet.

The spell on Richard was broken. He lunged forward.

Robinson's impetus was greater. Roaring and shrieking, he ran backwards into the closed french windows. An explosion of glass; a glittering detonation of whirling slivers. Plant pots and vines flew and toppled. Robinson's arms pinwheeled as Richard thrust through the ragged gap onto the balcony. His fingers caught the dummy's coat-tail as Robinson pinwheeled again. His unimpeded impetus brought him to the balcony rail.

'*No!*' yelled Richard.

Robinson screamed once. And then was gone, over the rail.

Richard grabbed the rail, sickened, and leaned over.

Robinson cartwheeled downwards away from him in a confused jumble of arms and legs, the dummy an indistinct mass around his face and throat. He could hear the horrific yammering all the way down.

He turned his head away before the impact.

Ten

In a dream, Richard watched himself walk out of the apartment. The lift awaited him. He rode down to the basement, walked out of the parking area and into the forecourt which fronted Brewster Dwellings. Distantly, he had expected the frenzied hubbub of a shocked yet blood-lusting crowd gathered round the body. He had expected to feel a hand on his shoulder and a uniformed figure suddenly spinning him round, saying: '*Do you know anything about this, sir?*' But he encountered no one. No one at all. It was as if time had stopped and Richard was enabled to escape from that scene of horror while everyone else was frozen in place. In a daze, he walked away from Brewster Dwellings and the mangled body that lay splashed on the concrete forecourt. He could not bring himself to look fully at the body or the insane, shattered remains of the murderous dummy. Something inside seemed to tell him that because Charlie had claimed a life, the motivating force behind it had been taken away.

He could only walk.

His car was parked in the town centre. Had anyone known that Robinson had arranged to meet him in the pub that day? Had anyone seen them there? If he could be recognised or traced, how could he convince the police that Robinson had been killed by a ventriloquist's dummy?

Well you see, officer,/ it's all quite simple, really. I've got this photograph which was taken about ten years ago. A photograph of a group of friends. Only they're vanishing from the photograph one by one, you see. And while I was visiting the scene of a murder . . . the two who have vanished were murdered, you see . . . a ventriloquist's dummy attacked Mr Robinson and myself . . . only it wasn't really Robinson it was after . . . it was me . . . and they fell out of a window . . .

They would lock him up and throw away the key.

Time and surroundings blurred and shifted. When Richard reached the car park, he had no idea how long he had been walking. He seemed to recall hearing an ambulance siren somewhere in the distance, but his mind was too filled with whirling, spinning images to identify it properly; images of blurred photographs and shifting faces. The pain in his savaged arm was only a minor irritation. In a few moments, he was driving mechanically and dazedly out of Durham towards Newcastle.

After twenty minutes, he pulled the car over onto the hard shoulder bordered by a tangle of impenetrable weeds and scrub, staggered out onto the grass and vomited. The nausea cramped him until he had nothing left to throw up. Ashen-faced and trembling, he leaned on the car door, resting his forehead on the cool upper frame. The shock had passed and his mind's defence mechanism, which had taken over to protect his sanity, had phased out. A terrible fear now gripped him. He climbed back into the car and sped off, resisting the urge to put his foot down and break the speed limit. At that moment, had he been stopped by a police car, he would have blurted out everything that had happened, regardless of the consequences.

He thought back to the Byker Chapter. He remembered the parties, the places they had been to, the holidays, the things they had done. Most of all he remembered how Charlie, the ventriloquist's doll, had been a sort of background prop. Derek had always dragged him along to the parties. They had all jokingly treated him as the eighth member of the clan. But now, the eighth member had come vividly and murderously to life, like something from one of those horror films back in the 1950s and early '60s that they used to see at the Imperial. Richard tried to shake off the feeling that he was playing a character actor's part in one of those films. Now, according to type, he should spend the remainder of his time in the movie telling himself that it was all just a dream or hallucination; that the booze had given him delirium tremens; that it was all some elaborate hoax; that he had suffered a nervous breakdown and that there was no such thing as the supernatural. He had seen all those old films and he also knew that while the victim was busily convincing himself that there was no such thing as a zombie or a vampire, the zombie or the vampire always crept up from behind and got him. Richard was not going to follow that cinematic cliché through to the end, although the temptation was great. He knew that he was faced with something outside the realms of normal experience; something supernatural (for want of a better term) and decidedly deadly. It was something that was killing his friends, something that was somehow wiping them from a photograph.

This time, he had managed to get away.

But when would it try again?

* * *

'*Gone*? What do you mean *gone*?'

The Sergeant-on-Duty stood, hands held imploringly at his sides, as the Chief Inspector stormed round the office.

'It must have been . . . ' began the Sergeant, dreading to have to use his next word '. . . stolen . . . '

'*Stolen*? From a police station? You have got to be joking!'

The Chief Inspector returned to the locker in which the suspected murder weapon had been locked. The door was buckled and warped, the lock dangling loose and shattered from its hasp.

'We found a small window broken in the Interview Room. Not big enough for an adult to climb through, but maybe someone really small, perhaps a child . . . ?'

'How the hell are we going to explain this?' The Chief Inspector looked in the locker again, as if hoping that the dummy might suddenly have reappeared.

The Sergeant opened his mouth to speak, but bit his tongue instead. He had fully intended to mention those noises he had heard over the last few days but now he could see no point in bringing it up. What possible use could it serve? In the dead of night, he had heard strange, scuttling, scratching and somehow sly noises in the locker room and had searched in vain for the source. Water bubbles in the central heating pipes? Some fault in the ventilator system? Yes, that was probably the answer. Why mention it at all?

Why mention that last night he could have sworn that those scratching noises had been coming from the interior of the cabinet where that bloody dummy had been locked?

Eleven

Richard sat in the same seat. Same drink. Same red and green spotlights. Same music.

It was Tuesday night, and he had gone to ground in the Imperial. Angie had tried to talk to him but it was obvious that something was wrong and that he needed time alone to think. She respected that and left him to himself for a while. Deejay was playing 'A Whiter Shade of Pale' on request, and a half-dozen dancers wandered slowly around the disco floor in their partners' arms.

The early edition of the *Evening Chronicle* poked out of Richard's jacket pocket. On page three was a small report of a death in Durham the previous Saturday. A college lecturer had apparently fallen to his death from the balcony of his flat. That was it. No reference to an earlier murder in the same apartment. No mention of a ventriloquist's dummy at the scene of the 'accident'. No mention of any suspicious characters seen leaving Brewster Dwellings. Nothing. Richard tried to piece everything together, to see if there was some kind of link that he had missed; some kind of thread that would make sense of the whole nightmare. Could it be that the dummy had killed Phil as well as Derek? How on earth could the bloody thing get all the way down to Shepherd's Bush under its own power and kill Phil before returning to Durham? Maybe Derek had had something to do with it? Maybe he had been behind everything? But Derek, like Phil, was dead. So where did that leave things? And now, what should Richard do? How could he stop these terrible things happening? The Byker Chapter itself was the key, of that much he was sure. And he was also sure that the nightmare had not ended and that there was more to come.

It was too much for him. He cast aside the Spectre, looking for something else to fill his mind.

The Imperial.

He looked around. This place had been very special to the Byker Chapter over the years. First as a cinema, when they were kids; then as a club. They had haunted the place in those days, even as it was haunting him now. Some of their best times had taken place inside these four walls. When the club had closed and the Imperial had become a run-down cinema again, the Byker Chapter had tried to retain its association with the place by making weekly trips to watch the latest double-bill. After a while, they had stopped coming. It only reminded them of the former glories, and watching it gradually fall into disrepair was like watching their favourite memories rotting and disintegrating. Pandora had once even tried to steal the Eric Burdon photograph from the wall but had been stopped by a vigilant commissionaire. Once again, he wondered what the Byker Chapter would make of this new nightclub.

You mean the dead ones, or the ones still living?

Stop it!

Who'll be next? When will you *vanish from the photograph?*

Stop it, I said! Stop it!

He became aware of a crowd of people entering the nightclub, laughing and chattering, but he paid little attention as they came up to the bar and ordered their drinks. A figure approached, but Richard was lost in his own nightmarish thoughts.

'You didn't strike me as the gigolo type!'

Richard looked up and saw Diane Drew standing in front of him. His surprise amused her. She laughed and put a hand on his arm as he shuffled uneasily in his seat. 'No, it's okay. I'm only joking.'

'Sorry. You startled me.' Richard realised that she had come in with the laughing group now at the bar. 'Celebrating?'

'No, not really. Just trying the place out. We'd heard some good things about it. You?'

'Certainly not celebrating, no. This is a sort of local for me, I suppose. I'm not really part of the disco scene, but I like to come here and unwind.'

'College-lecturer-seeks-solace-in-tinsel-town?'

'Yes, sort of. Can I buy you a drink?'

'No, it's okay, thanks. Someone's getting one for me.'

'Not the pimp in the Mercedes?'

Diane laughed. Richard decided that he liked the sound of her laughing very much. Very much indeed. 'No, not the pimp in the Mercedes. That was my cousin, actually. Why don't you join us?'

'Oh . . . no . . . no thanks. I appreciate it, but I've got to go shortly.'

'You're lying.' The words were softly spoken, mischievous. Again, that smile.

'Yes,' said Richard easily. 'I'm lying. But I'm not good company tonight, Diane. Really. If I joined your friends, they would have me categorised as a grade one pain in the arse and they—and you—would be glad when I made my excuses to leave. I'm . . . having a bad time, so please . . . '

Diane smiled again but Richard could not discern what she was thinking. Her ability to see right into him and what was going on there was really disturbing. What was she thinking now?

She turned and moved back to her friends and he returned to his glass of whisky, with the intention of finishing it off quickly and going away. His glass was full; he could not possibly swig it all at once. One gulp, two, three . . . and he was ready to move. But again, there was a hand on his arm and Diane was standing right next to him, was pulling up a stool beside him and sitting down. Resignedly, Richard sat down again.

'To be honest with you, Richard, I'm only here tonight with this crowd because I was pressurised into it. Nightclubs aren't my scene. I'm glad to see a friendly face.'

'Listen, Diane. Really, I'm not good . . . '

'Look, Eden, shut up and order me a drink. You couldn't possibly be a bigger pain in the arse than the ringleader of that lot over there. I've told them that you're a close friend whom I haven't seen for ages and they're going to have to bloody well respect that. So get me a drink!'

'Are you always so damned aggressive?'

'Tuesdays and Thursdays are worse, but generally . . . yes, I am.'

'Do you know that you've done nothing but insult me from the day I met you?'

'Maybe you deserve it?'

'Does everybody deserve it?'

'Most people . . . you more than most at the moment. Where's my vodka, then?'

Richard smiled in resignation and ordered two more drinks.
'I don't mean it,' she began again. 'It's a front, that's all. It's the face that I show to the world that helps me get by. There! You see . . . I've bared my soul and shared my secret with you. Now you're able to crucify me in public if I ever get too personal with you again. But be warned, I like to say things as I see them. I believe in honesty.'

'That's why you told me I was a fucking wreck?'

'Well you are, aren't you?'

Richard found it difficult to argue. 'Yes,' he said. And then, with conviction, 'Yes! I am! So what are you going to do about it?'

'A rehabilitation programme, that's what you need. I'm going to set you back on the straight track.'

'Nobody . . . '

' . . . knows the trouble I've seen. Sure, I've heard that one. It does no good, Richard. It's no use moping, you've got to pull yourself . . . '

' . . . up by the bootstraps? I've a feeling we're going to sit here trading clichés all night.'

'If you like. If it makes things better.' Again that smile. Diane lifted her drink, gave a mock toast to him and drank. Despite everything that had happened, despite everything that was going through his mind, this strange and intensely attractive girl with the marvellously arrogant approach to life was warming him. The icy chill of fear was momentarily thawed and, even though he knew that this could only be a temporary respite, he gave in to it and basked in it. He raised his glass to her in a return toast.

'I want you to believe this,' he said, 'and I also want you to believe that I'm not spinning a line when I say . . . I'm really glad that you turned up tonight. I feel better already.'

'Well, as long as it isn't a line . . . I thank you, kind sir. Now, come on and tell me the story of your life. The Doctor is "In".'

'Recently-separated-lecturer-struggles-to-find-his-identity-in-strange-new-world. End of story.'

'There's much more to it than that. I can tell.' Again, that extraordinary perception, that look that seemed to go right through him. 'Come on, out with it.'

'No, Diane. I won't bore you with it . . .' *Why is she looking at me like that? She can't possibly want to know me better* . . . 'Let's talk of arrogance and insult. Let's talk about you.'

Diane laughed loudly and with genuine humour. 'Okay, Richard. Question and answer. Begin . . .'

Twelve

They left the Imperial early, making excuses to Diane's 'friends' who seemed too preoccupied with themselves and their surroundings to care. Richard immediately concurred with her opinion of them.

Their conversation had flowed freely and easily. Richard found himself constantly surprised and delighted by Diane's frank attitude to life. She had graduated in Sociology at Nottingham—hence the slight accent—and after her post-grad course had taken up her first appointment at the college in Newcastle. Somehow, the horror of recent events had been pushed into the background and Richard was glad of this brief period of forgetfulness. The insanity and the doubt could wait for a couple of hours at least. But he had a feeling that, when Diane had gone, he would be plunged into even deeper despair. He now needed her company desperately to ward off the Spectre. Catching a taxi at the office in Shields Road, they were soon in Newcastle town centre. It was one-thirty; a light drizzle had begun. As they passed over Byker Bridge, Richard looked down at the Ouseburn as it wound its way to the River Tyne. When he had been a child, fish had swum in that water.

'This is going to sound like a line again . . .'

'Say it anyway.'

'Coffee?'

Diane smiled at him in the darkness. Her eyes were liquid, capturing the flare of the street lamps as they passed and throwing it back at him. It was another of those mysterious looks that could mean either 'of course' or 'you must be joking!'

Richard held his hands on his heart. 'Honourable intentions. Honest. I'll even pay for your taxi home afterwards.'

'Okay,' she said slowly, leaning forward. 'But, Richard . . .'

'Yes?'

'The first hint of funny business and I'll break your arm.'
'Karate expert?'
'I've seen *First of Fury* twice.'
'Hint taken.'
'At 1.45 am Richard led her into the reception area of his apartment block. For an instant, it reminded him of the controlled entry system at Brewster Dwellings and the horror swamped him again. There must have been a change in his demeanour, because he caught sight of an expression of concern on Diane's face. He decided that she would make a splendid lie detector and now regretted asking her back to his flat. Was his desperate need for company worth it? Would he end up giving everything away and convincing Diane that she had come to the lair of a madman?
'You'll have to excuse the place, it's in a . . . '
'No, I don't. If it's in a mess, we shall just have to tidy up.'
Richard laughed. 'You're really something.'
'I charge by the hour.'
'A very forthright escort agency, if you don't mind my saying so.'
'We aim to please, sir.'
The flat was not quite the mess that Richard remembered. It could have done with a good hoovering but, apart from that, everything was in order.
Except for two faces in a photograph. Richard clenched his teeth, telling himself: *Stop it!*
'Nice place,' said Diane, entering. With anyone else, the remark might have seemed trite, the polite sort of thing that people say. But Richard could tell that she meant it.
'Wall-to-wall carpets and back-to-the-wall rent. Yes, I like it.'
She crossed to the picture windows as Richard went into the kitchen.
'Coffee okay, or another drink?'
'Coffee's fine.'
When he returned with two cups, Diane was still standing at the window, looking out across the city. Her arms were wrapped round her body as if fighting to keep out a chill.
'It frightens me, sometimes.'
'What does?'

'The city. Sometimes it seems like a living entity. People are said to give a city character, but . . . I don't know . . . It's as if the city itself, the buildings, the streets, the back alleys, all had a life of their own. It seems more pronounced at this time of night when there aren't many people about.'

Her words startled Richard. They were much deeper than he would have expected of her—a spectral reminder of his own recent feelings.

When she turned round, he could see the serious expression on her face, but under his gaze the look dissolved warmly into a smile.

'Pretty heavy, eh?'

'I hope I'm not tempting a broken arm by saying this . . . but you're a strange girl. And I don't know why the hell you can be bothered with me.'

'Don't keep putting yourself down, Eden. You're not so bad.' She sipped her coffee, watching him over the rim of her cup. 'And as for me . . . yes, I agree . . . agree, that is, when you say you're tempting a broken arm.'

They both burst out laughing. It had a good, clean sound.

'I come from unusual stock,' said Diane.

'I sense a story coming on.'

'You're right. My mother was a medium. A psychic.'

'Really?'

'Yep . . . tea leaves in the bottom of cups, crystal gazing, all that sort of thing. They say it runs in the family. Maybe a little of the weirdness has rubbed off on me. She was an amazing woman, though. I learned a lot about life from her. An extremely sensitive woman, despite the baloney.'

'So you don't believe in the supernatural?' *Or ghost photographs . . . or walking, talking, killing ventriloquist's dummies . . . Stop it!*

'Not the kind of stuff that Mum was into. But . . . yes . . . I suppose there are certain kinds of phenomena that need closer examination. Precognition, sensitivity to certain atmospheres, that sort of thing.'

'So you were never tempted to follow in your mother's footsteps?'

'You mean gazing into the crystal ball?' Diane smiled that mischievous smile again. 'No, I could never see any future in it. But I often get feelings about things . . . about people . . . and it seems I'm seldom wrong. I've got a feeling about you, Richard. I got the vibes when we first met.'

'I do that to all the women. You must have missed the crowd of them outside. Can't keep their hands off me.'

'No, you're not reading me right. There's something about you, something that's bothering you, and I think it's more than your marriage breakdown. Something's hanging over you. Even when we were talking tonight, I could sense that it was always there. Now . . . it could be that I'm prying into territory that's too personal, in which case you can chuck me out on my ear. But I'd really like to know . . . maybe I can help.'

Richard sat silent for a long time. Diane, he decided, was probably the most remarkable woman he had ever met. He was being given an opportunity to share the nightmare, but no one could possibly believe anything he had to say, not even this Sociology teacher with the psychic background and the unnerving habit of picking up his thoughts and feelings with such uncanny accuracy.

'Come on, Eden. Spill the beans.'

'Diane, if I told you everything that's on my mind, you would be out of that door so fast it would make your head spin. You'd have the men in white coats and the police here in no time at all.'

'So try me.'

Yeah, try her. And before you know where you are you'll be in a padded cell, charged with murder. But . . . what the hell have I got to lose? I'm going to end up dead anyway, aren't I? Something's out there to get me. And, pretty soon, my face will have vanished from that photograph forever.

'I'm going to show you a photograph and then I'm going to tell you a story. After that, it's up to you whether you leave or stay.'

'Fair enough.'

Richard crossed to the bureau and opened the top drawer. The photograph was still there. His heart thudded in his chest as he examined the faces, half expecting that another one would be gone. But no, the photograph was as he had last seen it—with two faces missing. He turned back to Diane and gave it to her, prepared for her to go through the usual mediumistic ritual of clutching the photo, screwing her eyes tightly shut and trying to extract some psychic image from it. He did not know whether to be disappointed or not when she simply took it from him and examined it casually, with no trace of emotion on her face.

'That's a picture of the Byker Chapter . . . ' Richard began.

For the next hour, he related the events of the nightmare in full.

During the course of the story, they changed from coffee to vodka. Richard left nothing out, and more than once Diane's glance returned to the photograph which she held all the while. At last he finished speaking. He was standing at the window looking out across the city centre. Slowly he turned back to Diane, anxiously awaiting her reaction. She had not spoken for a long time.

'So that's it! The dummy was already there. I believe it was waiting for another member of the Chapter to come along. Crazy, I know, but that's what I believe. And that poor bastard got in the way. It killed him by mistake.'

Diane remained silent.

'Well . . . you did ask me. Now I've told you. I don't understand it . . . any of it, other than the fact that something . . . and it *has* to be something supernatural, is killing members of the Byker Chapter. And I've got to find out just what in hell it is and what it wants so that I can try to prevent it. Because I can't fight it if I don't know what it is. What do you think?'

'I think I'll have another drink,' said Diane, proffering her glass. Richard refilled it and waited for the response. When it was unforthcoming, his worst fears appeared to have been realised. He sat down heavily, running his hand through his hair, then reached for the telephone.

'I'm sorry,' he said, 'it was a mistake. I'll ring for a taxi . . . '

'No.' Again the silence. Diane was deep in thought. She sipped reflectively at her vodka. '. . . Put the phone down . . . ' Richard replaced the receiver. Then she said: 'You're in big trouble, Richard. You're all in big trouble if what you say is true.'

'Then you believe me?'

'Well, I've got two choices, haven't I?' Either you're a raving loonie, or else everything you've told me is true. And your story doesn't leave any kind of option for misinterpretation. If a ventriloquist's dummy tries to tear your throat out, that's not something you can explain away too easily, I should have thought. And I've seen the gouges on your arm. No, Richard, you're not lying. I can tell that.' She drank again. 'I don't understand any of it, either. Christ, you've given me the shivers. That business about the dummy . . . it's horrifying.' She stood up and began to pace around the room.

'More ice?' asked Richard, relief flooding over him. He had told his tale and Diane had not gone screaming to the door, begging to be let out. He had honestly believed an adverse reaction was inevitable and had steeled himself for the worst. Now, although the terror had not dimmed, he felt better for having spoken about it and been accepted.

'No, thanks. I've turned to ice inside already.'

Richard went into the kitchen to get ice from the freezer for himself, and Diane sat ruminating. What had started out as a potentially boring evening had become something else altogether; something that was, at least, far from boring. She had been surprised to see Richard propping up the bar in the Imperial, more surprised than she would have cared to admit to herself. Despite his shabbiness and tendency to keep to himself, she found him an extremely attractive man. Of course, he did not push himself like some others, but that only served to heighten her interest. She liked Richard, she decided; but she was not going to get involved with anyone again, not after her experience with Gary. They had been lovers for over two years and the pain of their 'split' had been something that would take a long time to heal. She also knew that Richard was having the same problems and was struggling with the same kind of depression that sometimes faced her.

These, however, were surface attractions. There was something else about Richard that she really liked and wanted to know better. Maybe, in time; but not straight away. And, anyway, after that story . . . *that story* . . . She believed it. It was crazy, she knew, but she believed it. She hardly knew the bloke at all. He could be psychotic; he could be some kind of maniac. He had admitted being involved in some way with a murder. He had even shown her the newspaper clipping from the *Evening Chronicle*. Everything he had told her could be a delusion. Perhaps Richard had gone insane and thrown Robinson out of the window in a fit of rage. Would she be next? Reason told her that she should grab her handbag and get out of that apartment as quickly as she could—the evidence all pointed that way. But Diane did not grab her things and leave hurriedly while Richard was in the kitchen. She believed him. And, secretly, she cursed the legacy left to her by her mother. She had never been wrong before, and she was not wrong now.

She walked round the apartment, thoughts milling in her brain. Absently, she pushed the outside door of the apartment shut with her foot. It had slipped its latch and blown open.

Returning to the sofa, she picked up the photograph again and looked at it intently, as if the answer could be there somewhere. She was drawn to the girl sitting in the middle of the sofa.

'Whatever happened to Pandora?'

'Pandora?' Richard came out of the kitchen. 'She was the first of the Chapter to go. I believe she moved down south and married some businessman. I can't recall where I heard it, but I've a feeling that's what happened.'

Diane returned to the photograph. 'And you say Derek was sitting on the sofa between Pandora and Stan?' Richard nodded. 'Where was the dummy?'

'It was behind the sofa somewhere, I think.'

'It was alive? The dummy was alive?'

'Very.'

Diane nodded. She looked for all the world like some detective at the scene of the crime, questioning witnesses. 'It does look as if something's out to get you, doesn't it? And the photograph's obviously the key.'

'My thoughts exactly. But I've been over everything. The Chapter. The party. Everything. And nothing makes sense. There's nothing to give a clue. Something's out there hunting us . . . stalking us . . . and, one by one, it's catching up with us . . . '

Something crashed in the kitchen.

Diane screamed and dropped her glass. Richard felt his heart leap. The terrifying sound resolved itself into a tinkle of broken crockery.

'Oh, God, it's the coffee pot. I left it on the edge of the bench. It's fallen off.' Richard hurried into the kitchen. The coffee pot lay scattered in broken pieces; coffee was splashed over the tiled floor. Apart from that, nothing. Richard felt his heartbeat return to normal. Diane was suddenly beside him, holding her chest, laughing nervously.

'That scared the living *hell* out of me. I suppose your story has got me spooked.' She picked up a cloth from the kitchen bench and returned to the living-room. 'I'd best mop up that vodka before it stains . . . So . . . anyway, what do you intend to do now, Richard?'

'Well, I can't just wait for whatever it is to come and find me. I think the most important thing is to track down all the other members of the Byker Chapter, wherever they may be . . . before it gets to them and me. Maybe one of them will have the answer.'

'It,' said Diane, stooping and rubbing at the spot on the carpet. 'Just what is *it*? That's the question, isn't it? And what does it want?'

'*You*?' croaked a voice from the top of the sofa.

Diane looked up.

The dummy squatted on the rim of the sofa, its mangled, shredded limbs dangling. Its glittering eyes were fixed on her, its shattered jaw hanging slack in an idiot grin. It giggled. Prehensile talons clicked from its cracked wooden hands like switchblades.

Diane shrieked.

The dummy dropped onto the sofa cushion, wagging its broken head from side to side and cackling in a high-pitched parody of childish laughter.

'*Richard!*' Diane could not move. She remained frozen to the spot as the dummy hopped towards her.

'*Jesus Christ Almighty!*' Richard was suddenly beside her, grabbing her by the elbows and flinging her to one side as the dummy shrieked insanely and flew at him over her head. Diane heard a crunching sound and saw the dummy crumple to the floor a yard away. Richard was standing, white-faced, his fist still clenched from the blow he had dealt. He dragged her to her feet and pushed her behind him. For the first time, she saw the trail of mud leading across the living-room carpet from the door. Somehow, the thing had pulled its shattered frame together again and had crawled all the way to Richard's flat without being seen. It had crawled in while they were talking in the kitchen. It had crawled in and waited for him.

Richard was stamping on the dummy, just as he had done in Derek's flat. It was now badly mangled, shattered, its life-force ebbing. Its attempt to take him had failed again; its croaking, babbling voice was slipping away. Richard stood back, gasping.

'Are you okay?' he asked.

'Oh, my God, Richard. What is it?'

'It's tracked me here like some bloodhound, Diane. It knew where to come. *It knew where to come.*'

Frantically, Diane scrabbled for the photograph. Richard knew what she was thinking and moved towards her nervously, one eye on the dummy, the other on the photo.

'No, Richard. It's okay. You're okay. The photo is just the same.'

'I've got to finish this thing, Diane. Will you help me?'

She nodded, fighting back a feeling of unreality.

'Get me a plastic bin-liner from the kitchen. Top cupboard.'

Diane went into the kitchen. As she pulled a black, plastic bag from the cupboard she heard a tearing sound, and when she returned, Richard was ripping the dummy apart with his bare hands. It was a revolting sight. It looked like a small child, and she fought to discard that horrible image as arms and legs were torn away. Richard kicked the head apart, sawdust spilling on the carpet. She opened the bag, realising his intention, and held it for him.

Piece by piece, Richard shoved the remains of the manikin into the bag, picking up each fragment as if it were still dangerous and poisonous. Soon, the shattered frame of the dummy was in the bag. Crazily, Diane was thinking of that old ventriloquist's routine when the act was finished and the dummy had to go back into the suitcase or whatever . . .

. . . I don't want to go back in the box . . .

'Get the door.' Richard hefted the sack in both hands as Diane opened the front door and they went out onto the staircase.

'Where?' she asked.

'Down to the basement. We daren't use the lift in case we're spotted. We're going down to the incinerator. I'm going to burn this bloody thing and destroy it completely.'

They stopped on the third floor when the sound of a door slamming echoed up towards them, followed by shrill laughter and the sound of movement. Fortunately, no one headed their way. They continued down the stairs until they had reached the basement. Richard had never been down here before, and had difficulty in locating the main door leading to the incinerator room. He was trying to shake off a series of hideous images flashing through his mind—images of the dummy crawling unseen in the night along ditches and through the shrubbery of motorway embankments. Deranged and vengeful, scrabbling in the shadows on its way from Durham to Newcastle. Crawling in the night, hiding in the day. He shuddered.

At last he found the right door and eased it open with his foot, still holding the sack away from him as if it contained a deadly snake. Reaching inside, he groped for a light switch, but Diane slipped past him, found a switch and then they were both through, closing the door quickly behind them. In the centre of the small brick room, amid coils of piping, stood the central heating boiler and the incinerator with its furnace door. The room was filled with a hissing sound; debris littered the floor.

Richard moved down some steps and laid the sack on the floor. He had no real idea how to open that furnace door or whether it would be dangerous, but he was going to do it. Diane stayed at the top of the small stone staircase, acting as a look-out, while he examined the locking mechanism; it seemed straightforward enough. He stood on the hinged side—the last thing he wanted was a spout of flame when he opened the door—and touched the handle, but it was too hot to manipulate. He looked around, found a rag and wound it round his fist. Moving back to the furnace door, he yanked at the lever mechanism and the door swung open. Roaring, orange light spilled out from the maw of the incinerator. He returned for the sack. The hair prickled on his scalp. Was it just the light from the incinerator, or was the sack writhing and squirming?

Is the bloody thing putting itself back together again?

He approached hesitantly. Diane had spotted the movement, too. 'Be careful, Richard.' Her words were lost in the roaring of the furnace. He moved stealthily closer. The plastic sack rustled and shifted to one side. Judging his distance, Richard seized the top of the sack and tossed it underarm towards the furnace door. The sack swung across the basement floor and flopped just in front of the door. The squirming became more furious. With a slitting sound, a taloned fingernail pierced the sack and began to cut a rip down one side. Richard heard Diane shout something behind him as he grabbed the sack again and heaved it up towards the mouth of the furnace.

Something inside the sack seized his arm in a sharp, tearing grip.

Richard pushed hard and bundled the sack into the furnace opening, feeling the fierce heat on his body, searing his face, singeing his hair and eyebrows. The thing inside the sack made an animalistic, mewling, howling sound, filled with hate and threat. The plastic sack began to melt.

A small, ragged arm shot out of the sack, hunting for Richard's throat. He seized the seeking claw by the wrist and pushed with all his strength. The sack slid into the furnace, plastic popping in a sudden blossom of flame. Richard fell backwards onto the floor.

Inside the incinerator, the dummy was screaming.

Richard pulled himself up again, flung himself at the furnace door and swung it shut. Diane ran to him and, without conscious effort, they were in each other's arms. The roaring of the furnace was the only sound now as they made their way out of the basement and back to the flat.

'Diane,' said Richard as they climbed the staircase, 'please don't go tonight. I want you to stay.'

'I want to stay, too, Richard. I'm not going anywhere.'

Thirteen

The following day was Wednesday, the last day of term. By tradition, there would be very little to do and, normally, Richard would enjoy a drink with some of his students, who would also be celebrating the end of another term. Today, however, celebration was far from his mind.

He and Diane made their way to college late. Richard stayed outside in the car park while Diane entered the building. The last thing either of them wanted at the moment was the sniggering and the snide comments of Ives and Potter. Richard stood and watched as Diane crossed the car park towards the main door. She was, he reaffirmed, someone really special. She was strong, and her strength gave him strength. Alone, he did not know whether he could fight the horror that had been visited on him and his despairing, hopeless world. With her . . . well, with her, he was going to face this damned thing and see it through. Their love-making on the previous night had been completely different from anything he had experienced before. Not in all the time before Denys, or with Denys, or in the terribly lonely days after Denys. Neither of them had promised anything, neither of them had lied or made false claims on the other. It had been a night without spoken commitment; but Richard knew that they *were* both committed in a sense that did not need words; they were committed to each other. Strangely, the horror had also served to bind them together. She could have walked away from him. God knew, it was terrifying enough. She could have left him to face this thing himself. But she had not. She had *chosen* to be with him; had chosen to help him. She wanted *him*. She was probably the best thing that had ever happened to him.

They met during the morning break. Under normal circumstances, their talk would have been light, happy and full of unspoken speculation about the future. But the shadow of the Spectre still hung over Richard and was the sole topic of conversation.

'How do you intend to track down the others? Do you know where they went after the Byker Chapter split up?'

'Derek was the easiest. I knew that he had taken up a job as a lecturer at Durham. Stan was a garage mechanic. God knows where he went. The old Byker addresses aren't any good any more. They pulled the place down and rebuilt it. I'm pretty sure that Joe got a job in an advertising agency in Liverpool.'

'I might be able to help there, then. I know Liverpool quite well.'

'Well, that's a start. But I haven't got a clue where Pandora or Barry might be. Maybe Central Records here have got some idea . . . or the Electoral Registration people at the Civic Centre.'

'It's worth a try. Have you got the photograph with you?'

Richard took it from his pocket and gave it a peremptory glance before handing it to Diane. 'I think it's probably best if I keep the damned thing with me all the time, now.'

'What the hell is going on, Richard? Why the photograph? Why hasn't . . .' And then, quickly: 'Richard, where's the negative? Have you got it?'

'No, Stan the Man was the photographer. He would have it.'

'That's a pity.'

'You're wondering if there's been any effect on the negative.'

'Yes . . . although even if there had, I don't see how it would help us. Oh, the whole damned thing is just insane. Where the hell do we start?'

Where do *we* start, she had said. Not where do *you* start? It gave Richard added strength to hear her say that.

'This afternoon I'll quiz Records and take it from there.'

He met Diane at the end of afternoon classes and they walked back to the block of flats where he lived, intending to grab a bite at the nearby Latin American restaurant. Richard's research at Central Records had borne no fruit at all. There was no clue to the whereabouts of the remaining members of the Byker Chapter. Diane had found a copy of the Yellow Pages for Liverpool; there were dozens of advertising agencies in there, but it was still worth a try.

'The dummy,' she said at last. 'Maybe, somehow, the whole thing was centred around the dummy. Now that it's been destroyed, everything's over.' She looked searchingly at Richard's face. 'Yes, I know, I'm kidding myself. The dummy was only a part of it. I can feel it.'

'Whatever killed Phil, I'm pretty sure that it wasn't the dummy. Something else did that.'

'After we've eaten, I want you to tell me everything about the Byker Chapter. I know we've talked about it a lot, but I want you to tell me absolutely everything you know and remember about every member of it. Everything that you did, in the smallest detail.'

They reached the end of the central pedestrian walkway where Richard's block of flats stood, straddling the main road. Beneath, the traffic growled restlessly. Ahead, the small Latin American restaurant looked cheerful and inviting. A cold wind snapped at their faces. Richard drew Diane closer to him. He realised now how selfish he was being.

'This isn't right, Diane. It's not fair. This whole damned thing is my problem . . . and I've just drawn you into it. It could be very dangerous for you. Maybe it's best if we call it a day and . . . '

'Shut up, Eden! I like you. I want to help.'

'Really, I want you to give it some thought. After all . . . '

'That promise of a broken arm still holds good.'

'Okay, lady. Far be it from me to change your mind.'

'That's better.'

They had reached the base of the apartment block. In the central doorway stood the figures of two men. One of them was slouched against the wall, his breath rising regularly in steaming clouds. The other was bearded, wearing a woollen cap, roll-necked sweater and reefer jacket. A small haversack hung on one shoulder. He was skipping backwards and forwards impatiently, as if to warm his feet. He clapped his hands together as they approached, and seemed surprisingly interested in them.

'We're just going to have to work out a plan of action,' continued Diane. 'Stan the Man is first on the list, because he's probably easier to trace than the others. He may still be in Byker. As for Joe, well I'm afraid your telephone bill may be quite high next quarter. But at least if we can find one member of the Chapter, that's a start. That could give us a lead to the others.'

'We've got a bigger lead than we think,' said Richard slowly as they climbed the steps to the entrance.

'How's that?' asked Diane.

The man who had been skipping in the doorway was moving towards them, pulling up the collar of his reefer jacket to keep out the cold.

'Because it seems that the Byker Chapter has found *us*.'

'Hello, Richard,' said the man in the woollen cap.

'Hello, Stan,' replied Richard.

The man slouching in the doorway waved drunkenly at them.

'Joe?'

'One and the same,' slurred the slumped shape. 'Good ol'

Trickie Dickie. You haven't changed a bit.'

A cold vortex of wind whipped at the base of the apartment block, ruffling their clothes greedily, like an animal. The man called Stan stood for a moment looking at them. He clapped his hands together against the chill.

'We've got to talk,' he said at last.

PART TWO
THE BYKER CHAPTER

How often are we to die before we
go quite off this stage? In every
friend we lose a part of ourselves,
and the best part.

Alexander Pope, *Letter to Jonathan Swift*

One

'Not exactly a happy reunion, is it?' said Stan reflectively, when they had settled themselves in Richard's flat. His reefer jacket was draped carelessly over a chair but he still wore the woollen cap, pulled down low over his ears. His long face was framed by a beard, making it look even longer. After preliminary introductions, they had ascended in the lift, saying virtually nothing. Diane's attention had been particularly drawn to the one called Joe. He had been slumped against the wall with a vacant grin on his face and seemed to rely heavily on Stan, even for simple prompting to move around. On entering the lift, Stan had propelled him into a corner where he had slumped again, mumbling rambling and disconnected phrases under his breath. Now, he stood in the corner of the room beside the picture window like a puppet dangling on one wire, eyes fixed on the city below. He was obviously stoned—by his behaviour, probably drugs rather than booze.

Richard had brought bottles of whisky and gin into the living-room, with American ginger and tonic as mixers. The silence between them seemed charged with latent energy.

'Been drinking a lot lately?' asked Stan. His phrasing seemed odd; there was more to the question than that.

'Yeah, some.' Richard replied evenly, expecting more.

'Been feeling nervous, depressed, down? Been feeling claustrophobic *and* agoraphobic at the same time?'

'What are you getting at, Stan?'

'Ha!' Stan's laugh was a short, sharp bark. There was no humour. 'Of course you have. And you think it's just the cares of the world, don't you? How about a persecution complex? Have you started feeling that there's something out there in the dark, stalking you, hunting you down? No? Well . . . you will . . . you will . . . Right, Joe?'

Joe waved ineffectually from the window, grinned and thumped his head against the wall. 'The Big Bad Wolf's gonna huff and puff and blow my whole fucking house down.' His words dissolved into boyish giggles.

'We're in trouble, Richard,' continued Stan, pouring himself a drink. 'Big trouble. I don't know how or why. But something's after us. A Spectre. And it's a big one.'

'The photograph,' said Richard simply. The straight whisky burned in his gut and went some way to quelling the fear inside.

'So you know? What else? What else do you know? What the hell is going on?' Stan's deep, green eyes were burning fiercely and intently.

'No, I don't know. Look, it's best if you tell me everything from your end. Then I'll tell you what's happened to me . . .'

'. . . to *us* . . .' said Diane from her chair beside the stereo. Incredibly, she was smiling.

Richard paused momentarily, feeling that strength inside again. 'To us,' he said.

'What's a Spectre?' she asked. Richard explained before turning back to Stan.

'I'm living in Middlesbrough,' said Stan. 'I'm a mechanic by trade. *Still* am, Richard. Oh, I know . . . I had big plans once about my photography. Big ideas. But it's still just a hobby.' He laughed again and continued. 'I had that photograph of the Byker Chapter enlarged from the negative.'

'The negative!' exclaimed Diane. 'Was there anything on it that . . . ?'

'Whoa, whoa!' Stan held his hands up imploringly. 'One singer, one song. Okay? All right . . . I had the enlargement framed and hanging on my living-room wall. Been there for years. Good memories from the good old days. I read about Phil's death in the newspapers; knew that it was him straight away. Then I noticed that the photograph had changed. He'd gone. I thought I was going crazy! I checked the photo over and over, tested my negative and everything. Nothing! Just as if he'd never been on the photograph in the first place. Then Derek vanished and I found out he'd snuffed it, too.'

Stan rummaged through his haversack and threw three colour enlargements on the coffee table. 'Still nothing. That's when I thought I'd better track down the other Byker Chapter members. I knew in general where I could find three others. You were the hardest, Teacher Man, even though you're still living closer to "home ground". Barry's a museum director in

Nottingham, and I knew that Joe here was a graphic designer in Liverpool. Barry was easiest so I set off to find him first. No dice. He's out of the country on holiday and won't be back until the end of the week. So my next stop was Liverpool . . . '

Joe had begun to sing 'Ten Green Bottles' in a curiously flat and bizarre monotone that sent icy tentacles creeping over Diane's skin. There was something very wrong with this man.

'Is he okay?' asked Richard.

'Yeah, he's okay. Shut up, Joe.'

Joe responded by smiling apishly and going through a drunken pantomime of sewing his lips shut with an invisible needle and thread. Richard went over to him and tried to guide him into a chair. Joe's reaction was surprising and alarming. He recoiled and lashed out, muttering, 'Just leave me, Dickie. Don't touch. Don't never touch . . . Just Stan . . . he's the only one who can touch . . . '

'Take it easy, Joe. No one wants to hurt you.' Richard stepped back.

'He'll be okay, Richard. Just leave him.'

Richard returned to his seat and sat down nervously, eyes still on Joe. The shambling, incoherent figure before him seemed a mere shell of the person he had laughed and joked with in the days of the Byker Chapter.

Stan continued: 'I knew the firm where Joe worked. When I got there I found that he'd been sacked the previous week for erratic behaviour. Kept telling everyone that something was following him around. Something that wanted him dead. I got his address from a sympathetic girl on the reception desk. When I found him . . . well . . . he'd barricaded himself in his flat. He wouldn't come out for love or money. Kept saying stupid things. He said that he knew it wasn't really me . . . '

'Jesus Christ,' said Richard, remembering Robinson's tale about Derek. Diane reacted, but said nothing. Stan had noticed, but continued with his tale.

'I finally managed to kick my way in there and narrowly avoided having my head blown off.' He produced two automatic pistols from the haversack and laid them on top of the photographs. Richard heard Diane's intake of breath. 'I don't know where he got them, but if I hadn't knocked him down I'd be filed away in one of those morgue drawers by now. He's okay now when he's high on smack, but he's almost paranoid when the effect wears off. Then the fear sets in.'

'What in hell's wrong with him?'

'The same thing that's wrong with us, only more advanced. Look at him. Look long and hard. Because that's how *we're* going to be soon.'

'Oh, my God.' Diane had moved to the coffee table and picked up one of the enlargements. 'Look at this, Richard.'

Richard joined her and followed the pointing finger to the figure of Joe, standing behind the sofa in Stan's flat. What had not been apparent in Richard's small colour print of the photograph was now instantly obvious. Joe had been standing at the centre of the sofa when the picture was taken. And now, a faint pink smudge could be seen on his chest and face—the colour of the pink pastel wall behind the sofa.

Joe was gradually fading from the photograph.

'That started to happen when I found Joe,' said Stan. 'He's next. He's the next chosen one.'

'What's going on?'

'We're being singled out one by one. Something is stalking us, hunting us down. And my guess is that as it gets closer, as it closes in, we can sense subconsciously that it's coming. Fear starts to eat us up because, deep down inside, we know that we're going to die. It's like . . . it's as if . . . it's eating us up bit by bit . . . eating up our sanity . . . eating up our souls. Look hard at Joe, Richard, because, pretty soon, when we're chosen, that's going to be us.'

Richard was looking at the image of himself in the photograph, desperately searching for any sign of transparency; any sign that he might be next after Joe.

'I know what you're thinking,' continued Stan, 'and it's already started with us. The fear. That's what I meant before, when I asked you about the depression and the drinking. That's the primary stage, I think. A premonition of death. Joe's done a great deal of talking since we met and I dragged him away from Liverpool. Mostly babble, because I've got to keep him high as a kite all the time. It's costing me a fucking fortune, but it'll be worth it if I can save him. Save *us*. But what I've been able to get out of him confirms everything I've said.'

'What the hell is it? Why is it doing this?'

'God knows,' replied Stan, 'and He isn't telling.'
'You'd better hear my side of things now,' said Richard.
Night crept over the city as he relived the horror.

Two

'So that's it. Everything.'
'Bloody hell . . . '
'I couldn't agree more.'
Stan turned to Diane. 'It's none of my business, but I've got a feeling that you're going to be better off out of this . . . '
'That's right. It's none of your business.'
Stan shrugged, then moved across to the window, looking out at the night. For a while, he seemed deep in thought. 'Derek's ventriloquist's doll! I can't believe it. What am I saying? Of *course* I believe it. But you're right—the doll was just an instrument, I think. There was a motivating force behind it.' He picked up one of the automatic pistols and handed it to Richard. 'I think you'd better hang on to this. I'll keep the other one.'
'I can't use this!' exclaimed Richard. 'I've never fired a gun before. The nearest thing I ever used was a water pistol.'
'Same principle. Point it and pull the trigger. Somebody gets wet.'
'And what good is this against a wooden dummy, for instance?'
'Don't quibble. It's much more effective than a plant pot, believe me.'
' . . . Stan . . . ' Joe seemed troubled again, making circular movements with his hands, like a child who was hungry and had to eat. 'Stan, you gotta let me . . . I've gotta have some more . . . '
'Oh, Jesus,' said Stan under his breath. He went to Joe, taking him by the arms and holding him firmly against the wall like a child. 'No more, Joe. Not for a while yet.'
'Gotta have some more. I can feel it. It's coming. *It wants me.*'
'No, it's not coming. We've run away, Joe. It doesn't know where we are. It can't find us.'

'Gotta have . . .'

'Look, Joe, there's a limit to what I can give you. Don't you see that? If you get too much, you're going to die.'

'Die? Yes . . . Oh, God, Stan . . . give it to me, man. Let me die. It would be better this way.' Joe began to cry.

Stan banged him hard against the wall. Diane winced at the sound.

'You're not going to die! I'm not going to let you die! Do you understand?' And then, more gently: 'You're safe with me. Richard's here, too. Nothing's going to get you.' Stan guided him to a chair, turned it round to face the television set and then switched on. A quiz game was in progress. 'There you are, kid. You watch that. It's better for you. You just concentrate on all those people and everything will be okay. Okay? You're in Newcastle now, Joe. We're far away from Liverpool. Nothing can find us here in Newcastle.'

Joe slumped in his seat, whimpering. Stan caught the look in Richard's eye as he crossed the room again to join them, picking up his drink on the way. 'Yeah, I know,' he whispered. 'It doesn't matter where the hell we are. Time and distance don't seem to mean a thing. When it wants us . . .' he shrugged.

' . . . it can take us,' finished Richard.

Stan motioned to them to move further away from Joe, who was now rocking backwards and forwards in his chair, eyes glued to the television screen.

'There's something else about this whole thing that convinces me we're up against something . . . well . . . I don't know . . . *weird*.'

'And what's that?' asked Richard.

'The dreams. I've been having the same dreams as Joe. Exactly the same . . . '

Fear began to eat Richard from the inside again.

'Dreams about the photograph,' continued Stan. 'And I've a feeling that you've been having them as well. Am I right? Our faces vanish . . . and then *we* begin to vanish . . . '

'And a voice,' said Richard, 'a voice that says the same word over and over again . . . '

'Spectre,' said Stan.

Richard swallowed a mouthful of whisky, grimacing.

'You realise,' said Diane, 'that we're on our own here? I

mean, where do we go for help? The police?'

'Of course we can't,' said Richard. 'You're right. We're on our own.'

'Is there any logic or pattern that either of you can see in this?' asked Stan, drinking direct from the whisky bottle and reminding Richard of himself not so long ago, on a drunken binge that he had seen at the time as a remedy for the acute depression caused by his separation from Denys, but which he now realised could have been the onset of the Spectre's influence.

'Well,' he said, 'there's the photo. The vanishings. The dummy. Phil and Derek, torn to pieces—Derek presumably by the dummy; Phil by someone—or something—else.'

'Then there's Joe,' continued Stan.

'So the only common element is the Byker Chapter,' said Richard. 'Where do we go from there?'

'It must have been something that happened on the night that photograph was taken,' said Diane. 'Something at the party.'

'Nothing happened,' replied Stan. 'Nothing bad, that is. Unless you know different, Richard? It was one of the best nights I've ever had.'

'One of the best nights *we've* ever had,' said Richard.

Stan shrugged again. It seemed to be a habit with him. Diane turned back to the window, chewing her lip as she looked out over the city, her gaze directed inwards. For a while, they were silent, lost in their own thoughts.

'It's like a focus, then,' said Diane at last.

'What?' Richard was jolted back to the present.

'That photograph is like a focal point for your friendship. One of the high points when you were all together.'

'So?' asked Stan.

'So . . . nothing. It doesn't give us any clues, I know. Unless, that is, you're both not telling me everything about that party for some reason. The party's important—I'm sure of it. A strong focal point for the Byker Chapter.'

'Talking abstracts is driving me crazy!' snapped Stan, finishing his drink and pouring another. 'There's something out there, something intangible but bloody deadly. And it's getting to us one by one. How the hell do we resist it or fight it if we don't even know what it is or what it wants? Why is it doing these things?'

Joe seemed agitated again. There was interference on the television set; the picture rolled and fluttered, buzzing angrily. Richard moved over and adjusted it.

'So what do we do next?' asked Diane.

'Drive down and speak to Barry in Nottingham,' said Stan. 'He'll be back from holiday soon. Maybe he's got an idea what this is all about.'

'It's easier to telephone,' said Richard.

'Oh yeah! Can you imagine that telephone call? Would you pay any attention to it, or would you think it was a crank? How long would it be before you hung up?'

'If the same sort of crazy things have been happening to him, we may not have to convince him.'

Stan shrugged again, turning to Joe. He was still sitting, hunched up, face glowing white in the light of the television. Richard moved back to the set, reaching for the controls. 'You're right. Let's just go. But we'd better move quickly if we . . . '

Joe shrieked, long and loud.

And then the lights went out.

The hissing snowstorm had suddenly become a howling, roaring maelstrom. The shuddering light from the screen changed everything into a stark, flickering black and white. Something barely visible whiplashed at Richard with an audible *snap*. Grunting in pain, he was jerked with terrible force half-way across the room in a cartwheel of arms and legs.

A shock! thought Diane in that horrified split-second. *An electric shock! All the lights have gone out. A fuse! The TV's live!*

But Joe was still screaming, frozen in his seat, knees bunched up under his chin; glazed eyes reflecting glassy light from the television like a drowned man. Then, as Diane ran quickly to Richard who lay crumpled and moaning on the carpet against the far wall, she looked back at the television set and saw for the first time what it was that had so terrified Joe and which now held her, too, frozen in shock.

The snowstorm on the screen had vanished. The screen *itself* seemed to have vanished. And inside the box, where there should have been a maze of wiring, conduits and tubes . . . was something born in a nightmare. Strangely amorphous coils of luminosity writhed within, an ethereal blue-white *something*, roiling and swarming like a living, electric storm-cloud.

Stan stared transfixed at the formless, twisting smoke. It emitted an ear-splitting gobbling, hissing noise and, as he watched incredulously, he sensed that the hissing apparition was *seeing* him with malignant, hostile eyes. Although he could see nothing with certainty, he had the horrifying impression that there were . . . mouths . . . in there, too; formless, gaping and hungry, with rows of uneven . . . razor . . . teeth . . .

The TV's live! Diane thought again in a kind of mocking counterpoint. Even though a part of her refused to accept what she saw, another part knew instinctively that the thing swarming and flickering in Richard's living-room was most definitely, most dangerously, alive.

And it was here . . . with them . . . *now*.

A coil of glowing phosphorescence was emerging from the aperture where the screen had been, curling in the air like a tentacle of fog, like some strange antenna, sensing their presence.

This is crazy! thought Stan. *TV pictures don't come to life! They don't float out of the screen into your living-room . . .*

The twisting cloud drifted slowly into the room; more tentacles of glowing smoke curled and writhed. Diane turned to scream at the others: 'Run! Get out! Get out before it . . . '

And then the nightmare was upon them.

A ribbon of smoke shot out of the set and coiled with deadly accuracy around Joe's throat. His screams turned to gurgling noises as he tried desperately to claw it loose.

Stan's reaction was instantaneous. With no time to think, he lunged towards Joe. The throttling *smoke* felt ice-cold and clammy, but it was somehow substantial as he fought to tear it from Joe's neck. Something from behind ripped at his collar and his woollen cap was suddenly snatched from his head. Joe fell to the floor, legs kicking. Stan followed him, clawing at the horrible grey coil around his neck, but the smoke-tentacle began to drag Joe back to the place where the television had been. Stan could not see the living storm-cloud behind him, but a nightmare image filled his mind of obscene, hungry mouths and barbed teeth champing in frenzy. He stamped on the coil and felt it flatten and tear under his boot; then another ice-cold rope began to curl around his own leg.

Jesus Christ!

Then Stan remembered the automatic pistol. Whipping it from his belt he frantically pulled back the chamber and held the muzzle against the glowing tentacle that was strangling Joe. Joe's eyes were starting from his head as Stan pulled the trigger. The report was muffled by the howling, gobbling noise that filled the room, but the tentacle flew apart.

'*What the hell is this?*' yelled Stan. The tentacle had exploded into a cloud of floating electric-blue flecks, like nothing that was alive at all. They were fading to nothing, like the sparks from an exploded firework. Joe kicked away from Stan, ripping the remnants of the squirming coil from his neck. The severed tentacle began to twitch on the floor like a beheaded snake; then it was gone, evaporating in wisps of grey mist. The coil of glowing smoke around Stan's leg spasmed and gripped relentlessly. Stan stumbled and cried out, swinging the gun upwards. Another coil flashed from the set and fastened on the hand holding the gun. Stan toppled over, clawing at it, trying to retrieve the pistol which was now effectively clamped to his hand. The gun discharged. Gloria Grahame's portrait on the wall exploded into fragments, the print fluttering to the floor. Stan bellowed, his voice lost in the uproar.

Richard had recovered sufficiently to understand what was happening. One second he had been leaning over to adjust the television control, the next he was lying against the wall. The muscles in his arm ached badly; the lacerations caused by the dummy had reopened. Now, as Diane struggled to lift him, he could see Stan and Joe in a life-and-death struggle with what looked like an insubstantial, nightmare tangle of twisting, writhing snake tentacles. They were being dragged towards what seemed, in the hellish, flickering light, to be a nest of glowing snakes that had once been his television set. Joe freed himself and was crawling away when another tentacle of fog whipped across the carpet and seized his ankle, dragging him back. Joe began to cry helplessly. Groggily, Richard saw Stan fighting to release the gun from his trapped hand. Then he remembered the other gun. He tore at his jerkin pocket. It was empty; the gun had fallen out when he had been flung across the room. Desperately, he scrabbled on the floor, tugging at Diane to help him.

'The gun! The gun!' he shouted over the hideous racket. The constant black-and-white, black-and-white, black-and-white was a nightmare image of Hell and he found himself thinking: *Just like those bloody pills! First I couldn't find those bloody pills and now I can't find the bloody gun!*

Stan's roaring was abruptly cut off as grey fog wreathed his head and shoulders in a smothering embrace. There was no more time. Richard staggered to his feet, blundered forward and swept up the coffee table, scattering bottles and glasses.

'*You bastard!*' he yelled, flinging the table at the roaring television set. The living storm-cloud billowed outwards instantly. Richard saw a jagged, crackling spider-web of lightning in the flickering mass and something from within the cloud lashed at the table. The impact shattered the glass and sent the table hurtling to one side, away from the television.

Richard found himself on top of Stan, tearing at the encircling grey mass. It flapped loose and struck at him like a shadowy cobra. Richard dodged, grabbed Stan and hauled him away. From the corner of his eye, he could see that Joe had been dragged almost to the base of the set.

Get away . . . we've got to get away . . . he screamed soundlessly, fingers pulling ineffectually at Stan's gun.

Now the room was filled with the living storm-cloud and its coiling tendrils of death. They swarmed over Richard's body, seeking, strangling, smothering, hunting for his eyes and throat. When they reached into his mouth, Richard knew that he was going to die.

A thunderclap exploded in the living-room, obliterating the flashing black-and-white in a brilliant-white blaze of electricity. Something screamed—an animal's scream, not human. Instantly, Richard felt a rain of sparks and glass on his face and hands. The fog-tentacles jerked away in a disintegration of hissing blue. The room was plunged into total darkness. The screaming ebbed and died away as if something had fallen into a bottomless pit.

The lights came on again.

Richard leaped to his feet. Stan was coughing and gagging, tearing at his shirt collar. Joe cowered in the far corner like a frightened animal. The living-room looked as if someone had thrown a hand grenade into it. The television set stood in the centre, its screen shattered, fragments of glass littering the carpet. Inside, Richard could see the exploded remains of wiring and tubes. There was no living, electric storm-cloud in there now, no nightmare fog tentacles from Hell; just a smoking, ruined piece of man-made equipment.

'Diane!' Suddenly he remembered her and twisted round to find her still standing where he had landed after the initial electric shock.

She was bolt upright, face set like marble, arms outstretched, holding Richard's gun in a two-handed grip. The barrel, still smoking, was pointed dead-centre at the TV screen. She pulled the trigger again. The gun barked flame. The television set imploded, crashing backwards in a wreck of glass, tubing and wires. Diane's lips were trembling as Richard took the gun from her cold fingers and held her face in the crook of his shoulder; she tried to control the shuddering that shook her from head to foot.

'It's okay, Diane. It's okay. Whatever in Hell it was, you stopped it.'

Joe began to babble again, clutching at his face. 'This would never have happened, Pandora . . . never . . . if you'd stayed with me like you said you would . . . you said you loved me better than the others . . . Just me . . . You said I was the one.'

'Take it easy, Joe,' said Richard. Stan was still gagging on the carpet. He held up a hand to Joe, trying to calm him.

'You'd never been with any of the others . . . Just me . . . You said you loved me, Pandora . . . you said you'd never leave me . . . But you did . . . if you'd stayed, this would never have happened. *I loved you, Pandora. I still love you!*' Joe bolted for the door, crying helplessly and snatching something from the table as he ran. He was gone before they could stop him.

A submerged feeling of dread began to swell in Richard at Joe's words. It seemed as if it had always been there, deep down and waiting. He quelled it, holding Diane closer. Stan was rising groggily to his feet as Richard lowered Diane to the sofa. He was poking the television set with his shoe when Richard moved to join him.

'Like my Mam used to say,' said Stan, 'too much television's not good for you.' He began rubbing his throat again.

'Did we imagine it, Stan? It's just an ordinary bloody television set. Did we just see things that weren't there?'

'Did I imagine this, then?' asked Stan. He pulled his roll-necked sweater down to show Richard a livid red weal across his throat. 'Or this?' He pointed to a similar mark on his wrist. 'Oh yeah, it was real all right.'

'It's insane.'

'Yeah, it's that, too.'

'Where's Joe?' Richard remembered his panic-stricken flight from the room. The door stood open in the hallway.

'Oh, hell!' Stan hurried across and looked out into the corridor. 'He's gone. The lift's on the way down. And he's got the car keys!'

* * *

The Spectre had found him. That was the only thing that Joe could be sure of as he clawed in panic at the security door and let himself out into the night. His twilight world allowed him to focus rationally only on very rare occasions, but of that one indisputable fact he was sure. Stan had been wrong to say that he was safe here in Newcastle; the Spectre had come to take him.

The chill night air crowded in on him as he spun in the courtyard, his overcoat flapping around him. The tall concrete and glass buildings towering around him seemed about to collapse inwards, burying him forever. Desperately, in his terror, he remembered that he had snatched the car keys. Where had Stan parked the car? Footsteps ringing on the concrete walkway, he plunged downwards to the car park. There were too many cars here. Too many! He bounced from car to car, scrabbling furiously at locks, whimpering in fear, expecting to feel the presence of the Spectre again at any second, just as he had felt it in that stranger's living-room. Stan had had no right to take him away from what he knew; if he had been left alone, the horror would have passed him by. He was sure of it now.

What colour was the car? Green? Blue? Red?

Red? That's it! Yes, it was red!

Joe collapsed against the bonnet of a blue car, knocking the air out of his lungs. Gasping, he raised himself as he saw a familiar red car parked next to it. Two large dice hung above the dashboard. He remembered the dice instantly and realised that he had found the car at last. Whimpering, he fumbled at the lock until it opened; then he was inside, gunning the engine frantically into life. He became aware of movement on the walkway. There were three figures up there; one of them was running towards him, arms flapping. He was shouting at him to stop, to come back. Terrified, Joe slammed the gears into first and drove at the figure hurtling towards him. It was the Spectre again, sending things to kill him. The figure loomed large and then twisted to one side as he floored the accelerator and the car roared over the ramp and down the walkway to the central motorway. No Spectres followed him.

* * *

Diane and Richard helped Stan to his feet as the car vanished from sight, tyres screeching on the tarmac. He had been grazed, but seemed not to be hurt. The car passed on, weaving crazily from side to side.

'We've got to stop him,' said Stan breathlessly. 'Have you got a car?'

'It's being repaired,' replied Richard.

'I've got a car,' said Diane, 'but it's parked at the college.'

'Shit!'

'How shall we find him?' asked Richard.

'I know where he's heading. He'll be going back home to Liverpool again. Sanctuary. If he doesn't smash himself up on the way there, of course.'

'Come on, let's get my car.'

Three

Joe drove almost instinctively, neon light washing the car. He had found some of Stan's stuff in the dashboard and had greedily swallowed it. Soon, the fear had crawled away again. His instincts seemed to have been deceptively heightened as he sped down the central motorway.

'Automatic pilot,' he giggled, switching on the radio. Derek and the Dominoes were playing 'Layla'. He switched off quickly. It reminded him of Pandora, and the memory of Pandora brought back that nightmare in the flat. He fumbled among the cassettes on the dash, found a Rolling Stones recording and jammed it into the slot. Smiling, he swerved around a van, horn ringing angrily, and thought about Liverpool. He would be okay when he got there. Nothing would find him if he could only get home again.

* * *

By the time Diane had swung her Fiat down from the flyover and onto the central motorway, it had begun to rain and Joe had gained a fifty-minute start. Secretly, but without voicing their thoughts, they all believed that he would never make it as far as Liverpool. Stan had told them about the drugs in the dash—a foolish risk, he admitted—and no one doubted that Joe would have taken the lot by now. It could only be a matter of time before his sanity or concentration—or both—sent him over the central reservation, across a parapet and into the twilight zone.

They would be on the outskirts of Liverpool by eleven-thirty if Diane kept her foot down, and back at Joe's flat half-an-hour after that. They had hardly uttered a word in over an hour. At last, from the back seat, Stan spoke up.

'What the *hell* happened back there? What was it?'

'I've seen something like it before,' said Diane in a voice that seemed too calm, too composed. All she really wanted to do was scream and let the terror out. She had been waiting for someone to break the silence. 'It was at a séance a long time ago, when I was a child. Like I said before, my mother was a medium.'

'What was it, Diane?' asked Richard from the passenger seat next to her.

'Ectoplasm.'

A car's headlights, coming from the other direction, momentarily dazzled them. A horn blatted nearby.

'You mean . . . table rapping, voices from the grave? All that stuff?' said Stan.

'That's what I mean.'

Richard could see the whites of Diane's knuckles as she gripped the steering wheel. There were memories there, behind her eyes, memories that she wanted to remain hidden.

'The way that horrible stuff glowed, the way it looked. I just knew that it was some kind of ectoplasm. But I've never seen anything as hellish or deadly or *big* as that in my life.'

'Mediums produce it in séances, isn't that right?' asked Richard gently. 'A sort of smoke that forms into apparitions or spirits, or something.'

'Not quite. It's tissue. Some scientists say it's formed from the body cells of mediums when they're in a trance. When I was small, I once saw my mother in a trance. I wasn't supposed to be there. She didn't like to involve me—or even talk to me about it. But I was hiding in the hall, peeking round a door into the parlour. Mother had three customers that day. I saw . . .' Diane suppressed a shiver, took a deep breath and continued, 'coils of glowing smoke—like snakes—come out of her nose and mouth. They crept over the parlour table, twisted and knotted together, changing into the face of an old man. I remember screaming and screaming, just before I fainted. My mother kept as much as possible from me after that. Afterwards, though, she did tell me about ectoplasm, and how it can form pseudopod 'limbs'. She wanted to explain that much to me because she was worried about the effects of what I'd seen; she didn't want it to scar me. I was only seven, but I'll never forget it.'

'Ectoplasm,' repeated Stan. 'But from a *television* set, for crying out loud!'

'And ectoplasm implies a medium or psychic of some kind, doesn't it?' conjectured Richard.

'Nothing human could make anything like the thing we saw back at your flat,' said Diane.
'And it doesn't explain wooden dummies that suddenly come to life and try to tear a chunk out of your throat,' said Stan.
Richard's thoughts returned to that hideous wooden monstrosity and Robinson's horrific death. Then he remembered Joe's babbled, barely coherent words after Diane had blasted that insane apparition in his flat. The implications had thrown him into a quandary. How could it make sense? *You said I was the one, Pandora*, he had said. *You said that you would always love me. You said I was the one.*
Richard remembered that final week before the end of term, back in the days of the Byker Chapter. It was the last week the Chapter would ever have together: a bitter-sweet time. Things had changed then, and would never be the same again. The disintegration, the feeling that they no longer seemed to belong together had mysteriously set in during those last few days and—somehow—the best thing in their lives had turned completely sour.
It had been an evening in Mark Antony's Coffee House, he remembered. Pandora, Phil, Derek and himself had gone for something to eat after college and work. Derek and Phil had left together, leaving Pandora and himself to finish their coffee. They both had nothing better to do that evening; so they'd talked, and had more coffee, and talked, and talked . . .
And Pandora had told him that the Byker Chapter meant a great deal to her, as it did to them all. It was a great thing, a small group bound together by friendship. No pettiness, no rivalry, nothing expected from any individual member . . . except friendship. No jealousies . . . and particularly, no sexual jealousies over her. She led her own life outside the Chapter. They both agreed that the moment she 'scored' with Phil or Derek or any of the others, then that would result in the disintegration of the Byker Chapter. An advantage would have been taken; the bond between them would snap. Richard had always felt in his heart that this was true, and so he was completely unprepared for what Pandora told him next.
She was in love with him.
She had felt that way for a long time now, but had refrained from saying anything for the reasons she had just given.

Richard had been surprised at the depth of his own feelings, bursting through at her words.

They had only a few days before the end of term; they must not tell the others, as they both knew that would be the end of the Chapter. They had given in to their feelings. But despite their well-kept secret, the Chapter had still dissolved, never to reform. It seemed almost as if the Chapter itself was a living organism, drawing its vitality from the sum of all its individual parts. Somehow, it had sensed that it had fallen prey to a dread disease, of which its component parts were unaware. It had sensed that something had gone wrong. And it had died.

On the last day, when the Byker Chapter had ceased to exist, Pandora had also gone from Richard's life. No reasons, no answers. She had left him and he had never seen her again.

Now, after a living nightmare had attacked them in Richard's own home, Joe had begun to babble those words which only Richard himself should have known. Was Joe insane? Had the fear and the drugs completely destroyed his mind? Was he merely delirious? Had he somehow read Richard's mind? Or could it be that Pandora had . . . Pandora could *really* have . . . ?

'What is it?' Diane was looking at him intently from the driving seat. 'Come on, Richard. Let's have it.'

'What?'

'Something's eating you.' Again, that penetrating insight. 'You've got some idea what this is all about, haven't you?'

'Not really. But something that Joe said has made me wonder.'

'And that is?' asked Stan from the back seat.

'You heard what he said?'

'No, I was too preoccupied trying to get the air back into my lungs.'

'It was all a little garbled. But he seemed to be saying that Pandora and he were in love. She'd told him that she'd never leave him—things like that—which is pretty crazy.' Richard paused, feeling the accumulated guilt of many years bearing down on him. 'You won't know this, Stan, but . . . just before the Byker Chapter disbanded . . . Pandora and I had something going.' Richard looked over at Diane again, wondering what her reaction might be. Her eyes remained fixed on the road; he could read nothing there. 'We kept it a secret. Then she left and I never saw her again. But the way Joe was talking it was if he . . . '

Richard turned in his seat to look at Stan. Neon light and shadow chased over his long, bearded face and there was an expression there that baffled Richard. He was slumped back heavily in his seat, his eyes fixed on his fists as they clenched and unclenched in his lap.

'What's wrong, Stan?'

'What's wrong? *What's wrong?* Everything's fucking wrong, man! Everything. Pandora came to me . . . *me!* . . . ' Stan banged his fist against his chest. 'She told me the same thing. We had the same secret affair.'

'Then the three of us . . . ?' stammered Richard.

'Why only three? Why not all of us?'

'There's the answer,' said Diane calmly. 'Pandora's the key to everything that's happened to you.'

Four

It was after ten o'clock when Joe reached the outskirts of Liverpool, having been responsible, both directly and indirectly, for two car smashes and the destruction of a 'Little Chef' restaurant sign. Somehow, he had escaped the attention of the police on all three occasions. Oblivious and deliriously happy, he swept into his home ground. But the sight of the Mersey River reminded him somehow of his flat. A vivid impression of its empty, claustrophobic darkness and the television set in the corner beside his stereo unit, threatened his mood of euphoria. Playing the same Rolling Stones cassette for the umpteenth time, he performed a maniacal three-point turn in the middle of the road, destroying a traffic bollard, and headed towards the only place where he could find real sanctuary.

The studio.

He had not been there for many weeks now. When the bad feelings had started, he had begun to feel uneasy in that self-contained, glass-panelled structure standing in the grounds of a private estate, which he rented, dirt cheap, from the eccentric recluse who owned the 23-bedroomed Tudor mansion in the middle of the estate. Joe suspected that his annual rental on the studio probably payed for one quarterly electricity bill at the house. When the Spectre had begun to seek him out, the glass frontage and windows of the studio had made him feel vulnerable, somehow on display. Finally, he had been driven into the fearful seclusion of his flat, leaving behind the creation on which he had been working. Now, however, the glass windows did not seem so threatening. And, of course, the studio had no television set.

As he roared through the wrought-iron gates to the estate, the euphoria was in full flood again. He needed to be working again; needed to be absorbed in his creation. And the thought of the unfinished, partly formed clay standing in the centre of his studio, fuelled his elation.

Parking the car beside a dilapidated wooden fence, and losing the paintwork along one side in the process, Joe hurried quickly through the darkness, refusing to be intimidated by the closely crowding, spectral trees. He left the driving door open with the Rolling Stones blasting 'Brown Sugar' into the night.

Frantically, he opened the main doors and found the central switch bank. Sharp yellow light dissolved the darkness and chased the shadows. The familiarity of the place was soothing—the drawing board and easels, the scattered canvases, the racks of materials. And, in centre stage, draped with a white sheet—the statue.

Joe slammed the door carelessly, a smile on his face. He hurried to the figure and tugged the sheet away. He could not really understand why he had started this one in the first place. It had not been commissioned; there was no real purpose in its creation. But once commenced, as a kind of creative therapy from the largely basic work he did to earn his bread and butter as a designer, he had been enthralled by its potential and his desire to make, for once perhaps, something really beautiful.

It was to be the image of a woman, standing lifesize, with a flowing gown and flowing hair, arms held out in a kind of mysterious appeal. Imitation Greek goddess, perhaps? Joe did not really know. And that was most of the fascination. The body was completed, but although he had tried many times in his preliminary sketches to get the face just right, he could not achieve what he was after. Latterly he had attempted to work on the face 'blind', using only his instinct. But each effort had been merely adequate and he had torn the clay from the framework. He was after something very special, even though he did not know what that 'something' would be. Tonight, on his 'high' and with all the bad memories far away, he would finally get it right.

He threw his overcoat on the floor, kicking it out of his way as he moved to the bench. He lit the small oil-burning stove to ward off the chill and to prevent his fingers becoming cramped while working with the cold clay and the lukewarm water he would need to shape it. Pulling off the lid of his clay bin, he could see that the material was still good and fresh. With trembling fingers he fiddled with the portable radio on the bench beside him until he had found some good music, then turned back to the figure in the middle of the floor. Within minutes, he had begun work under the bright, clean strobe lights. Outside, the darkness crowded around the studio, but Joe was unaware and unconcerned. Inside was only light, and that was all that mattered.

Tonight, he would breathe everything he had into his creation. Every line, every contour of that special, unknown face would occupy him. He was the Creator. And from Clay he would create Beauty.

Five

'It's the answer, I'm sure of it,' said Diane, giving voice to what they all believed. The statement hung heavily in the air. After Richard's revelation, Diane knew that it had been a painful hour for both of them. Now, she wished that she had not stated the obvious. Richard had begun to talk about his affair with Pandora, revealing conversations and memories that he had kept close to his heart all these years. Bitterly, Stan had been able to complete half-stated sentences and heartfelt promises. Pandora had said the same thing to Richard that she had said to Stan; and also, presumably, to Joe . . . and perhaps to all the other members of the Byker Chapter. With her attention fixed grimly on the cat's-eyes in the road ahead, Diane had listened to a two-way reminiscence and realisation of betrayal that was heart-rending. What Richard and Stan had always believed to be personal, intimate and deeply felt had, in fact, been exposed as a shared experience. During it all, she had been aware of Richard's eyes occasionally flashing towards her, searching for some sign of a reaction. God, how she'd wanted to react sometimes. The events of the last two days had turned her life upside-down: the attraction to Richard, the dummy, the nightmare, that bloody insane television set. The chance for normal rationalisation and order had been overthrown; she was operating on pure adrenalin and instinct. But her instinct drew her closer to Richard, closer than she could ever have believed possible. When he had thrown her those searching glances, for a deep reason, unknown to her, she had been forced not to respond, even though she wanted to show him that it did not matter, his affair with Pandora did not matter. Not to them; not to the way things were going to be for them from now on. Curiously, it seemed as if Richard's ex-wife Denys had never existed at all. From now on, they were going to be together.

If he stays alive, of course.

She refused even to acknowledge that thought. Of course he would make it. Together, they would solve this damn' thing. They would find this Pandora—whoever or whatever she was—and they would solve it.

After they had talked themselves to a full-stop, the silence had descended like a sorrowful cloak. Diane cursed herself for intruding with her stupid, unnecessary statement. But the silence was agonising and she had to break it.

'Will Joe make it back?' *Damn, more unnecessary statements!*

Stan shrugged; Diane could see him in the mirror above her. He seemed unconcerned whether she saw him or not, and now, it angered her. Richard seemed to sense her thoughts. He suddenly recalled the powerful image of Diane standing with that pistol held in a classical shooting pose, even though she had never fired a gun before.

'Diane,' he said after a while, 'you've got more guts than both of us.'

She turned to look at him, caught his smile and returned it.

Richard turned back to Stan. Their eyes held for a long time and it seemed as if all those years between the Byker Chapter's break-up and their reunion had never been. At heart, the friendship was as strong as ever; it had been in cold storage, that was all. Stan was the same as he remembered him from all those years ago. Stupidly, he heard himself ask:

'So how the hell have you been, man?'

Stan seemed puzzled by these strange, incongruous words. His eyes searched Richard's face, like a man just woken from sleep. Then realisation dawned and his face split into that very familiar, toothy grin.

'Fine, man.'

They both laughed.

'Married?' asked Richard.

'Me? Nope. Never signed a form, anyway.'

'You go for blondes, right?' asked Diane, eyes still on the road but now sparkling with a kind of joy.

'Right! How the hell did you know?'

'She knows more about you than you can probably guess. Intuition's a fine art as far as Diane's concerned.'

'Yeah? You a natural blonde, Diane?'

'Nice try, smooth guy,' replied Diane, smiling.

Richard leaned secretly across and squeezed her arm.

'You lucky bastard,' said Stan quietly from the back.

Whatever water had passed under Byker Bridge, whatever had happened to them in the days since the Byker Chapter—it was as if no time had passed at all. They had no real need to discuss their lives—the ins and outs of ten years' experience—Richard could tell just by looking at Stan. His eyes were glowing. Richard found himself reaching across the back seat to Stan.

Instinctively, Stan took his hand in a strong grip.

'We're gonna sort this thing out, Stan.'

'Too bloody right we are, Teacher Man.'

In that instant, as Stan clasped his hand, Richard was transported back in time to a coppery-hot summer day in old Byker. He was nine years old, Stan a year older, and Spider Parker had just double-dog-dared them. A dare was challenge enough. A double-dare could not be ignored. But a double-dog-dare had to be faced and met if any honour was to be retained.

Spider Parker had earned his nickname for his amazing agility and the fact that heights—*any* height—just did not scare him. He had tied a one hundred and twenty foot rope swing to one of the 'underhang' struts on the railway bridge while the kids below, in the cradle of the Ouseburn valley, had looked up and watched him scurrying and skipping from girder to girder. Richard remembered the tingling fear in his toes and fingertips when Spider had swung one-handed in empty space. Now, all a kid had to do was grab the rope and climb the rubbish tip on the valley side until he had reached the point where the bridge girders plunged into the earth. A simple jump into the air could send you hurtling out into dizzy space, hundreds of feet above the valley floor.

And Spider had double-dog-dared Richard and Stan that they could not fix up a similar swing under Byker Bridge, which ran parallel to the railway viaduct spanning the valley. Richard had climbed into the lower struts on the valley side many times before. It was easy. All you had to do was use the coal merchant's fence as a beginning.

There was no fear as both Stan and he slipped quickly over the huge, hot steel plates with rivets as big as a nine-year-old's fist. But fear was waiting nevertheless, curled up and crouching like an invisible gargoyle on a particular great grey girder, spotted by pigeons' droppings. Richard had never been beyond that girder before. Now he would have to climb past it, higher and higher. Stan was leading the way, rope coiled massively over his shoulder and trailing away behind him over the girders as he moved, like some umbilical cord to safety. Richard was too ashamed to let his fear hold him back. He scrambled after Stan.

Don't look down . . . that's what Professor Challenger had told the other explorers in *The Lost World* as they inched along a precarious cliff edge above a boiling cauldron of molten lava. He had seen that film with Stan and Phil and the others at the Imperial the previous week. *Never look down* . . . *just keep going* . . .

The metal beneath his fingertips seemed alive as they moved. It was sending little electric shocks through his arms and legs, robbing his strength, turning his spine to mush.

Don't look down!

Stan had stopped now and was feeding the rope down between two girders.

Richard could only watch, electrified, motionless with fear. It did not matter whether he looked down or not; he could imagine it, anyway. He could still see the patchwork roofs on toy houses; the great slate factory roofs; the Ouseburn oozing along and glinting black in the fierce sunlight like liquid coal. The smell of tarmac from the bridge road just above his head was dizzying and cloying his brain. The top of the leadworks chimney, with its twelve-foot round garden of weeds where no foot had trodden since it was built, seemed terribly close. The rope had snagged in the metal lattice-work beside Richard, and Stan was telling him to pull it free and stop farting about . . .

. . . Richard was not really here. He was at home in bed and just dreaming. He watched his hand move for the rope and knew, just *knew*, that the nightmare demanded that he should fall. It was the logic demanded by every nightmare that only the worst could happen and that he was bound to tumble screaming and twisting into empty air, down, down, down . . . shattering the sparkling black mirror of the river below.

His hand was still moving. Light from the steelwork beside him was shining directly into his face. His hand closed on the rope.

And then his legs slithered beneath him and he fell between two girders.

Everything 'whited-out'. It always did in the worst nightmares. When the bad thing eventually happened, you 'whited-out' and woke up. Except that in this dream, when Richard awoke, he was hanging in the air with one hand clamped on a loop of rope, dangling just beneath the struts of a bridge, the world tilting distantly below.

Stan was hanging onto one end of the rope, the other end was still snagged in a girder.

'Jesus, no . . . Stan . . . no . . . let me back . . . let me back . . .'

And Stan, face white in the dark underhang, was hauling him back, hand over hand.

'Don't let go, Stan! Don't . . . DON'T LET GO!'

Stan's hand on his wrist felt like a man's hand—like his father's hand, somehow—the strength that hauled him into the girders again was a man's strength. And only the fierce, cruel adult bullying that Stan used to make him crawl back beneath the bridge to the side of the valley could have budged Richard from his tightly-held perch.

Richard and Stan had been ill for a week after that, absent from school. They had never spoken of that incident since. They had almost met the Spectre that time. It had been much too close even to speak of in hushed whispers. It might easily scent them if they talked about it; scent them and return.

Perhaps, Richard thought, death had always been the Spectre. He knew now, as an adult, that it had been shock that had made them ill. Stan had saved his life then and they had been mysteriously bonded ever since. Now, in a car speeding towards unknown horrors . . . unknown Spectres . . . Richard remembered that day as he grasped Stan's hand. There was a strength, a power, in that handshake; something that defied description.

But could that power dispel the Spectres?

* * *

Diane had switched on the radio as they travelled. A sudden fog had descended over the highway. At first, ragged wraiths had whirled and plucked at the car; now, in a suddenly dense shroud, the fog had smothered them.

'Joe's *never* going to make it in this,' said Richard.

Diane half-turned to speak.

And then something solidified from the swirling fog and reared in the headlights before them.

Richard cried out in alarm and Diane swung the wheel to the left before they could see exactly what it was. Tyres screeching, the car hit the hard shoulder and began bouncing precariously along the embankment on two wheels. Diane tugged desperately at the steering wheel. The embankment suddenly vanished and Stan's head slammed into the roof as the car jerked back onto four wheels again. Diane jammed on the brakes, but it was too late to prevent the car from nose-diving down a grassed slope and into a dilapidated fence. The fence cracked and splintered. The jerk on the safety belt knocked the air out of Richard's lungs.

For a long time, they all sat, too dazed to move. On the radio, the theme music from *Midnight Express* continued to play. Then Diane said:

'What was it? Did I hit somebody?'

'No,' said Richard.' You didn't hit anything.'

'What was it? Could you see?'

'No, we were moving too fast. Where the hell did that damned fog came from?'

Just as suddenly as it had come, the fog had vanished.

Diane could see Stan in the rear-view mirror, rubbing his head and groaning.

'You okay?'

'Yeah . . . just about . . . '

'What the hell is that?' asked Richard. Reflected in the mirror, Diane could see something moving outside the rear window. She turned round, taking in Richard's mystified expression, and looked back.

The fog had not vanished. It had formed into an unnatural, undulating, shapeless mass in the centre of the highway. It seemed to be about thirty yards long at its thickest, evaporating to nothingness on either side after another fifty yards or so. It had a strange, unhealthy look. Even now, it had begun to swell and curl away from the highway like a living thing. To Diane's horror, it appeared to be groping with tendrils of smoke down the embankment after them. It reminded her of those hideous tentacles back in Richard's flat.

'I don't believe it,' said Richard. 'That bloody fog's following us.'

'Oh, my God,' said Diane. *'It's glowing!'*

Stan twisted round to watch as the outer tendrils of the fog found the car. When he spoke, his voice sounded ridiculously normal, calm and composed. 'It's alive. It's the same thing from Richard's flat.'

Now they could hear the same sibilant rattling and gobbling. Somewhere in there, somewhere in that pulsing mass, were the hellish eyes and barbed, ravenous mouths.

Diane reached for the starter. The car engine coughed and died, coughed and died again.

Terror swamped her. She could almost taste her fear as the impending horror swirled down the embankment towards them.

'Richard!' she shouted suddenly. 'Roll up the window!'

Startled, Richard took heed of her warning and rolled up the glass just as the first billowing clouds and squirming tendrils reached his door. Seconds later, the car had been swamped in a dense grey blanket as if some giant spider had suddenly spun them into a grey, webbed cocoon. Chill air crept into the car through the air conditioning unit. Diane snapped it off quickly. The car sat on the embankment like some strange submarine at the bottom of the ocean. The tentacles had withdrawn somewhere out of sight.

Something scraped the roof.

'For God's sake, stay in the car!' hissed Stan.

The car began to shake vigorously from side to side. Richard brought out the automatic pistol from where he had placed it in the glove compartment. He had no idea what he could do with it after their previous experience in the flat, but the positive action made him feel better. The shaking stopped abruptly, followed by a viscous, slithering sound.

'The roof,' whispered Diane, 'it's on the roof.'

Stan shrank back in his seat, craning his neck upwards at the window to get a better view. Something whiplashed at the glass, cobwebbing it. Stan leaped back, uninjured. Richard found himself holding the gun at the window, waiting for the next sign of movement.

The car lurched again, once, rocking on its suspension.

'It jumped off,' said Diane.

'What the hell *is* it?' Richard peered into the murk. There was no sign of any movement; just the billowing, poisonous fog.

Somewhere in the murk, something laughed.

The sound was hollow, somehow echoing. And Diane knew immediately that nothing human had made that sound. She reached for Richard. He took her hand, squirming round to find the owner of that voice. In the back seat, Stan was doing the same. The laughter came again, this time from the rear of the car, terrifyingly close.

'It's playing with us,' said Stan.

'It wants to frighten us into leaving the car,' said Diane, as steadily as she was able. 'If we do, we're dead.'

Again the inhuman laughter; a bubbling, poisonous sound. It echoed and rippled, suddenly emerging as words. Horrifying, sickening, *dead* words.

'Necrolan . . . Absavel . . . Gorgus . . . '

It laughed again.

'One by one by one by one by one . . . '

Diane bit into her fist. 'Oh, my God, what is it?'

'What is it?' came an echo, and then that terrible laughter yet again: *'Seek and find. Hide and seek. Hide. Seek. Find . . . find . . . FIND!'* The words changed abruptly from their rambling sing-song tone to a voice thick with menace: *'One by one was better. But now, you know. No matter! There is no further need to eat you piece by piece, one by one. Not any more.'*

The voice was silent. Richard was aware of the blood buzzing in his ears. A vein twitched on his temple. He could see droplets of sweat on Stan's rigid face. Diane held his hand in a painful grip. When the words came again, they were on the other side of the car. There was still nothing to be seen.

'Too late! Too late to save Joseph!' More of that hideous laughter. *'All of you . . . '* The voice dropped to a low, cunning, brooding bass, echoing in the fog. *'. . . all of you will die! Every one . . . of the Chapter . . . every one . . . The Sins of the Fathers . . . every one . . .'*

The fog was becoming denser now, swirling close and thick.

'It's coming,' said Diane. 'I can feel it! It's moving in . . . Oh, God! What are we going to do?'

Richard twisted from side to side in his seat, looking for any sign of movement in the billowing greyness beyond the windows.

Closer . . . closer . . .

'Midnight Express' continued to play on the radio as Richard's mind skipped crazily over the last few days.

Phil: 'The police were summoned following complaints from neighbours concerning excessive noise from Mr Stuart's television and radio which were still playing at maximum volume when entry was forced into the flat and his body was found . . . '

Creeping death . . . even now probing the car . . . sliding hungry and evil over the roof . . .

Robinson about Derek: 'And he had his television set in the sitting-room blasting away like hell.'

'Midnight Express' on the car radio . . . soft and melancholy . . .

The nightmare in his flat. The insane monstrosity from the television screen.

Tendrils from Hell . . . ravening for death . . . Now . . . Now! NOW!

The television . . . the radio . . . 'Midnight Express' . . . the car radio . . .

Richard lunged for the dial as the first thin, poisonous wisps of the thing outside began to curl through the grille and into the car. Something bit savagely at his fingers, drawing blood. He ignored it, snapping the radio off. The tendrils disappeared.

Outside in the fog, something shrieked. The noise was almost too intense to bear.

The shriek faded and, even now, Richard could see that the fog had begun to lose its density. Cobweb wisps began floating away from the car windows. The voice, now hollow and fading, echoed distantly.

'A brief respite . . . brief . . . But you! The Woman! You are as one of them, now . . . you will also die . . . soon . . . soon . . . too late for Joseph . . . too late . . . too late . . .

'It's going,' said Richard, his blood chilling at the explicit threat to Diane. 'It can't hurt us now.'

And then the fog had disappeared as quickly as it had come.

'How . . . ?' began Stan, gazing out into the clear night.

'The radio,' said Richard. 'Don't ask me how, but this thing can use television or radio to track us down. If something's switched on and we're around, it can use it as a "homing device" to search for us. And somehow, it can come through to take us.'

Diane threw the gears into reverse. The car started straight away, lurching out of its rut and roaring back up towards the hard shoulder. Seconds later, they had joined the 'slow' lane before rejoining the main highway traffic. They said nothing for a long time.

* * *

'They have discovered. But it is of no matter. It will soon be strong enough to stalk them without the need for man-made contrivances. But there is one who was not with them. You must turn the key again and open the cage.'

'Why are you doing these things? What does it want?'

'The flesh is the cage and you are the flesh. It is time for the Stalking again.'

The hissing snowstorm. The whining and buzzing of invisible forces in the air. Somewhere out there the brief sound of cruel laughter. The hissing of snakes. A blizzard of electric snow.

'I can't do it. I won't do it. Not again.'

'You will do it. You must be whole. Gorgus . . . Imago . . . Pacter . . .'

'It makes me ill.'

'No, it makes you whole. Every time, it makes you more whole. Dark-Out now . . . Dark-Out . . . Necrolan . . . Absavel . . . Gorgus . . .'

Six

Time had lost its meaning for Joe. The nightmare threat of the Spectre had been submerged deeply in his mind as if it had never existed. All that mattered was the work on which he was engaged. He might have been working for hours or days, it was immaterial; all that mattered was the clay and the shaping of the clay. Gesture by gesture, inch by inch, he continued to mould and form. It was a painfully slow process, but that mysterious, elusive face was finally beginning to come to life in his hands. The lips were perfect: the shape, the slight pout, the promise. Everything was perfect. The chin had taken longer but he had succeeded at last in capturing that certain delicacy. He had taken no rest; he needed no rest. The curls of hair above the high cheekbones were points of detail only; they had taken a lot of time but there had not been the same need for concentration. The forehead had been next, the gentle slope of the forehead. The nose had presented a great deal of difficulty, much more than he might have envisaged. But at last he had perfected that slightly aquiline shape.

The eyes.

He knew that this would be the biggest challenge of all, and he prepared for it—the final, most important touch. Did they not say that the eyes were the mirror of the soul? The eyes had consumed him. He was lost in them, more deeply than he had ever been lost in Pandora's eyes . . .

Pandora . . . Pandora . . . Pandora . . .

Who was Pandora?

The name brought back unfamiliar, unpleasant memories. He cast them aside and delved deeply into his work. The eyes were watching him as he proceeded. They were pleading with him; imploring him to do them justice. Only under his hands could the image come to life. Feelings of unease began to grow in him; the drugs were beginning to wear off and unpleasant memories kept threatening to return. Deeper and deeper, he threw himself into his work; concentrating everything on the image of the dream woman. As long as he could give it everything that was in him, give it his soul, breathe his very life into it, the bad, dark memories and places would stay away. And he would gladly give a rib if it would make his creation perfect.

The eyes were coming to life. Joe began to laugh as he worked; wild, hysterical laughter. Feverishly, insistently, his fingers flicked and shaped, curved and hollowed. Rapidly, his small scalpel danced over the irises and lenses. Breathless, he stood back, face still thrust forward, to gaze upon his creation. It was finished! He had given her a face, a face that had lived in his subconscious all his life; the face of a woman who had never lived. He laughed again and it seemed that the image's eyes sparkled with glee at being given such life. He threw his hands wide in joy and was in no way surprised when the image did the same.

Drinking in the beauty he had created, he moved into his creation's embrace. His arms closed around the clay. The clay enclosed his own body.

And then Joe's vision finally came into focus. A wave of dizziness engulfed him. He started, as if waking from some strange dream; he was back in the real world again. The darkness and the fear were suddenly crowding and claustrophobic. The only thing that could protect him was his creation. He felt the cold clay around him as if for the first time and raised his face lovingly to the face of his image.

And then Joe began to scream as he had never screamed in his life.

It had been a fantasy, his image of creating the perfect woman. His hands had been directed by another source. His eyes had been blinded to the horror in clay that he had created.

The clay closed round his head, greedily sucking his face into its cold maw, muffling his screams of horror. The arms of the image locked fast and consumed his struggling body in an immutable embrace. The momentum of Joe's death struggle tipped over the oil burner. Flames devoured his legs, spreading liquid fire over the bare wooden floor to the drawing board and the curtains.

Clay oozed and dripped.

In minutes the studio was ablaze, obliterating the dead sculptor and his nightmare in clay.

Joe had finally seen the face of the Spectre.

Seven

'It *hunts* using television or radio?' repeated Stan.

'I think so.'

'How?'

'How the hell should I know?' Richard had been struggling to control the trembling in his fingers ever since they had resumed their journey.

'I think I can envisage it,' said Diane, surprised at the calm in her voice. 'Something out there—a Spectre, to use your own Byker Chapter slang—is hunting you one by one (*Us! It's hunting* us *one by one. Oh, God!*). We don't know what it is, or why it's doing these things, but it could be anywhere in the country. If it can use television or radio waves, that would make every receiver an *eye* . . . looking for us (*There, I said it!*).'

'But there are millions and millions of television and radio sets,' said Stan. 'How the hell could it find us . . . ?'

'We're not dealing with anything human, Stan,' said Richard.

'I don't know . . . ' Richard could see Stan in the rear-view mirror, shaking his head. 'It's mad. All of it. It's like one of those X movies we used to sneak into the Imperial to see when we were kids.'

'You know we're dealing with something evil, Stan, something supernatural. You were probably the first to come to that conclusion.'

'Yeah? Well let's send for Peter Cushing. He'd know what to do.' Stan laughed in that curious, barking fashion as orange highway lights flashed over his face. 'Wait! What about that dummy? How does a television or radio come into that?'

'I think . . . ' began Diane. She swallowed hard, gripping the wheel tightly and yielding to that horrible *instinct* that she had been hiding since she was a little girl. 'I think . . . that when the Spectre came out of Derek's television, or radio, or whatever . . . it went into the dummy. I think that after the dummy killed Derek, it stayed there. When the police took it away, some kind of . . . *force* . . . stayed in it, waiting. The dummy managed to get away from the police station and crawled away and came back to the flat . . .'

'Come on, Diane! How the shit can you know all that?'

'Shut up, Stan! Let her finish.'

' . . . back to the flat because it knew . . . it *knew* that someone else . . . another Byker Chapter member . . . would come to find out what had happened. And you did, Richard.'

Stan was suddenly silent. Richard and Diane sat waiting for his response. When the silence continued, Richard looked back. Stan was sitting, head down. When he looked up, his face was ashen. Richard could see that he was holding a copy of the Byker Chapter photograph in his hands.

'It's Joe,' he said. 'He's vanished from the photograph.'

* * *

There was no sign of Joe's car and the door was locked when they finally arrived at his flat, well after midnight. When there was no response to their knocking, Richard and Stan broke down the door, but once inside it was obvious that he had not arrived. Then Stan remembered the studio. Joe had rambled on about it a lot on their way up to Newcastle. Now they were faced with two choices: either the car had cracked up on the highway, or Joe had somehow made it to Liverpool, panicked at the thought of returning to the flat and had gone instead to the studio.

The fire brigade had finally extinguished the flames by the time Diane pulled over on the opposite side of the road from the estate. Two fire engines were parked on the other side, and access to the studio was impossible. Red lights blinked in the darkness. Three hoses had been strung out through the wrought-iron gates. Beyond the stone wall bordering the estate, thick black smoke shrouded the trees and Diane suppressed a shudder; it reminded her of the fog they had encountered on the highway. The police and firemen were too involved to notice the Fiat and its three occupants.

'Oh, Christ, no . . .' moaned Stan, clambering out of the car.

Two ambulance-men were carrying a stretcher down the driveway. The body was completely covered by a white sheet, but as they manoeuvred the stretcher into the waiting ambulance, a charred arm flopped out. Richard felt his stomach roll. Stan slumped against the car, hands on thighs, head down. 'Oh, Christ.' After a while, he climbed back into the car.

'Where next?' asked Diane, already knowing the answer.

'Barry Clark.'

'If he's still alive,' said Richard.

'He's still in the photo, Teacher Man,' said Stan.

They roared off into the night.

* * *

A memory in Richard's mind.

A Sunday afternoon in Byker. The Byker Chapter lay on a grassy bank beside Ouseburn Primary School. The air seemed vibrant with heat as Derek emerged from the pub with a tray of drinks, walking carefully towards them. The school's strangely arabesque turrets and towers pierced a cloudless blue sky. Kids were playing football in the park behind the school known, for some strange reason, as Granny's Park. Beyond, traffic glittered on Byker Bridge. To their left, a ship was coming into the River Tyne, its masts moving slowly above the buildings that blocked the river from view.

Pandora lay on her front, elbows planted on the grass, chin cupped in her hands. Barry was chewing a piece of grass. Richard watched Barry watching Pandora and wondered what was going through his mind. The others struggled from their lazy poses to take amber-golden pint glasses of beer from Derek's tray. Somewhere in the grass, a grasshopper chirred industriously. Pandora smiled secretly and flipped onto her back, taking a chilled glass of wine from the tray. Her eyes were as blue as the sky.

Barry saw that Richard was watching him and smiled.

'Deep thoughts, Barry?'

'Yeah . . . ' He turned to look at the school and then the figures on the grass. 'I was thinking about Ouseburn School. Except for Pandora, we all went there. We've all grown up in Byker. All stayed together. It's good. But life's not like that. Everything changes, eventually. I mean, look at Byker: they're tearing it down around us. It's a shame that things can't stay the same forever. But they won't. Soon, all this will be gone. And so will we.'

Pandora rolled over again, dandelion seeds in her hair. She kicked Barry's foot. 'We've got the sunshine, we've got a drink and we've got ourselves. Let's live for today.'

Richard smiled, raising his glass. 'The Byker Chapter won't change. We'll always be together. We'll always be friends.'

'I think I'm going to be sick with all this sentiment flying around,' said Stan, chortling into his beer.

Barry laughed, his pensive air evaporating.

Of us all, thought Richard, *Barry's most vulnerable. He needs friends more than any of us. Something inside him sometimes resists it.*

'I don't care what you say,' said Pandora, grabbing Barry around the neck in an arm grip. 'As long as we all have each other, nothing can go wrong. What we have is special. It's magic.'

'You believe in magic?' asked Phil.

'Newcastle Exhibition ale,' interrupted Derek, sipping his beer, 'now *that's* magic.'

'Of course I believe in magic,' replied Pandora. 'With a name like Pandora I'd have to believe in magic, wouldn't I?'

'Yeah, what kind of name is that, anyway?' asked Joe.

Pandora released her hold on Barry, making a playful lunge at Joe, who evaded her.

'It's a fine old Cornish name. I'm not Byker stock, remember? I'm a foreigner.'

'You're adopted,' said Richard. 'We've adopted you.' He sat back again, looking out across the River Tyne. He felt good today. Really good. It was a fine thing to have such friends. They all believed in the Chapter. They all believed in friendship. He turned back to Barry, sipping his beer. Something about the half-smile on his face reaffirmed Richard's feeling: he was the most vulnerable; his insecurity required

protection—their protection. And they would always give it.
The Byker Chapter would survive.

Eight

The Imperial staff had finished their cleaning-up chores and had been ferried away by taxi into the darkness. Glasses had been washed and stacked, ashtrays emptied. Deejay had locked the nightclub's supply of LPs and singles in the office, taking his own records away with him, as usual. The disco lights had been switched off and disconnected. The security doors had been locked, the burglar alarm activated.

The Imperial lay shrouded in the same engulfing darkness that it had known in the years when it had stood derelict, awaiting transformation into its latest guise.

And, at the heart of that darkness, drinking in the silence in the centre of the disco floor, stood Pearson—the Under-Manager.

He stood there a long time, hands clasped before him, head lowered. He was savouring the night, smelling the silence; breathing deeply. Now at last, after so many long years of waiting, everything he had prayed for was about to come to pass.

He shivered in anticipation. Somewhere outside, a car rushed past, its headlights shining briefly on the main entrance doors; sending long, stray shafts of amber light chasing over the nightclub walls and the mosaic tiles behind the bar. Turning briskly, Pearson walked back across the floor, unimpeded by the blackness that he loved, and quickly ascended the staircase. His echoing footsteps were quickly swallowed by the gloom.

The security door at the top of the staircase opened of its own volition before he reached it, throwing his outline into stark relief; slabs of orange light invaded the darkness. From somewhere beyond the doorway, at the core of the light, a woman's quiet voice said:

'The third father is dead.'

Pearson paused on the threshold.

'Then we are ready to begin,' he said.

A small figure stepped into the doorway. It stood for a long time, facing Pearson. Pearson held out his hand. The small form took it. Together, they descended the stairs again. The door behind them closed silently. They crossed the disco floor and pushed through the padded double-doors into the reception area. Within seconds, the burglar alarm was de-activated.

The man and his small companion stepped outside onto the rainwashed pavements. Dirty water swirled and chased litter in the gutters. A full moon sailed the sky in ragged streaks of cloud. They began to walk towards the main street.

Traffic lights changed silently on the empty street—Red, amber, green, amber. Red, amber, green, amber—just like the disco lights inside the Imperial. Pearson and the small figure stopped beside a shop window. Together, they turned to face it.

'Our emissary is within,' said Pearson.

'Yes,' said a small voice.

'*Imago . . . Pacter . . . Emergo . . .*' began Pearson, lifting his hands in the air. 'Come forth!'

The traffic lights on Shields Road gleamed blood-red in the shop window.

'*Gorgus . . . Imago . . . Absavel . . .*'

'*Come forth!*'

On the other side of the glass, something moved.

* * *

Graham's Garments stood between a freezer centre and a pub on Shields Road, within a minute's walk of the Imperial nightclub on Byker Bank to the east, and another minute to the police station on Clifford Street.

Consequently, when the burglar alarm was activated that Thursday evening, a police presence was guaranteed in a very short time. Contacting the manager, however, proved less easy and, by the time that he arrived, Police Constable Brewer's professional detachment had been severely taxed by the persistent clamouring of the alarm. The manager, Mr Benson, was dishevelled, eyes still full of sleep. He had flung an overcoat on top of his pyjamas; he wore shoes, but no socks; his hair was awry.

'Sodding hell,' was all he could say as he surveyed the damage. The main windows had been shattered. Glass sparkled on the pavement.

The cold night air had penetrated deeply into the shop when Benson opened up and they entered, their breath hanging in clouds. Brewer looked around as Benson frantically checked the safe and the stock. It was a small shop which had seen many forms of commerce in its lifetime. It had been a newsagent, an off-licence, a second-hand bookshop. At present, it was a clothes-store; multi-coloured cardboard signs promised a 'Once-and-for-All' sale that had been ongoing for thirteen months. Half a dozen battered tailor's dummies stood in awkward poses. Trousers and shirts hung in neat ranks on both sides of the shop.

'Safe's okay,' said Benson at last, emerging from a back room, 'and as far as I can tell, no one's stolen any of the stock.'

Brewer was standing by the shattered shop window.

'Possibly drunken kids,' said Benson, joining him. 'The bastards! Must have chucked a brick through the window.'

'No sign of a brick,' mused Brewer. 'Must have used . . . '

'Shit!' exclaimed Benson suddenly.

'What?'

'The dummy. They've stolen one of my dummies.' He spun round, seeking confirmation. Stooping, he picked up a jacket and trousers from the floor. 'I don't understand it.' He held up the clothes for Brewer's examination. 'The dummy was wearing these. Why the hell have they stripped a dummy? Why would they nick a battered old shop dummy and leave everything else?'

'Kids,' said Brewer. 'Probably kids . . . ' His attention remained fixed on the shop floor and the pavement outside. He felt uncomfortable and uneasy without being able to understand why. It had to do with the window.

'Funny, isn't it?' he said at last.

'What is?'

'There's no glass on the shop floor. It's all on the pavement outside.'

Benson harrumphed emphatically. 'Maybe the dummy just decided to walk out of here, then.' *Bloody police!* he thought. *They all think they're Starsky and Hutch.* 'But they just don't do that, do they?'

'No,' said Brewer uncomfortably, staring out into the night. 'Of course they don't.'

Nine

It was quieter than usual for a Friday night in the Imperial and, for the first time, Angie wished that there was more custom. Normally, the jostling for position at the bar, the raised tempers, the stupid patter and the inane remarks got on her nerves. She would be so rushed off her feet that she hardly had time to think. And that was the very reason why, tonight, she wanted lots of activity to occupy her mind. Things had been getting her down lately; although she had developed an immunity to the drunken lines, the clichés and the try-outs, tonight she would actually have welcomed them.

Jason, her two-year-old son, was unwell. He had developed a fever two days ago and was burning up. If it were not for her mother, she did not know how she would manage. The night-club hours were lousy and she had just about decided that she had had enough and should try to get a job somewhere else. But God knew, jobs were hard enough to come by these days, without throwing one away. She occupied herself in furiously polishing glasses that did not need cleaning. Josh was making small-talk, telling her about a new nightclub on the other side of town that had just opened, but Angie barely listened to what he was saying. Across the way, on the disco floor, Deejay was mechanically playing records with a minimum of jive talk; there were too few punters in tonight to develop his patter sufficiently. Occasionally, she could see him looking over at her. He had tried it on with her in the past, but she had given him her best cold shoulder and he had never tried again.

In her time, at the ripe old age of twenty-two, Angie had been a waitress, worked in a laundromat and for a while had sung as part of a double act on the working mens' club circuit. That was how she had met Johnny—Johnny with his big ideas about where he was going and where he would take her. She had got pregnant, and Johnny had cleared off out of her life, taking his big ideas with him. In her darker moods, like tonight, she longed for the day when he might walk into the Imperial. She had often fantasised about what she would do if that ever happened. On impulse, she scanned the small clusters of customers at the bar and on the disco floor. A Medallion Man stood with his back to the bar, shirt open almost to the waist, watching two girls dancing together. His intention seemed written all over his face. Now, there was a Johnny-type, if ever she saw one. She hoped that he would move across to her bar and try a few lines. Maybe she could pretend that he was Johnny. She would delight in using him for practice. Just let the sucker try. She finished drying a glass and placed it on the counter.

And then that guy walked in.

She had never seen him before, but something seemed to happen inside when she caught sight of him. He was tall, immaculately dressed and with a healthy tan—certainly not acquired in Newcastle. Something about him was instantly appealing. With a perfunctory glance around the nightclub, he made his way straight to the bar. He saw her and smiled. A beautiful, sexy, inviting smile. Angie felt years of bitterness slipping away. *Can this be happening*? she thought. She was entranced by that smile. He held her with his eyes as he pulled up a stool and sat down. She moved across, feeling as jittery as a fifteen-year-old in the presence of a film star. *This hasn't happened to me in ages? What's going on?*

'Drink?' she found herself asking.

'Whisky, please.' Again, that smile. Perfect, white even teeth. Sparkling eyes. There seemed to be an aura about him, an almost magical aura. Angie was already captivated. She turned back to him with the glass of whisky.

'Your name's Angie. Right?'

' . . . Right . . . ' *Why is my heart thumping like this? Why am I so nervous?* 'How did you know?'

'I'm a friend of Mr Pearson . . . and the Woman. I know all about the Imperial and who works here. I've been hoping that I might meet you . . . ' When he handed her a five-pound note, his fingers held hers for a long time. Puzzled, yet still exhilarated, she looked directly at him. When he smiled again, that curious feeling inside seemed to swell and surge. A shivering brought her out in pleasant goosebumps.

'We've got things to talk about, Angie,' he said.

'Things?' asked Angie breathlessly.

'About you and me.'

Suddenly, Angie did not want to let go of his hand.

* * *

Josh had realised that Angie's thoughts were elsewhere, but he had gone on speaking to her anyway. She was pretty moody and there were times when he could not get through to her at all. But tonight, he was feeling just as bad as she was and he needed somebody to talk to—it did not matter what about. All right, Angie was depressed, but so was he, and he kept on talking, even though he knew she was not listening.

Josh lived in Heaton, the suburb of Newcastle which was separated from Byker by the main street, Shields Road. He had shared a flat with David for three years now and the strain was beginning to show. They had had their huffy patches before, of course, but this was something else, something with deeper roots. Josh knew that it was all because David could not get a job. He had been working as a finance clerk with a shipping firm; not great money, but enough to live on comfortably. Then the firm—which was based down on Newcastle Quayside—had gone bust. David had been made redundant and after that everything had gone wrong. Obviously, it was bound to lead to friction when Josh was working, bringing in the money, and David was unable to contribute. Josh had tried to make him see that it did not matter, but things had gone from bad to worse in recent weeks and he could see the big split-up coming. It was heart-breaking, but it seemed completely unavoidable. David was so much more aggressive than he was and Josh could sometimes see him bubbling over with rage and frustration. One day soon, there would come the final argument—the argument to end all arguments—and then David would walk out of the flat and out of his life forever.

Josh stopped talking when the new fellow came in. He was unmistakably attractive and Josh tried to catch his eye, but the guy just walked straight to the corner of the bar and began talking to Angie. Josh slipped under the bar, picked up a tray and decided to do a circuit of the nightclub, hunting for empty glasses. Not that they had sold many drinks that night, but Mr

Pearson seemed rather particular about efficiency. At the main entrance, he could see Paul and Andy, the bouncers, lounging against the wall in their black suits and dickie bow-ties. He tried to keep as far away as possible from Paul. Short, stocky and built like a boxer with his classic broken nose and pig-like eyes, Paul's straight fair hair was combed savagely back over small ears. The man was an ignorant, surly thug who revelled in being a 'queer basher' and had often dangled vague—and not so vague—threats over Josh's head. He was trouble, and the greater the distance between them the better. Even now, he had spotted Josh as he rounded the bend to the disco floor. He said something to him, but Josh did not hear over the sound of the music. Nor did he look up, because he knew that would only be inviting trouble. He just went on collecting the few glasses he could find, aware of Paul's sniggering from the doorway. Behind him, Andy was laughing, too.

'Queer bastard,' said Paul. 'I reckon they should fit him up in a skirt and spangly tights. That would suit him better.'

Andy laughed again. It was a polite, uneasy laugh, but Paul did not notice it. 'Just let him go, Paul. He can't help it.'

'You fancy him, like?' Paul turned back to him, eyes glinting with that same look of stupid, ignorant savagery that Andy knew so well. Chance remarks could be a dangerous thing around Paul.

'That poof! Come on, Paul. You know what I mean. He's just not worth the trouble.' Andy could feel sweat curling around the neckband of his bow-tie. He loosened his collar. Paul growled under his breath and slumped back against the wall, arms folded. Danger had temporarily been averted.

'Should be a law. Should be some way to keep them off the streets.'

'How's your brother then, Paul?' asked Andy, changing the subject. 'He recovered after that car smash?'

Paul appeared not to have heard. His gaze remained fixed on the nightclub beyond the reception doors. 'And her! That bitch behind the bar. She's another one who needs a seeing-to. Thinks she's so bloody high and mighty. One of these days, she's gonna get it from me and she's gonna like it . . .'

Andy had seen him like this before. He had been at the booze again, and if Pearson smelt it on his breath there would be hell to pay. Not that Paul had the brains to be intimidated by the Under-Manager, but there had been times when Andy wondered whether another remark from Pearson might result in him getting a fractured skull. He knew what Paul was capable of; the man was just a fucking monster. Whenever he had been drinking he became even more surly, and that usually meant big trouble for some poor sod. Andy knew for a fact that Paul had traced the driver who had been involved in the car smash that injured his brother, and that he had broken the guy's legs with a cricket bat.

'They ever find the other driver . . . ?' he began again, but it was too late. Paul had suddenly bulldozed away from the wall and into the nightclub, with that intimidating, stocky walk.

'Oh, Christ . . .' Andy turned his face to the wall. He moved to the entrance door for some fresh air. If there was going to be bother, then he would rather know nothing about it. Chucking out drunken punters was one thing, but just looking for somebody to give him a good hiding because you did not like his face was another matter . . .

Paul made his way straight across the nightclub floor to the bar. The bitch was talking to some mealy-mouthed bastard he had never seen before. They were both chattering away and smiling; smiling, bloody smiling. She was smiling at him in a way that Paul had often wanted her to smile at him, but she had always ignored him whenever he spoke to her. The sight of that skinny bastard making her smile was just too much for him. Josh was now forgotten. Paul knew just what he would do when he got to the bar. The scenario was playing in his mind as he stomped across the nightclub.

This guy bothering you, Angie?

What? No . . . no, he's not. We're talking . . .

Come on, mister. You've had too much to drink. Time to go.

What are you talking about? I've just bought my first drink. I'm not drunk. I'm just talking . . .

This is your last chance. You go now, or I make you go.

Leave him alone, Paul. We're just talking. There's no harm being done. Just leave us alone.

Yes, there's no trouble. Please, I'm not making a fuss.

One more chance.

Really, I'm not . . .

Thud! Crash! Out you go you mealy-mouthed . . .

Angie looked up as Paul drew level with the bar. The smoothie did not move at all. Paul said: 'This guy bothering you, Angie?'

'What?' asked Angie with that tone of arrogance that really got under Paul's skin.

'All right, mister. You've had too much to drink. It's . . .'

And then Paul's potential victim looked up at him.

It's the disco lights, thought Paul in panic. *It's just the disco lights making his eyes look like that. A trick . . . a trick of the light . . .*

'Yes?' asked the man.

His eyes were black. A wet, shining, fathomless black, like black marbles glinting in the half-light. There were no pupils, no irises, just that deep, deep black. The man was smiling at him, and the smile made Paul feel that he was standing on the rim of a bottomless pit. The ledge was about to crumble, he was about to fall.

'I was just wondering . . . wondering . . .' he heard himself mumbling. Angie was still looking at him, had not seen the stranger's face.

'Why don't you go and find somebody to bounce, Paul?' she said. 'That's what you're paid for, isn't it?'

'Wondering what?' asked the stranger. And Paul felt his balance on that precarious ledge begin to falter. He was going to fall; fall and fall and fall into those hellish, bottomless black eyes.

'Nothing . . . nothing . . . ' He reeled away from the bar as if *he* was the customer who had had one drink too many. All he wanted to do was get away from that bar and back to the reception area before the floor beneath him disintegrated, taking him with it. He was unaware of Angie's snort of derision as she turned back to her companion.

He was smiling at her, with a faint shrug at the behaviour of the bouncer.

'Don't bother about him, he's just weird,' said Angie. She leaned forward, both elbows on the bar, hunching over to reveal more of her cleavage. She had not realised just how good-looking this new fellow was. And those eyes of his were something else. Those deep blue, smiling, crystal-clear eyes.

* * *

Josh was returning to the bar with his burden of three half-pint glasses and an empty crisp bag when Paul hurtled past him without a word, heading for the reception area. Josh jumped out of the way, arm moving to protect his face, but Paul was not interested in him at all; he did not even seem to see him as he blundered past. Josh felt his heart hammering as he watched Paul vanish from sight into the reception area.

Recovering his composure, he slipped quickly under the trap door of the bar. Angie was still deep in conversation with that guy and, by her demeanour, it seemed that she was more than interested in him. For a reason he did not understand, Josh felt a twinge of sadness. He disregarded it and began to wash the glasses from the tray, his thoughts returning to Paul and his peculiar exit from the nightclub. He had probably been at the bottle again. Josh had occasionally seen him out in the yard where the booze was delivered. Paul kept a bottle out there—probably stolen from the stock—and often availed himself of it. Perhaps he had had too much tonight and had suddenly . . . *come over all queer* . . . thought Josh, laughing as he dried the glasses. He looked back at Angie and her new boyfriend. She was getting him another drink. And her boyfriend was looking over at him . . . looking and looking . . . with a nice smile on his face.

No . . . no . . . that can't be right. He can't be looking at me as if he's really interested in me. He's chatting up Angie. He couldn't be interested in me. Could he?

But he *was* looking at him and only glanced away when Angie returned with his drink. As she moved reluctantly to serve another customer, the new fellow tipped his glass at Josh in a toast. He seemed to sip at his drink teasingly.

'Cheers,' said Josh, feeling his heart hammering and a flush rising to his face. Then Angie came back and the new guy resumed his conversation with her. Josh turned to serve another customer, breathless and excited.

* * *

After he had vomited in the toilet stall, thankful that none of the punters were in there to see him, Paul washed his face, standing, arms braced on the basin, head down, until he had controlled the trembling. He did not know what had happened back there in the nightclub to make him react that way. The light had been playing tricks, that was all. The lights and the bloody music had made him dizzy. That last mouthful of rotgut in the back yard had probably been too much all at once. He scooped up another handful of water and threw it over his face, shaking his head vigorously like some great bulldog, rubbery jowls flapping. He began to drag in great lungfuls of air, blowing out noisily. That seemed to do the trick. He wiped his face and then took out his comb, brushing his blond hair firmly back into place. A punter came in behind him and moved to the urinal. Paul watched him carefully in the mirror as he combed his hair. If the bugger so much as looked at him and noticed how ragged he felt, he would be out on his ear before he knew what had hit him. Luckily for the punter, he was preoccupied with the business in hand. Paul snorted and went out to the reception area.

Andy was quick to notice that there was something different about his manner. Something about his piggy eyes; something there that he had never seen before, that Paul was unsuccessfully trying to conceal. He moved to the reception door and looked into the nightclub. Everything seemed normal enough. Angie was still talking to that guy; the guy was still smiling. Perhaps he was a karate expert, or a copper, or something. Whatever he was, he was still alive and should probably count himself lucky.

A crowd of punters with free tickets had suddenly appeared at the main doors and Paul was grudgingly allowing them past. Andy held the doors while they moved through towards the cloakroom. Somewhere inside, little Jackie Trent was reading a paperback, quiet as a dormouse as usual.

Paul joined Andy at the nightclub doors and glared inside. Andy watched his face, knew that he was looking at the guy talking to Angie and wondered just what the hell was going on. Paul was mumbling angrily under his breath, but his anger was somehow at a distance: 'I'm gonna get that fella. He tries to get in tomorrow night and I'm gonna find any reason to rough him up and chuck him out. Any reason! His shoes, his tie, the colour of his bloody hair . . . '

Andy knew that the rage was just a cover-up for something that Paul had never in his life experienced, more from ignor-

ance and insensitivity than bravery or courage.
That thing was fear.

Ten

At 2.00 am it was a fairly easy job to clear the nightclub. Custom had been poor and the punters who remained were soon collecting their coats at the desk. Andy noticed that, despite everything he had said earlier, Paul kept well away from the bar-side of the club. Andy spoke only once to the guy who had put the frighteners on Paul. He seemed ordinary enough. Quite pally with Angie, but so what? When Andy had asked him to drink up, please, because the nightclub was closing, the stranger had simply smiled and lifted his glass to his lips in acknowledgement. So where was the problem? Andy had moved on, asking the other punters to finish their drinks.

At the reception area, holding the doors open while the customers filed out, chattering and laughing, he noticed that the stranger was still sitting at the bar while Angie washed up the glasses that Josh had collected. Instinctively, he looked for Paul and saw him standing not far away beneath one of the large mosaic prints on the nightclub wall. His gaze was directed at the bar and he was trembling, but Andy could not tell from that distance whether it was with rage or fear. Either way, he had a feeling that something was going to happen after all. If it was, he was going to look the other way. Paul had his excuse to act tough now if he wanted. The stranger had been asked to move and he was still sitting there. Paul had the perfect reason to go over and sort him out if it made him feel better. But Paul was just standing and staring, clenching and unclenching his fists.

The sound of a door opening drew Andy's attention to the staircase just beyond the disco floor. A flood of light angled down the stairs and almost immediately a gaunt shadow appeared on the threshold, descending quickly from the Woman's quarters. It was Pearson. He looked like some spooky undertaker. Obviously, he was checking to see if the closing up was going smoothly. Selfconsciously, Andy began to bustle the customers along; he had to be seen to be doing his job. Pearson nodded at Deejay as he crossed the disco floor, revolving splashes of red and green orbed light dancing over his sober black suit and snow-white hair as he moved towards them.

As Andy watched, Paul came forward. Apparently, with the boss there to see, he was going to make a big professional show of throwing the stranger out. But no. Andy noted with surprise that Paul was not making for the bar at all, he was making for Pearson. He could not hear what Paul was saying from that distance, but the words became clearer as Pearson continued to move towards the reception area, evidently unconcerned about Paul's interruption.

'. . . been told to leave, Mr Pearson.'

'Is that so?' And then, to the customers: 'I hope you've all had an enjoyable evening. Please come again.'

'Shall I throw him out, Mr Pearson?'

'No, Paul. You may not throw him out.'

'But it's two o'clock, Mr Pearson. He's been told to leave and he's still there.'

'The Woman says that he can stay.'

Smiling, Pearson turned from the reception doors and headed for the bar. So the guy was a friend of the management! Andy watched expressions of puzzlement, rage and brutality shifting and changing on Paul's face in a comical kaleidoscope. He looked ready to explode! Andy fought to control his laughter. If Paul saw him, he would probably end up in the gutter on Byker Bank in a pool of broken teeth. He watched as Pearson walked past the bar, raising his hand slightly in recognition as he passed the stranger. The stranger smiled back and then Pearson had vanished into the deeper shadows of the nightclub.

The last customer disappeared into the night. Paul burst into the reception area, kicking the toilet doors in rage before storming inside.

Andy moved back to the desk, lit a cigarette and leaned back against the wall. Tonight had certainly been a strange one.

* * *

Josh had never felt so good. All night long, this new face had been chatting to Angie. They had been laughing and talking just like a couple of lovers. But all the time, whenever Angie had to serve a customer or go for another drink, the stranger had been giving him those looks. Once or twice, Josh had tried to involve himself in their conversation, but Angie had made it plain that he was poaching on her ground. Accordingly, he had been more or less forced to keep his distance to avoid a scene. Angie could be extremely difficult if she chose. Josh knew nothing of Paul's encounter with the stranger, but he did notice the slight wave that Mr Pearson gave him as he passed. When the Under-Manager was out of earshot, he heard Angie make a mock-impressed sound; a little murmur of appreciation. The stranger smiled back.

'Friends in high places,' he said.

'I've finished here. Okay if I go?' Angie seemed to be in a hurry, and Josh felt his spirits deflate as the stranger began to rise from his seat. Was he taking her home?

'Sure,' he replied. 'Everything's done, I think. What about your taxi home?'

'Don't need it. My friend's giving me a lift.'

'Okay.' Josh could feel a terrible, crushing pain in his chest as Angie pushed past him and ducked under the flap on the bar. It had all been a terrible, terrible joke. It was just more of the pain that he had endured since school-days. He should have known.

But suddenly, the stranger was standing directly opposite him on the other side of the bar. He was still smiling and, just as suddenly, he leaned across and took Josh's hand while Angie was still scrambling under the bar. Quickly, he pressed something into Josh's palm, smiled again and turned to meet Angie as she emerged.

'Goodnight, Josh,' said Angie.

'Goodnight.'

'Goodnight, Josh,' said the stranger. Why did that simple phrase seem to hold so much promise? The stranger turned as Angie linked her arm with his and they headed away across the nightclub towards the exit.

Josh looked down to see what the stranger had pushed into his hand. It was a small, scribbled note, written on the back of a barmat after the pattern had been stripped off.

'Don't go home. Wait for me outside. I'll see you at 2.30, when everyone's gone.'

Still puzzling, Josh watched them leave.

Eleven

When Angie came out of the stranger's embrace, she knew that at last everything had changed for the better. She felt exhilarated, dazed almost; weak and dizzy. She laughed and pushed closer to him. They were feelings she had read about in the magazines. The harsh realities of life and the bad cards dealt her by fate had convinced her early on that this kind of experience, this kind of feeling, was all fairytale bullshit. Now she realised that she had been wrong.

They were standing on the crest of Byker Bank, looking down the steeply sloping road to the Ouseburn. At the bottom of the valley, the Bank sloped tightly upwards again into the night. On their right, Angie could see the night traffic glittering on the Bridge spanning the valley. A metro thundered overhead, joining the mid-air race in parallel with Byker Bridge. They began to walk again, down the Bank. She clung tightly to him as they moved.

'Where's your car parked?' she asked.

'At the bottom, down by the Ouseburn.'

'Why not the car park just opposite the Imperial?'

'Too easy a target for vandals.'

'Oh.' It did not matter where he was parked, really. She was just making small talk and she was enjoying the walk. The canyon walls of the Byker Wall housing development stared blankly from their left, everyone abed. She was glad of the steep descent, it gave her a reason to cling to him as they walked. *As if*, she thought, *I need a reason.*

'Hundreds and hundreds of people used to live here,' she said, 'in red-brick houses on either side of the Bank. They pulled it all down. Said it was a slum. Some of the people were rehoused in the Wall, but lots of them were scattered all over Newcastle on different housing estates. Sad, really.'

'I know.'

They reached the bottom of the Bank, and the bridge that spanned the Ouseburn. Small boats crowded the angular, concrete banks of the river, greedy for the glittering black water. The stranger guided her across to the other side of the road, towards the shadowed places where the boats were moored.

'My car's down here.'

'The Ouseburn,' said Angie dreamily. 'That's what the water's like down there, now. Ooze. It just oozes out of the hill under here and into the River Tyne over there. The water used to be clear—fish and everything. Not any more, though. It just oozes along.'

They moved down the lane into the shadow.

'My Grandad told me that it used to be called the Ewes Burn in the olden days when this was all valley and grass and trees and cottages and things. . . '

The stranger suddenly stopped. He bent to kiss her and she melted into that fantastic embrace. Dimly, she could see the silhouette of the Imperial, perched at the top of the Bank, overlooking the valley. She closed her eyes. She was swimming again. It was an exciting, dizzying feeling, almost as if she had been drinking too much. When they moved apart, his eyes seemed almost liquid in the dark. It was a strange effect; probably the black water from the Ouseburn glinting in his eyes.

'You're the first,' he said quietly.

Angie laughed. 'Come on, don't give me that. You must have had lots of girls in your time.'

She moved closer to him again, snuggling at his chest against the cold.

But now, strangely, his chest was not warm and inviting. It was hard. Hard and cold. The arms around her were no longer comforting; they were too tight, almost crushing the breath from her body. His hands on her shoulder and the small of her back were digging through her raincoat and into the flesh; sharp and cruel. She smelt his breath: cold like frost—and fetid, like something long dead.

She whimpered, struggling upwards to look at his face.

'*You're the first*,' it said.

She never had time to scream.

* * *

Josh stood nervously in the car park of the Plough directly opposite the Imperial. At closing time, he had walked round the block, still clutching the stranger's note in his hand. Fortunately, he had been able to avoid Paul, whose surly mood seemed to have reached new heights tonight. From the darkness of the car park, he had watched as a taxi ferried the pig away.

Was it all just a cruel hoax? Were the stranger and Angie in bed, even now, laughing at the thought of him standing there in the cold? Why the hell was he hanging around here, anyway? He had been through this sort of treatment before and he had been hurt many times before. Why was he setting himself up again? Because, he knew, he was searching for something. Searching for a way to be happy; searching for something he thought that David and he might have been able to achieve, but which he now knew was not possible. That was why he did not just make his way to the taxi office on Shields Road and drive away. Figuratively, there had been many car parks, many promises, many chances. They had all come to nothing, but Josh would never let the pain of failure keep him from trying again, over and over, however hopelessly.

He looked at his watch. It was 2.25 am. Knowing his luck, Paul might suddenly lurch round the corner, fists bunched, piggy eyes glaring. Five minutes and no more. He would be strong. If it was a joke, he could take it. He would never let on that he had kept the assignment. If Angie mentioned anything, he would tell her that he had seen right through their little plan. He would tell her that he had thought they were friends, that she should be ashamed . . .

'Hello, Josh.'

Josh jumped. As if from nowhere, the stranger had suddenly materialised beside him. Tall, dark, shadowed; the street lamp on the other side of the road silhouetting him in a yellow aura. The only light appeared to come from his eyes: small sparks of blue light.

'Hi,' said Josh, composure regained.

'Sorry to keep you waiting. I had business.'

'Yes, I know. I work with her.'

The stranger laughed, a harsh, humourless sound. Josh noticed curiously that although he could see his own breath in the crisp, early morning air and the faint glow of the street lamp, he could not see the stranger's.

'It's not like that, Josh,' said the stranger at last. 'Angie's had a hard time, what with the kid and all. I'm a friend of the management of the Imperial. I know about everyone who works there. Angie was depressed tonight. Upset.'

'I never noticed.'

'Believe me, she was. I took her home.'

'And came back?'

'Yes, I came back. I want to be your friend.'

'I stopped passing notes when I was at school.'

'I see. You'd rather Paul saw me talking to you.'

'Oh, I'm sorry. You know about him, too, I suppose . . . I hadn't realised . . . '

'I've been watching you all night, Josh. I'd really like to know you better.'

'I noticed you, too.'

'Let's go back to my place for a drink.'

'Where?'

'Shieldfield. It's not far from here.'

'Okay. There's a taxi office just round the corner.'

'No, let's walk across the bridge. I'd like to talk.'

'Okay.'

They walked to the top of the Bank, turned left on Shields Road and in seconds were on the deserted bridge.

'So you know what Paul is like?' asked Josh at last, looking for something to say to break the silence. 'He does have a reputation, doesn't he?'

'He's a dangerous man,' replied the stranger, looking out to the distant River Tyne, flowing dark and lonely. 'He doesn't understand people like us.'

'Like us?'

'You know what I mean.'

'So it *was* really just sympathy for Angie?'

'Of course.'

They had reached the highest point of the bridge. Below, the Ouseburn glistened blackly past factories and the small municipal farm, curving sinuously and elusively before it met the Tyne, less than half a mile from where they stood. Below and to the right was the roof of the Ship pub.

'Used to be a popular spot for suicides,' said the stranger. Josh moved forward to look over the trestled parapet of the bridge. 'The highest spot is over there. Right into the Ship's back yard.'

'That's macabre,' said Josh, shivering.

'Here, let me warm you.'

The stranger took him in his arms before Josh could react. He was surprised at how easily he let himself be taken. His lips were hungry and the stranger reciprocated in a way that allayed his previous fears. When they moved apart, Josh could see that a woman was walking towards them from the other side of the bridge. He pulled away in embarrassment, but stayed close as they resumed their walk. His natural pessimism, his belief that the stranger's scribbled note had been just another terrible joke, had disappeared. He could be himself, truly himself, at last.

He tried to speak, tried to find the words as they walked. But nothing would come when he looked at that haunting face. The stranger was half-smiling, and Josh could see that he was feeling the same as he did. There was no need for words; they both knew. That was enough.

'I don't even know your name,' said Josh. The stranger took his hand. Smiling, Josh pushed closer, feeling that he should be embarrassed—after all, that woman had almost reached them. But he did not care what she thought.

When the stranger suddenly stopped walking, so did Josh, looking questioningly up into that dark face with its strange, liquid eyes. Was he going to do it again just for devilment? Just *because* the woman was walking towards them? She was obviously a drunk because she seemed unsteady on her feet. Josh moved back into the stranger's ready embrace.

'Josh . . .' said the approaching woman in a slow, dragging voice.

He looked round and stared intently at her for the first time.

It was Angie.

Her face seemed white, almost spectrally white. And she was smiling in a strange way: her face was smiling but her eyes were like glass. She seemed demented, insane. She had lost her mind.

'Angie?' asked Josh uneasily. Something was wrong.

She came towards him and Josh suddenly found that he

could not move from the stranger's embrace.

Her lips were smiling, smiling, smiling. A crimson gash around white, white teeth. She snarled.

And then, just before she reached him, Josh saw that terrible, terrible smile across her throat.

* * *

Arthur had been thrown out of the Salvation Army hostel on City Road two hours earlier for starting a fight.

He had protested his innocence all the way from his room, down the corridor and the stairs and then out onto the pavement. At that stage, he had thrown his second bottle of Brown Ale through the reception window, yelling back at them that yes, he had smashed that first bottle over Andy Crabtree's head. The bastard was so ugly, he had just been trying to improve his face.

Spinning on legs made of rubber, he had dramatically buttoned up his patched overcoat and walked away, his bulging pockets laden with a night's supply of that popular Brown Ale brew, known for its effects throughout the North-East as 'Journey into Space'.

Arthur had no conscious recollection of making his way down under Byker Bridge. Nevertheless, he was there and he did not question it. Huddled under some bushes by the municipal farm, and fortified against the cold by the warming properties of the Brown Ale, he stared into the Ouseburn, remembering how, as a kid, he had waded in that water, catching small fish in a jam jar.

' "Plodging", that's what it's called,' he slurred to himself, repeating the word over and over, mimicking the sound of bare feet in the water.

'Plodge, plodge, plodge, plodge, plodge . . . '

The sound of screaming silenced him and made him look round in alarm. From his vantage point, he had a good view along the valley bottom. But although the screaming went on and on, he could see no one.

Ghosts? Down here?

Then something heavy thudded into the water just upstream. A plume of dirty yellow water spiralled high, showering Arthur and stinging his eyes.

'Shit!'

He wiped the wet away from his dirty, bristled face, leaving a grey smear. He squinted, trying to peer into the darkness for some explanation, but remained sprawled in the bushes. He was incapable of movement. For a long, long time, he sat waiting. From his position, he could see down into a ten-yard stretch of black water. The half-submerged skeleton of a bed-frame jutted from the burn on his left, and now, he could see that a black, glistening bundle of rags had been caught in it. He drank from his Brown Ale bottle, wondering whether that bundle had been the reason for the big splash. Someone must have chucked it over Byker Bridge. The bastards, it could have hit *him*.

The current tugged at the bundle and Arthur watched, fascinated, waiting to see if the water would wash it free from the rusted frame. When it eventually did, he clapped his hands drunkenly and toasted the bundle as its air-pocketed mass floated his way. Now, even the drunken stupor could not blur his perception of what that bundle was.

It was a body.

For the first time, Arthur became aware of the ice-cold chill of the early morning air. With the bottle half-raised to his lips, he sat watching as the bundle turned and rolled lazily in the filthy ooze. A blue-white hand beckoned from the water as the corpse turned face down.

From nowhere, two people had suddenly materialised on the other side of the burn's concrete bank. A man and a woman. Arthur could only see their silhouettes as they stood, staring at the body as it floated towards the Tyne. Something about the way they stood made him shrink back further into the shadows. Hands held stiffly by their sides, heads bowed and watching, they looked so terribly *hungry*. Instinctively, Arthur was dreadfully afraid of that hunger.

Oh, God, God, God . . . don't let them see me . . . don't let them . . .

A faint splash from the burn distracted his uneasy gaze. The bundle in the water was moving, twisting around.

Slowly, awkwardly and with great effort . . . the corpse stood up in the water.

But he was dead . . . he must be dead . . . how can he not be dead?

The black water flowed around the corpse's waist as it stood, head bowed, unmoving. A frozen tableau in the cold street light: the man and the woman on the bank and the dripping, dishevelled man in the water.

The corpse turned away from Arthur, head still lowered, and began to wade mechanically towards the watchers on the bank.

Plodge . . . plodge . . . plodge . . . plodge . . . plodge . . .

The corpse hauled itself from the water and clambered up the bank to join its companions. As one, they turned and walked away into the dark shadow of the bridge.

Arthur remained where he was for a long time, eyes screwed tightly shut, clamping the Brown Ale bottle against his forehead with both hands.

'Journey into Space' he thought. *That's what's doing it. I didn't see any of it. It was all the booze. Things like that don't happen. People just don't walk around like zombies . . . unless they're drunk, like me . . . Hah! But they weren't drunk. God Almighty, they weren't . . . No, no . . . it was a dream. I'm pissed, that's all.*

The night and its Spectres were too much for Arthur. He would get rid of his remaining booze—all one bottle of it—and go back to the Sally Army headquarters. He would give up drinking, he swore to God. No more of that stuff. He would go back and beg for his bed. They would let him in.

After a long, long time he staggered to his feet, clutching at the undergrowth for support, his mind spinning. He shook his head, pulling himself out of the bushes. And stepped straight into Josh's widespread, waiting arms.

Twelve

Barry Clark had arrived home in Nottingham on Friday. Two weeks in Italy had finally dispelled the strange cloud of depression that had hung over him recently. It had been one of the oddest moods he had ever experienced. Everything had been working out well for him in his life—both personal and professional. On the personal level, he and his wife Sheila had been getting on fine. On a professional level, everything was going his way. Why, then, had he become so withdrawn and moody?

Why had he felt as if he just wanted to lock himself away from the world and never open his front door again? It was crazy. Sheila had sensed his confused bewilderment, had diagnosed it as overwork and had convinced him that a holiday would cure him. She had been right. Once in Italy, he had felt as if some terrible, dark burden had been taken away from him. For a while he feared that, back home again, his mood might return; but he had shrugged it off and was now ready to start work with a renewed vigour.

Sheila was still at home unpacking as he sat in his office at the museum. Although it was Saturday morning, he had been keen to catch up on his work. Sheila had been heartened by his sudden return to good health but his anxiety about his job had worried her. His good mood, however, had dispelled her fears. After checking with the security caretaker, Barry had eagerly let himself into the museum and was soon lost in the correspondence, papers and committee reports that had accumulated since his departure. The museum was closed for internal redecoration, although the contractor had not yet put in an appearance.

It was three o'clock and the afternoon shadows were lengthening when he decided to call it a day. Locking the office door, he made his way down the stone balustraded staircase from the upper gallery to the reception area, his footsteps echoing through the empty building. As he passed the first glass cases housing geographical exhibits, a rattling sound drew his attention to the main doors. There were three people standing in the outside foyer: two men and a woman. One man, with a beard and wearing a woollen cap, was peering through the glass at him, shielding his eyes and rapping on the door.

'We're closed,' said Barry loudly, his voice echoing to nothingness.

The man in the woollen cap said something, his voice muffled by the glass. Exasperated, Barry approached the glass door and, as he did so, the second man moved into view. 'I'm sorry, we're closed for renovations. There's a timetable on the . . . ' He paused, suddenly recognising the two men in front of him. 'Richard,' he said. 'Richard Eden.'

'What's happened to the hair, then?' asked Richard, pointing at Barry's receding hairline and smiling that familiar smile.

'My God! And Stan the Man, too. I don't believe it.'

'Seeing's believing, Bazza. Let's in, man! We're freezing to death out here.'

Quickly, Barry found the keys in his hip pocket and admitted the three visitors. For one heart-stopping moment, he almost believed that the girl with the blonde hair was Pandora, her hair lightened from its natural brunette. He did not know whether he felt disappointed or relieved when he realised that he had never seen her before.

Stan clapped him on the shoulder as they entered. 'Nice place you've got here, Barry. Furniture's a mite old-fashioned.' Barry laughed but noted the strangely tense tone in Stan's voice. He was glad to see them; more than that—he was bloody glad to see them both after so many years! But something was wrong. He could sense it immediately from the strained way they returned his smile.

Barry led them into the main gallery as Richard introduced Diane. There were seats in there. Not the maximum comfort, perhaps, but he sensed that they would be more than welcome to three people who looked as if they had not slept for days. While they sat down, he leaned on the display table facing them, his good humour fading as he studied their strained faces. He sighed dramatically.

'All right, what do you have to tell me? Obviously, something's wrong, so you'd better just spit it out and get it over with.'

'Remember the Byker Chapter?' began Richard.

'Of course.'

'Apart from Pandora—wherever *she* is—we're the only ones left. We don't have a great deal of time, so I'll get straight to the point. Derek, Phil and Joe were murdered. And whatever murdered them is trying to kill us, too.'

Barry remained silent, perched on the edge of the table, displaying no reaction at all to Richard's statement.

Stan broke the silence: 'Do you remember that photograph I took of us all back in '72? Back at my place?'

'Yes, I remember the photo,' said Barry guardedly.

'Have you still got it?'

'No, my copy was destroyed in a fire at home.'

Stan reached into his haversack, found the envelope containing the photographs and handed a print to Barry.

'Notice anything wrong?'

'Look, just what's going on here?'

'Do you notice anything *wrong*?' asked Richard forcefully.

'Of course there's something wrong. Someone's been tampering with it. Derek, Phil and Joe aren't in it.'

'Exactly. Every time one of us dies, his image fades from the photo.'

'What's this all about?' There was anger in Barry's voice now.

'Listen Barry,' continued Richard, 'I'm sorry if this all seems bloody crazy or if what I'm going to ask you now seems indiscreet, but if you'll pardon the cliché—our lives may depend on it. During that last week of term, did you sleep with Pandora?'

Barry looked at them for a long time, sighed and moved slowly to the telephone on the other side of the table. He lifted the receiver.

'What are you doing?' asked Diane.

'I'm going to ring for the police. I don't know where this conversation is going, but I can smell blackmail a mile off.'

'Blackmail?' snapped Stan. 'Doesn't the past count for anything with you, Barry? You remember how it was? We were all pretty close.'

'That was a long time ago, Stan.'

'Maybe. But why would we blackmail you? How the hell do we profit from making statements like this?'

'I don't know. I haven't sussed your angle yet. It could be that you think my sleeping with Pandora all those years ago might just carry some weight with my wife . . . '

'No, no, no, no . . . ' said Richard in exasperation. 'Look, Barry. We *all* slept with Pandora in that last week. For some reason we don't understand, she tricked each of us into believing that we were the most important thing in her life. She kept it secret . . . *we* kept it secret from each other. God knows what's going on, but somehow that whole crazy situation is the reason for all these deaths. You remember how it was in those days, Barry. The Byker Chapter was special. We all knew that Pandora was one of the pivotal characters. You remember? We used to say that if any one of us broke the . . . what was it? . . . the *code*, yeah, the code . . . by making a play for Pandora, or vice versa, the Chapter would fall apart. Well, that's exactly what happened. We all knew something had gone wrong with the Chapter but we couldn't identify it. It wasn't that one of us had slept with Pandora . . . we *all* had. All in the space of that one week.'

'Barry,' continued Stan, 'this is on the level. Straight up. We don't know what this thing is or how it operates. But for some reason, it wants us dead.'

'You keep saying "thing" or "it". What the hell are you getting at?'

For the next fifteen minutes, Richard, Diane and Stan recounted the nightmare. Shadows lengthened in the museum as they talked. When they had finished, there was a long silence while they waited for Barry's response. When he looked blankly from face to face, sighed and ran his hand through his hair, Stan's angry reaction startled them all.

'All right, Barry! I know it sounds like a whole load of shit! But we've seen these things—I've seen these things—and you've just got to believe us or you're going to end up dead like Joe and the other poor sods! This isn't some elaborate con-trick, believe me. We can just leave if you want us to, but if we do you're on your own. At least if we're together, we're stronger. There's something out there, Barry. It's not human. It can do things—weird things—and it wants us dead. It's the biggest bloody Spectre we've ever had to face.'

'Spectre,' said Barry, remembrance twitching a faint nerve of humour in his jaw.

'We heard it,' said Diane. 'In the fog. It told us it had . . . changed its tactics . . . it somehow doesn't have to hunt us down one by one any more.'

'If we can find out just what it is and why it wants us,' continued Richard, 'maybe we can find a way to stop it.'

'Pandora's the key,' said Stan. 'That much we're sure of. If we only knew where she is.'

'I know where she is,' said Barry resignedly.

'*What?*' Richard felt his pulse begin to race.

'Well, at least I'm pretty sure I know where she is,' continued Barry. 'During that last week, she told me that she had found somebody else. She was leaving me for some guy she'd met in the town. I was . . well, pretty devastated . . . I was really stuck on her . . . ' Barry cleared his throat, removed his spectacles and began polishing the lenses. Diane could sense a familiar pain. 'But there was something about the way she told me that convinced me she wasn't telling the truth. I made my own investigations. I was right, she was lying. There was no one else. I found out, when she left college, that she'd gone back home, back to her parents in Mevagissey. That's in Cornwall. I wanted to run after her, beg her to change her mind. But the fact that she'd told me an elaborate lie to get rid of me was too hurtful. I respected her reasons—even though I didn't know what they were.'

'Mevagissey,' echoed Richard. 'I've been there once, on holiday.'

'We've got to find her, Barry,' said Stan. 'She may have the answer to this whole damned business.'

'I don't know, Stan. I just don't know. I have to think about it.' Barry began fingering the print again. 'What about the negative?'

'It's the same as the prints. Just as if the others had never been there. But I want to have another look at the negative, do some experimentation again. See if there's been any change since Joe's death.'

'You can use our facilities here, if you like.'

'You've got a dark room?'

'And all the materials you're likely to need.'

'Great. I'll start now, if that's okay.'

'Help yourself. I'll show you where it is.'

'Barry?' said Richard.

'Yes . . . '

'Whether we like it or not, we're dealing with something supernatural here. And we're not talking about ghosts rattling chains in the attic, or heads-tucked-underneath-the-arm. We're talking about something that's real . . . and deadly . . . *and it knows us*.'

'I don't know . . . ' said Barry hopelessly. 'I just don't know. Can I watch while you're in the dark room, Stan?'

'Sure. Let's go.'

The dark room was situated at the far end of the ground floor gallery. Barry gave Richard the key to the tea room next door and Diane accompanied him there to boil a kettle, while

Stan and Barry clattered past the glass cases of owls, bears, hyenas and eagles and down three stone steps, to where the dark room was hidden discreetly between packing crates which had until recently contained a selection of animal skins awaiting the skills of a taxidermist.

Diane plugged in the kettle and leaned against the bench, stroking her hair back into place, rubbing her eyes. When she looked over to Richard, she saw that he was watching her. There was a wistful look on his face, a kind of resignation.

'Remember me?' she asked after a while.

Richard laughed and moved over to her. When he stood back and began making tea, he said: 'I'm sorry, Diane. I shouldn't have dragged you into all this.'

'Don't be,' she replied. 'I'm a big girl. And as I said before, it was my choice.'

'We haven't even had a chance to get to know each other properly. We've been thrown in at the deep end.'

'You mean we haven't had to go through the usual bullshit from each other.'

Richard laughed again. 'I've *never* known anyone like you before.' He handed her a cup. They sipped their tea.

'You feel up to travelling down to Mevagissey?' asked Richard.

'Yes. I'll make some telephone calls. I'll be all right.'

'Well, I don't want you doing any more driving. You'll be worn out. Stan and I will take turns.'

'Richard?'

'Yes?'

'Will we really be safer if we stay together? Or will it just mean that it'll take us all at once?'

'It's not going to take you, Diane. I promise you that.'

* * *

'People are dying, aren't they? I can feel it. It's killing them one by one.'

'It is necessary. Their deaths are necessary to make you whole.'

'You mustn't let it come through again. I won't let you!'

'NEVER DEFY ME! It is time again. We have no further need for manmade devices. The photograph is enough. Look deeply and Dark-Out.'

'Please, not again.'

'Look deeply and search. You must be whole. Gorgus . . . Imago . . . Pacter . . . '

'Please . . . please . . . ' And then, *' . . . Yes . . . yes . . . YES!'*

Thirteen

Barry watched as Stan prepared everything with the true touch of a professional. Hastily, he had checked the available equipment, the jars of chemicals which he would need for the job and the paper on which he could reproduce prints. Barry's attempts at conversation were greeted by simple grunts and nods of the head. After a while, he gave up and let Stan get on with the job.

The dark room was a converted store-room and, as such, was much bigger than the usual purpose-built room. The walls had been treated to ensure that there could be no light seepage. The multi-level sink and basins occupied one wall with a central developing bench unit and sink jutting out into the centre of the room. Bill Tavistock, Barry's assistant, had been taking wildlife pictures for the gallery and various prints were still pinned to the walls. When Stan was ready to begin work and had taken the negative from his rucksack, he looked up and motioned to the light switch. Barry switched off, plunging them into absolute blackness. A second later, the room was suddenly bathed in a deep red glow as Stan pulled the light cord hanging above the developing unit. He began his preparations. Barry found that he could not remain silent any longer.

'All right, Stan. What's the game?'

'What do you mean?' asked Stan distantly, engrossed in his work.

'You can't really expect me to believe what you've all told me. What's the real reason behind this ridiculous charade?'

Stan looked up at him for several long, measured seconds. Returning to his work, he said: 'Look, Barry, I've been through enough hell for the past few days and I've got no further intention of trying to convince you that this is not a hoax. Everything we've told you is true. It happened . . . it's still happening. I know we all used to be great mates. But, I've got to be honest, I'm at the stage now when I don't give a shit whether you believe me at all. We've told you how it is—it's up to you whether you believe it or not. Something inhuman is out there. And it wants us dead. Together, we may have a chance against it. If not . . . who knows? If you won't believe us, then you're on your own. It's your choice. Make it. I don't have any more time to waste trying to convince you.'

Barry watched as Stan skilfully operated the enlarger and transferred a sheet to the washtray, scrutinising it intently. He tried to find some way of replying, but just could not get the right words together. A dim image began to grow on the paper. The details of the remaining members of the Byker Chapter swam into view. There were four people in the photograph now: Stan, Richard, Pandora and Barry. Stan moved to the larger developing tray and rolled out an enlarged printing sheet.

'What are you doing now?'

'I want to make a substantial enlargement. There may be more to see on a larger print.'

He transferred the print from the enlarger to the washtray and Barry moved over to join him as the blank white became a blurred smudge. Barry watched the enlarged details of the photograph begin to swim into view. He remained watching, engrossed, as Stan moved back to the original print in the smaller tray, lifted it out and pegged it onto an overhead rail.

Barry found himself studying the faces of the remaining four Byker Chapter members. Stan, Richard, Pandora and himself, all of them smiling at the camera as if everything was all right. He looked at Pandora for a long time. Could it be true? Could she really have lied to him? Could she really have led him to believe that he was somehow special while, at the same time, making out with every other member of the Chapter? Or could it be that Stan and Richard had somehow found out about his affair with Pandora and were conducting this whole elaborate trick as a kind of jealous revenge? Barry did not know what to think as he studied that beautiful face. What was she doing now? Where was she? And why had she simply left him without any explanation or reason?

He looked at his own image. The years between then and now had melted away; the photograph might have been taken yesterday. How had Stan managed to fix the negative that way? How had he made the other images vanish from the photograph? If it was a trick, then it was an extremely complex and mysterious one. There were no background smudges where the figures had previously been standing or sitting. It was as if they had never been there; the background details of Stan's flat which had previously been obscured by the Byker Chapter members were perfect in every detail. Barry looked closely at his own face again, studying the features. Maybe Stan had carefully rigged a room to look like a duplicate of his own room all those years ago, had cut out the figures from the original photograph very carefully and then superimposed them onto the new set-up. If so, perhaps he would see details in the outline of his own figure where the scissors had been. It was an enlargement, surely such details would be much clearer. Barry moved closer, studying his own old-fashioned hairstyle. The head was turned slightly at an angle, away from the camera, even though he had still been looking at the camera when the flash went off.

And then, as Barry watched, the image of his face in the photograph turned, shifted its gaze and looked directly at him.

Barry recoiled, eyes swimming, feeling dizzy. He had been bending over too long, the blood had rushed to his head and blurred his vision. He looked again at the photograph.

His own image grinned back at him, eyes gleaming. He cursed softly, rubbing his eyes with the backs of his hands. This red light was affecting his vision. He looked again.

The image was still grinning, the eyes sparkling liquidly. The grin began to spread, revealing long white teeth. The eyes narrowed as the grin widened over the face, distorting it. Barry's face was changing. The lips parted in an ever-widening, red crescent. The teeth were elongating, sharpening. Saliva began to run from the corners of the mouth, dripping from the chin. The ears were now somehow pointed. The old-fashioned haircut had also somehow spread while he had been watching that changing face. It had spread and grown over the neck and inwards towards the face, until the entire head was fringed by a tangled, shaggy mane. The eyes were now not human eyes; they were sunken, yellow orbs bisected by black crescent irises. The face had become the face of an animal, an insane, mutated parody of a feral wild beast. Obscene, claw-like hands moved from the image's sides and braced on the sofa.

The figure moved slowly round from behind the sofa. It began to walk towards the camera.

Barry broke from the almost trance-like spell with a sudden, involuntary cry. Stan had just pegged another print to the overhead rail.

'What's wrong? You clarting around with those chemicals?'

'The picture . . . ' said Barry weakly.

'What about the picture?'

'Nothing . . . nothing . . . ' Barry steeled himself, cursing himself for a fool and looked back at the enlargement lying in the washtray. Instantly, he recoiled from it and blundered towards Stan. The image of himself had crossed the room in the photograph and was peering hellishly and directly into the camera lens.

'This isn't funny, Stan! Just stop fooling around and tell me what you want. I've had enough party tricks tonight to last a lifetime . . . '

'What the hell are you on about, man?' asked Stan, then remembered the enlargement: 'Did you see anything in that photo? Something we've missed . . . ?'

'Listen, you bastard! I want to know what's going on! I want to know what you want from me and why you're saying and doing these things! Tell me! Tell me! TELL ME!' Barry seized Stan round the throat and pinned him against the wall. Stan tried to pull his hands away as they whirled round, exchanging places. Stan banged him hard against the wall, remembering in a flash how he had banged Joe against Richard's living-room wall in an attempt to calm him down. But now Barry's hands had fallen away from Stan's neck and Stan could feel his whole body going limp against him. Even in the hellish red light that bathed the dark room, he could see the change that had suddenly come over Barry. His eyes were filled with abject fear, fixed on something behind Stan in the direction of the large washtray. He began to moan, a low whimpering sound. Quickly, Stan turned round.

There was a sound of sloshing liquid and he became aware of some kind of movement in the developing tray itself. He took a step forward, then halted, paralysed.

A hand was emerging from the tray.

Clutching, curling fingers were rising into the air, coated in a black, sludge-like substance which could not be the chemicals he had placed in there. The dripping hand rose vertically and smoothly out of the tray. Now, Stan could see the tar-coated arm. Another hand appeared on the rim of the tray, taloned fingers feeling and groping for purchase. Something was climbing out as if the tray itself had suddenly become some trap-door into Hell.

Stan moved to the light switch and flicked it quickly a dozen times. The light would not come on. He looked back at the developing tray. In the eerie, ruddy glow, he could see a head-like shape emerging from the tray as the thing began to climb sinuously out into the dark room.

Barry was crouched in the corner, saying the same thing over and over again: 'I won't believe your stupid tricks . . . I won't believe your stupid tricks . . . I won't believe your stupid tricks . . . '

Stan threw himself at the dark room door. The handle remained fast and immovable. It seemed to have been sealed shut. Frantically, he tugged and beat at the panelling.

'Richard! Richard! Diane! Help us! For God's sake, open the door!'

Behind him, Stan could hear a dripping, slopping sound and looked back hastily to see a grotesque, man-like form crawling slowly from the tray onto the bench. It was huge. Black sludge dripped and splashed to the floor as it moved. In seconds, it would be free. Barry suddenly broke out of his immobility and flung himself rabidly at the door beside Stan, shrieking and tearing at the wood. Stan began to hammer with the flat of his hand, shouting Richard's name again and again.

From behind him came a soft *thump*.

Feeling terror crawling on his back like a living thing, he turned and saw that the creature was free from the developing tray. It had slumped down on the far side of the table and was now hidden from sight. Stan had a sudden, hideous impression of an atrocious birth. The tray had been a womb. The thick, sludge-like slime covering the monstrosity was some gruesome travesty of a mother's birth fluid.

Slowly, menacingly and with a terrifying suggestion of

growing strength, the thing began to rise from the floor on the other side of the table. The sludge had trickled from its face enough to show Stan dull yellow, evil eyes, shrouded by a face of vaguely wolf-like features. An insane, dripping grin revealed rows of irregular, barbed, yellow teeth. It snarled as it rose, saliva dripping from its jaws, eyes now turning in their direction. The thing had to stoop as its head approached the low ceiling of the dark room. It started to growl with a low, savage gurgling. It moved towards them. The growl became words; words from a loathesome mouth that was not meant for speech.

'*Necrolan . . . Absavel . . . Gorgus . . .* ' And then, a horrifying echo of the thing in the fog: '*Hide and seek . . . Seek and find . . . EVERY ONE!*'

Stan turned and began to hammer on the door again, knowing that they were both going to die. Something crashed on the floor behind them as a table was pushed roughly to one side. A shelf of chemicals shattered. Barry began to shout hoarsely and wordlessly at the top of his voice. A hideous shadow fell over them.

'*. . . GOOORRRRGGGUUUUSSSS . . .*'

Then the door was open and both men had fallen through into the gallery. Stan was vaguely aware of Richard and Diane as he turned quickly and slammed the door shut. Frantically, he began to drag the empty packing crates up against it. Barry remained where he had collapsed on the floor, gasping for breath.

'Who locked the bloody door?' Stan shouted as he desperately tugged the crates against it.

Richard was beside him now, helping him unquestioningly. 'No one. The door was open. We heard you shouting. What's going on, Stan . . . ?' His voice faded as something threw itself at the dark room door from the other side. The wood panelling bulged and splintered with a loud, cracking noise. They all stood, frozen at the impact. For a while there was silence and Stan could not shake off the feeling that the thing on the other side, whatever it was, was now contemplating its next move. With a savage impact, the door splintered on its hinges, jolting them into action again as they dragged up more cases.

'*What the hell is it?*' Richard shouted, but their danger was too immediate for an answer. The attack continued, blow after blow raining on the dark room door. Hellish red light splintered through the massive rents in the woodwork.

'We've got to get out of here!' yelled Stan. 'The door won't hold much longer.' One of the packing crates fell heavily from the barricade to the floor. Hinges squealed. Behind the sounds of destruction, Richard finally became aware of throaty, abominable snarlings and gurglings.

He turned to grab Diane and pull her away; Stan poised himself for flight, then remembered Barry and began to move towards his prone figure. Suddenly, the door split apart, boards whirling into the gallery. Packing crates tumbled and the room was filled with an immense roaring and bellowing. A spar of wood caught Richard on the shoulder, spinning him away from Diane. A packing crate fell across Stan's legs, pinning him to the ground. And as he lay there, he knew that the horror in the dark room was finally free and that the Spectre had found them again. He waited for death. The roaring sound became a raging wind filled with the same howling, echoing, mocking laughter that they had heard in the fog.

But death did not come.

The roaring and the raging wind abruptly disappeared.

Richard pulled himself to his feet, grabbing for Diane. She had fallen beside him but seemed unhurt. Barry lay moaning beside Stan who, even now, was pulling the crate away from his legs. They looked at the jagged gap where the dark room door had been. The door itself had been shattered completely, wood and plastic littering the gallery floor; a single tattered board hung creaking from one hinge. Beyond, in the wrecked dark room, there was no sign of the thing that had emerged from the developing tray. It had vanished as surely as one of the ghost images from the photograph. Stan kicked aside the packing crate and moved unsteadily back to the dark room, peering quickly around for any sign of the monstrous apparition. Picking his way inside, he snatched up the remains of the large print which now lay, ripped to pieces, on the ruined dark room floor, and studied it desperately. Richard could tell by the look on his face that there had been no change at all. Hopelessly, he looked up at them.

'Nothing. Just the same as it was before.'

He came towards them, holding the print. 'I don't understand. We didn't have a radio or television on. How did it find us?'

'You heard what it said in the fog,' said Richard. 'Perhaps it doesn't need to use them any more. Perhaps it's strong enough to do its own . . . hunting.'

Barry clambered to his feet, surveying the destruction with utter bewilderment. Richard saw the bewilderment blossom; very soon it would become abject terror again . . . and then . . . perhaps insanity? Barry fought to regain control. Holding himself erect, he turned on them.

'Get out! All of you! Get out of here!'

'Take it easy, Barry . . . ' began Stan.

'Get out or by God I'll call the police! You think I'm stupid? You think I'm taken in by this carnival of fucking horrors? Get out! Get out . . . '

'You saw that thing in there,' said Stan. 'You *saw* it! Surely you're not going to turn your back . . . '

'Get out, I said. Get out . . . get out . . . GET OUT!'

'You idiot! You saw it, didn't you? I'm surprised we're still alive. It could have taken us all. *But it's just playing with us, don't you see that?* We've got to stick together. We've . . . '

'If you're not gone in ten seconds . . . ' Barry's entire body was trembling as if with some terrible palsy.

'At least tell us where in Mevagissey we can find Pandora,' said Richard as calmly as he could.

' . . . Get out . . . '

Stan made to lunge forward and take Barry by the lapels. Richard caught him and held him back. 'It's no use, Stan. Can't you see? He can never believe us, even if he wanted to. We just can't save him.'

The image flashed into his mind again of that sunny afternoon when the Byker Chapter had lain on a grassy bank beside Ouseburn School; of that instant when he had thought how vulnerable Barry seemed; how, of them all, he was the one who needed the Chapter most but who questioned how long their friendship could last. His terror and rejection of the Chapter now seemed the only, fated, logical outcome.

He took a pen from his inside pocket, scribbled on a scrap of paper and pushed it into Barry's top jacket pocket. 'We're staying in a motel for the night, Barry. You can ring us at that number if you change your mind or . . .'

Barry's eyes remained filled with wild rage. Richard knew that it was hopeless.

Seconds later, they had left the gallery. Barry stood among the packing crates and the shattered remnants of the dark room door, head bowed, body trembling.

He was alone.

Fourteen

For a long time, Barry remained standing outside the dark room, trying to rationalise everything that had happened. Eventually, he made his way to the store-room at the other side of the gallery. In one of the boxes, next to the cleaning fluid and piles of mops, he knew that there was a half-bottle of whisky left over from the previous Chritsmas Eve celebrations. He retrieved it and, walking back through the gallery without looking at the remains of the dark room door as he passed, made his way up the stone staircase and let himself into his office again. Sitting behind his desk once more, he took a long drink, then another, as the lengthening shadows of evening crept stealthily over the gallery, up the balustraded staircase and across the carpet of his office. What he had seen was beyond all rationalisation, but his mind needed to make sense of it somehow.

Gradually, as the evening progressed and the drink took hold, he became convinced that it had all been some strange, bizarre practical joke or failed blackmail attempt. They had all looked stoned when they had arrived at the gallery. Perhaps they had been shooting up? Perhaps, in some way he did not understand, they had all hallucinated the monstrous thing from the photograph, and somehow it had been communicated to him. Yes, that must be the answer. He had been in that dark room with Stan for quite some time, and there had been long periods when Stan had been busying himself with the developing process while Barry had been scrutinising the enlargement. Perhaps Stan had somehow introduced some kind of hallucinogenic chemical into the air. He had been using chemicals in the washtray, and while Barry had been examining the photograph in the tray, the vapour from those chemicals had affected him. Yes, that was it. That must be it. The nightmare of his own image coming vividly and monstrously alive had been a hallucination. Now, the effect had worn off and he had sent those bastards packing. Everything was going to be all right.

The whisky felt good inside him. Now that he had explained everything to himself he was able to ring Sheila. Controlling the odd waver that somehow remained in his voice, he told her that there was a great deal of work he wanted to finish that evening. Worried, she tried to convince him that he should come home as soon as he possibly could. Barry promised that he would be back in an hour. Replacing the receiver, he drank three full measures of whisky. He switched on the overhead lamp on his desk and breathed deeply. He was feeling better now . . . the nightmare was over . . .

The sudden sound of a footfall on the landing outside his office brought the terror crowding back. The office door began to open slowly. Something was coming in. Barry muffled a cry, rising to his feet. And then a voice said:

'That you, Mr Clark?'

Barry slumped back onto his seat as the familiar figure of Frank Jameson appeared in the doorway. The security caretaker.

'Yes, Frank, it's me. God, you gave me a fright.'

'Sorry,' said Frank, moving into the light. 'I heard movement up here. Thought I'd have a look. What the hell's happened downstairs in the dark room, Mr Clark?'

'Oh . . . that . . . yes . . . '

'Didn't you hear anything?'

'Hear anything? Yes . . . yes . . . I did. Vandals, Frank. They must have broken in through the back exit. When I got down there, they were gone.'

'Back exit? That can't be, Mr Clark. Locked the bugger myself. It's still locked.' For the first time, Frank saw the whisky bottle on the desk, could smell it on Barry's breath. Cautiously now, aware that something very peculiar had been happening, he said: 'You all right, Mr Clark? Something happened that I should know about?'

'Yes, I'm fine. Look, none of this is your fault, Frank. You left me up here in charge. So I don't want you to think that the responsibility for this falls on your shoulders. It's entirely my . . . '

'*Shhhhhh* . . . ' Frank held a finger to his lips, turning back to the office door. In a low voice, he said: 'Did you hear that? A noise downstairs in the gallery. I think the buggers are back again.'

He made for the door. Involuntarily, Barry rose to his feet, the fear crawling over his flesh again. 'No, Frank. It's nothing . . . look, let's call the police . . . they'll sort everything out . . . ' He lifted the telephone receiver, but Frank was already out of sight. Barry could hear his soft footsteps on the stone staircase as he made his way down to the gallery. Suppressing a sob, he hurried after him.

Frank was half-way down the stairs when Barry emerged at the stairhead. Anger swelled within him. They had come back; they were going to try their tricks again. From somewhere below, he heard a distant scuffling sound. Frank had heard it, too, and was hurrying softly downstairs. Rage swamping caution, Barry clattered down the staircase after Frank who, hearing him, turned back and motioned that he should be silent. Barry swept past him, footsteps echoing and ringing through the dark museum. Purposefully, he strode straight into the gallery, Frank hurrying to catch him up.

'They've heard us for sure now,' wheezed Frank, a trace of contempt in his voice.

Barry reached for the light switch which would illuminate the Natural History Exhibition and was not entirely surprised when the light would not come on. More tricks. The glow of a street light could be seen in the corner of one of the far windows. It threw slanting orange light over the glass exhibition cases and the photographs on the wall.

'All right!' exclaimed Barry angrily, still trying to control the tremor in his voice. 'Come out, Stan! That's enough, Richard! Party's over!'

Frank stepped forward, trying the switch again. 'You *do* know something about that mess beside the dark room, don't you? You been having a party or something, Mr Clark?' Frank moved past him, striding into the gallery.

'Come out!' His torch beam played among the exhibits but there was no further sound. The darkness seemed to have swallowed his voice.

Barry followed and, between them, they conducted a rapid search among the glass cabinets, moving to the lower area that gave access to the store-room and the ruined dark room. There was nothing. Frank hurried down into the storage room and then the dark room, emerging seconds later when it was obvious that there was no one in there. He crossed rapidly to the back exit, tried the bar across the door and found that it was still locked. He tried the light switch and found that it would not work in there, either.

'Must be a fuse or an electricity cut or something . . . '

Barry had just decided to take Frank into his confidence about the whole insane business—the visit of his former friends and the conjuration of that dreadful Spectre—when a movement off to his left caught his attention. He turned quickly. It had been a slow, rolling kind of motion near the glass case standing by the wall. He concentrated on the spot where he thought he had seen it. Frank noticed his reaction and quickly played the light onto the glass case. Inside reared the enormous form of a brown grizzly bear, muzzle bared in a fearful snarl. It reminded Barry of the nightmare he had seen—that he *thought* he had seen—in the dark room. The bear's glass eyes reflected the torchlight. But there was no further sign of furtive movement at the base of the glass cabinet as Frank took a step forward.

And then Barry was suddenly swamped with that terrible, nauseous feeling of fear that had assailed him before he had left England for his holiday in Italy. The effect was instantaneous and sickening. He clutched his stomach and bent double, retching with fear.

'What's wrong . . . ?' began Frank.

A glass case beside the exit suddenly exploded with the force of a bomb, and something began whirling and fluttering around the gallery.

Another case exploded on the other side, and Frank's torch beam swung round just as a rain of glass rattled on the floor tiles. Utterly amazed, he saw a tawny owl burst through the glass and go fluttering around the upper reaches of the gallery, shrieking raucously.

'What the hell is going on?' he exclaimed as another case exploded; then another, and another. The gallery was suddenly full of huge birds, flapping and shrieking and buffeting against the other glass cases. Ten feet away, a seagull crashed through its glass case, wings beating loudly. It snapped at Frank as it passed. He lashed out with his torch and it was gone overhead.

'*They're coming alive*,' Barry said. '*The exhibits are coming alive*.' He spoke as if it was somehow the most normal and ordinary thing in the world. Another glass case detonated and Frank jumped back as he felt something soft scamper over his feet. He kicked out. Suddenly, the tawny owl swooped down from the ceiling and attacked Barry. He beat out at it, calling desperately to Frank as it flurried at his head. He staggered round and dashed for the exit. The owl swooped again and Barry fell to the floor. Screaming, it circled away towards the ceiling. Barry clasped his hands over his ears, trying to block out those terrible sounds, while the gallery echoed to the shrieking and hooting of a living menagerie.

He looked up from the floor and saw Frank still standing with his back to the bear case. He was gazing blankly at Barry as feathered bodies swooped and dived overhead, shaking his head as if totally refusing to believe what he saw.

And then Barry saw the movement again and realised that the nightmare had not gone away; it was still here in the gallery and had only been waiting for him to return. The first furtive movement he had seen had not come from in front of the grizzly bear's glass exhibition case . . . but *inside* it. It was the same look that he had seen in the dark room; the same leering, frozen snarl. Whatever had been in the dark room, whatever form it had taken in there, it had not vanished in a raging whirlwind. It had come out into the gallery and it had been there all the time, looking for a form in which to host itself. It had turned to the glass case on the far wall . . .

A fearsomely large, hooked claw clenched and unclenched with a brittle, crackling sound. *Trying it on for size*, thought Barry. *It's trying it on for size*. The bear's head turned to look down at Frank, who had heard the crackling noise but had not noticed the movement, being too preoccupied with the noisy, swirling birds overhead. He turned quickly, torch held high like a club, hunting for the source of the new noise but still with his back to the monstrous form in the glass case. Barry could not move, could not speak. He could only watch in horror. He tried to whisper a warning to Frank, tried to tell him to run, tried to run away himself. The rearing bear-thing slowly moved again.

As he struggled to rise from the floor, the black shape in the glass case behind Frank suddenly reared up, and in the same second Barry found his voice.

'*Run, Frank! For God's sake, run!*'

The bear case burst apart. Glass splintered and cracked in a glistening shroud around Frank as an abominably loud, echoing, roaring sound filled the gallery. The black shape lunged forward, the vaguely man-like arms descended on him. Barry screamed aloud as the caretaker's body was suddenly smothered in a horrifying embrace that swept him off his feet and towards that terrible, roaring head. Frank's screams were drowned by a horrible snorting and growling.

The tawny owl was suddenly slashing at Barry's face and he fell again. It was joined by others, all shrieking and hooting raucously, tearing at his flesh. Barry lashed out, felt his fist make contact. Shielding his eyes, feeling something tangling in his hair, he blundered across the gallery. He seized it, felt something slash the palm of his hand and then lunged to one side, slamming the feathered body against the gallery wall, again and again, until the slashing, flapping thing ceased to move. Sawdust pattered to the floor. But then another night-dark bird was flapping at his collar, pecking and slashing at his neck. Another fluttered past his face, seeking his eyes. Crying out, Barry spun away from the wall. From the direction of the shattered bear case came the sounds of crunching glass and ripping cloth. Frank's screams had ceased and Barry could see that the hunched black shape was tearing at a tattered mass between its claws which was somehow much too small to be the security caretaker. *He's got away*! thought Barry. Then the shape threw the tattered mass away and it thudded wetly only a few feet from Barry. In the orange light cast by the street lamp, he could see that it was Frank's upper torso—the head and the lower body had been bitten away. Now, the hunched, abominable shape was moving towards him.

Barry fled from the gallery and reached the main outer entrance. He flung himself at the main doors. They were locked—and his keys were upstairs. Looking around, he found an ornamental waste paper bin, picked it up and heaved it at the glass pane above waist height. The glass shattered outwards. Quickly he picked his way over the broken glass and tried to clamber out. Off to his right, a terrifying black mass appeared in the gallery entrance, rearing upwards, sharp claws scraping on the wall panelling. There was no time. Barry fled to the stone staircase and leaped upwards faster than he would have believed possible of himself. From behind came the muffled grunting and heavy breathing of a large animal.

Inside his office, he pulled a filing cabinet across the carpet to the door, breath coming in a frantic, whining wheeze. He pushed it up hard against the door, and began to back away until he had reached his desk. He strained to listen for any sound, unable to hear because of his whining breath, the pounding of blood in his ears. From below, he became aware at last of a padding sound and the dry scrape of claws on stone.

Frantically he grabbed for the telephone, hunting desperately for the scrap of paper in his top jacket pocket.

* * *

Richard had just opened the door of their motel room when the telephone rang. They had been to a local store to stock up before their trip to Mevagissey; nothing too heavy, just enough to last them for their journey down. Diane bumped the door shut with her hip as Stan made his way to the connecting room door and the separate apartment beyond. Richard looked at Diane, puzzled for an instant, before lifting the receiver.

'Hello?'

'Richard, it's me! What do I do, for God's sake, what do I do?'

'Barry? What's wrong? Calm down. Tell me what's . . . '

'In the museum. My God, Richard. The exhibits. The birds, the bear—*they've all come alive.*'

'Barry. Get out of there now. It doesn't matter how. Just get away. Is there another way out?'

'*Shhh* . . .' whispering now. ' . . . The bear . . . it's outside my office door. Oh, God . . . I can see it through the fluted glass . . . weaving from side to side. Oh, God . . . I'll be quiet . . . it'll go away . . . I'll wake up and it won't be there . . . I'll . . . ' A sudden, furious pounding, a splintering noise. The sound of wood being torn apart, of something being pushed screeching away from a door. 'OH, GOD HELP ME, RICHARD, IT'S BREAKING DOWN THE DOOR!' Tearing and splintering, ripping and clawing. And above it all, the throaty, abominable roaring and growling of a large animal.

'Run, Barry! For God's sake, run!'

The sound of stentorian breathing. Padding footsteps. A crashing of furniture. A throaty snarling. A terrible, desperate scream ululating loudly and then changing abruptly into a *liquid*, muffled gurgling. Snorting, ripping.

And then the buzzing tone of a disconnected line.

Diane took the receiver from Richard's nerveless fingers and pushed him back into a seat. His face was white with shock. Diane turned to look at Stan, feeling sick. Stan looked ashen, too. And then, suddenly, Richard was scrabbling in his inside pocket and had pulled out a print of the Byker Chapter photograph.

'Oh, my God . . . look . . . look . . .'

Stan pushed across to look at the photograph as Diane grabbed Richard's wrist and stared, not believing her eyes.

Like a cheap special effect from a B feature horror movie, Barry was fading from the photograph. The plain, pink pastel wall of Stan the Man's flat could be seen clearly through his transparent form. And then, he was gone.

Richard raised his eyes from the photograph.

'Let's just get the hell down to Mevagissey, now,' he said.

PART THREE
CHILDREN OF THE NIGHT

Listen to them—the children of the night.
What music they make!

Bram Stoker, *Dracula*

One

Deejay was enjoying his own patter tonight. He was really in the mood; everything was going just fine. The Imperial was packed and that always brought out the best in him. For someone who had been born in the shadow of dock-yard cranes on the River Tyne, he had affected one of the weirdest Mid-Atlantic accents ever heard in the North-East. When he was playing records, it veered crazily from the local dialect—Geordie—to Memphis, Tennessee. Tonight was going to be a good night, he could feel it. There were two hen parties and one of the local lads was leaving his factory to move 'down south'. His mates had decided to throw a party for him. Record requests were coming thick and fast. Any requests for records that Deejay did not have in his collection were promptly ignored. He had already identified a possible three women from the crowd as potential 'scores' for later on that evening. He felt really, really good.

Why, then, should Angie be bothering him so much tonight?

She was doing nothing out of the ordinary; she was just working behind the bar as usual. Saying very little to any of the customers; serving drinks, washing glasses. She looked whiter than normal and was wearing a black satin choker around her throat. Josh seemed very quiet, too. By the looks of things, they had probably had an argument. They had not exchanged a word all evening. Time and time again, Deejay found his attention wandering to Angie. There was something about her . . . *something* . . . that disturbed him and threatened to disrupt his good mood. What the hell was it?

There was a new face in the Imperial tonight. Pearson had taken on some old guy to wait at the tables. Even now, he was silently moving from table to table collecting glasses. He looked crammed into the Imperial uniform; the bow-tie around his throat seemed to be biting into his flesh. Deejay could not help thinking that Pearson had chosen the most unlikely-looking person for the job. Take away the uniform and the guy looked like one of the drunken bums you often saw hanging around down by the Quayside.

His attention returned to Angie and Josh. They were working mechanically and efficiently behind that bar like bloody zombies. He looked at his watch. Normally, around this time he had a short break. He had intended to follow through with his mood tonight; he did not really need a rest. But the uneasiness, the nagging, illogical feelings about the bar staff were threatening to put him off his stride. Perhaps if he went down there and had a little chat with them? Just enough to settle himself . . .

Deejay fixed the record deck and switched over to tape.

'All right—now it's a whole lotta soul. Back real soon!'

Deejay slipped out of his booth in the centre of the disco floor and boogied between two of the girls he had been keeping his eye on. Neither of them seemed to react, which only made his mood worse. Sullenly, he moved across the floor towards the bar. The new guy walked straight past him as if he were not there, glassy eyes fixed on the next table and its empty glasses. The odour of sweat made him wince as he passed. There was something else about that smell. Something sickly-sweet . . . sweet and . . . not quite right. Deejay shrugged it off and positioned himself on the stool at the end of the bar.

'How about a vodka, Angie?'

Angie moved to the bottle without acknowledging him and began to pour. She looked even more vacant than she usually did. Up close, she was whiter than he had imagined. Her make-up could not hide the deep hollows beneath her eyes. *Late night last night*, thought Deejay. *The sugar-daddy must have had a lot of fun.*

'How's it going?'

Angie placed the drink in front of him, moved off and began to wash glasses again. Beyond her, Deejay could see Josh as he mechanically served another customer. Still no reply from Angie.

Bitch! 'Lots of people in tonight . . .'

The bitch was treating him as if he did not exist! Deejay swigged his vodka and turned to look back across the room. In the reception doorway, he could see that Paul the bouncer was leaning on the wall and watching his every move as he tried to talk to Angie. Deejay gulped down his vodka and moved away.

He knew that Paul fancied Angie pretty strongly. It would be like him to move over here and give Deejay a good hiding, just for showing an interest. The man was an animal.

He strolled to a nearby table. The young couple already seated there were too engrossed in each other to pay him any attention. He raised his glass, cursing Angie and that great bloody hulk in the reception doorway. Turning to watch the dancers, he suddenly saw a gaunt figure emerge from the crowd and walk briskly towards the bar. It was Pearson, obviously on another of his 'is everything going well?' circuits of the night-club. Hastily, Deejay checked his watch and confirmed that he was taking his break during the allotted time. He watched as Pearson reached the bar and beckoned to Josh and Angie. They moved forward and Deejay watched as Pearson talked to them. They remained expressionless, nodding in agreement when Pearson turned and began to walk his way.

'Evening, Mr Pearson.'

'Good evening, David. You're doing very well tonight.'

'Thank you.'

'I wonder if you would be so good as to have a few private words with me. Upstairs.'

'Upstairs?' *Nobody* was allowed upstairs.

'That's right. Shall we say . . . ' Pearson looked at his watch. 'Ten minutes?'

Deejay finished his drink quickly. 'Ten minutes. Sure. Right.'

Pearson vanished into the crowd again. Straining in his seat, Deejay watched as the Under-Manager quickly mounted the stairway leading to the Woman's rooms. He appeared to look back, smiling, but in this light it was difficult to be sure. Then he had vanished behind the door. Deejay stood up for a better view. The door had been left open. And that had *never* happened before. That big green door was always shut; nobody but Pearson ever passed in or out. Deejay had often watched him meticulously locking and unlocking the door; had often sung softly under his breath: 'Green door, what's that secret you're keeping?' Now, he had received a direct invitation and he did not know whether to feel honoured or apprehensive. Maybe it had something to do with what he had just said to Angie and Josh? Deejay looked over to where Paul had been leaning against the wall. He was no longer there. Good! Deejay moved quickly back to the bar and waited until Angie had finished serving a group of young girls.

'What's going on, Angie? What did the Big Man want?'

Angie still acted as if he was not there.

'Come on, what's it all about?' Angie turned to serve another customer. Cursing, Deejay moved along the bar to Josh.

'Okay, Josh? What's going down?'

Josh finished wiping a glass and went to serve a customer, looking straight through him.

'You turds!' Deejay spun away from the bar and hurried back to his booth on the disco floor. Keying in a second tape, he slipped away again to the foot of the stairs. He looked at his watch. Ten minutes, Pearson had said. Only five had passed but, what the hell, he might as well go up there now as the door was open. Briskly, he sprinted up the steps to the green door. A slab of orange light spilled underneath. He paused briefly at the top, savouring the moment, and looked back across the disco. From here, he could see everything. The disco, the bar, the seating area, the reception. Everything. *Mistress of all she surveys*, he thought wryly. And then he slipped past the door.

Ahead of him lay a corridor. The walls were covered with heavy-duty veloured wallpaper; the floor smothered in deep-pile carpet. An orange shade on the overhead light dangled tassles. There were two doors set in the corridor walls on either side. They were both closed. But at the end of the corridor, facing him, was another green door, standing slightly ajar. Deejay walked forward, footsteps muffled by the carpet. Behind him he heard a soft *snick* and turned to see that the outer door had closed. Shrugging, he moved on, adopting an air of jollity that somehow did not come easily. The doors to left and right made him feel uneasy. It was almost as if he expected one of them suddenly to be flung open and someone to jump out at him.

Someone . . . or something? Now, why the hell am I thinking like that?

The inner green door loomed large. Deejay leaned forward and touched it. It began to open slowly.

'Mr Pearson . . . ?'

He stood on the threshold for a long time, looking inside. He could see two richly upholstered armchairs and a sofa. A gas heater had been installed in a make-shift recess on the far wall. A photograph hung on the near wall—a photograph of two blokes and a girl, sitting on a sofa.

'Mr Pearson? It's me, David.' Deejay walked into the room and became aware of the soft hissing and the flickering light. In the corner stood a television set. It had been switched on, but not tuned in. A snowstorm buzzed angrily on the screen. 'Mr Pearson?' Deejay moved towards what he presumed to be a bathroom door, feeling a little guilty that his presence should have gone unnoticed for so long. Now, he felt like an intruder. Anxious to be discovered, he peered through the door opening. There was no one in the bathroom, but he could see a row of female toiletries on the cabinet shelf. Maybe he was going to meet the Woman herself?

The click of a latch followed by the hiss of a door on the carpet drew Deejay's attention back to the corridor. Moving quickly, he opened the living-room door again and looked out.

He had expected Pearson or, at best, the Woman. He was not prepared for what met his eyes. Startled, he drew back.

It was a small boy, perhaps ten years old. His sandy hair was brushed severely to one side, against the natural growth. He was wearing a black blazer and trousers which accentuated his white, freckled face. He was the saddest looking kid Deejay had ever seen. His large, liquid eyes seemed to capture and reflect the orange light from the corridor. He still held the handle of the door nearest to the living-room and looked up in surprise when he saw Deejay.

For a long moment, they stood there, saying nothing.

Then the boy glanced nervously back at the room from which he had come and quietly pulled the door shut. He looked at Deejay again with those big, liquid eyes.

'Are you my Daddy?' he asked quietly.

'What?' Deejay was disconcerted by the question. 'No . . . no . . . look, where's Mr Pearson?'

The liquid eyes clouded with disappointment. Deejay could see the beginning of tears. The child hung his head. 'I thought you might be. I've been waiting for him.'

Deejay began to move forward.

Suddenly, the door was snapped open again. The kid jumped nervously and Deejay turned to see Pearson on the threshold.

His face looked swollen with rage. Instantly, the anger dissipated when he saw Deejay standing there.

'David!' he beamed. 'You're early. I haven't yet prepared for you.'

'Sorry.' Deejay made a weak attempt to look at his watch.

'Never mind, never mind. Come in.'

Pearson held the door wide. The room was approximately the same size as the living-room Deejay had just left but was sparsely furnished. A fake electric coal fire provided the only light and its fake orange flame curled and danced in the grating, making flickering, crawling shadows on the walls. Off to the left, shrouded in deeper shadow, was a high-backed wicker chair. Someone was sitting in it but Deejay could make out no details, only the silhouette. Pink fingers curled strangely on the arm rests. Could this be the Woman?

He heard the door shut and saw that Pearson had guided the child protectively into the room.

'Let's sit down,' said Pearson, gesturing to the seat directly opposite the wicker chair and its occupant. 'I think that you will find this interesting.'

'Interesting?' queried Deejay, sitting.

'Oh, but yes. This must seem very mysterious, but bear with me, young man. All will become clear in a very short while.'

Pearson pulled another chair into the centre of the room and motioned to the boy. He sat quietly, swinging his feet and gazing at the carpet, that same look of sadness on his face. Pearson moved to the wicker chair and turned it slightly to form a triangle with the others. The electric firelight spilled over the figure seated there.

The indefinable crawling feeling that Deejay had first felt when the green door had closed behind him, shutting out the disco music, was now tangible and very unpleasant. More than anything else, he wanted to get up and walk out of that room.

He cleared his throat. 'What's with the shop dummy, Mr Pearson?'

Pearson turned to look at the manikin in the wicker chair and then back at Deejay. There seemed to be an air of affected puzzlement when he spoke, as if he was deliberately teasing him. 'I beg your pardon?'

'The dummy.' Deejay cleared his throat again. 'It's a shop dummy.'

'So it is,' smiled Pearson, moving to the battered pink manikin and readjusting the arms on the rests, as if trying to find a more comfortable position for it. It was an old department-store manikin that had obviously seen a lot of service. That oval grey-pink head bore only the slightest contours of a human face: a horizontal groove for the mouth, slight hollows for the eyes, the ears closely shaped to the head, slightly raised ridges to suggest hair. The nose had been badly chipped, pink paint flaking away. Pearson finished arranging the mottled grey-pink hands and stood back.

'Look, I've put a tape on downstairs, Mr Pearson. I can't really stay for very long, you know. The tape will run down. I've got to change it, put some records on . . . '

'Commendable, David. Always putting your job first. But this won't take long, I promise you.'

'Yeah?' Again, the half-hearted glance at the watch.

'Of course. Now, please . . . I just want you to sit quietly for a few moments.'

Pearson moved over to the child and Deejay watched as he tilted the boy's face upwards with a finger under the chin. He looked like some kind of doctor as he examined the young face.

'Are you feeling well, Timothy?'

So that was the kid's name.

The boy nodded, shyly averting his eyes from Pearson's penetrating stare.

'I want another Dark-Out, Timothy. Do you understand?'

'Yes.'

'Good. Then we'll begin. Empty your mind. Find a spot on the carpet to look at. Pick one of those spirals, there. Good. Then empty your mind. Just like when you're watching that blank television screen . . . '

What the hell is going on here? thought Deejay. *I don't have time for this.*

'Good. Now, Timothy. Dark-Out. *Absavel* . . . *Dark-Out* . . . *Imago* . . . *Dark-Out* . . . *Pacter* . . . let it come . . . *Gorgus* . . . let it take over . . . let it come . . . '

The boy's head was lowered, staring at the carpet beneath his feet. His legs had stopped swinging as Pearson continued to talk in that odd, hypnotic, crooning way. Deejay shuffled uneasily in his chair. What was this weirdo up to now? *Why don't I just tell him to piss off and find another DJ? I've got contacts. I can get a job somewhere else. There are other nightclubs in the town. And I bet I can make more money than that bastard pays, I'm sure of it. What about that advert in the* Evening Chronicle *for a new disc-jockey at the Tuxedo Princess? Yeah, that would be . . .*

The boy looked up.

At first, Deejay thought that the lack of light and the thick, black shadows were playing tricks with the kid's face. His eyes looked just like glistening, jet-black marbles. Pearson was standing back, smiling, arms folded smugly across his chest as if he had just pulled off some really neat conjuring trick. The kid sat straight and still, eyes oddly insect-like in the dark. Yes, those eyes were just like the black, glistening eyes of some hungry, waiting insect; waiting for Deejay to move so that it could spring nightmarishly out of its web to ensnare him.

That's enough! Deejay stood up and strode briskly towards the door. 'This is all very . . . interesting . . . Mr Pearson. Just like you said. But that tape's got about twelve minutes left before it runs out. So, if you don't mind, I'd like to get back down there to the disco. Perhaps we can have a chat some other time . . . '

The door was locked.

Deejay turned back, sighing deeply. Pearson was still standing, straight and unmoving, smiling.

'Well?' asked Deejay, feeling his anger starting to swell.

'Well,' replied Pearson as a simple statement.

'The door's locked.'

'Of course it is, David. I locked it.'

'Will you open it, please?'

'No.'

'No?'

'No. We haven't yet finished. *Absavel, Timothy. Otmo Nos Andophant Vermini Pacter Imago . . .* '

Deejay could feel something in the air, like a sound; but there was no sound. It was like a vibration, but there was no vibration. The air was charged with energy and it was like standing next to some massive dynamo, throbbing with invisible power. Then he saw something that his mind refused to accept.

Smoke was pouring from the kid's nostrils and mouth. Thick, blue smoke that swirled as if he was puffing on some huge cigar. It curled through the air, thick and plumed. And, as Deejay watched, it twisted across the room towards the department-store manikin sitting in the wicker chair. Somehow, the smoke seemed almost alive. Alive . . . *and glowing*. It began to shroud the dummy in a dense, blue haze. Suddenly fearful, Deejay tugged at the unyielding door handle.

'*Imago Palcusat Non Enno . . . Absavel . . . Gorgus . . .* '

'Pearson, what the hell are you . . . ?' His words faded to nothing.

The shop dummy was suddenly standing in the centre of the room, facing him.

Pearson stood it up. He picked it out of the chair and propped it up like that when I wasn't looking. Shop dummies don't move by themselves.

The dummy began to move jerkily towards him, joints squeaking. Its arms reached towards him.

And now Deejay knew that it was no trick of the light that made the dummy's face swarm and shift like that. The pink-grey face was a canvas, and some invisible painter was changing and rearranging; creating faces and wiping them as the dummy walked towards him. The effect was hypnotic. He watched the swirling, shifting oval of eyes and teeth; hundreds of faces were there, twisted and contorted, oozing and flowing. It was a mirror into Hell and its denizens were crowding for position to peer through at him from the other side.

Deejay screamed, eyes still riveted on the approaching horror.

'Really, David,' said Pearson, 'you of all people should know that we're soundproofed up here.'

Just before those savage arms enfolded him and that terrible face swarmed to engulf his own, Deejay saw a face that he recognised. At the last, just before his sanity and his life were ripped away, he recognised that face.

It was his own.

Two

Paul had been keeping a close eye on the street doors all night. Each time a new crowd of punters queued for admittance, he checked them over sullenly, searching for that smarmy smooth-talker who had been chatting up Angie the night before.

He had been fantasisng about what he was going to do to that bastard; after the previous night's humiliation, he wanted to hurt him, hurt him badly. He had decided that he would let him in, keep an eye on him and, as soon as he left his seat and went to the toilet, Paul would move in. He could visualise quite clearly the look of surprise on that smarm's face as he turned from the urinal, prick in hand, the surprise quickly turning to fear. The first punch would take out his teeth. The second would rupture his gut. The third, the fourth, the fifth . . . Then Paul would take the half-bottle of whisky from his inside pocket and pour it over the bastard's mashed face. If Pearson turned up, his alibi would be perfect: the man was pissed out of his skull and had attacked him. Andy would back him up—Andy had *better* back him up. Paul smiled and moved away to the inner reception doors.

Deejay had been gone for some time now. Paul scanned the nightclub, wondering where he had disappeared to. Angie was silently dispensing drinks at the bar, but there was no sign of Deejay there—which was just as well for him. In fact, there was no sign of him anywhere in the milling crowd. It could not be long now before the tape ran down. Pearson would not like it if Deejay was skiving. Paul grunted in amusement. He hoped that he *was* skiving. The smarmy little git deserved everything that was coming to him.

Beyond and above the dancers, the green door opened. Paul watched, expecting to see Pearson emerge.

Deejay stepped through and walked calmly down the stairs.

Paul stared in disbelief. What the hell was he doing upstairs in the Woman's private rooms? Could the bastard have scored with her or something? Was he her personal little gigolo? Paul's mind was racing with possibilities as Deejay moved across the disco floor, shouldering calmly through the dancers towards the bar.

Josh had moved forward, was leaning across the bar as Deejay drew level and began whispering confidentially, just as Pearson had done earlier. What the hell was going on here? Some kind of conspiracy? Deejay flitted quickly back to the disco floor and swung into his booth, hands dancing quickly over the tapes and turn-tables.

'Dave Johnson's the name, music's the game! DJ, the Deejay!'

Paul's surprise and curiosity were developing into a familiar rage. Something was going on. No one but Pearson ever went beyond that green door. Paul had never been up there, and if anyone was to be invited, he should be. People were whispering all the bloody time! Angie and that stranger; Pearson and Angie and Josh; now, Deejay and Josh.

Josh had dipped under the bar after Deejay returned to the booth, but Paul was unaware as he approached him, collecting glasses on a tray. Josh watched him every step of the way, pale face reflecting green and red disco light, until he was standing ten feet away, silently watching him.

Josh whistled.

Paul looked at him, glaring. There was a faint expression on Josh's face: sarcastic and taunting.

'What the hell do you want, you little tart?'

Josh stood silently watching him.

'I thought Pearson had signed on that weird old git to collect glasses,' Paul continued. 'A weird git and a fruit. What a collection.'

'Why don't you admit it, Paul? You're just a closet queen. Don't hide it.'

For the second time that night, Paul was stunned into disbelief.

'If you want an education, I'll meet you back in the delivery yard,' said Josh. 'How about it?'

Paul's rage bubbled outwards. Growling, he moved forward. Andy's sudden appearance and the hand clamped on his arm brought him to a halt. 'Take it easy, Paul. Not here. It's not worth it. You'll lose your job.'

'Don't fight your feelings, Paul,' continued Josh. 'Even an ugly turd like you needs a little fun sometimes.'

'You little bastard . . . '

Again, Andy's restraining hand, fighting a losing battle.

'Ten minutes,' said Paul through clenched teeth. 'Out back in the yard.'

Andy could feel Paul's body shaking with rage; there was no way he could stop him if he decided to tear the little idiot apart. What the hell was Josh thinking about? Paul would kill him for this.

Josh laughed; a curious, hollow, empty sound. He swung away, his retreating back a mocking insult. Andy had never seen him do anything like this before; he always kept well clear of Paul.

'Ten minutes,' repeated Paul again, bunching his fists. 'Ten minutes.'

Josh moved back to the bar and placed the tray there. For a few moments he and Angie stood, staring at each other and saying nothing. Then, suddenly, Josh turned and looked across at them. Slowly and deliberately he raised two fingers and gave Paul a 'V' sign.

Paul tore free from Andy's grasp and began to stalk across the nightclub.

'Oh, no . . . not here, Paul . . . for God's sake, not here.'

Josh whirled round and made for the exit leading to the back delivery yard. Paul followed. And Andy, arguing with himself that he was going to keep out of it, was going to stay in the reception and supervise the punters as he was paid to do, went after them.

* * *

It had begun to rain when Paul bustled past the exit door and out into the yard. Overhead, an arc light illuminated the brewery crates and the sacks of debris awaiting collection. Pearson had installed the light to deter potential gate-crashers or burglars. The brightly lit, rusted bins, the gleaming black plastic bags brimming with rubbish and the encrusted stone walls were a startling contrast to the streamlined chrome and chic velour of the nightclub, only feet away. But Paul was in no mood for comparisons as he stepped outside into the drizzle, looking for Josh. The little bastard was nowhere to be seen. Where was he?

Over there, behind the pile of rubbish bags.

Paul strode across, kicking a bag aside. The plastic ruptured, spilling rubbish.

Josh was not there.

Paul looked round. By the time he had finished with the little squirt, they would have to take him away in six of those black plastic bags.

'Come on out, you little git. This won't take long.'

'*I'm over here.*'

Paul whirled round as Josh stepped calmly out from behind the packing crates. Paul grinned and moved quickly forward, head down.

And then he stopped.

The yard was brightly lit by the overhead lamp and Paul could see every detail of the slight, white-shirted, black-trousered poof. The rain was soaking through Josh's shirt, revealing the spare, pink flesh beneath. His hair was plastered to his head. He was smiling. Everything about him looked familiar; everything, except the eyes. They were black, a shining, wet black; just like that stranger's eyes the night before. Paul could only stand, frozen, as Josh began to walk slowly towards him. He was unaware of the warm gush of urine on his legs as Josh advanced.

Smiling, smiling, smiling.

* * *

Andy hit the exit door with both hands. The door banged wide and he was outside before it snapped shut behind him again. His worst fears were immediately confirmed. Paul was kicking the living shit out of Josh.

Andy could not see them, but he could hear them, all right. They were behind that mound of plastic rubbish sacks; he could see the sacks heaving and shifting with every blow. There was a horrible, animal-like grunting coming from behind there. Andy saw a shoe flap into view in the rain, heard a drum-beat of legs on the solid concrete paving of the yard.

'Leave him, Paul! That's enough!'

He sprinted through the rain, dodging another sack as it fell from the pile in front of him. He braced himself to grab Paul and pull him away. Then he rounded the pile and confronted them.

Josh was crouching over Paul as he lay on the ground, arms held wide and shivering in surrender. Paul's legs were twitching spasmodically and Andy knew that it was Paul, not Josh, who was making those horrible, gurgling, *dying* sounds. Josh looked up, his face a twisted snarl, black eyes gleaming. His mouth and chin were spattered with blood—Paul's blood. Andy could see blood spurting from the ruin of Paul's throat onto the concrete, washing away in the rain. His glazed eyes had already submitted to death.

'*Oh, Jesus . . . no . . . no . . .* '

The hands that were now claws seized Andy's face, propelling him backwards; he fainted only seconds before the thing that had been Josh smashed his head against the yard wall.

Soon, two bodies lay lifeless in the rain.

But the husks would not remain empty for long.

Three

The house stood alone in a shroud of tangled willows, its crumbling walls decaying under the onslaught of the harsh Cornish winds. Whoever had built it seemed to have little regard for the ravages of weather and season. The town road petered out as the remnants of the Byker Chapter finally wound their way up onto the cliffs surrounding Mevagissey harbour. A niche had been carved from the rock overlooking the bay and the house's foundations had been laid within. The building nestled inside the niche as if it had actually grown out of the cliff, its crumbling façade facing outwards towards the sea. Once, perhaps, it had been quaint Olde English. But now it had fallen into neglect; the rutted, overgrown track that had once been the road bore testimony to the fact that the house, and whoever lived there, had been long forgotten.

Below, seagulls skimmed over the shadowed water for pieces

of fish thrown from the mackerel boats, or the discarded debris of the few holidaymakers who had braved the off-season months. It was warmer than usual today and the haze hanging over the harbour was the same colour as the sea. Together, they seemed to have blended into a vast nothingness; a blue-grey void flanked by the steeply rising rows of houses on both promontories overlooking the harbour.

When they had eventually arrived in Mevagissey after driving all night, it had seemed to Richard that the sea and the sky had vanished; that they were somehow perched on the edge of the universe, perhaps on the edge of reality itself. Finding the Ellisons' house had been easier than they had expected. They had stopped at the first pub they came across for something to eat and the landlord had given them directions at once.

'You tax collectors or something?' he had asked, with a sarcasm that seemed to be appreciated by the regular customers leaning against the bar.

'No, why?' returned Richard.

'Nobody but the grocery boy or the postman been up to the Ellisons' in donkey's years.'

'Is their daughter still living with them? Pandora Ellison?' asked Stan, perhaps too eagerly.

'Little Pandora?' Couldn't say. Ain't seem 'em for years. Could be.'

Further enquiries had elicited nothing. Finishing their meal, they had left for the Ellisons' house, but not before Richard had noticed a particular record on the jukebox: 'Layla' by Derek and the Dominoes. It seemed strange to see that Byker Chapter record on a jukebox at the edge of the world, so far from Byker. It seemed somehow portentous.

Stan was driving when they rounded the bend above the harbour and the Ellisons' house came into view. He pulled up well before they had reached the house. It was the end of their journey, and they all knew it. The shadow of the Spectre had never left them and the whispering of the sea and buffeting of the wind sounded ominous.

Richard felt Diane's hand on his arm. He grasped it. She was shivering. 'Last stop,' said Stan grimly, turning to look at them in the back seat. 'Think we'll get any answers?'

'We've got to,' said Richard determinedly, as Stan drove on.

They parked the car off the track, in an alcove at the side of the house. Willow branches tapped on the car roof. Stan strode to the dilapidated front door, grasped the ornate knocker—a grinning gargoyle—and rapped sharply, skipping from foot to foot in the same nervous manner that Richard remembered from their first meeting. The door opened without hesitation, as if whoever lived there had seen their approach and anticipated their arrival. Stan stood back apprehensively.

A frail, elderly man appeared in the doorway. His hair was thick, wiry and snow-white. Two tufts of white balanced precariously over thick spectacles. Despite a permanent stoop, he was still a tall man. His brown, knitted cardigan had been buttoned wrongly from the top button down. He seemed radiantly happy.

'Mr Ellison . . . ?' asked Stan.

'Yes . . . yes . . . '

'Err . . . my name's Stan Shaftoe. This is Richard Eden and Diane Drew. We're from Newcastle. We've come to see . . . '

'Pandora?' asked the happily agitated old man. 'Am I right? It's about Pandora?'

'Yes,' said Stan, a nervous smile creeping over his face, looking back at Richard for support.

'Yes, Mr Ellison,' said Richard steadily. 'Pandora.'

'Come in, come in.'

The door swung wide to admit them. Stan entered first and, as Richard pushed into the darkness with Diane, a moist, foetid smell assailed his nostrils. The warm, damp smell of an animal's den.

The room was dark and Richard struggled to make out the details. Somewhere a clock was chiming softly. He became aware of the elderly man fumbling in the corner. In the next instant, a standard lamp had been switched on, throwing the interior of the room into dingy relief. Richard realised that for some reason the curtains had been drawn, even though it was bright daylight outside. One wall of the room had been shelved. Rows of tattered books stretched from floor to ceiling. Other volumes lay scattered on the sparse furniture: an oak table, a small sofa, an armchair. There were four used tea-cups on the table.

'Please, please,' said the old man, 'be seated.' Flopping into the dishevelled armchair, he waved vaguely at the furniture. Diane sat nervously on the sofa, as if expecting to make a break for it at any second. Richard joined her, but Stan remained standing, still hopping nervously from foot to foot. The old man had the demeanour of someone who was about to be informed that he had won the football pools.

It became apparent that Mr Ellison was waiting for someone to speak. 'Is Pandora here?' asked Richard at last, looking curiously at the strange oak door set in the far wall. The old man appeared not to have heard.

'Well, it had to happen, didn't it?' he said. 'It's a shame, a shame. But it comes to us all, eventually. You're her Byker friends, I expect? Ah ha. Yes, a shame . . .'

'Mr Ellison,' said Richard again, carefully, 'we've come to see Pandora. It's been a long journey. Can we speak to her, please?'

Mr Ellison's expression clouded as Richard's words finally seemed to register. He looked at them in puzzlement, as if aware of their presence for the first time. He shuffled forward in his seat, scrutinising them.

'What is this?' he asked at last. His mood of euphoria appeared to have evaporated, to be replaced by a sullen, aggressive and intimidating manner. 'What do you mean, "Is Pandora here?" You know very well that she isn't here. You're here to tell me that she's dead, aren't you? You've come to tell me that our daughter has died at last.'

'Dead?' asked Stan. 'What do you mean, Mr Ellison?'

'You're her friends from Newcastle, yes? I've been waiting for you for years. I knew that you would come at last. She must be dead.'

'Mr Ellison,' said Richard, 'I went to college with Pandora. But that was ten years ago. She came back here to live, didn't she?'

'Of course she came back!' shouted the old man, now quivering with rage. 'And she brought that damned thing back with her! How could we ever forget that? But she's not here now, you know that! It's ten years since we saw her. She *must* be dead! Please tell me that she's dead. We can't live with it any more . . . ' The old man suddenly collapsed into racking sobs. 'She must be dead . . . she has to be dead . . . she has to release us . . . '

They shifted uneasily in their seats, unable to give any comfort. From somewhere in the interior of the house came the sound of a regular, muffled thumping. Mr Ellison was suddenly quiet, stifling his anguish with a stained handkerchief from his cardigan pocket. He wiped his eyes, listening intently. The thumping came again. Quickly, he left his seat and scurried to the heavy oak door in the far wall. In an instant, he had vanished from sight, closing the door behind him without a word.

'Well, what the hell do you make of that?' asked Stan, non-plussed, striding around the room, hands in the air. 'What the hell was he talking about?'

'She's obviously not here.'

'So we've wasted our time . . . ' Stan's words were cut off by the sound of raised voices from beyond the door. They could make out no words. One of the voices belonged to Mr Ellison. The other was unmistakably a muffled woman's voice.

'Could it be Pandora?' queried Diane. And then the voices ceased.

The door opened again and Mr Ellison entered. When he spoke, his voice was thick with emotion. 'She wants to see you.'

'So Pandora *is* here?' said Stan.

'No. Not Pandora. My wife, Margaret.' Mr Ellison held the door wide and beckoned to them. 'But I must ask you, please, to keep your distance. My wife suffers from a . . . disease . . . She has seen no one but myself in more than ten years. Personally, I think it's a mistake, but she wants to see you, and when she wants something, she can be a very wilful woman . . . ' Mr Ellison stifled another sob and stood, head lowered, as they rose and made their way to the door.

'Richard,' whispered Diane in his ear, 'I don't like this at all. There's something wrong about this house. Something not right. I don't think we should go in there.'

'What option do we have, Diane? We've come this far. We have to find out what this is all about.' Richard passed through first, Diane close behind and Stan last. Beyond the door was a ramshackle wooden staircase which groaned under their weight. A rusted storm-lamp hung inside the door jamb, providing just enough illumination to guide their way. The moist, sickly, damp smell was much stronger in here; the rotting timbers leading upwards reminded Richard of the interior of an ancient galleon. At the top of the stairs was another storm-lamp, hanging above a landing. A door stood open, throwing another feeble wedge of light onto the bare wooden floor. Behind them, Richard heard Mr Ellison gently closing the door. Subconsciously he waited to hear a key turning in the lock, imprisoning them inside forever. There was no sound. At the top of the stairs, he reached out and touched the second door. Mildew coated the rough, stone wall. Inside was a single chair, a small table and, in the far corner beside a shuttered window, a four-poster bed. A moth-eaten, threadbare blanket had been hung from the tester overhead, screening the occupant.

'Come in,' said a muffled voice from the bed.

A candle had been lit and was standing on the shuttered window-sill. Its bare light cast the shadow of the woman in the bed against the blanket that screened her from view.

'There's only one seat, I'm afraid, but please try to make yourselves comfortable.'

Diane looked at the matted, stained chair and could not bring herself to sit on it. Stan perched himself on one arm-rest. Diane kept close to the door, dreading what her reaction might be if it suddenly swung shut.

'Arnold tells me that you are all friends of Pandora from Newcastle.'

'That's right, Mrs Ellison,' said Richard. 'We were all very close some years ago. Where is she now? Your husband seemed to think that . . . '

'My husband,' said Mrs Ellison reflectively. 'Poor Arnold is not quite right in his mind, I'm afraid. He has been praying for Pandora's death for many years now. He thinks that her death will end our suffering. Poor man. He knows so little. He used to be so strong. And now . . . well, now . . . '

'Where is she, Mrs Ellison?' asked Stan. 'It's very important that we find her.'

'Something evil has marked you for death. I know it. And you are right to search for Pandora. But she is not here.'

'How did you know . . . ?' began Richard.

'I have been waiting for many years now for the horror to begin. It is strong enough now, I think. You are the ones who called yourselves the Byker Chapter, am I right?'

'That's right,' said Richard quietly. 'What is happening to us, Mrs Ellison?'

The shadow behind the blanket quivered in a palsy of diseased coughing. Eventually, it began to speak again. 'I knew that you would come here at last, seeking the truth. But I am afraid that it will do you no good now. It has had ten years to grow strong. What is happening to you? Well, you are dying, are you not? But why? And how? These are the questions to which you seek answers. Very well. Listen . . . '

There was a long pause and the sound of fumbling as Mrs Ellison pulled herself into a more upright position. Richard had the impression that she had prepared herself for this speech for many years. Finally, the shadow began to speak again:

'You think that you knew my daughter very well. She was a popular girl. She wrote to me quite often when she started college in Newcastle, told me all about her friends in Byker. I was glad that she was happy and I could tell that she had completely pushed to the back of her mind the terrible thing that happened to her when she was a child. Of course, it was our fault that it happened, but . . . I am digressing . . . She was a good, normal, happy girl at college. Or so I convinced myself. But she had not overcome her experience. It had remained with her, hidden deep inside.

'My husband and I were foolish when we were younger. Extremely foolish. Arnold was an attractive man and I . . . I was once a very beautiful woman. At that time we were, as they say, persons of "independent means": a bequest from Arnold's aunt. We squandered it. Our tastes were excessive; we indulged ourselves at every opportunity. We were very popular then, and we attracted people with the same penchant for extravagance. If we wanted something or someone, we obtained it. Our greed became excessive, our desires more and more outrageous.

'At a time when we had become bored with our range of . . . experience, shall I say? . . . we met Hugh Barnard. We had heard of his unsavoury reputation, of course. Respectable people shunned his company. But this very fact drew us to him and his circle of friends.

'Barnard's forte was mysticism. In the popular journals, they refer to it as "black magic". Both Arnold and myself were convinced that he was a sham and that his elaborate pretence was a put-on for his friends. Nevertheless, we began to join in his "parties", going along with the whole rigmarole. It was exciting and amusing. It gave Arnold and myself an opportunity for interesting sex with a number of different people. That was the big attraction. Barnard, of course, took the whole thing very seriously. "Hurling the Stone", he called it. You are familiar with the term? Perhaps not. It's an elaborate sexual ritual, where both partners throw out power and achieve their wishes at the point of orgasm.'

Diane shuffled uneasily at the old woman's unusually forthright language. Somehow, it did not seem right. And her words were chilling Diane to the bone. She pushed closer to Richard.

Mrs Ellison continued: 'Barnard's parties provided us both with the special thrill we were looking for. We never believed for one moment that he was completely serious about everything he said. The sex and the drugs, the play-acting, the rituals and the dressing-up—it was all part of a new diversion for us. Barnard used to tell us that "Hurling the Stone" was only a mild form of something much greater which he intended to prepare; something he called the "Ritual of the Scarlet Woman". He was a great believer in Alasteir Crowley—probably the most notorious magician of modern times—who claimed to have established contact with what he called "transmundane entities", also known as the "Deep Ones'. He had personally perfected the ritual, Barnard claimed, which involved sexual relations with a carefully selected female member of a coven, who was supposed to take on the symbolic form of a gateway to the void. As I understood it, the intention was to establish an opening in space through which outside forces—the "Deep Ones"—could enter and become manifest on earth. Barnard told us that the thing he was trying to bring to earth had once existed here thousands of years ago. In myth, it was known as the Gorgon . . .'

The Gorgon, thought Richard. *The creature with snakes instead of hair. It could turn anyone looking at its face to stone.* He felt Diane's grip tighten on his arm. He remembered the ectoplasmic, snake-like tentacles from the television and the monstrosity in the fog.

'Of course,' continued the old woman, 'I never believed any of it. But I guessed from the way that Barnard looked at me when he told me the tale that it was all a device to allow him to sleep with me. But Barnard wasn't thinking that, at all. He believed every word of his tale. And if I'd known then what I know now, I would have killed him there and then.

'He teased us all about the Scarlet Woman. Who was it going to be? Who was going to have the honour? He told us that he had studied the alignments of the stars, he had discovered the correct form of the ritual which Crowley had devised. He even sacrificed a rabbit and drank the blood! Right here, in this house. How we all laughed.

'A night was chosen for the Ritual. I felt sure that he had chosen me.

'Then, when Pandora didn't come home from school that day, I knew what had happened. I think I'd known all along that Barnard was insane. But I never believed that the scum would do anything to hurt Pandora. She was only a child, ten years old. She was missing for two days. Of course, we went straight to the police and told them about Barnard. When they got to his house, everything, including Barnard, had gone. There was a massive police search; road blocks, everything. But they never found him and we never heard anything about him again. And then, just when we'd given up hope of seeing Pandora alive, she turned up on our doorstep, ragged and dishevelled as if she had been out there on the cliffs for the entire two days. She was suffering from exposure, she had been beaten.

'And, of course, she had been raped.

'We never told the police about Barnard's rituals. We would have been too deeply implicated ourselves in other . . . incidents . . . We never told them that he had used Pandora in his Ritual of the Scarlet Woman. But we fabricated something that made it plain Barnard was responsible for her abduction and assault.

'Pandora couldn't remember anything that had happened to her. She had blocked it all out of her mind, or else Barnard had somehow been able to make her forget. The last thing she did remember was leaving school for home. Her next memory was of reaching home, dazed and tired. Thank God she had been spared the memory of whatever happened to her at Barnard's house.

'The police doctor told us that she would have to have hospital treatment. Not only had she been raped, but things had . . . had been done to her . . . things inside . . . After two operations, we knew that Pandora would never be able to have a child.

'We did everything we could to protect her. We had always hidden our worst excesses from her; we wanted her to grow up normally. We encouraged her. She managed to put the bad time behind her. When she wanted to move away from home, away from Cornwall, we encouraged her in that, too. When she was awarded a place at a college in Newcastle, she was overjoyed. It seemed so far away, a chance to spread her wings. In that we also encouraged her.

'Years passed. The shadow of what had happened to Pandora changed Arnold and myself. The fire inside us had died. We realised that it was for the best. We tried to change our lives. Pandora kept in constant contact with us from college and we were glad that she was so happy. That's how we came to find out about the Byker Chapter. She was confident that she would pass her final examinations.

'Then, in that final week, something changed. Her letters seemed to be written by a different person. They were rambling . . . vague . . . troubled . . . She told us that she was losing confidence and she didn't know why. At first, I thought it was examination pressure. But then it became apparent that it was worse, much worse than that. Something was happening to Pandora. Her letters became vicious, obscene, threatening. It seemed as if she was having some kind of nervous breakdown. She threatened to kill us if we came up to Newcastle to see her. I was convinced that she was losing her mind. Then, everything changed again. She apologised for her previous behaviour, telling us that it had been stress. Everything was fine. She was confident again, just like the Pandora we knew and loved. But I wasn't completely convinced that everything was all right. The shadow of what had happened to her had always stayed with me. I felt, somehow, as if everything was coming to a head.

'Without any warning, she arrived on our doorstep at the end of term. Something was wrong. I could tell by her eyes. She had come home for good, she said, because that was where she belonged. But she was different. She was changed.

'And, God help me, she was pregnant.'

There was another long pause. The shadow behind the curtain had hung its head and Richard thought that he heard a stifled sob. The candlelight guttered and the shadow swelled grotesquely. Beside him, Diane's face was pure white in the faint light. Stan's expression was firmly set. The shadow coughed and spat phlegm.

'Of course, it was not possible for Pandora to conceive. We knew that categorically. It was just not physically possible. I knew that that monster Barnard's depraved corruption of my daughter was responsible. In one of her lucid moments, she told me that something had happened to her at college in that last week of term. Something inside had compelled her to do it. Something inexplicable. Any one of those men could be the father, she had no way of knowing. Filled with guilt, when that strange possession left her, she had fled back home. Back home to me . . . her mother. God forgive me, that her mother could be responsible for this.

'Barnard's ritual had failed. He had wanted to use my own daughter, my own virginal daughter, as his Gateway. He wanted her to give birth to one of the "Deep Ones"—the Gorgon—but he had failed. And in that failure, he had rendered her incapable of ever conceiving her own child. But Barnard had sown the seed and it had lain dormant for years. It had blossomed again, years later, making Pandora re-enact the ritual; making her take lovers . . . yes, *you* . . . her lovers . . . so that your own seed could help give life to the One Beyond. I knew that she could not be carrying a human child. Oh yes, you are all fathers of that thing which she carried . . . but the real father was the one who fed upon your seed from beyond and used it to achieve its own rebirth through Pandora—the Gorgon.

'We could not let anyone know, of course. I knew the child would have to be delivered at home, delivered by me. We kept Pandora with us. She never really understood, poor child. The pregnancy was not easy. It was not a normal child. It was the essence of the Gorgon, one of the Deep Ones . . . '

* * *

Pandora's white face was beaded with sweat. Her eyes seemed fixed on some inner point, perhaps on the focal point of the pain itself—her as yet unborn child—as Margaret moved her daughter gently to the bed. Pandora gave one short, sharp intake of breath through gritted teeth as she was helped onto the counterpane. The contractions began again.

Downstairs, in the kitchen, Pandora's father knelt on the floor in the centre of a chalked pentagram. Black candles guttered flame. Outside, in the night, a chill wind from the sea rattled at the window-panes. He drew a jewelled knife from the scabbard lying on the floor before him. The keen edge of the blade felt like ice on the flesh of his arm. Blood ran freely, dripping onto the floor within the pentagram.

'*Protect us this night . . .*'

Upstairs, Margaret dabbed at Pandora's brow, her hand shaking. Her daughter's face seemed sculpted from marble. Mechanically, instinctively and with no prompting from Margaret, Pandora was now fully into labour. There was a bottle of gin on the bedside table. Margaret picked it up and drank deeply, wiping a trembling hand across her mouth. Tonight was the culmination of nine months of fear. As Pandora had become increasingly withdrawn, sitting night after night in silence as if contemplating the life that grew inside her, Margaret's inner fear had also been growing. As one had grown, so had the other—like identical twins growing separately in different mothers. Margaret prayed that Arnold was performing the ritual correctly downstairs. There was no margin for error in any of the invocations if protection was to be assured.

Pandora was clenching fistfuls of the blanket, her back arching, dragging in and forcing out lungfuls of air. The baby was coming.

'That's the way, Pandora! That's the way!' *Protect us this night from the unborn.*

Pandora was trying to speak now, trying to vocalise her rapid, desperate breathing. 'Muh . . . Muh . . . Muh . . . MOTHER!'

The scream fed the fear inside Margaret. She was shaking with terror, but something drew her forward to bend down between her daughter's widespread legs.

'*Mother . . . help me . . . help . . .*' Pandora writhed, sweat glistening on her face. Margaret was reaching downwards, watching her own hands as if they belonged to someone else. A head was emerging. Some force was impelling Margaret as her hands touched the small, glistening dome. The baby began to slide outwards.

It's all right! thought Margaret frantically. *Everything's all right! It's a baby, that's all. Just a baby . . .*

And then she really saw what it was.

Where is its face? WHERE IS ITS FACE?

She sensed only vaguely that she was staggering away from the bed; that she was holding aloft the thing that had just been born, and that she was screaming. Screaming, screaming, screaming—like a mad woman. Vaguely, she was aware that her body was juddering and spasming as if she were having a fit. Something had swarmed into her body, into her brain: a terrifying, pulsating, living power; a power that emanated from the *thing* she was holding—except that she was not holding it, it was holding *her*. And that power was coursing through her mind, surging through her nervous system, pulsing in her veins. It was probing, searching and examining.

'*God help me . . . help me . . . what do you want? Leave me alone . . . please . . . PLEASE!*'

Sexless, indiscriminate, hungry to live, it swarmed and analysed, taking from her what it needed. She could sense now that it had chosen. She was a woman; it would be a boy. It began to take what it required. She could feel the thing examining the living tissue of her body, her vital organs, her heart, her brain.

Her face.

'*No . . . please . . . no . . .*'

A savage, muffling darkness descended on Margaret. She was drowning in a black, poisonous, suffocating mire. The screaming was now only in her mind. Vaguely, before consciousness left her, she became aware of another noise. The lustful, healthy crying of a new-born baby . . .

* * *

The old woman had gone silent, engrossed in her terrible memories. They waited for her to continue. When she did not, Richard spoke up.

'What is it, Mrs Ellison?' His voice sounded dry and rusty. 'What is the Gorgon? We know the legend, I think, about the woman—Medusa—who could turn people into stone . . . '

'Forget the myths!' snapped the woman, breaking from her trance. 'The Gorgon is Master and Mistress of the Shape-Changers. You have heard of shape-changers, of course? Such creatures have existed since the dawn of time. They have lived here with us in the dark places of the world, the dark places of the soul. Once, they were called vampires or werewolves. Barnard dismissed these as minor entities only, able to change their form in a very limited way. He told us that the Gorgon had once presided over the shape-changers here on Earth, before its physical body was slain and its spirit sent to limbo with the other Old Gods. The Gorgon was the Supreme Shape Changer . . . for the Gorgon had no real form of its own . . . it could change the shape of other things . . . could inhabit other things and make them do its bidding . . . '

My God, thought Richard. *The dummy. The bear.* And then suddenly he realised with alarm that Diane was moaning. He turned to see her weaving from side to side, her eyes closed. She staggered, putting one hand to the wall to steady herself. Quickly, Richard held her; how cold her flesh seemed, she was shivering.

'The Gorgon could give shape to the shapeless,' continued Mrs Ellison, 'life to the inanimate. If it could be born here again . . . '

'The Gorgon . . . the Spectre . . . ' Diane began to speak as if in a trance. Richard tried to shake her out of it, but whatever force was compelling her had taken over. 'That which has no form or substance. That which does not physically exist. Yet it wishes, it hungers, to exist, above all else. It is evil. What better way to live than in man's discarded dreams, hopes and desires? Man fashions life in clay, in paint and stone. He bequeaths a secondary life to the inanimate. A motive force within him is to create. This unholy thing takes the images and brings them to life. And if this formless, shapeless thing which craves life could be born into the real world, what then? If the circumstances were right, might not that which was formless have form, that which was shapeless be given shape? Incomplete, yes; but able to grow. Able to feed on that which has given it life. And having no *self*, it must feed and grow on the personalities, the individualities of its fathers. The Sins of the Fathers . . . ' Diane slumped against Richard in a dead faint.

'She knows!' exclaimed the old woman in an excited, asthmatic wheeze. 'She has the sight! The Gorgon *was* born again—here, in this house. I delivered it myself. And I know what manner of thing it is. I know that it has been building strength over the years. Weak at first, it must kill and absorb the fathers who gave it life. It must kill you all before it can really be free, before it can attain the full power that will enable it to live here forever.'

'How can we stop it?' asked Stan.

'Stop it? Stop it?' laughed Mrs Ellison. 'But you can't stop it. Don't you see? You *must* die. How can you stop something that is able to do this on the very instant that it is born . . . ?'

With a billow of mildewed dust, the shadow suddenly ripped aside the blanket that screened it. Stan was the first to see it properly as it thrust its face towards them. With an involuntary cry of nausea, he recoiled from the bed. At first, the deeper shadow hid it from Richard's view as he struggled to hold the semi-conscious Diane. When he did focus on it, he was glad that Diane could not see.

'You see? You see?' croaked Mrs Ellison. 'And you think that you will be able to stop it?'

The shared nightmare of the Byker Chapter had become real as they stared at the hideous spectacle of a face that had been *wiped smooth like potter's clay*. The old woman's eyes and nose were gone, leaving only a smooth, pink mask with a ragged gash for a mouth. She was gasping for breath, making a mewing sound that could have been laughter or grief, as she pulled the blanket back to hide her terrible non-face.

'It took what it needed from me,' wheezed the hideous form behind the blanket. 'It took what it needed to live from inside me. *And then it took my face!'* Richard remembered the dreams of smooth, featureless faces and felt ill.

Hurried footsteps clattered on the staircase outside. The door swung wide and Mr Ellison stood there. In his hands, he held a double-barrelled shotgun.

'I knew that it was a mistake, Margaret! Get out, all of you! Get out of here before I kill you!'

Richard bundled Diane past the old man, noticing the mad glittering in his eyes as he moved the barrel of the shotgun back and forth between Stan and himself. The old woman was still making that asthmatic tittering sound that filled him with revulsion. Stan came over to him and together they helped Diane down the rickety wooden stairs to the main room. Behind them came muttered voices, followed once again by the unhealthy gasping noise. The bedroom door slammed and Richard heard Mr Ellison descending. He had no wish to remain in this house any longer. Somehow, he sensed that it could only do Diane more harm to stay here. She had been right, there was an unhealthy influence in the house; they had to get away. He blundered across the room, upsetting a small table and scattering empty tea-cups on the floor. He had just reached the door when he heard a commotion behind him. With Diane's arm still over his shoulder, he turned and saw that Stan had hidden behind the door at the bottom of the stairs. As Mr Ellison passed into the living-room, he had seized the barrel of the shotgun, twisted it out of his grip and pushed him back into the armchair. The old man crumpled there like a bag of rags.

'Leave it, Stan!' shouted Richard, only wanting to get away from the place as quickly as possible.

'No, Richard! We can't just leave it!' Stan levelled the shotgun at Mr Ellison's face so that the barrel was only a couple of inches from his nose. He shrank back into his seat, trying to push himself as far away from the gun as possible.

'Listen, old man . . . ' Stan held the gun firmly. 'I've no intention of letting this thing just pick us off one by one. There must be a way to stop it. Now . . . your wife told us that Pandora came back here to have a . . . a . . . *baby*. What happened after the baby was born? Where did she go after that?'

'You can't fool me with stupid questions! I don't know what else you want, but you know very well where she is . . . '

Stan pulled back the hammers on the shotgun with a brittle and threatening click.

'*Where is she?*'

'But you know where she is,' blurted the old man. 'She's been living in Byker. She went back to live there after the . . . thing . . . was born. She manages a nightclub on Byker Bank. A nightclub called the Imperial.'

'Oh, my God . . .' said Richard faintly. 'Oh, my God . . .' She had been there all along. They had hunted for her while something inhuman had hunted for them. And all the time, she had been almost on their doorstep.

The Imperial.

'The Woman,' said Richard.

Four

It was night-time. They had been driving for hours.

'We'll have to stop.' Richard turned the car up the slip-road from the motorway. A neon sign beckoned just ahead: '*Food. Petrol. Motel.*' 'Even if it's just for coffee. We can't go on at this rate. We'll be burned out before we get to Newcastle. After this stop, we can take turns driving and sleeping.'

'You're right,' grunted Stan from the back seat. 'We need some rest before we . . . '

Before we what? The thought hung heavily, unspoken.

There were plenty of parking spaces in the quadrangle behind the service station. Richard swung past three cars and then about ten motor-cycles which were propped haphazardly against the service station wall. He parked beside them. Seconds later, they were ascending the staircase in the multi-purpose block, following two arrows on the wall which directed them to the cafeteria. Their experience at the Ellisons' house had drained them physically and mentally; a persistent headache had throbbed behind Diane's eyes ever since. She pinched her temples between thumb and forefinger as they reached the cafeteria door.

'Are you all right, Diane?' Richard was instantly concerned.

'Yes . . . ' she replied weakly. 'But we have to be careful, Richard. It's very close to us. Not in the physical sense. But *psychically*, it's very close. We can't afford to take any chances.'

'The child,' said Richard remotely.

'*Our* child,' echoed Stan.

They entered the cafeteria. The harsh, bright light in the antiseptic, tiled room made them squint as they pushed past rows of empty chairs and tables. The cafeteria was empty, except for a huddle of black-leather-jacketed motorcyclists—presumably the owners of the machines in the car park—crowded round the tables nearest to the serving counter. An exasperated woman in an apron was trying to understand the garbled order of a straggle-haired girl in jeans and teeshirt. The girl seemed unsteady on her feet: drunk or drugged, or both.

Stan volunteered to go and get the coffees. Richard chose a table and Diane and he clambered into the tubular-frame chairs. Richard took Diane's hands across the table and squeezed.

'It's like being in a nightmare and not being able to wake up,' said Diane at last. Richard could feel the involuntary shuddering that suddenly gripped her—as if a bitter wind had suddenly swept into the room.

'You sure you're okay?'

'I felt it back there, somehow. I could feel how *hungry* it is; how hungry it is to have us dead.'

'How in God's name do we stop it?'

A sudden disturbance at the serving counter drew their attention. Two of the black-jackets appeared to be jostling Stan as he moved away from the counter with three coffees on a tray. Stan said something to one of them, who spat at his feet and gave a two-fingered 'V' sign. The other black-jackets began to laugh. Stan moved off towards Richard and Diane.

'What's wrong?' asked Richard when he joined them.

Stan shot a fierce glare at the black-jackets as he handed out the coffee. 'Bikers. Hell's Angels—I don't know. Just trying to hassle me.'

The black-jackets were silent now, staring sullenly in their direction. The straggle-haired girl was standing, head down, swaying from side to side as if dancing to inaudible music. Richard could feel their surly mood and did not like it. Three of the bikers rose from their tables and moved slowly towards them. Richard and Stan watched all the way as they passed, the bikers' eyes dulled with drugs or booze and full of the threat of mindless violence. They stopped at the cigarette machine by the exit, where one of them began to fumble for change in his jeans pocket.

All at once the cafeteria was filled with the sound of strident, heavy-metal music, a guitar solo shrieking harshly—someone down at the front had switched on a radio. The black-jackets' resentful glare was now turned away from them. Richard felt Diane's sudden, intense grip on his fingers.

'Oh, God, Richard. They've got a radio. *It'll find us!*'

Richard spun round to face the bikers.

'Excuse me. Could you turn the radio off, please?'

The hostile stares were now redirected towards them. One of the bikers, a hunched, bearded man with 'Motorhead' stitched on the back of his studded jacket, leaned over to the radio and turned it up. Reverberating keyboards joined the screeching guitar.

'*Please? Will you turn it off?*' shouted Diane.

One of the black-jackets hawked and spat on the floor.

'Shit!' said Stan. 'Come on. We've got to get out.'

Quickly, they pushed back their seats. Diane's coffee cup clattered over; a steaming brown pool spread on the table.

'*It's coming, Richard!*' exclaimed Diane. '*It's hunting!*'

They hurried towards the exit door. Richard saw the three black-jackets standing beside the cigarette machine, leaning in the exit door-frame, and knew what was coming next.

'What's wrong, then?' said an acne-covered face as they drew level. 'Don't you like our music?' The black-jackets were blocking their escape.

'Can we get past, please?' asked Richard. Behind him, he became aware of shuffling feet as the other black-jackets left their tables by the counter and began to come up behind them. The music was growing louder. They were bringing the radio with them.

Stan moved forward threateningly. From nowhere, steel glittered in one of the bikers' fists and Stan stopped. The biker grinned and began to pare dirt from under a fingernail with the wicked-looking object in his hand. Richard could see that it was a steel comb. The teeth had been removed to form a grip. The end of the handle had been sharpened to a stiletto tip.

'It knows we're here,' said Diane evenly. '*It's coming!*'

'We don't want trouble,' continued Richard. 'Please, we just want to leave.' For a second, he recognised Joe's glazed stare in one of the biker's eyes; recognised also the cold, inherent brutality that he had seen in the eyes of the bouncer at the Imperial nightclub.

Diane twisted round, gasping, and Richard turned to see that the other bikers were directly behind them. One of the men had bent down, put a hand between Diane's legs and cupped her sex. The others giggled or brayed laughter. There was a loud *whack!* as Diane hit the man across the face, making him stagger away, clutching his cheek. The laughing stopped. The man took his hand away from his face and Richard could see the rosy imprint of the slap on an unhealthy white skin.

'*Get them!*' shouted one of the bikers. And then everything started to happen.

Stan jerked an elbow backwards and Richard heard the crunch as it flattened a bearded biker's nose. He reeled backwards, clutching his face. The steel comb whickered in the air. Richard grabbed the arm and wrist wielding the improvised knife and spun wrestling away. Somewhere in the background, the waitress was screaming: 'Police! Police! I'll call the police if you don't . . . ' A table crashed. Stan was rolling on the floor as two of the black-jackets started to lash at him with their feet. Dimly, Richard was aware of Diane grappling with the straggle-haired girl who was shrieking like a banshee. He whirled the biker away from him. His opponent staggered and slipped on the tiled floor but quickly regained his balance. They squared up to each other. Then the biker grinned as Richard's arms were suddenly pinioned from behind. Richard struggled and kicked to no avail. The biker with the 'knife' began to move slowly forward, grinning, licking his lips. The heavy-metal music blasted insanely . . .

Overhead, the strobe lights suddenly flickered and grew dim. Shadows leaped and crawled on the tiled floor.

'*Richard!*' It was Diane's voice, mortally fearful. '*It's here! It's found us!*'

The lights went out.

The heavy-metal music spiralled away to a garbled squeak and was abruptly snuffed out. Richard became aware that the fighting had stopped.

Somewhere on his left, a new light began to glow. The grip on his arms was suddenly gone and he spun away, grabbing Diane's hand and pulling her back. He turned to look at the source of the light.

It was the radio.

One of the bikers had placed it on a nearby table. Now, it was pulsing with luminous blue light and Richard could hear distant, crackling static growing steadily louder. Stan was on his feet, backing off. The black-jackets seemed entranced by this strange phenomenon; one of them was actually smiling as if, somehow, his music had come to life. The growing static began to resolve itself into a terrifying, familiar noise: the sibilant hissing of hungry snakes; an obscene, avid gobbling. Even as they watched, glowing electric-blue tendrils swarmed from the radio speaker, crawling over and encircling the radio like some barbed, living cage.

Richard pulled Diane away step by step, icy terror in his veins. Diane seemed as entranced by the spectacle as the black-jackets. The girl with the straggling hair was laughing, stepping forward, arms outstretched towards the radio.

'No! Don't!' exclaimed Stan, now at Richard's side.

It was too late.

The girl touched the radio with both hands; laughing, laughing, laughing. Then the laughter became a high-pitched, desperate screaming as crackling, hissing blue coils swarmed over her hands and curled upwards over her arms. The black-jackets stood transfixed in horror while the ravenous, swarming terror rapidly engulfed the girl's writhing body in a smothering embrace.

'*Come on!*' Richard heard himself yelling. Pulling Diane with him, Stan grabbing her other arm, they blundered towards the exit. Blue-black shadow flickered and crawled on the walls amid crackling flashes of light from the radio. The manic hissing, rattling and gobbling was growing steadily louder. The girl's dreadful screams were rising to an unbearable pitch as they burst through the double doors and clattered down the stairs.

They ran across the tarmac towards their car. Looking back, Richard saw the upper windows of the cafeteria flickering with flashes of blue lightning, as if an electric storm was raging inside. Even from here, he could hear the angry hissing of the

Spectre and the terrified screams of the other black-jackets as the thing swarmed and spread hungrily.

In seconds, they were in the car; it started immediately. Richard reversed out quickly and swung the car towards the car park exit in a screeching swerve, leaving a track of burned rubber behind. They would have to pass below the cafeteria windows and he cast an anxious glance upwards as they roared past.

A blur of motion and the sound of distant screaming was followed by an explosive shattering of glass.

'*Look out!*' yelled Diane.

The torn, twisted figure of a biker slammed with horrifying impact onto the car bonnet.

'*Bloody hell!*' Richard swerved, crumpling the left wing of the car against the cafeteria wall. The biker's broken body rolled from the bonnet, arms flapping lifelessly, and was gone from sight. Richard floored the accelerator. In top gear, the car hurtled out of the parking lot and down the slip road towards the highway.

Soon, the horror in the cafeteria was far behind them.

* * *

Their car broke down just outside Darlington; it coughed and wheezed to a standstill in a layby. To Diane it seemed just another nail in the coffin of that terrible destiny that awaited them. They had talked and debated all the way back from Mevagissey without arriving at a definite course of action. But of one thing they were sure: they had to get back to Newcastle, fast. They had no idea how much time they had left; but the hovering shadow of the Spectre seemed ever-present, watching, waiting, toying with them. After thirty minutes under the car hood, Stan pronounced the engine unserviceable and they caught the first available train to Newcastle.

'What the hell *do* we do?' said Stan after a long pause, as the train sped onwards to their destination. 'We've been over it all so many times, but we're still no further forward. How are we going to stop it?'

'She said it couldn't be stopped,' said Richard.

'Well, screw that!' snapped Stan. 'I won't believe it. There must be a way.' His furious burst of energy was good for them, revitalising. But there was still no solution to their dilemma.

'The child,' murmured Diane as if it were their answer. 'It all revolves around the child.'

'But what kind of child?' asked Stan. 'Richard told you about Mrs Ellison's face. What the hell kind of child can do that to somebody the moment that it's born?'

'We've been talking about this for hours,' said Richard steadily. 'But we all know that there's only one thing we can do. We have to go back to the Imperial. We have to meet this thing face to face.'

'And then it'll kill us,' said Stan matter-of-factly.

Richard rapped a bunched fist on the table. 'There's nothing else we can do. The only other alternative is to keep on running or to lock ourselves away. And you know yourself that running or hiding isn't going to stop it. Sooner or later it'll get us anyway.'

'The devil or the deep blue sea,' said Diane.

'It's the devil, all right,' said Richard. 'A devil of our own making.'

Stan bumped the canvas bag beneath him with his foot to make sure that it was still there. Inside were the two pistols and the shotgun which he had taken from Mr Ellison. The feel of solid, destructive metal was only faintly reassuring. But it was reassurance, nevertheless. He was unsure just how much impact a double-barrelled shotgun would have on a shape-changing phantom, but he would not have swapped it for a bunch of garlic cloves, a crucifix or a phial of Holy Water.

The air in Newcastle Central Station seemed frozen with the breath of winter. They made straight for the taxi rank through crowds of milling, Monday morning commuters. Richard sidestepped a man with a strangely haunted face and a walking-stick—he looked like a walking phantom—and hurried Diane into the nearest taxi.

The Spectre was waiting for them here in Newcastle as the taxi roared away towards the other side of town. They could feel it every inch of the way. It lurked in the shadows and the dark places of office blocks, shops and car parks. It stood watching from every street corner. It glanced from every flitting reflection in each passing shop window. They could feel its touch on their minds and in their souls.

It's here and it's always been here. It's waiting. It has time. It doesn't have to rush. Richard knew these things and, looking at the others, he knew instinctively that they knew it, too. But more than anything else, he knew with mounting fear that the thing . . . the Spectre . . . the Gorgon . . . was *aware* of them. *It knows we're back. It's just sitting there, waiting for us to return. Because if we don't come to it, then it will come to us.*

They stopped at Diane's flat so that she could change her clothes and they could grab something to eat. The food tasted like ashes in their mouths. Their next port of call would be Richard's flat, and then . . .

And then we face the Nightmare.

Five

For the past six weeks, business for Harrow Electrics had not been good. Apart from really minor jobs, repairing domestic appliances, there had been hardly anything at all. The situation made Eric Harrow very depressed, which meant that 50 per cent of Harrow Electrics' workforce was in the doldrums. The other 50 per cent, Tony Jameson, was not exactly a barrel of laughs, either. Not a soul had been into their small shop on Shields Road for three days, except for one little guy who had wandered in by mistake, looking for a newsagent. Things were pretty depressing, with the rent and electricity bills to be paid.

Which was why Harrow Electrics had been ready to spring promptly into action when the telephone rang on Saturday and the Under-Manager of the Imperial nightclub asked if they would be able to undertake a job requiring prompt and speedy attention. Eric had lived in Byker for most of his life but, strangely, had never been to the Imperial during its incarnation as a nightclub. He had seen a few films there when it had been a cinema, but that was all. Pearson seemed a strange sort of fellow, but was obviously someone who knew what he wanted. The Imperial was undergoing a change of management; could Harrow Electrics replace the neon sign on the frontage of the nightclub by Monday?

'Well . . . I don't know, Mr Pearson. Neon signs are a bit tricky, you know. It's not like changing a fuse or something . . .'

'I require a replacement urgently. If you are not able to meet this deadline, then I shall have to find someone who can. Good day.'

'No! Wait just a second, Mr Pearson. I'm sure that we can work something out. I suppose it really depends on how elaborate you want it and whether we can get the materials together.'

'Monday, Mr Harrow?'

'Yeah . . . yeah . . . first thing on Monday morning, we'll be there.'

'Good, I wish to have the work completed to celebrate a change of management. It is imperative that it should be ready for the evening.'

Pearson had agreed to Eric's first estimate, which was deliberately and grossly inflated. The money was staggering, but Pearson had accepted without question. How the hell could they possibly afford to miss out on a chance like this? And so it was that Eric and Tony found themselves working on the frontage of the Imperial throughout Monday. The neon name sign had been easier to arrange than Eric had assumed. Pearson's requirements were not too elaborate, using basic tube filaments, nothing fancy. All he required was a simple name change for the nightclub. As they worked on the scaffolding which had been hastily erected at the front, Tony had said: 'Funny bloody name for a nightclub, innit?'

'Not really. What's so strange about it?'

'I dunno. It just seems funny, that's all.'

'Well, what about all the other nightclubs in Newcastle? Some of them have got funny names, haven't they?'

Tony had said no more, but Eric sensed that he was in a strange mood. Maybe he had been having another argument with Yvonne? Best leave him alone and he would come out of it.

Tony had been trying to shake off a bad feeling all day. He could not put his finger on it, but ever since Eric had taken on this job, he had felt . . . well . . . *creepy*—that was the only word he could find to describe it. He had only felt like that once before in his life: a few years ago, when he had felt for two days that something bad had happened, before the news came through that his brother had been killed by an Exocet missile in the Falkland Islands. Tony had *known* that something had happened, perhaps he had even known *before* it had happened. He had that same feeling now as he worked on the electrics of the Imperial.

On top of everything else, his imagination was playing tricks on him. Just beyond and below where they worked, he could see right through the glass frontage of the nightclub. Everything inside was black as pitch, but Tony could not shake off the feeling that there were people in there, standing together silently in the darkness, watching them as they worked on the new sign. Once, he was sure that he had seen the outline of a head. But, of course, that was bloody stupid. Why the hell would people stand there in the dark like that, just watching? It was crazy! Even so, he was glad when the work was completed. Was it just coincidence that Pearson walked out of the night-club onto the street at the instant they had finished and were starting to take down the scaffolding? Eric had been the one to check the internal wiring. Tony had remained outside in the street, refusing to go inside. Pearson paid them cash in hand and Eric was over the moon about the fee. The old idiot had even paid them a bonus for finishing ahead of time! But Tony could not share Eric's enthusiasm when Pearson offered free tickets for the new management's opening night. Eric took six, but Tony did not want any. He had something else to do that night. *Like staying at home, locking the door, having a few cans of lager and refusing to open up, no matter who says they're out there knocking on it.*

As they were packing away their gear into the van, Tony could not bring himself to look Pearson in the eye. There was something unnatural about those eyes, something not quite right. He left all the talking to Eric. He had already moved off to the van when he overheard Pearson's last conversation with Eric. Their words somehow only intensified that bad feeling.

'So you will bring your friends tonight, Mr Harrow?'

'You bet. Never been to the Imperial before.'

'But it's not the Imperial now, of course. Is it?'

'Oh, yeah!' laughed Eric. 'I forgot.'

'I can promise you an evening you won't forget. It will be a very special night tonight.'

'I can hardly wait, Mr Pearson. I intend to have one hell of a night.'

'Oh yes, Mr Harrow,' said Pearson. 'I think I can promise you that.'

Six

'Can you feel it?' asked Stan.

'Yes,' replied Richard, ' ... yes ... It's attacking ... attacking my mind. It's trying to break down my mental defence.'

'It wants us to lose hope, Richard. It wants us to despair.'

'It's launching a *spiritual* assault, just as it did on Phil and the others.'

'All the times we've been suffering depressive bouts, all the times we've felt that we were going slowly out of our minds—it's been the Spectre. Hunting us down. Draining us.'

'We can fight it! We've got to fight it ... '

'Oh, my God, Richard ... '

'What? What is it, Diane?'

'Look ... the photograph ... you and Stan ... you're both ... starting to fade ... It's barely perceptible, but if you look closely enough ... '

'Phil ... Barry ... Joe ... Derek ... All dead. All vanished from the photograph as if they'd never been. It's bloody insane.'

'Do we sit and wait for it to find us, Stan? Or do we seek it out ourselves?'

'And when we find it, what do we do?'

'We're still alive, aren't we? As long as we're alive we can fight back!'

'But how, Teacher Man? How? It's just sitting there in the Imperial waiting for us. Like some bloody horrible spider in the middle of its web. How do we fight it? We've seen what it can do.'

'There must be a way. Somehow ... some way ... we have to find Pandora. She's the key to everything.'

'And the child—whatever in Hell it is.'

'God help us.'

Seven

The nightclub sat silently waiting.

Winter brooded ominously in the December sky, the short day fading early into darkness. Soon, the night-time people would be on the streets, looking for entertainment.

And the nightclub was ready to entertain.

It was raining again and the street lamps cast strange, angular shadows at the top of Byker Bank. Somewhere inside the nightclub, someone pressed a switch and the new, blue neon sign flickered into life, joining the wash of colour on the wet streets. The sign beckoned invitingly.

In the Plough, the pub across the street, an early evening customer noticed the blue light and turned on his bar stool to the man behind the bar. 'Hey, what about that?'

'What about what?'

'The Imperial. It's had a name change.'

The bartender finished pulling a pint from the pumps and moved slowly round to the other side of the bar. He crossed to the windows and looked out into the night. 'So it has.' He shook his head. 'Weird bunch in there, I reckon. A woman who never shows her face. Really weird. And that Manager isn't much better. What's his name again?'

'Pearson?'

'Yeah, that's right. Pearson. He's not from around here, is he?'

'No. Well, he's not a Byker lad, put it that way. Nor Newcastle either. Strange kind of accent. Kinda southern, like.'

'Bunch of spooks, if you ask me.'

'In that case, the new nightclub name suits them.' The customer grunted in semi-amusement and returned to his pint of bitter. Soon, the conversation had turned to Newcastle United football team's chances in the next game.

Outside on the street, the blue neon sign flashed its one word solemnly onto the pavement over and over, patiently waiting for its children of the night.

'SPECTRES'.

*   *   *

Eric Harrow was thoroughly enjoying himself. He had not been to a nightclub in donkey's years but he was sure he could get used to being a smooth man-about-town. His wife, Shirley, had bought him a new shirt and tie especially for the occasion. She was dancing with his cousin, Jack, and seemed to be having an equally good time. She had suggested that they use two of Mr Pearson's six free tickets and ask Eric's cousin and wife to the big 'Opening Night'. Eric had wanted his workmate, Tony Jameson, to use the other two, but Tony had cried off, saying that he was unwell. Eric had noticed how white and shaky he seemed after they had finished working on the 'Spectres' neon sign. Maybe he had caught a touch of 'flu. Shame. Still, the four of them were making the most of their night out. Beside him, his cousin's wife, Doreen, laughed at Jack's exaggerated dancing style. Eric clinked her gin and tonic glass with his own and looked out across the nightclub.

Although there had been no publicity about the change of management, the place was pretty full, and the free-drink vouchers being given out at the reception desk guaranteed a party mood from the word 'go'. The flashing disco lights dazzled Eric, the thudding music made conversation virtually impossible, and he wondered how the galaxy of male and female posers, all trying very hard to look casual and chic, were able to communicate. The resident DJ was working almost mechanically; his smooth patter—apparently a prerequisite for the job—was pruned to the minimum and he did not affect the mid-American voice that most DJs adopted. He was wearing a white polo-neck pullover, which struck Eric as a little strange in the hot atmosphere. Didn't he ever sweat? Still, he seemed very popular with the clutch of young girls dancing just below the booth that housed his record deck and LPs. Eric remembered his previous visits to nightclubs in the good old days, when he was still a young'un. Then, the bouncers on the door had been surly, gruff, no-nonsense types, whose intimidating manner was enough to put you off even before you entered. But the bouncers in the Imperial (or Spectres) seemed to be a different breed. They were smiling when the party entered. They took coats, they held the doors open and, although they hardly spoke at all, they still had time to wish everyone a good night. Shirley had really been impressed with that. The bar staff were also unusually quiet. The blonde girl had smiled at the lads' few lines of joky patter, but had not said a word.

Eric's attention wandered to one of the four television/video sets at each corner of the disco floor. They were showing the latest selection of videos from the Top-Twenty record charts, and one of his favourite tracks was showing now, even though he could not hear what was being sung. Bloody silly. Why have a DJ playing records *and* a video screen?

It was nine o'clock when the DJ—who was cornily nick-named 'Deejay'—turned down the music and spoke into the microphone.

'If I could just interrupt for ten seconds, good people, and have your attention. I can see a selection of old and new faces here tonight, and I expect that you may have wondered about the change of management as well as the change of name for the nightclub. Well, I'd like to introduce Mr Pearson, who's the Under-Manager for Spectres . . . '

A gaunt sixty-year-old man had suddenly stepped up into the booth, hands clasped before him, stark white hair rinsed green by the overhead disco light.

' . . . and he'd just like to have a quick word to explain.'

There was a smatter of applause, a few drunken hoots and the man called Pearson moved to the microphone and began to speak.

'It's more gratifying than you'll ever know to see so many people here tonight. As you know, we're under new management now and I think I can promise everyone something very special. Very special indeed.'

Another smattering of applause from a group by the bar, who were not actually listening to him.

'You are privileged to be here. Privileged to be the first. Privileged to enact something that has been delayed for thousands of years . . . '

'*What the hell is he on about?*'

'*Don't ask me . . .* '

'It has not been possible until now. Circumstances were not right. However, now there is enough power. You will be the Great Sacrifice to the Deep Ones, which will presage the Beginning of a New Age.'

'So, anyway, Michelle said to me: "Listen, if he thinks he can push me around like that, he's got another think coming. I mean, who would put up with that kind of treatment from somebody who . . . " '

'Only two fathers remain to be consumed. Once that has been accomplished, the child will have completely converted. There will be no further delay, no more reason to hide and wait, gaining strength through the years. The child's power will be complete and he himself will be able to finish what you are privileged to begin.'

'What's the stupid old fart on about, anyway? Look, I'll have a pint of scotch if you're going to the bar . . . '

'What about this surprise, then?'

Pearson smiled and turned to Deejay. 'Lights.'

Eric had only half-heard what the Under-Manager had been saying, but the little he had grasped seemed to make no sense at all. Now, the DJ was turning down the lights until the only illumination in the nightclub was provided by the four television sets above the disco floor. There was nothing to be seen on the screens; only a blank, white, hissing snowstorm. Pearson had suddenly slipped away, darting up a staircase on the other side of the room and vanishing from sight behind a green door.

* * *

'It is time again, boy.'

'No . . . please . . . '

'I have told you what must be done.'

A snap. The hissing white snowstorm of a blank television screen.

'Look deeply and Dark-Out, Timothy. You are not complete until all the fathers are dead, but now you must begin the Vengeance that was promised.'

'No! I won't do it! I can't *do it!'*

'Absavel . . . Imago . . . Pacter . . . Gorgus . . . '

'No, no, no, no. No . . . '

'Otmo Nos Andophant Vermini Pacter Imago.'

'No . . . no . . . ' And then: 'Yes . . . yes . . . Absavel . . . Imago . . . GORRRGUS!'

* * *

People were growing restless. The lights had been out for too long and the punch-line was a little late in coming. The four television screens over the disco floor still flickered and flashed emptily. When was something going to happen? Eric hoped that this was not going to spoil the party mood.

Somewhere, a girl gave a mock scream as someone touched her leg; beside Eric, Doreen shuffled uncomfortably as they listened to the crowd's impatient grumbling; nothing seemed to be happening. Someone shouted: 'Hey, why are all the doors locked? Come on, man, I've got to go to the toilet.'

And then Eric's feelings of unease swelled into something approaching panic. Vaguely, he became aware that the bar staff had slipped under the trap door on the bar and were positioning themselves beside the doors, as if waiting for something. The disc jockey was nowhere to be seen. Eric knew, without having to look, that he had joined the bar staff at the exits.

Sure enough, there he was; he could see him more clearly because of his white polo-neck. Someone nearby screamed, but this time there was no humour, only terror. And as the knot of partygoers shrank back from the figure, it seemed to Eric that the DJ was . . . well . . . no, surely not, it must be the dark. Surely his body could not be contorting, surely his face could not be writhing and changing like that? It must be the dark, it could not be anything else. Then someone else screamed from the other side of the nightclub and the fear began to spread like some wild, contagious disease. Another group of people beside the disco floor were retreating from a figure approaching from the opposite side of the booth. Vaguely, Eric recognised one of the bouncers from the reception. And again, just before the image was blocked from view by milling, frightened customers, he had the impression that the figure was *changing* as it moved.

'Shirley!' he shouted, desperately seeking his wife in the crowd on the dance floor. Then he looked up at the nearest overhanging video screen and saw what everyone else, all over the room, could see. Panic finally took over and the nightclub patrons became a screaming, frightened mob. The hissing white screen had suddenly become the backdrop for a movie clip. *It's a horror film, that's all*, thought Eric, as a writhing mass of tentacles and teeth rattled and gobbled against the screen.

The noise was deafening. Even now, the tentacles were twisting from the screen, writhing over the rim of the television set and hunting in the crowd. On the far side of the disco, he saw the changing image of the bouncer, eyes gleaming, take a young man by the shoulder and bury his face in his throat. Just beyond, a knot of twisting tentacles had grabbed a girl by the arm and was dragging her up, through the air, towards the horror on the television screen.

The nightclub had become Hell.

Eric could hear the screaming, the shattering of broken glass, the cries of terror as *shapes* blocked the exit doors. A blood-flecked face collided with his own and he went down under dozens of trampling feet. Dazed, he cowered on the ground, protecting his head. Suddenly, the crowd swarmed away from him as they were herded to the centre of the room.

'Help me . . . help me . . . help . . . ' Eric had one arm raised, begging, blood running from his nose.

Something took his hand.

Eric looked up and screamed. It was the girl from behind the bar, the girl who had been smiling reflectively at the lads' patter only minutes before, the girl with the long, blonde hair. But now, the tresses of blonde hair were snakes and the eyes were black portals into Hell. The snakes curled around his wrist, biting and encircling as he was drawn slowly to his feet. More hissing, spitting snakes were reaching for his face as he died of fright.

Eight

'Now?' asked Richard.

'Now,' replied Stan.

Richard dialled the local taxi firm and, within ten minutes, they were climbing into a blue Morris Marina. Stan kept the canvas bag on his lap. Fear was eating at them from the inside as Richard told the West Indian driver their destination.

'The Imperial. Byker Bank.'

Diane gripped his hand. It was as icy as her own.

Richard felt another emotion flooding over the chill inside as he looked at Diane; at her firmly set, white face and her sparkling, beautiful eyes. Temporarily, it thawed the fear and made him more glad to be with her than he could have put into words. Meeting her, he realised, had been one of the best things that had ever happened to him.

It might be the last good thing that will ever happen to me. And then, angrily: *You selfish bastard! What about her? What have you done to Diane? If she had never met you, she wouldn't be going with you to die!*

He opened his mouth to speak. Diane shook her head and smiled.

Don't, she mouthed. *Don't.*

I love you, Diane.

'Big night out tonight?' asked the taxi driver.

'You might say that,' replied Stan, shifting the canvas bag on his lap.

'I just did, man.'

'Much business tonight?'

'Slowest night I can remember for years. Not a soul about. Really weird.' The taxi shot from the flyover and onto the stretch of Shields Road leading to Byker Bridge. 'The town seems dead tonight.'

Why the hell did I feel like throwing up when he said that? thought Stan. *Because*, said a small voice, *Death is abroad. And that death will spread through the night. Spreading . . . searching . . . finding . . .*

A metro train rumbled past on their right as the taxi whizzed through amber traffic lights and hit Byker Bridge with a thud of tyres and a rattle of suspension. Beyond, the glitter of lights from living-room windows in the Byker Wall beckoned to them.

Below, the Ouseburn wound silently to the River Tyne; giant, dinosaur cranes crowded the water in the distance. Ahead and to the right, the black silhouette of the Imperial stood shrouded in phosphorescent will-o'-the-wisp blue from its hidden neon light.

The taxi reached the end of the Bridge. Shields Road and its closely crowded shops were deserted. Richard leaned forward and tapped the taxi driver's shoulder as the car drew level with the top of Byker Bank. 'Just here will be fine.'

'Don't you want me to turn down Byker Bank? The Imperial's only round the corner.'

'No, thanks. This is okay.'

They scrambled out of the taxi and stood in the chill night air, closing the taxi doors with a heavy *chunking* sound that was swallowed by the darkness. The taxi pulled away as they crossed the empty street, the overhead lights making the resin sparkle in the asphalt beneath their feet.

Richard heard Diane's intake of breath and pulled her close as they reached the top of the Bank. He was instantly aware of some kind of change. Spectral blue light soaked the wet pavements around the Imperial.

'Something's different.'

'What?' asked Stan, eyes darting.

'The sign's been changed. It's different.'

Keeping to the other side of the road, they drew level with the nightclub. For the first time, they saw the neon sign.

'Spectres,' said Diane. '*Spectres.*'

'It's laughing at us,' said Stan.

'Don't go in,' whispered Diane. 'We mustn't go in there.'

Stan pulled out the shotgun, bunched the canvas bag over his shoulder and broke open the gun chambers, checking the shells. He snapped the gun shut.

Diane steeled herself. 'I'm sorry, Richard. We *must* go in.'

'Let's go, then,' said Richard, fingering the automatic pistol in his jerkin pocket that Stan had given him earlier. His heart was hammering as they crossed the road towards the nightclub. They reached the reception doors. Inside, only blackness.

'Diane, maybe you should . . . ' began Stan.

The sound of an electric guitar suddenly drowned his words. Someone had begun to play a record in there. It was instantly recognisable—Derek and the Dominoes playing 'Layla'.

Green and red lights began to swirl against the doors.

'We're expected,' said Richard, pushing open the doors and stepping inside. Diane and Stan were close behind, and now Eric Clapton's guitar was deafeningly loud.

The reception area was empty.

Stan moved quickly to the desk and looked over into the cloakroom, shotgun held like some kind of probe. The racks were filled with coats. The double-sided mirror on its castored stand reflected the green and red light from the disco beyond. There was nothing else in there.

'Pandora? Where are you?' shouted Richard and then

wished that he had kept silent. There was no point in drawing attention to their presence. *But it knows we're here*, he thought. *It knows every step we're taking.*

Stan moved forward and nosed open the inner doors with the barrel of the shotgun.

'*Oh, my God . . .*'

Richard pushed past him and looked inside.

The nightclub had become a slaughterhouse.

Twisted and broken corpses lay strewn about the club in grotesque poses. Furniture had been shattered; glasses and tables smashed to atoms. Some of the shredded, torn figures were no longer recognisable as human. The red and green disco lights swirled over a scene of abominable carnage, reflected in dark pools of crimson on the nightclub floor. It was the aftermath of a Masque of the Red Death; it was a scene from Hell. Over it all, the thud and pound of Eric Clapton's agonised music. Richard felt his gorge rising and turned back to Diane, the stench of death in his nostrils. She stood, eyes screwed shut, sweat beading on her forehead.

'I know,' she said. 'I felt it.'

Richard pushed through the double doors and the others followed.

Stan moved ahead like some jungle fighter on manoeuvres, stepping over the bodies sprawled on the floor, skidding in one of the glistening pools. He reached the bar and looked over quickly for any crouching danger. There was no one there. Richard swallowed hard and took Diane's arm, keeping close to her as he walked slowly towards the record booth in the centre of the disco floor. A dead, white face seemed to grin at him from the floor, red light swirling in dead eyes. He looked away and kept moving. They reached the empty booth, 'Layla' blasting through the nightclub. The record glinted black from the turntable as it spun. Richard leaned in and lifted the pick-up arm away from the disc. The music stopped.

'Welcome home,' said a quiet voice behind them.

Richard snapped the automatic from his pocket and pointed it at the figure which had suddenly materialised on the disco floor. Instantly, Stan was beside him, shotgun levelled.

The figure stepped forward into the green and red light, hands clasped before him in a prayer-like gesture.

'Pearson,' said Richard as he recognised the Under-Manager.

'No, it's not,' said Diane, her voice breaking slightly. 'It's not Pearson. His name is Barnard. Hugh Barnard.'

'What a remarkably perceptive aura you have, my dear. I've never come across one quite like it before.' Barnard took another step forward, smiling that benign smile. His white hair seemed to swirl in the disco light, eyes sparkling red. Stan cocked the hammers on the shotgun.

'Really,' said Barnard, 'such manners. Well . . . I see that Margaret has been telling tales. But then, I knew she would.'

'You knew we'd been there?' asked Stan.

Barnard burst out laughing, swaying from side to side. 'My dears, I've known where you've been for some time now. Your deductive powers are to be commended. After Barry's death, we were strong enough to hunt without man-made devices; although, I must admit, the presence of that radio in the motorway cafeteria proved too great a temptation.' Barnard laughed again and waved his hand at an overhead video screen. 'Seven fathers—six Byker Chapter members. Yourselves . . . and the Gorgon, which has fathered itself. Margaret told you about the child, of course. It was necessary—*is* necessary—for the six human fathers to die and be ***absorbed*** by the Gorgon. With each death, the power grows.'

'What in God's name has happened here?' asked Richard.

'Hardly in God's name,' replied Barnard in amusement. 'In the name of the Gorgon; a sacrifice. To pave the way for the Deep Ones' emergence.'

'Where's Pandora?' asked Stan.

'Pandora?'

'Cut the crap, Barnard. You've got her here with that kid. Now, where is she?'

'Such impatience, young man. Don't you realise that this is a time to be savoured? We mustn't rush things now that you're here.'

'Show me Pandora, you bastard! Or I'll blow a hole in you big enough to drive a lorry through.'

Barnard laughed again as if he was enjoying every moment. He turned towards the staircase on the other side of the disco and beckoned.

'Pandora, my dear. You have visitors.'

The silhouetted figure of a young woman emerged at the top of the stairs and looked down at them. She was wearing a light gown, her hair blowing in an invisible breeze. They could not see her face. She descended quickly and began to move over the disco floor towards them. Stan was the first to see her properly.

'Pandora?' he said, incredulity in his voice.

The woman smiled as she stepped into the light, and it was as if all the intervening years had never been: her beautiful hair flowing on her shoulders; that pale, lovely complexion and the blue eyes.

'Stan,' she said. Then, turning: 'and Richard.'

Richard was not aware that Diane had let go of his hand and was standing back as Pandora glided towards him, arms held wide. It had been so long and, God, so much had happened to them all. Now they had found her at last.

'Richard,' she said again as they embraced.

But something was wrong as she leaned up to kiss him.

Her arms were solid and unyielding. The hands felt like claws. Even as Richard watched, her face was shifting and spreading like a terrible, melting wax mask. Her beautiful, even teeth were elongating, sharpening. A forked tongue flickered from the gaping red maw that had been her mouth.

'*Jesus Christ!*' Richard tore himself free before that face could fasten on his. He jerked the abomination away from him, staggering back. And then Stan squeezed the shotgun trigger and the echoing roar made Richard's ears *whang*! The thing took the full blast at point-blank range, spinning away across the nightclub floor in a ragged, liquid pirouette. It slumped forward, the face shifting and altering as it crawled towards the bar. Richard saw dozens of men's and women's faces on the ever-changing visage. He saw the furrowed snout of a bear, the ragged teeth of a hyena, the malevolent eyes of a spider. He saw the snake's tongue again as the thing coughed blood that turned to acid, scouring the floor. It started to crawl up the bar; the mouth opened and emitted a roaring, howling sound filled with abominable rage. The thing stood erect again, turned and began to advance towards them, face swirling and changing. The flowing white gown had become a torn, rotting graveyard shroud. Frozen in fear, they watched as the thing raised its arms wide to reveal a torso suddenly alive with squirming, hungry mouths armed with dagger teeth. The shotgun blast had blown a hole in its chest. Writhing tentacles twisted and crawled within.

Roaring, it swept forward to take them.

'*Absavel, Imago! Terminet!*' shouted Barnard suddenly.

The thing stopped. The roaring sound dwindled to a liquid gurgling.

'*Terminet!*'

The swirling images on the thing's face faded. Its arms dropped to its sides. The body began to spasm. It dropped to its knees, racked by convulsions, head bowed, arms hugging its body as if in pain. It quivered, uttering a soft, poisonous, hissing sound, and slumped over to one side.

It was dead.

And now, twisted and torn, with the ragged hole in its chest cavity still smoking, they could see for the first time what manner of creature had attacked them.

It was a department store manikin. A shop dummy.

'A shame,' said Barnard, still smiling. 'It has served us so well until now.' He began to move towards the mutilated dummy.

'Stay still, Barnard, or I'll blow your head off,' warned Stan. Barnard paid no heed as he moved past the ruined, smoking dummy, dipped behind the bar and casually began to pour himself a large whisky.

'I'm warning you!'

'You won't use that on me, Stan. Not until you know everything that's going on.'

How the hell does he know our names? thought Richard.

Barnard laughed, sipping at his whisky. 'It's still very much a mystery to you all, isn't it?'

'Images,' said Diane vacantly.

'Images,' repeated Barnard, sitting on a stool behind the bar. 'You really are so perceptive, my dear. I shall have to find a use for you. Yes, images are the key.'

'And the child,' said Stan. 'What is it?'

'It? Really. How uncaring. But yes, the child is also the key. He is the flesh that houses something very special. Margaret told you, of course, about the Ritual of the Scarlet Woman. I'm afraid that I rather botched that twenty years ago. If I'd known then what I know now . . . Still, no use crying over . . . '

'Spilt blood?' said Richard without humour.

'Yes . . . very good . . . Where was I? Oh, yes. The Ritual was only partially successful. At the time I thought that it had failed completely. But it had not. You see, I succeeded in *sowing the mystical seed*, if you like. It remained dormant in Pandora until ten years ago, like a time bomb . . . or an alarm clock . . . whatever delay simile you care to choose. She was impelled to do what she did. She slept with you all and took your seed. The mystical seed and your own seed allowed her to give birth—remarkable under the physical circumstances, wouldn't you say?'

'You bastard,' muttered Stan, stepping forward. Richard stopped him.

'You, the fathers, were partly responsible for the *physical* birth. I, in my own way, provided the means for the Gorgon to plant its own seed.'

'The Gorgon,' said Richard. 'Just what in Hell is it?'

'Your phraseology is so perceptive, Richard. It is one of many terms used to describe the force which is about to be fully unleashed. Its real name is quite unpronounceable, I'm afraid. Together, the Gorgon and yourselves fathered the child. But the child, although housing the spirit of the Gorgon within his physical shell, is nevertheless human. The power has had to be coaxed from him. He is a split personality in the true sense of the word. Using the correct formula I have been able to summon the darker side of his "personality". With the death of each father, his strength has grown. He has not only killed them, he has *absorbed* them as part of his self, his totality, his whole. When all the fathers are consumed, the Gorgon will then truly be reborn.'

'How the hell did you find us?' asked Stan, knowing the answer but wanting to hear it from Barnard's own lips.

'Remarkable devices, the radio and the television set. The child has been able to use mankind's own technology in his quest. When I allow his dark side to emerge, it is able to search the airwaves.'

Richard remembered the television set that had suddenly become a living, deadly nest of snakes. *The cloud, the teeth, the snake-like tentacles. Snakes. The Gorgon's head. Instead of hair, it had snakes.*

Barnard poured himself another drink, smiling at them. 'It is so pleasant to be able to talk about my life's work after so many years spent in secrecy. I hope that this isn't boring you . . . '

'Keep talking, Barnard,' said Richard.

'The most remarkable thing about my vocation has been the ability to explore and discover the truth behind man's oldest superstitions, myths and fears. "Every legend has its basis in fact"—isn't that how the cliché goes? Well, like all clichés, it has an underlying truth.'

'Spare us the history lesson,' snapped Stan.

'No, let him talk,' said Richard.

'Thank you. According to ancient Greek myth, the Gorgons were sisters: Stheno, Euryale and Medusa. Their gaze could turn a man to stone. Perseus, the hero, slew Medusa by looking at her reflection in a polished shield. According to Barnard, the Gorgon—for want of a better term—is a single entity, expelled by man from earth before history began. Its gaze could certainly terrify a man to death, but the "turning to stone" business is merely a symbolic interpretation. The Gorgon has many other names and is known in many other cultures. To the Jews, it was known as the Golem; in the Indian culture it is Kali, Bringer of Vengeance; to the Egyptians, it was Anubis. But for you these names all mean the same thing: Death. Soon, when you are dead, it will walk the earth again, its banishment at an end. In a very short time, my dears, mankind will be an extinct species.'

'And what about you, Barnard?' asked Diane. 'What good does it do you if everyone is dead?'

'You cannot begin to imagine my rewards.'

'You're sick,' said Diane.

'And the images?' asked Richard. 'What about the images?'

'Shape-changing,' said Barnard. 'I believe that Margaret acquainted you with the term, did she not? The Gorgon has the ability to breathe life into images. It can animate the inanimate—dummies, statues, museum exhibits—you have encountered the various guises; and, as you've already surmised, the photograph of the Byker Chapter was the focal point: the child was able to maximise his powers by concentrating upon Pandora's copy of the photograph. I would imagine that you've heard of psychics using the same technique to trace missing persons.'

'Every time one of us died—was killed—we didn't only die, we were . . . ' Richard eased the pressure on the trigger of his gun. It would be so easy to kill this perverted maniac.

'Your identity was assimilated into the Gorgon. The fathers were consumed. And the images faded from the photograph.' Barnard sipped his drink. 'Did you know that certain aboriginal tribes will not allow their photographs to be taken because they fear that their souls will be stolen and entrapped within the photographic image? How apt, under the present circumstances. Of course, until all the fathers have been consumed, a guiding hand is needed to direct this wild talent in the child: to guide it, nurture it and bring it fully to life.'

'Why here? Why the Imperial?' asked Richard.

'You mean "Spectres"? A long story. To cut it short, Pandora left home after the baby was born—she was not in her right mind, of course. She was guided to seek me out, which wasn't easy. Following the unfortunate publicity in Cornwall, I had been forced to adopt a low profile elsewhere in the British Isles. But she found me: greater powers than herself were at work. The first few years were easy enough. The baby's power was largely dormant—after Margaret's unfortunate encounter—but as it grew, its psychic strength grew also. Pandora and the child were always extremely close, both physically and psychically. She exercises, shall we say, a limited amount of "mother control". But her mind had unfortunately been permanently affected—naturally enough, I suppose, under the circumstances. She drew great strength from her memories to sustain her. She acquainted me fully with the exploits of the Byker Chapter. Eventually, it reached a point where her desire to return to Byker was too strong to be obviated. Her "peace of mind", to use a misplaced phrase, was essential to the development of the child. So . . .

'My enquiries revealed that this nightclub—the Imperial—Spectres—was up for sale again. I bought it, poured my resources into it and made it a viable concern, with our headquarters upstairs. Pandora's happiness in her surroundings proved exceptionally beneficial to the boy's development;

I, for my part, have enjoyed playing the role of Under-Manager. It has been a refreshing change from skulking in a small country house in the middle of nowhere. And I have been so looking forward to this day, when the fruits of my endeavours are to be plucked.'

Barnard drank again, then burst out laughing. 'Richard . . . Richard . . . how amusing! You have been a regular customer of "Spectres" for so long. We could have taken you long ago. When the child and I were . . . *hunting* . . . it was a great temptation. The Gorgon has taken the Byker Chapter one by one . . . *in order of sexual intercourse with Pandora.* Philip slept with Pandora first. He was therefore first to die. Richard, you were last, and so you must be the last to die.' He laughed again, choking on his whisky. 'I must say that I had some difficulty in restraining Charlie, the ventriloquist's dummy. It would not have been appropriate for you to die at that stage, but the Gorgon was so hungry . . . And what of the dreams you have all shared? You remember the *faceless* dreams? That was a little amusement on my part. A taunt, shall we say?'

'The nightclub sign . . . ' began Stan.

'A little in-joke for the Byker Chapter, my dear. Pandora acquainted me with your Chapter slang, during her ravings. I trust the humour was not lost on you.'

'So Pandora and the child are . . . '

'Upstairs,' finished Barnard.

'You mean that you've kept them both—Pandora and the child—locked away up there all these years?'

'But of course! Any contact other than with me is forbidden. It was necessary to maintain the correct rituals, the necessary . . . shall we say "magic"? The child needed solitude to develop. The human side of his nature has been more than a little rebellious, I'm afraid. My rituals took from the mother and gave to the child. Also, the child must be protected.' Barnard finished his drink with a flourish. '*Perseus Amago non Imagi Palcutat.* The child has an aversion to mirrors.'

'It's monstrous,' said Diane, 'monstrous.'

'Ah yes,' continued Barnard. 'You remind me: it's time to return to matters in hand.' He stood up, scooping a handful of peanuts from the bar and feeding them lasciviously to himself one at a time: *chop, chop, chop.*

'Richard and Stan. You must die, of course. But, Diane . . . your arrival is timely, my dear. The mass sacrifice has created a perfect atmosphere for the Gorgon's emergence. I think the added performance of a *quality* ritual, with your good self as the centre of attraction, will be pleasing to the Gorgon before it finally metamorphoses within the child, after the death of the last father.'

Barnard's eyes seemed to be glowing, reflecting the disco light. Richard could see that his hands were trembling with excitement.

'It's so good to be able to talk. You are such patient listeners. And now I will reward your patience with the greatest revelation of all. I am Pandora's Epimetheus, guarding the box which unleashed all evil upon the world. But the Gorgon, when it emerges completely after your deaths, *is also a Gateway*, a Gateway between worlds! The Deep Ones who were consigned to another dimension will be summoned again when the Gorgon is completely reborn. The Old Gods will return to Earth. They will reclaim possession of their world—and mankind will become an extinct species. You ask my reward? *I, too, shall become a God!*'

Barnard pointed a shaking finger at the disco floor. 'The Gorgon will create a tunnel through space and time. The Deep Ones will emerge and grant my reward.'

'Oh, God, Richard,' said Diane. 'Look at the disco floor.'

For the first time, Richard noticed that the corpse-strewn floor was shaped like a five-pointed star.

'It's a pentagram,' said Diane.

'Again, so observant!' said Barnard. 'The mystical pattern. A perfect place for worship . . . and sacrifice. First, Diane, my dear, you will die. Then, we shall have sex. I believe that the Gorgon will find that pleasing.'

'And I believe I'm going to blow your fucking head off with this shotgun,' said Stan.

'Perhaps you should save your firepower for something else,' said Barnard quietly.

Four shapes had emerged from the surrounding darkness, hemming them into a tight quadrangle. Richard recognised the nightclub staff immediately: Angie and Josh, the bar staff—Paul and Andy, the bouncers.

'Dead people,' said Diane instinctively. 'They're all dead people.'

Even now, as they began to move in towards them, Angie was unwinding the black satin choker from around her throat to reveal the gaping wound.

'Aren't they just the perfect images of themselves?' chortled Barnard. 'As I told you—as Margaret told you—the Gorgon animates the inanimate, breathes life into images. What superb images, then! Empty shells, images of their former selves, just waiting to be filled with a motivating force. Almost poetic, don't you think?'

'I'll kill you unless you call them off!' exclaimed Stan, shotgun wavering between Barnard and the approaching, hellishly grinning and demoniac Spectres.

'It won't stop them, Stan.'

'You're bluffing!'

'Try it, then.'

'You bastard!' Stan swung the shotgun and levelled it at Andy. The gun roared, spitting sparks. The shot shredded Andy's right arm, tearing it away from the shoulder and hurling it across the nightclub. Andy staggered under the force of the blast, collapsing to his knees. Grinning, he stood up again and continued his slow advance. Barnard slipped under the bar and out of their way, scurrying past the advancing figures. Richard snapped his arm upwards and fired. The bullet gouged a splintered track along the bar. Barnard vanished into the darkness. Laughing, laughing, laughing.

Diane snatched an ornamental ashtray from the bar and flung it at Angie. It snapped her head to one side, leaving a gash parallel to the gash in her throat. Still, she came on. Richard pulled Diane closer to him, levelling the pistol at the approaching figures, terror breathing in his face. He was aware of Stan jamming fresh shells into the shotgun breach, then Josh's spectrally white, grinning face, with its malevolent black, marble eyes, thrust quickly towards his own. In horror, Richard struck out with the gun, at the same time squeezing the trigger. The gun barrel and the bullet connected simultaneously with Josh's face; he staggered backwards, a swilling black hole foaming where his eye socket had been, a ragged mass at the back of his head.

'*Richard*!' screamed Diane.

Paul was already reaching for her throat. Richard flung himself desperately forward as the twin explosions of Stan's shotgun *whanged* in his eardrums. A claw-like hand connected with his head, groping at his hair. His face was slammed hard against the bar; blood-red, purple pain filled his head. Completely helpless, with Diane's screams ringing in his ears, he sank into a black, enfolding pit of unconsciousness.

It was the end.

Nine

Blackness. Only blackness.

Richard was conscious again, but the all-enveloping darkness precluded any real feeling of awakening. *Am I dead?* he thought. *Is this what it's like to be dead? No. Because if I were dead my arms wouldn't be hurting so much and my head wouldn't be banging like a tin drum.*

Then he realised that he was lying on his arms. They had been tied behind his back and the lack of circulation was causing him agony. His forehead felt crusted—probably dried blood from the blow on the bar. He tried to scuffle round, causing the pain to bite again, and found that his ankles had been tied as well. He was lying on a rough wooden floor; a splinter had wedged itself under the flesh of his wrist. Groaning, he rolled over onto his side, searching for non-existent light. The sound seemed hollow, somehow muffled—he was obviously in a small, enclosed space, a large cupboard, perhaps, or a small room. The last moments before he had lost consciousness crystallised in his memory and he was swamped by panic to get free and find out what had happened to the others. 'Diane?' he said aloud. *Oh, God, please let her be here with me now.* 'Stan?' He rolled back onto his front. The blood began to flow into his arms, bringing fresh agony. Bracing his swollen forehead on the floor, he brought up his knees and rose painfully to a kneeling position. He tried to shuffle forward but only succeeded in slumping to the floor again. It was hopeless.

'Diane, are you there?'

Only the blackness. The suffocating blackness and the silence.

A sliver of light suddenly pierced the dark, accompanied by the creaking of wood. Someone had opened a door. The crack grew wider as Richard twisted round to face it. Slowly, the door swung wide to the wall and in the oblong of orange light stood the silhouette of a small child.

God! The child! The Gorgon! In a piercing stab of terror, Richard was convinced that he had died and that this was Hell. The Horror had come to claim him at last and would bind him for all eternity. The child moved forward quietly into the room. The angled light from the passage outside illuminated him, and Richard could see the blazer and trousers, the neat tie, the auburn hair and the large questioning, liquid eyes. The eyes of a child, not a monster.

'Are you my Daddy?' asked the boy.

'Where's Barnard?' asked Richard, studying the child intently. So this was the core of the nightmare? This was the focus of the Horror that had claimed most of the Byker Chapter. This was Pandora's child. Their creation.

'Who?'

'Barnard . . . Mr Pearson. Where is he?' Richard struggled to keep the panic and the urgency out of his voice.

'He's down in the disco where I'm not allowed to go. Are you my Daddy?'

'What's your name?'

'Timothy.'

'Your mother, her name is Pandora, right?'

'Pandora, yes. But . . . but . . . ' The child's liquid eyes were now somehow glazed. He cocked his head to one side as if listening. ' . . . But . . . ' His head was rolling slowly upwards, breath expelling from his mouth in a slow hiss.

Something was happening.

The boy's head dropped, chin on chest.

Fear began to wrap Richard's soul in a shrouded cocoon. He knew that he was now in the presence of the thing that had hunted so hungrily for the Byker Chapter.

The child looked up, marble black eyes glistening. It smiled. Richard tried to squirm backwards, feeling the bindings cutting into his flesh. The child's lips moved awkwardly, as if the process of articulating took an immense effort.

'*Rich . . . Rich . . . RICHAAARD*!' The thing that had once looked like a child spoke in a deep, horrific, growling baritone that sent shivers of ice piercing into Richard's soul. '*Now . . . now . . . I have you!*' The child-thing began to laugh. Richard recognised that voice. It was the voice of the monstrosity in the fog, that had attacked them on the highway. '*Soon I will be whole. I will be fully reborn. And then the Deep Ones will return to reclaim their . . . their . . . their . . .*'

The black eyes now seemed dulled. A puzzled expression clouded the child-thing's face. It began to shake its head, as if refusing to accept something. Richard could sense that a great struggle was taking place. 'NOOOO . . . *No* . . . No . . . ' The child-thing's chin was resting on its chest again, hands held stiffly by its sides, fingers clenching and unclenching.

The child looked up. The face was beaded with sweat. But it was the face of a child again, not a monster. He was breathing heavily as if he had undergone some terrible strain. When he spoke, it was in the voice of an ordinary little boy.

'I've . . . I've . . . made it go away again. You asked about my . . . my mother. Yes, her name's Pandora.'

Richard struggled to keep his voice even, trying to subdue the terror inside. 'Is she here?'

'Yes.'

God, what do I have to lose? I've got to try a gamble. How else shall I get free?

'Will you untie me?'

A pause. Then: 'Yes.'

The child moved softly to Richard's side and began to tug at the cords that bound his wrists. The questioning eyes never left his face.

'There was a woman and another man with me. Do you know where they are?'

'I might.'

Don't force it! Don't anger the kid until you're untied!

'Mr Pearson hasn't started anything yet,' the boy continued. 'You don't have to worry about your friends. There's time. Are you . . . ?'

'Take me to your mother,' said Richard. *If I can find her, she might be able to stop him. I don't know whether the Gorgon will come back to possess the kid . . . my kid . . . But Barnard said that Pandora has a limited amount of 'mother control'. Maybe she can stop this insanity . . .*

The cords were now loose around his wrists. He sat up, plucking them away and working hastily on his ankles. He massaged his arms and legs and then staggered to his feet, resisting the instinctive impulse to lean against the child for support when the pins and needles in his legs threatened to unbalance him. The child went silently ahead into the corridor beyond and Richard realised that he had been lying in a bedroom of some kind. Dust sheets covered the furniture. It had obviously not been used for some time. The child was opening another door directly opposite and looking back at him. Pandora must be in there. He hurried after the child as he slipped into the room.

It was a sitting-room of some sort. There was no light, save that thrown by an electric fire against the wall. A high-backed wicker chair stood next to it, its occupant obviously a woman—but shrouded in shadow. Richard moved into the room as the child closed the door behind him. Slowly, he approached the silent, unmoving shape in the chair. Its fingers flexed on the arm rest and a head turned to look at him from the shadows.

'Pandora?'

'Richard?' The voice was agonisingly familiar, uncertain, trembling. It was Pandora's voice, but something was very, very wrong. Drawn forward almost against his will, Richard found himself standing before the wicker chair looking down. *What's wrong with her voice? It sounds so . . . so . . . so old.* The woman leaned forward to look at him, her face revealed in the firelight. Richard felt emotion swelling inside him, bursting from his chest in racking sobs. He dropped to his knees.

'Pandora. Oh, Pandora. What has he done to you, my love? What has he *done*?'

It was Pandora who beckoned to him with her arms held wide, tears coursing down her face. It was Pandora who shared his sorrow at this heart-rending reunion after so much pain, so many years and so much terror. But it was the face of a Pandora who was eighty years old, not thirty. Her aged, creased face was the face of a grandmother, not a former friend and lover. Instinctively, as Richard sank down beside her and cradled her frail body in his arms, he knew what had happened.

The child needed solitude to develop, Barnard had said. *My rituals took from the mother and gave to the child.* Pandora's vitality had been drained; her life had been rechannelled to feed the supernatural power of her own son.

'That bastard, Barnard,' sobbed Richard. 'He did this to you.'

'It's been so long, Richard. So long.'

Richard felt hot tears on his hands. The boy had knelt beside them and was silently taking Pandora's hand and squeezing it to his cheek. Again, he found himself thinking: *Can this kid really be the focal point for all the horror?*

'Pandora. Can you stop Barnard?'

He read the hopelessness in her eyes before she spoke.

'No.'

He turned to the boy. 'How long was I unconscious?'

'Not long,' said the child, eyes riveted on his mother's face.

'You're worrying about the woman. But he hasn't started yet. There's time.'

'Are those . . . things . . . still downstairs with Barnard . . . with Pearson?'

'Only one,' replied the child, liquid eyes still fixed on his mother. 'The others have been terminated. He has no further use for them.'

Richard remembered how Barnard had withdrawn the motivating force from the shop dummy at a vocal command.

'Can *you* stop him?' he asked the boy.

A sparkling tear formed on Timothy's eyelashes. It quivered there and then spilled over his cheek. 'No. He controls everything. And whatever's in me is stronger than I am. It's growing stronger all the time.'

'Where's Stan?'

The boy was silent.

'Help him,' said the old woman. The child and the woman looked at each other for a long time. 'Help him,' she said again. 'You must resist what's in you, Timothy. I know you can. You must not allow it to take control again.'

'I don't . . . I don't know if I can, Mother. I don't . . .'

'Do you *love* me, Timothy?'

'Yes.'

'Then you must resist it. And you must help this man. You will, won't you?'

The boy took a deep breath, steeling himself, an almost unearthly determination in his eyes. Slowly he wiped the tears from his face. Then, quickly, he left his mother's side and flitted from the room into the corridor. Richard followed. The child pushed open another door and stood quietly as Richard burst past him into the room.

Like the others, it was sparsely furnished, but Richard's attention was drawn immediately to the centre of the room.

Stan was sitting on a wooden chair, his arms strapped to the struts in the back rest. He was conscious, but he had been gagged. He began to struggle and groan as Richard hurried over to him. In seconds, the gag was loose and Richard was working on the bindings.

'What the hell happened down there?' hissed Richard as he plucked at the knots. 'I thought we were dead.'

'Those bloody things,' gasped Stan. 'Christ, Richard, I've never seen anything like it. One of them took that shotgun from me and tore it to pieces in its bare hands. After you'd been knocked down they dragged us up here. Barnard tied me up and went back downstairs.'

'Diane?'

'One of the things kept her down there. She's still there.'

'He's going to kill her first, Stan.'

'He's going to kill us all.'

'Why the hell didn't he do it there and then?'

'He wants to savour it,' said the child from the doorway.

Stan stared at the boy with a look of fear that Richard recognised as his own first reaction.

'It's okay, Stan, the kid's okay.'

'Is Pandora here?' asked Stan at last, still watching the boy.

'She's back there. But we don't have time.'

'How the hell do we stop him?'

'We've got to get down there to Diane,' said Richard, ignoring the question. 'She needs us.'

'We can't just blunder down there. Those bloody things would tear us apart.'

'There's only one down there now,' said Richard. He hurried into the corridor again, taking the boy by one arm and hissing in his ear: 'The power really comes when he makes your dark side emerge. Is that right?'

'He makes me "Dark-Out", yes.'

'How does he make you do that?'

'He says words. Foreign words. After that, I don't know what happens.'

'How are these zombies of his—or whatever in Hell they are—walking around and doing his bidding? You're not "Dark" now, are you?'

'He conjures them up through the Dark side of me. Once he's got them he can make them do anything he wants without me.'

'And there's no way you can control them?'

'No. Only when I "Dark-Out".'

'So you can't control that thing downstairs?'

The boy shook his head.

'Timothy, you heard your mother. She told you . . . '

'Are you my Daddy?'

' . . . told you to help me. And you will do that, won't you?'

The boy nodded.

'I want you to go down there into the nightclub when I say. I want you to . . . '

'I'm not allowed down there! I've *never* been downstairs. It's forbidden!'

' . . . want you to go down to Mr Pearson and tell him you're losing the power. Tell him that you're dying. And draw him away from the disco floor. Do you understand?'

The child was searching Richard's face as if for the answer to some unfathomable question.

'Your mother wants you to help us. You'll do that, won't you, Timothy?'

'Yes.'

Stan joined them as they talked. Together, they moved down the thickly carpeted corridor to the outer green door. Richard pulled it open carefully.

* * *

Downstairs, the disco lights illuminated the five-pointed star on the floor: a shining, astral body glowing red, green, red, green, red, green. The corpses had been cleared away and heaped in a corner. Barnard stood at the tip of the star, head bent, apparently in prayer. In the centre of the floor, Diane lay spreadeagled and unconscious. The light reflected on a tin bowl that had been placed beside her head. To her left, light sparked on the wickedly sharp butcher's knife that Barnard had taken from the restaurant area. Richard almost lost control and blundered forward; only Stan's restraining hand on his arm brought him back to rationality.

'All right, Timothy,' said Richard through clenched teeth. 'Do it.'

For a few seconds, the boy hesitated on the threshold. Then, taking a deep breath, he stepped round the door. Richard and Stan shrank back as his footsteps rang on the tiling. Instantly, it seemed, Barnard had spotted him.

'WHAT ARE YOU DOING?'

The child's footsteps ceased. His voice, lost and frightened, drifted back to them. 'I'm not well. I feel ill.'

Richard found himself thinking: *It's not fair. He's just a frightened little boy.*

'GO BACK!' thundered Barnard's voice again.

'Go on, kid. Go on!' hissed Stan under his breath.

'My power's leaving me, Mr Pearson. I can feel it. It's dying inside.' Again, the sound of footsteps as he continued his descent.

'You're lying to me, Timothy.' Barnard's voice again; quieter, but filled with sly, treacle-thick menace. 'You couldn't possibly know that. You must go back to your mother. There are too many dangers down here for you.'

'I'm sick, Mr Pearson. I can feeling something bad inside. I think I'm dying.' The sound of his footsteps had changed. The child had reached the floor at the bottom of the stairs. 'Mother won't listen. I need help.'

'You can't be sick. It's important that you be well.' An edge of doubt had crept into Barnard's voice. 'You are the host, my child. You are the flesh that houses the Great One, the Deep One. We're too close to the Final Enactment for you to be ill.'

Richard sneaked a look around the edge of the door. Timothy had walked round the disco floor until he had reached the reception doors. Facing the stairs, he was doubled over and clutching his stomach. Barnard had turned to watch him, his back to the stairs. On Barnard's right, Richard could see Paul the bouncer. He looked like a corpse hanging from a meathook, head bloody and sagging. Diane lay unmoving on the floor.

God, let her be all right.

Barnard turned to Paul, raising his hand in the beginnings of a gesture of command. Richard shrank back, but Timothy had anticipated the possibility of discovery and, uttering a choking sound, sank to his knees. Barnard twitched forward, reaching for the child.

In the next instant, Richard and Stan were on the stairs, moving fast and low, the boy's moaning covering their footsteps. Richard sprinted down and across the five-pointed star, eyes fixed on the bouncer for any sign of movement. At his side, Stan kept between him and Paul as Richard scooped up Diane from the floor. The scuffling alerted Barnard, and Richard had a glimpse of a furiously snarling, white, almost animalistic face as he turned from the boy, still crouching. He laughed. It was a sound of derision, not humour.

'How resourceful you are, my dears. I can see that my delay in killing you was a mistake. No doubt the boy's little charade indicates his alliance with your interests.' Barnard's hand tangled in Timothy's hair, jerking him back. The boy squealed. 'I see that I shall have to rectify matters at once.' He turned to the corpse of the bouncer. 'Let us reward the Sins of the Fathers, Paul. *Kill them! Kill them now!*'

Paul's head rose slowly, eyes glinting black, and turned to look at them. He stepped forward, slowly and stupidly at first, as if his body needed to be coaxed into movement after its period of inactivity. It grinned, strength returning.

Richard hurried back towards the stairs. There was a strange smell on Diane's lips: she had been drugged. Stan was suddenly between Paul and Richard again, pushing Richard away towards the stairs, his eyes fixed on the slowly approaching figure.

'Get her upstairs!' he hissed. 'Lock that door. I'll try to keep it back. If only I knew where he'd put those sodding guns . . . '

'KILL THEM!' shrieked Barnard. 'KILL THEM ALL!'

In a sudden blur of motion, Paul struck with the speed of a snake, seizing Stan by the shoulders. The force of the impact cannoned Stan into Richard, pushing him onto the stairs.

Richard fought for balance with Diane a dead weight in his arms, and regained it as Stan and Paul whirled away, grappling. Paul's ghostly white face lunged at Stan's neck. Richard heard a ripping of cloth and looked back to see part of Stan's shirt collar clenched between the bouncer's blood-encrusted teeth. The head was moving for another strike, its idiot's grin widening, breath hissing like a cobra.

I can't leave him!

Stan twisted, grabbing the thing's throat, trying to push it back.

I can't!

The head began to move closer; Stan's grip was useless to halt its slow, hissing progress. Somewhere behind, Barnard was laughing.

No!

Richard laid Diane gently on the staircase.

No!!

He launched himself from the stairs. The impetus tumbled all three of them onto the floor in a writhing, twisting bundle of thrashing limbs. Richard had the thing's arm and held it with all his weight, one knee on the elbow. Stan prised himself loose and held the other arm. The thing's head lashed from side to side, teeth champing furiously, saliva spraying. Its feet beat a tattoo on the shining floor.

It was too strong.

It began to rise, lifting them both on its arms like struggling children. The thing swung Richard away on one arm. Grip broken, he sprawled on the floor in an ungainly breakdance imitation, body sliding. The thing fastened its free hand on Stan's throat again.

Richard grabbed a chair leg for support to haul himself upright. When it moved in his hand, he remembered that the chairs on the fringe of the disco floor were not fixtures. Sweeping the light tubular frame up with him as he rose, he swung it high in both hands and brought it down full on Paul's back. The thing blundered against the booth in the centre of the floor, its flailing arm shattering an overhead globe light. But the blow had not stopped its assault on Stan. It pushed him against the booth, throttling him. Stan clawed at the relentless grip. '*Barnard . . .* ' he choked. '*Get Barnard!*'

Richard whirled towards Barnard, who was still crouching beside the boy. He appeared to be talking to him, like a schoolteacher explaining a simple problem.

'*Tekel . . . upharsin . . . Gorgus . . . Imago . . .* '

Timothy huddled beside him, shaking his head as if trying to ward something off.

Richard stepped forward. Behind him, Stan uttered another strangled gasp as he wrestled with the man-thing. Caught uncertainly in the middle, Richard took a step towards Barnard and then back to Stan.

And then: '*God damn it!*'

He sprinted over the disco floor to Barnard who began to turn as Richard drew level with him. A precise and savage kick to the side of Barnard's head sent him sprawling in a grunting heap. The *crack* of the impact seemed to echo in the nightclub. Richard hurled himself back. Stan was holding the thing's face from his throat. Richard twisted an arm away. They collided with the booth again. Somewhere inside, the mechanism was jarred; a needle *zipped* across an LP and suddenly Eric Clapton was pounding 'Layla' from the overhead speakers.

The lights began to spin as they thrashed away from the disco floor, towards the bar.

The thing twisted savagely, and suddenly Stan was flung headlong over the tables. It turned and fastened on Richard. Tables and glasses crashed, the music pounded, the lights circled and spun. Green, red, green, red, green, red. Richard felt talons sinking into his throat. The thing was holding him aloft, fingernails biting into his flesh. Hissing, it strode forward, holding him in the air like some bizarre offering. Red lights were flashing behind his eyes. The thing slammed him against the bar; the terrible white face struck. Richard's shirt ripped apart; pain boiled from his left side. When the thing's face came into view again, he could see that there was blood on its teeth. His blood. *And it was chewing.*

Glass shattered at Richard's right. Stan suddenly loomed into vision. He had seized the whisky bottle that Barnard had left on the bar and smashed it. Savagely, he jammed the broken bottle into the thing's face. It hissed. Stan stabbed again. And again. The thing lashed out once more and Stan was suddenly gone.

Christ, don't let it . . . Stan . . . For God's sake . . . help . . .

Suddenly, it was as if Richard was a kid again. He was hanging on a strut beneath Byker Bridge, death waiting for him below. But Stan's hand was not there to save him. The thing's eyes glittered black like the water of the Ouseburn below and Richard knew that this time he was going to fall. The gory face moved in again, blood-flecked lips writhing, teeth champing.

Something roared close to Richard's face, something that spat flame. It roared again and the thing's head snapped away. Richard felt himself falling, recognising the sounds as pistol shots. He expected to see black water rushing up at him and was surprised when his hands touched the tiled floor of the night-club. Turning, choking and gasping for breath, he saw that Stan had found the automatic pistols. *They must have been on the bar*, he thought. He could see Stan standing against the bar, face set and grim, holding the gun in the same way that Diane had used it. He was not snapping off panic shots now; there was a grim purpose in his eyes as he fired again. The thing was slowly closing in on him, juddering under the impact of the bullets. Stan squeezed off another methodical shot and a piece of the advancing thing's face blew away.

Still gasping, unable to speak, Richard nodded: *Yes, yes . . . that's it . . . the head . . . the head . . .* And then, crazily: *You've seen the film, you've read the book, now live the nightmare.*

Paul took another step.

Stan fired again, backing off. A chunk of scalp whipped away into the nightclub.

Another step.

The gun roared again. The face was unrecognisable as anything that had ever been human.

Another step. Faltering.

Stan dropped the first pistol, fumbled at the second. Four deafening, ringing gunshots in quick succession.

The thing's head disintegrated. It stopped, arms juddering, and sank to its knees.

Again, in Richard's mind, more crazy thoughts: *Paul's not the man he was. He's just an image of his former self.*

The thing slumped to one side and lay still.

For the second time, Paul was dead.

Stepping around the hideous mess on the floor, Stan picked

Richard up and guided him to a bar stool. His fear seemed to have solidified like ice inside him. It remained there, cold and hard, but controlled. He drew Richard's jacket away from his side and examined the ragged wound there. The thing had bitten a chunk out of him and the gash was bleeding copiously, shirt clinging in a scarlet mass to his side. Stan grabbed a clean cloth from the bar counter, folded it into a wad and pressed it against the wound to stop the bleeding.

Something moved on the stairs.

Stan whipped round and snatched the pistol from the bar, heart thudding, fear thawing instantly from ice to a more liquid, volatile terror.

An old woman was sitting on the bottom step. She was nursing Diane like a child, rocking backwards and forwards, crooning. Stan snapped forward, gun ready.

'No!' Richard caught his sleeve. 'It's okay. She's not one of them.'

'Who . . . ?'

'It's Pandora.'

Is he raving? thought Stan. *He must be in shock. What the hell does he mean? That's an old woman. Pandora is the same age as me . . .* And then he saw the old woman's face for the first time. That face could certainly be an eighty-year-old version of Pandora. *No . . . I can't . . . I won't . . . believe it.* But something purely instinctive told him that Richard was right. A feeling of despair filled him. His gun hand lowered. When he spoke, grief choked his words.

'Oh, my God, Pandora. What's happened to you?'

'Stan!' yelled Richard suddenly. 'Stop Barnard!' Richard's warning shocked him into action. Instantly, he looked across to where the nightclub manager had been lying and saw that Barnard had recovered consciousness and dragged himself back to the child, blood glinting on his forehead.

'*Absavel . . . Imago . . . Gorgus . . .* ' he was croaking, hand on the child's collar. Timothy was still crouched beside him, face down, listening but shaking his head as if he did not want to hear the words.

'Stop him,' gasped Pandora from the stairs, eyes suddenly glinting and wild. 'He's making Timothy Dark-Out. He'll recall the Spectre.'

Stan checked his gun, feeling the ice forming inside again. Briskly, face set and determined, he walked purposefully across the disco floor towards Barnard and the child.

'*Imago . . . Impactus . . .* '

He reached them, raised the gun and pointed it at Barnard's head.

The child looked up.

Stan saw the insect-black, gleaming eyes and knew that he was too late. The kid had Darked-Out. There was *power* in the air now, radiating invisibly from Timothy and swamping Stan. He could not move. Something held him in an invisible embrace. The child's hair was whipping in a wind that had blown up from nowhere; it crackled as if with static electricity. A roaring filled the air and the disco lights whirled crazily. It was like standing in the eye of a tornado. There was pain in Stan's outstretched hand, a relentless pressure like a vice on his fingers. The pressure changed, pulling his fingers open. Stan struggled to squeeze the trigger, but it was useless. The gun rattled to the floor.

'Kill him,' coughed Barnard. 'Kill him now.'

* * *

Still leaning heavily on the barstool, pain eating into his side, Richard saw the whirlwind materialise in the centre of the room. He struggled to move forward as he saw Stan drop the gun.

'No, Timothy . . . no . . . '

The child raised his arms slowly. Richard could only watch helplessly as an invisible force seized Stan and lifted him into the air, legs dangling. Wisps of blue smoke seemed to be curling from the boy's mouth and nostrils. There was a loud *snap*! like a discharge of electricity, and Stan was hurled thirty feet across the nightclub. He crashed through the reception doors and vanished from sight.

'*Oh, God, no!*' Realising that Stan must be dead, Richard staggered towards Barnard, careless now of whatever might be done to him. His rage conquered the pain and kept him moving. The Byker Chapter. All dead. One by one, dying hideous deaths. And it was all because of that insane bastard

Barnard. He was the source of the nightmare. A foul child rapist. A stealer of souls. A thing that should not be allowed to live. Richard would grab that gun from the floor. He would pump those remaining bullets into that monster's brain. He would finish the nightmare once and for all . . .

The child whirled towards him. Richard felt a roaring blast of invisible power scorching across the nightclub, smothering him, holding him in its grip like some mighty fist. The child smiled as Richard struggled in vain. Behind him, Barnard was giggling, 'Good, good, good . . .'

The boy raised his arms again and Richard's feet left the floor. The invisible fist began to close. His side was on fire; he could feel his entire body being crushed. He screamed aloud and Barnard's giggling intensified. The hellish wind plucked at the child, ruffling his hair and clothes. Red and green lights swirled around them like a kaleidoscope from Hades. Richard's lungs were compressing, he could not breathe. He began to gasp for air, crying out when something *cracked* inside. It could only be a rib breaking under the pressure.

Barnard clambered to his feet, laughing. 'You can't stop him. Nothing can stop the child now. Kill him. Kill him and emerge in your full Glory. The fathers will all be absorbed and you will have returned in all your Power. Kill him and recall the other Old Ones. Begin the Vengeance on those who would have banished you forever. *Absavel . . . Imago . . . Tekel . . .* '

Richard could taste salt in his mouth and knew that it must be blood. His vision was misting over. Death could not be far away. *Is this the way it ends?*

There was a blur of motion beneath him and he saw that Pandora had staggered to the boy. She was kneeling at his feet. Above the whirlwind, Richard could hear her speaking to him.

'Timothy. Help us. Don't let it win. Don't let it through. Stop it.'

'Stop it, you bitch?' Barnard was laughing again. 'Nothing can stop it. The human part of him has served its purpose. It no longer exists. The Gorgon is emerging.'

'Help us, Timothy. Don't kill him. Don't let it come through.'

The child was looking at Pandora, hair flying.

Barnard, angrily: '*Impactus . . . Imago . . . Dursit . . .* '

'Please, Timothy. Help us!'

Ten

Diane's mind floated and drifted in dark, dangerous places. She knew, even while unconscious, that she had been drugged. She remembered how Barnard had forced that abominable liquid between her teeth. Her subconscious mind was exploring and she knew that she was close to the answer, close to the source of the Spectre.

Suddenly, she had found it. It was so simple! Her mother's legacy had sensed the Nature of the Beast. Desperately, she fought the drug-induced stupor that had made her conscious mind a prisoner yet had allowed her subconscious to expand and seek.

'Wake up . . . *Wake up!* . . . WAKE UP!'

Red, green, red, green, red, green.

She was crawling on a smooth, dark, puddled floor. Above and around her raged a whirlwind. The presence of a great Danger cramped her stomach with fear, but the certain knowledge that someone she loved was close to death spurred her on. She knew what had to be done, if only she had the strength.

She continued to crawl.

* * *

The red, buzzing pain behind Stan's eyes dissipated slightly and he was awake. When he was seven years old, he had been making his way to school, walking on a high brick wall. He had missed his footing and fallen, banging his head on the concrete pavement. He had gone on to school and, half an hour into the arithmetic lesson, had collapsed. He was concussed. Now he remembered that pain again. His vision swimming and blurred, he wondered if he was still seven years old, lying on the pavement. He moved onto one elbow, brain seeming to throb in a paper-thin skull. He looked around. He was lying in the reception area, at the foot of the cloakroom desk. Red and green lights winked through the glass of the inner doors. Incredibly, there was a whirlwind in there, a howling, raging wind.

Stan remembered.

He turned his head and saw his own face, upside down. He crawled over and painfully began to pull himself to his feet, clawing his way up the desk; he realised that he had been looking at his own reflection in the full-length double mirror which stood behind the counter. He hugged the rim of the desk, leaning over it and gasping for breath. He watched his mirror image doing the same thing on the other side of the desk.

It looks nothing like me, he thought crazily. *That wild, white face, the tousled hair.*

He became aware of movement behind him. The double doors leading into the nightclub were juddering open. A dishevelled figure began to crawl through.

It was Diane.

With pain like a cancer eating into his brain, he staggered towards her. She was moaning as he hauled her to her feet, trying to guide her into one of the reception seats. He could just make out her words.

'The Gorgon . . . images . . . reflections of fear . . . the photograph . . . vanishing images . . . mirror images . . . mirrors . . . ' She was trying to push past him, reaching out for something behind him. 'Perseus, the hero, slew Medusa by looking at her reflection in a polished shield . . . '

Nausea cramped Stan's stomach as he tried to restrain her. 'We've got to stop it, Diane. We have to . . .'

And then he saw what she was trying to reach.

The full-length mirror behind the cloakroom desk.

'It's the only way, Stan,' she gasped. 'The only way to stop the Gorgon is to use its own power against it. We have to . . . have to . . . *reflect its own power back against it.*'

Stan looked at their own battered reflections in the mirror. Diane was still groping out towards it. He seemed to hear Barnard's words: *'There are too many dangers here. The boy has an aversion to mirrors.'*

At last, he understood.

Diane was suddenly limp in his arms, breathing heavily. He laid her gently across the reception seats. She was still moaning, unintelligibly now, as he turned to look back at the mirror.

The nightmare flashing lights from the disco reflected back at him.

He staggered round the desk and moved towards the mirror.

Eleven

'Imago . . . Impactus . . . '

'No, Timothy. Please, I love you. Try. Don't let it through. Help us. Fight what's inside you!'

The boy remained in the same position, hair swirling, eyes black. Pandora clung to his hands, staring up at him.

'*Palcutat . . . Emergo . . . Non Enno . . . '* Barnard's eyes were ablaze with an unholy glee.

Something was happening in the air above the pentagram-shaped disco floor. A shimmering haze had formed, blurring and shifting.

'Come forth!' shouted Barnard. 'Eris, Phobos, Metus, Demius, Pallor . . . The Gorgon has prepared your way!'

A twisting, bubbling mass of ectoplasmic cloud was appearing in the haze. Shifting and swelling, ethereal and insubstantial, but growing . . . growing . . .

'Chimaera! Hydra! Come forth!'

'Stop it, Timothy! You promised! You must fight back!'

The boy continued to stare at Pandora. A flicker of something vaguely human crossed his face.

'Pandora!' shouted Barnard. 'I am your Epimetheus! You will obey me! Leave the boy. The Gorgon hungers to return . . . the Deep Ones hunger to return! And I will become a God, as they are. It is promised. This is to be my reward. *My reward!*'

Above the disco floor, strange new lights had appeared in the billowing cloud, mixing with the disco lights in a hellish kaleidoscope. They shifted and moved like living things. Impatient. Waiting. But the cloud's substantive growth seemed to have been temporarily halted.

Barnard turned back to the boy, raging. 'Kill her! Kill her and then kill the last father! It must be done.' He stood apart from them, hands clenching and unclenching, fury on his face. Why was there hesitation? Why was the child staring down at his mother like that? Was that *doubt* on the boy's face?

He strode to where the gun had been dropped, picked it up and swung round to Pandora.

'Bitch!' He pulled the trigger.

The shot hit Pandora in the side of the head. The impact of the bullet sent her sprawling away from the child. A dark pool spread beneath her. Still held aloft, Richard began to weep. Barnard was smiling now as he looked at the boy.

'*Absavel . . . Imago . . . Gorgus . . .*'

Timothy had not moved. His head was still bowed as Barnard spoke. The cloud above the disco floor hovered, unchanged, keeping its impatient vigil. But now there was a low moaning noise, audible even beneath the roaring of the storm. It was coming from Timothy.'*Absavel . . . Imago . . .*' Barnard commanded.

Richard felt the invisible power that was holding him disappear. He dropped to the floor like a stone, sprawling in a shaken heap. The pain in his side had muted to a dull, red burning. His broken rib throbbed with every breath. Barnard fell silent. He was looking at Richard with an expression on his face that mixed rage with bafflement.

'*Imago! Tekel! Dursit!*'

A visible war for possession was reflected on the boy's face. Shades of the human and the inhuman passed in turn over his features. The moaning grew to a crescendo; the ever-shifting, contorting alternation of small boy and beast rapidly accelerating. One moment the eyes were black and filled with hate; the next, crystal-clear, human and anguished. Timothy's head fell to his chest again. Above, the bubbling, insubstantial cloud was waiting.

'*Absavel! Impactus!*' Barnard took a step forward.

The boy's head flew up. 'Muh . . . muh . . . MOTHER!' Richard could see the ferocious snarl on his face, the gleaming black eyes now filled with hate. Barnard's smile dissolved.

'No . . .'

The boy flicked his head savagely. Barnard was flung, screaming, across the nightclub, tumbling head over heels through empty air. Richard watched as he hurtled over the bar and crashed against the mosaic-tiled wall. He was held there, fifteen feet above the ground, a struggling fly trapped in the centre of a cobweb of broken tiling.

Timothy walked slowly past Richard towards the bar. Barnard was moaning, struggling uselessly to lower himself from the wall. The boy reached the bar and looked up.

'Timothy,' moaned Barnard. 'Let me down . . . let me down . . . please . . . '

A living symbiosis of child and Gorgon, Timothy gazed at Barnard. The forces were somehow equally balanced, momentarily not in conflict. When the boy spoke, it was with two voices: the voice of Timothy filled with a child's anger and vengeance and the voice of the Gorgon—the Spectre—that inhuman voice from the fog, reaching across the aeons.

'You killed my muh . . . muh . . . mother . . . *Baaaaarnard! Why have I waited so long?* You . . . you . . . killed her . . . you . . . *You ask for your reward? You say that you are Epimetheus to Pandora? Very well, your reward is to share the fate of your brother, Prometheus . . .* You'll pay, Mr Pearson! I'll make you . . . make you . . . *Chained to a crag on Mount Caucasus and devoured by a vulture for thirty thousand years. I shall* . . . make you pay . . . *shall be your vulture, Barnard!*'

'No . . . Timothy . . . no . . . '

Richard watched as the boy flicked his head again and Barnard began to scream hoarsely. His arm was torn away and flung across the nightclub; his leg was ripped from his torso. Richard turned away in horror and crawled across the floor to Pandora. He caressed her arm. 'Pandora . . . Pandy . . . ' It was just a matter of time before he himself followed her. Behind him, Barnard's screams were diminishing now. He struggled to his feet. He had to get to Diane and drag her away from this hellish place. But Diane was no longer lying on the stairs. She was nowhere to be seen.

'Diane . . . '

A blast of invisible power from behind flung him to the floor again. His broken rib burned red-hot, the wound in his side was bleeding heavily. Cursing, he twisted round and saw that Timothy was walking slowly towards him. Behind the boy, Barnard was gone: only a large crimson smear remained in the centre of the cobwebbed mosaic. Above the disco floor, the living cloud seemed to swarm with renewed vigour.

'Timothy . . .' began Richard, holding up his hand. And then the invisible power seized his ankle and twisted him into the air again, upside-down and dangling. He was turned around in the air like a doll, to hang upright and looking down on the boy. Helpless, he could only watch as snakes of blue smoke began to curl from Timothy's eyes and mouth. The relentless, terrible pressure on Richard's body returned. Now, he knew that he must die; he would be crushed to death. The child had been subdued, following Barnard's horrible death, and the Gorgon was finally about to emerge.

Slowly, Timothy began to change.

The boy's face darkened, hollowed eyes suddenly alive with black fire. His skin seemed somehow reptilian as the tendrils of blue smoke curling from his eyes and mouth swarmed around his head in a wreath of twisting, ectoplasmic snakes, hissing with poisonous threat—a living image of the mythological Medusa.

'Timothy,' croaked Richard, 'remember what your mother said. She wanted you to help us.'

The snakes hissed again, plainly audible through the howling wind. They were the same deadly, luminous snakes of fog that Richard had seen before.

'Help us, Timothy. Stop it from coming through.' The pain was now somehow dulled. *I'm dying. It's killing me.*

The thing that had been Timothy seemed wrapped in a shifting shroud, monstrous and hideous. There was nothing remotely human there now. Above, the boiling cloud began to swell and grow. The internal, flickering, *living* lights from the spectrum of another dimension were hungry . . . the Deep Ones were coming. The Gorgon emitted a triumphant howl.

'*Timothy!*' came a shout from the other side of the nightclub.

The power faltered as the creature looked up at the figure that had emerged from the reception doors. With a great effort, Richard turned his head to see a familiar form advancing towards them.

It was Stan.

He was not dead. And he was holding the full-length mirror from the cloakroom in front of him as he came. The disco lights were gleaming in it as he advanced.

'Look at me, Timothy! Look at the mirror!'

The thing remained standing, watching Stan as he drew closer. The wind still howled and whirled in the nightclub and, to Richard, it seemed that its force was now being directed at Stan. He was struggling forward against it. Debris flew through the air towards him. A wine glass shattered on the frame of the mirror, a tubular frame chair began to bounce across the disco floor.

For the second time, Richard dropped to the floor, the impact reactivating the agony inside him. Lying on his back, he could dimly see the bubbling cloud above him seething and spreading. He twisted round. Stan was forcing his way towards the Gorgon, mirror still intact and held aloft. Behind him, Diane was leaning in the reception doorway. She was trying to shout, but the raging whirlwind snatched her words.

'Face yourself!' shouted Stan above the howling wind. 'Look at yourself!'

The Gorgon's reflection was suddenly caught in the glass and, to Richard, it seemed to be frozen, arms flung up across the monstrous face to ward off the approaching mirror. The wind still plucked and swirled in the nightclub, but its full fury was no longer directed at Stan. The sight reminded Richard of a vampire confronted by a crucifix in one of those Hammer horror films that they used to watch in the Imperial, all those years ago. The reflected disco lights momentarily dazzled him, recalling instantly the time when he had crouched beneath Byker Bridge and the sunlight had flashed in his face; the time when Stan's grip on his hand had saved him from death. He was trying to save them now.

'Look at the image, Timothy! Face it! Fight what's inside you. It's the only way.' Still transfixed, arms shielding its face, there was a look of inhuman horror on the Spectre's face; Richard could sense a screaming in the very air itself. The thing's power was somehow being reflected back at it from the mirror, building and boiling to a white-hot intensity. Stan, too, seemed to be conscious of that raging power, like the rumbling approach of water from a burst dam. He moved forward. 'Face it, Tim! Face it!' The very structure of the nightclub was groaning under some immense pressure. The shattered mosaic behind the bar started to fall apart in cascading shards. Dust was drifting down from overhead. The disco lights were exploding one by one.

'Fight it, Timothy! *Fight it!*' Stan stepped forward again.

The spinning Krypton globe above the disco floor plunged downwards, shattering into a million pieces. Glasses hanging above the bar exploded on their racks. A shard glanced, stinging, across Richard's face. Gaping cracks chased up the walls.

An inhuman roar issued from the Gorgon's mouth. The mirror disintegrated, imploding towards Stan in a whirling scythe of dagger-like shards.

'*No!*' yelled Richard at the top of his voice. The mirror frame tumbled away into the darkness. Stan, his body pierced in a dozen places by spears of broken glass, slumped to the floor.

The wind shrieked like an animal in mortal pain. The thing still stood, arms outflung, black eyes staring.

'Stan . . . ' Richard crawled forward.

The nebulous cloud overhead was moving downwards and outwards in an undulating mass of grey fog. It enveloped the Gorgon in its billowing grey shrouds; curled and swarmed throughout the nightclub, quickly engulfing everything in a poisonous, rolling smoke. Blinded, Richard clutched at his eyes, coughing at the bitter, *dead* taste that clogged his nose and mouth.

Silence. The shrieking wind and the abominable howling of the Gorgon were suddenly gone.

The cloud was evaporating, dissolving into curling grey wisps. Richard's eyes streamed, each cough racking him with agony. He buried his face in his hands.

There was a sudden rattle of footsteps on the debris beside him and someone took his arm, helping him up.

It was Diane.

'Richard, thank God! Are you . . . ?'

'Yeah . . . yeah . . . I'm okay . . . '

The grey cloud and its invisible denizens had vanished. Richard looked across to where the Gorgon had been.

A small, frightened boy was standing in the centre of the nightclub, rubbing his eyes.

With Diane's help, Richard picked his way over the littered disco towards the inert figure lying crumpled on the floor not far from Pandora.

'Stan? Stan . . . ' *He can't be dead. Not him, too. He mustn't be dead.*

He knelt and turned Stan over to face him.

'I stopped it, Teacher Man,' said Stan in a whispered,

pained voice. 'We didn't need Peter Cushing after all.'

His face was a mask of dirt and blood. He coughed, and Richard could hear the sound of blood in his lungs. For the first time, he saw the spear of glass imbedded in Stan's chest.

'Don't move, Stan. Don't . . . '

'You joking?' he smiled, coughing again. Blood flecked his chin. 'My pocket . . . pocket . . . ' He began to fumble at his jacket. Richard reached inside and drew out the crumpled photograph of the Byker Chapter. 'Let me . . . let me see . . . '

Richard held it up. 'Oh, Christ, Stan. No . . . '

Pandora had vanished from the photograph. Richard's image was faded, but seemed somehow to be solidifying. Even now, Stan's image was fading rapidly. Stan coughed again, grimacing in pain.

'*Goddammit!*' snapped Richard. '*I won't let this happen! It's over! It's finished!*' He gripped Stan's hand. The horror was finished. It *had* to be finished. Suddenly, it was as if they were kids back beneath Byker Bridge again. Only this time, Stan was slipping away and Richard was trying to haul him back.

Stan's image continued to fade.

'The Gorgon's gone! It's been sent back to where it came from, along with those other hellish things. How much more death does it want? Hasn't there been enough?'

' . . . Look . . . look . . . ' Stan was gesturing at the photograph again.

His image was solidifying, losing its phantom transparency.

' . . . Look . . . '

Richard watched as, one by one, the other members of the Byker Chapter began to reappear in the photograph.

'Thank God,' said Richard. 'Thank God.'

The photograph was complete. Seven smiling faces, seven friends from a party held a decade ago.

'Thanks to Diane . . . we beat it, Richard,' said Stan. 'We stopped it.' His grip was weakening.

'No, Stan. You can't die. Not now. Not after everything that's happened, everything we've been through.'

'Do my living for me, Richard.'

'No, Stan. I won't let it happen.'

'This is one fall I'll have to take alone. See you around, Teacher Man.'

Stan's grip relaxed. He coughed again. His eyes closed.

'Stan . . . '

Diane was at Richard's side as he placed Stan's hand gently on the floor. He stood and took her in his arms. She was weeping.

'It's over, Diane. It's over.'

Diane braced herself, stemming the tears. But somewhere, they could still hear the sound of weeping. They turned and saw that it was the boy, Timothy. He was crying, hands held to his face, stifling the sobs on his sleeve. Richard went to him, gently taking his hands away from his eyes. Timothy looked up at him. His eyes were a crystal-blue, slightly bloodshot from the tears and the swirling dust. Richard pulled the child towards him and Timothy fell into his embrace. The tears were flowing freely now. Richard stroked his head, gazing in the direction of Stan's body. Stan had done it. He had despatched the hellish thing back to where it had come from. They owed their lives and souls to him. All around, the Imperial—Spectres—groaned and settled.

Twelve

They walked down Northumberland Street together.

The nightmare in Byker was over. Their secret flight from its ruined nightclub, just before the police arrived, had happened three days ago. Timothy walked between Richard and Diane, holding their hands as shoppers streamed around them. He would never have believed that there were so many people in the world.

Richard looked down at him, ruffling his hair. There was a big world ahead of the kid, a world rich with experience. Diane watched Richard, knew what he was thinking and leaned over to kiss him. The whole event had haunted his sleep these last three nights and would continue to haunt him for a long time. Last night, he had awoken shouting hoarsely, with sweat beaded on his face. But together they would make it.

Timothy looked up, eyes sky-blue and clear. He had been silent for a long time, studying the crowds, his memory of everything prior to these last three days gone. It was as if he had just been born.

'Are you my Daddy?'

Richard searched his face, squeezing the boy's hand gently.

'No, Timothy,' he said at last. 'I'm not your Daddy.'

Their reflections were caught in a shop window as they passed.

Startled, Diane drew in a hissing breath.

Timothy's reflection was not there.

And now, Diane could feel a cold, familiar terror inside. She strained forward to get a better view of the shop window, but a passing bus obscured it. Now they were moving on. *It must have been imagination! Surely it was imagination!* Even now, she could see the child's reflection in another window. Yes, it was just a trick of the light. Wasn't it? But why did that bad feeling remain as she searched Timothy's young, innocent face? Why did the Spectre's shadow still seem to hang overhead? She shook it away, burying it deep inside.

She felt Richard's grip on her hand tighten and looked up. He had been watching her. Glancing down at the child, he returned her look. They were communicating without words. Richard looked down at Timothy again.

'You're not my Daddy?' repeated the boy.

Richard paused, squeezing Diane's hand once more.

'No,' he said. 'I'm your Guardian.'

They walked on. An elderly couple passed them in the street. The old woman looked up at her companion, smiling at the charming family group.

'Did you see that child?' she asked. 'What a lovely boy.'

After a while, she looked back and smiled again.

'He's the image of his father,' she said.

AUTHOR'S POSTSCRIPT

The district of Byker in Newcastle upon Tyne (in the North-East of England) exists—as its inhabitants are well aware. I was a Byker kid, so I can testify first-hand to the remarkable community spirit which was and is a strong feature of the area. The descriptions of places and landmarks in *Spectre* are factual, but the characters depicted therein are purely fictional and any resemblance, as they say, to persons living or dead is purely coincidental.

The Imperial cinema did exist. It showed its last film in 1962 and, apart from housing a community group for a short while, remained largely derelict. Its incarnation as bingo hall and nightclub are fictional inventions. Owned by a garage and used as a warehouse of sorts for the last few years, it stood, battered and dilapidated at the top of Byker Bank, awaiting its next incarnation; a forgotten temple of cinematic dreams.

As I write, the bulldozers are about to move in and reduce it to rubble. The Imperial will be gone by the time that you read these words, but for many the memory will linger on. Particularly for one kid, whose imagination was captured and fired by the flickering images on its haunted screen.

S.L.
November, 1985